VEILBREAKER

BECCA SULLIVAN

DEDICATION

To my husband and family—thank you for standing beside me through every moment of this journey. Your love and support made this possible.

To my friends—your encouragement meant more than you know. You kept me going when the path felt uncertain.

To my readers who took the time to read and review *Guardian*—I am endlessly grateful. It brings me so much joy to know these characters are loved as deeply by you as they are by me.

And to my Nana—though you are no longer on this side of the Veil, I carry you with me always. This is for you.

Welcome to the celestial realm....

Stories of angels and demons have existed for centuries—both through scripture and myth. They are often told in absolutes: beings of pure light, or creatures born of darkness. Good or evil. Heaven or Hell.

But I have never believed our world, or the things beyond it, were ever that simple.

In *Veilbreaker*, angels are not untouchable creatures, nor are demons merely monsters to be feared. They are shaped by choice, by loyalty, by love—and sometimes, by loss. And some walk the fragile line between what is right and what they believe in.

Demons, too, are not all the same. Some are born of chaos. Others are what remains of something that once knew grace.

This story is not a retelling of any single belief or tradition, but a reimagining. A world where the lines between light and dark blur.

So here is a glossary of the celestial beings in the Seraphic Hearts Books:

Guardian: Celestial angel protectors assigned to watch over human souls. Bound by strict laws, they are forbidden from interference beyond their purpose.

Fallen: Angels who have turned from their original purpose. Some fell by choice, others by consequence. Their allegiance is no longer to the divine order, but to their own will.

Nephilim: Half-human, half-angel. Their existence is considered unnatural by celestial laws.

Archnephilim: Half-human, half-angel except their souls were taken before birth to be made into an angel.

Demon: Entities born from darkness, chaos, or the remnants of something once divine.

Watcher: Ancient angel observers tasked with monitoring humanity. However, they fell in love with humans and taught them magic.

Archangel: A superior rank of angels. They are considered leaders of angels.

Cambion: Half-demon, half-angel.

Throne: A higher order of angels. They are known for their wisdom and mercy.

Ossaris: Humans with traces of angelic blood, originally given by the Archangels Michael and Gabriel. They were created to safeguard supernatural boundaries and maintain balance within the Watchers.

Principalities: A higher order of angels who guide Ossaris.

Veilbreaker: An Ossaris with special powers. They can unravel the boundary between realms—intentionally or not and banish both angels and demons.

Chapter One

Rhiannon

I sat quietly in the first pew of Nan's church, the polished wood cool beneath me, reflecting the dim glow of candlelight. The faint scent of incense drifted through the air, mingling with the subtle perfume of aged wood. Nan was tucked away in the confession booth, her whispered words barely audible, slipping through the ornate lattice of the small booth. I had asked to come along, seeking some semblance of solace in this sacred space. I wasn't sure if walking into this hallowed building would grant my prayers to be answered because the emptiness inside me felt as vast and silent as a black hole. I doubted I could ever hear or feel any type of divine connection.

My fingers twisted together anxiously, the knuckles turning white as I grappled with my unease. Churches always made me nervous, a lingering effect from the fire and brimstone sermons I had endured with my mom at her chosen church, where every word seemed to echo with judgment. But here, the atmosphere was different; the soft glow of candles flickered gently, casting a warm, soothing hue over the intricately carved pews and the stone walls that reached up towards the vaulted ceiling. The quiet reverence of the space was palpable, a silent invitation to breathe and be still.

"Relax, Rhi," Kiran whispered beside me, his voice a quiet reassurance. "Nothing will hurt you."

I turned to glance at him, his black jeans and scuffed Doc Martens a stark contrast to the somber setting. He didn't resemble the serene angels depicted in the stained glass windows, blues, reds, and golds casting a mosaic of ethereal light across the stone floor. Yet, he was my angel, my protector. My eyes drifted to one of the towering stained glass windows behind him, the colors dancing as the sunlight filtered through.

Kiran murmured as his warm hand brushed over my tightly clenched knuckles, stopping my fingers from tracing the star-shaped scar that marred my palm. I paused, feeling a sudden, electric pulse between us that made every nerve in my body stand on edge.

Ever since Azreal, the grim angel of death with dark, imposing wings and eyes like storm clouds, had declared me the warrior's child, everything had shifted. In just a couple of months, life had twisted in ways I never imagined. Now, with only two days until school would start, I sat on the cool, polished wood bench beside my Guardian Angel in The Lady of Swords Catholic Church, waiting for my grandmother to finish confession. What secrets that sweet lady had to confess was beyond me, but I couldn't help but wonder.

She seemed slightly shocked that I had requested to come with her, but quickly said yes. "Father McKinnley is a kind man, new to our parish, and very young for a priest," she had said. "He might understand you better than we old folks do."

With a playful eye roll, I had agreed to accompany her, but gave a hard pass to confession. How could I possibly tell a priest that I had a Guardian Angel that I could see and touch? One who was strikingly handsome, with a gentle demeanor and a fondness for vintage band t-shirts. How could I explain that I had survived the torment of a Fallen Angel, befriended a Watcher, and counted a witch among my best friends? And let's not forget the Nephilim who happened to be my boyfr—

A sharp ache twisted in my chest, a painful reminder of Justin's absence. I hadn't received a single word from him in over two weeks. Each unanswered text and call felt like a silent accusation, a heavy weight on my heart. When I asked my cousin Taylor if she or Scott, Justin's brother, had heard from Justin, she had said no. Then, they proceeded to bombard me with questions on what was going on.

Again, what do I tell her? If a priest who believed in celestial beings would probably think I was mad, how would my sweet, normal cousin take it? Justin had witnessed the truth firsthand, yet he still clung to denial, unable to accept his half-angel, half-human lineage as a Nephilim.

Kiran's gentle touch on my knuckles pulled me from my spiraling thoughts. "Let's light a candle," he suggested.

I allowed him to guide me toward the wall of flickering red votive candles, their soft glow casting a comforting aura. Kiran picked up a slender wooden stick, igniting its tip from an already burning flame. I watched, transfixed, as he lit one of the tiny votives and then handed me the stick with a reassuring nod. Mimicking his actions, I lit the candle beside his, feeling a small sense of solace in the simple ritual. A warmth lingered in his gaze as he took the stick back, nestling it into the sand-filled bowl. His lips moved soundlessly in a silent prayer, and then he made the sign of the cross, his fingers brushing his forehead, heart, and both shoulders with practiced grace.

I stood there, eyes fixed on the flickering flames, wondering if my prayers would ascend beyond the ceiling and be heard. I had prayed repeatedly since that fateful day at Vince's. The day I almost lost Kiran and the day I lost Justin to all of this craziness. I prayed for Justin, hoping he would find peace and accept himself. But, mostly, I prayed for Kiran, who had sacrificed so much for me and lost his grace, and was now a Fallen. I knew it tortured him, even though he wore a mask of strength and hid his pain well.

I sighed heavily and followed Kiran's example of the sign of the cross. His fingers glided gently down my back, stopping at my waist, where a soft warmth spread through me at the intimacy of his touch. My whispered prayers hung in the air, and Kiran stood beside me with an understanding look that seemed to say he knew exactly what I had prayed for.

"Rhi?" My grandmother's hushed voice startled me, making me jump involuntarily. "Who were you praying for?"

I turned towards her, taking in her small frame standing right next to Kiran, totally oblivious to his presence. I couldn't tell her. Not about so I settled on the only thing I could. "Justin."

Her lips curled into a gentle smile as she rummaged through her worn purse, the crinkling of the leather echoing softly in the quiet space. She pulled out a few bills and pressed them into my hand. "Here. You should leave a small donation."

I took the bills from her outstretched hand and carefully folded them into the donation box. As I turned back to her, my eyes drifted to the stained glass window behind her, where sunlight poured through, illuminating the scene with a radiant glow. The glass depicted a majestic angel, clad in ornate armor and flowing golden robes that seemed to ripple with life. In one hand, he brandished a gleaming sword high above his head; in the other, he held a set of scales, perfectly balanced. A halo encircled his light brown hair. I stared at it, mesmerized. He was large, and if I was being honest, frightening. His sword was aimed at what I could only think was the Devil. The devilish figure had dark, twisted horns jutting from his head and raised an arm defensively, as though trying to ward off the angel's impending blow. Yet, what captivated me the most were the angel's wings. They were crafted from a vivid red glass, a shade so rich and deep that it seemed to pulse with life. At first glance, they were simply beautiful, but the longer I stared, the more they began to resemble wings drenched in blood. A shiver crept up my spine, leaving a trail of goosebumps in its wake. Chills worked their way through me, and Kiran took notice. So did Nan.

"Are you all right, Rhi?" My grandmother asked as she followed my gaze. Her eyes softened with a hint of reverence. "Ah, Saint Michael, when he threw Lucifer out of Heaven. He is one of the most powerful angels."

"She's right," Kiran's voice echoed softly in my mind, brushing against my consciousness like a whisper in the wind. *"Michael is very powerful."*

My skin prickled at Kiran's words. Michael was called the warrior, and Azrael had said I was the child of the warrior. I didn't remember anything about my father, and my mother never spoke of him but, still. The idea seemed absurd, even to me, now entrenched in this mysterious world of the supernatural.

"I cannot believe it," I responded to Kiran in my mind.

I felt a gentle touch on my cheek as Kiran's hand caressed my skin. The warmth of it was comforting, and I found myself yearning to sink into that touch.

Nan's old green sedan creaked as she pulled into our driveway. I glanced over to see my neighbor Mia lounging on her weathered porch swing, her laughter mingling with the warm summer air as Sam leaned against the porch railing, his hands shoved deep into his pockets. I hadn't seen Sam since the night everything happened. I think he was avoiding me, and now was my chance to talk to him. Just as I unbuckled my seatbelt and swung the car door open, Nan's voice

broke through my thoughts. "I guess they put Mr. Hollander's house on the market," she said with a sigh, her eyes drifting toward the end of the street.

I followed her gaze down the street to the dilapidated house three doors down, its dark brown paint fading into an eerie, almost black hue. The wrought iron fence that enclosed the front yard was rusted and twisted, adding to its unsettling presence. I always thought it looked spooky and oddly out of place with the other cheerful homes on the street. "We always thought that house was haunted," I remarked as memories of childhood tales flooded back.

She scoffed, dismissing my comment with a wave of her hand. "He was just an eccentric man. I never heard anything about it being haunted." With a firm click, she shut her door and turned to face me, her eyes gleaming with mischief. "Now, the McKenzies' house down the road, that place is haunted." She brushed past me as she began her ascent up the stairs.

I stood there, a mix of confusion and intrigue swirling in my mind. Who would have thought that Nan, with her sensible demeanor, actually believed in haunted houses?

"I'm going to see what Mia is up to," I called up. The late afternoon sun was casting long shadows on the sidewalk. As I approached, Sam caught sight of me, and his face visibly paled, a look of panic flashing across his features.

"Oh no, you don't!" I shouted, quickening my steps up Mia's stairs, "I have questions for you." My voice was unwavering as I closed the distance between us.

Sam's dark eyes darted nervously between me and Kiran, who had appeared beside me, and for a moment, I thought Sam might vanish into thin air, like he was prone to doing. Reaching the porch, I pointed an accusing finger at him, trying to muster a look that could pass as menacing. "Angel or not, I will stab you," I promised.

Sam raised his hands defensively, palms out, and turned to Kiran with a pleading look. "Can you not keep a leash on your ward?" he asked, his voice laced with exasperation, eyes narrowing at me as if I were a particularly puzzling riddle.

Kiran chuckled softly next to me. "You know as well as I do, she would never allow that," he replied.

I nudged Kiran in the ribs with my elbow, never breaking eye contact with Sam. "You have answers to some questions I have." I folded my arms over my chest and stood tall, trying to project an air of authority, despite knowing the futility of intimidating a Watcher. Sam had been around since the dawn of time, a fact he reminded me of often, and I was convinced he held the secret of my father's identity. A mystery I was determined to unravel.

Sam let his hands fall to his sides and leaned lazily against the weathered porch railing. "I may have such knowledge, but I am not at liberty to say," he drawled.

Mia sprang up from her seat on the porch swing, determination etched on her face as she positioned herself between us. "What do you know about my Lady Bug, Sam?" She mimicked the stance I had taken moments earlier.

Sam cocked an eyebrow, his gaze flicking between us with a hint of amusement. "Ganging up on me, are you?" he teased.

Mia rapidly tapped her foot against the porch.

"Look, I'd love to tell you more about your father," Sam began, his tone turning serious, "but I am bound by the vow I took."

Mia was skeptical. "What kind of vow?"

"The kind that, if broken, lands me in the sixth circle of Hell for heresy," Sam replied darkly.

Mia's arms fell to her sides, a look of concern washing over her as she turned toward me. "Oh girl, that's bad. Don't push him for an answer," she warned.

Kiran appeared beside me, his gaze fixed intently on Sam. "And who did you make this vow to, Samyaza?" he inquired, suspicion lacing his words.

Sam feigned shock, placing a hand dramatically over his heart. "Kiran, after everything we've been through, are we not friends?" he exclaimed, a hint of playfulness within the hurt. "Please, call me Sam."

"Okay, Sam. Who was it that you made this vow to?" Kiran pressed again.

"Her father, of course," Sam stated plainly, his words hanging in the air like a heavy curtain.

"Oh, so her father has enough power to send you to Hell then," Kiran said with a sly grin.

Sam's expression darkened. "I've said too much already."

"I don't know that I believe you," I said, narrowing my eyes at him. "And wait a minute. When you say the sixth level of Hell, are you referring to Dante's Inferno? Like what the poet Dante wrote?"

Sam's lips curled wickedly, a knowing glint in his eyes. "Dante is a Watcher."

"So, it's real? What he wrote in the Divine Comedy?" I pressed, searching his face for any hint of deceit.

"Mostly," Sam replied with a nonchalant shrug.

Mia shook her head, her expression a mixture of disbelief and concern. "Girl, I'm not taking the chance that he's telling the truth and ends up there," she said softly, her voice dropping to a whisper as she pointed her finger downward. "The punishment for breaking a vow would be either shaming you or having your mouth sewn shut, unable to eat, drink, or speak." She turned to Sam, seeking confirmation. "That's correct, right Sam?"

Sam nodded solemnly. "Indeed it is," he confirmed.

I rolled my eyes, feeling exhausted by the tangled web of celestial politics and games. All I wanted was to know my father. It shouldn't be this difficult. "Your friend, the one we met in the caves the night we went dancing. He was about to say who my father is. He isn't bound by the same vow," I insisted, my voice tinged with desperation.

Sam turned his piercing eyes on me, fury burning in their depths. "He was, and I've since bound him to my vow. It's crucial that the wrong people don't find out."

I stepped closer. "And I'm supposed to be the wrong people?" I hissed.

Sam's expression softened, his gaze losing its edge. "No, sweet cheeks. It's all for your protection." He paused, drawing in a deep breath as though steadying himself. "If the wrong people knew... well, that would be catastrophic."

"Don't call her that." Kiran seethed, bearing his teeth.

"Lighten up, Guardian," Sam replied, his eyes glinting as he regarded Kiran. "It only means how easily she blushes."

I rolled my eyes at them. "Can we take the testosterone down a level?" Mia, standing just behind Kiran, let her fingers drift down his arm. "I kinda like it when this one gets all protective," she purred as her hand came to rest on his bicep. "Blondie, you are one hot angel."

Kiran pulled his arm away, but Mia feigned wide-eyed innocence.

"Alright, Sam," I conceded, "Kiran and I will uncover the truth one way or another."

Sam's eyes darted towards Kiran, a silent warning flickering in their depths, cautioning him not to probe too deeply.

"What about Justin?" I asked.

"I really don't think..." Sam began. I cut him off.

"Sam, he hasn't answered any of my calls or texts. I need to know he is okay." My voice wavered slightly, betraying my anxiety.

Sam scowled, his lips pressing into a thin line. "He is fine."

"Where is he?" I pushed.

Sam sighed heavily. "He is at Vince's house. However, I would advise you not to go there looking for him." It was a sharp warning.

"Why?" I asked.

"You may not like what you see." He said simply.

A knot of anxiety twisted in my stomach. What was it that I wouldn't like? Was Justin really okay? The fear must have been swritten all over my face, as Sam added, "He is fine, Rhiannon. He's just...angry."

I turned to Kiran, desperation creeping into my voice. "I need to see him. I need to explain...I need..."

"Shhh," Kiran whispered soothingly, "He's safe, Rhi, and probably needs time to process everything. It's a lot to take in."

I felt a wave of warmth; Kiran's calming energy was like a soft blanket. Reluctantly, I nodded, accepting his reassurance.

"You two really need to get a room," Mia teased.

"Mia," I gasped. "He's an angel."

"I get that Lady Bug, but obviously angels get it on with humans, or we wouldn't have all these Nephilims walking around."

"True that." Sam chimed in.

"And," I added, leaning forward with a curious expression. "What about your girlfriend, Jess?" I asked pointedly, my eyes narrowing as I turned to Mia.

Mia huffed and plopped back down, crossing her legs in front of her, her colorful toe polish peeking out from between her sandals. "We broke up, we're friends though. I can't start my senior year tied down, I gotta play the field." She turned her gaze toward Kiran. "So, blondie, now that you're cool with us seeing you, when are you going to let the rest of the world in on your hotness?"

"Actually," Kiran began, his cheeks tinged with a hint of pink. "I was thinking of doing just that."

Sam and I turned in unison, "What?" We both exclaimed, the surprise evident in our voices.

Kiran shrugged, "It's only that you will be starting school in a couple of days, Rhi and I thought maybe I should accompany you."

"Wouldn't you already be with me?" I asked.

"Well, yes." He lowered his eyes, allowing his thick lashes to shield them from view. He seemed shy. "I just thought...since you don't really know anyone..."

"Hey now, she knows me!" Mia quipped. "And I won't let her just flounder her way through school."

"Yes, but I can manipulate things so I am in all of her classes with her, and people will be less likely to bother her with another person she seems to know around."

Sam let out a soft chuckle. "Don't you really mean that boys will be less likely to bother her?"

"Or girls, Sam," Mia interjected. "It's not like girls won't notice the new girl and want to get closer to my Lady Bug."

"Enough of all of this," Kiran snapped. "I just think it would be easier for everyone if I appear in my human form alongside Rhi at school." He hesitated, rubbing the back of his neck. "But I'm not sure how to explain my appearance. I don't want to lie to anyone…"

Sam cut him off. "Listen, Guardian, you aren't using your powers for anything nefarious. Just create a simple backstory. It's not a big deal."

Mia suddenly sprang to her feet, her eyes lighting up. "I have an idea! Why don't you say your family moved into Mr. Hollander's house? It's for sale, and that would make perfect sense!"

Sam stroked his jaw thoughtfully, glancing over at the weathered old house with its faded paint and overgrown garden. "That could work, Guardian. If anyone asks about your family, just tell them you're an only child, and your parents travel for work a lot," he advised. "I can handle getting you the place."

"Um, no," Kiran replied firmly, shaking his head. "I'll contact the agent myself and ensure she gets paid. I'm not glamoring my way into that home or lying."

I loved the idea of Kiran being by my side. His presence would anchor me in the bustling sea of unfamiliar faces. I loved Mia, but the idea of being paraded around like a shiny trophy to all her friends made my stomach churn.

I turned to Kiran. "Well, Kiran, I guess you get to experience one pretty big human rite of passage." I raised an eyebrow and giggled, "Going to high school."

Chapter Two

Rhiannon

I sat cross-legged on my rumpled bed, the quilt bunched beneath me, staring at the screen of my phone. My thumb hovered over the keyboard as I scrolled back through the litany of unanswered texts I'd sent to Justin.

Twenty-nine messages, each with no reply. Maybe the thirtieth would be the charm. I rotated the phone anxiously between my fingers, the smooth surface cool against my skin, and nearly dropped it when a sudden ping broke the silence.

Kacey: *We're going out! Last weekend before school starts.*

I really wasn't in the mood to go out. I wasn't really in the mood for anything, quite frankly.

I don't know Kace. I'm not really feeling it. I texted back.

I'm not taking no for an answer! Steve and I will be there at eight to pick you up. Be ready!

With a deep, resigned sigh, I imagined my cousin Kacey marching up to my door, her fiery determination dragging me out by my hair if necessary. I knew resistance was futile, so I texted back a simple fine, accompanied by a grumpy-faced emoji. Her response was swift, a cascade of pink heart emojis filling my screen.

I grasped my phone tightly between my fingers, deciding to send text number thirty. Justin. I typed. Please talk to me. I know how hard this is. My fingers hovered over the screen. And I miss you. I waited a moment and then hit send.

I stared intently at the screen, willing a reply to appear. The seconds ticked by, each one stretching longer than the last.

Nothing.

My heart sank and I flopped back onto my bed, the last shred of hope that Justin would reach out slipping away.

I picked back up my phone and texted Mia: *My cousins want to go to some party. Wanna come?*

Hell yes! I'm in.

I let out a heavy sigh and willed my body to rise from the cozy confines of my bed. My fingers skimmed over the spines of my CD collection, searching for the familiar cover. Finally, my hand landed on the Papa Roach CD, and with a satisfying click, I slid it into the player and cranked the volume.

I rummaged through my dresser, thinking I would just put on a pair of shorts and a t-shirt. I paused when I pulled out a particular one. It was the one Sam had dressed me in the night we went to the club. The black cotton shirt emblazoned with the bold phrase Half Angel Half Devil sprawled across the front. Justin had completely flipped when he saw me in that outfit, his eyes wild with jealousy.

The memory of Justin's explosive reaction gnawed at me; he had spiraled out of control over the mere thought of me spending time with Sam, who had simply been my babysitter during Kiran's absence in the Veil. Sam was just a friend who wanted to enjoy a night of dancing, but to Justin, it was a betrayal. I decided I was done wallowing in my feelings for him.

In a moment of defiance, I tossed the shirt onto my bed, the fabric landing in a messy heap, and turned toward the closet. I retrieved the flirty skirt, also from Sam, its soft fabric shimmering slightly in the light. I quickly slipped into the ensemble, opting for my comfortable sneakers instead of the heeled boots I had previously worn with the outfit.

This party was going to be my escape, a chance to enjoy myself without Justin's shadow looming over me. I whisked a coat of mascara onto my lashes, watching as they darkened and lengthened, and dusted a soft blush across my cheeks to bring some color to my pale complexion. I grabbed my strawberry lip gloss, the sweet scent wafting up as I applied a generous layer to my lips. I stuffed the tube into the pocket of my skirt before picking up the curling iron, creating soft waves that cascaded down my back.

I turned to admire my reflection in the mirror, feeling a flicker of confidence, just as Kiran suddenly appeared behind me.

I yelped in surprise, my heart racing as I caught sight of him in the mirror. Kiran grinned, his eyes sparkling with mischief. "You would think you would be used to it by now," he teased.

With a slight frown, I quipped, "I think I'll just put a bell around your neck."

He let out a deep, throaty laugh. "I'd like to see you try." His gaze shifted to my shirt, an amused eyebrow arching. "Really?"

"Sam gave it to me...well, more like he snapped his fingers and magically dressed me in it," I explained. "I like it."

Kiran frowned, "Are we going out tonight?"

I fluffed my hair out over my shoulders, letting the dark waves cascade down as I met his gaze in the mirror. "Yes, Kacey and Steve want to go to a party before school starts on Monday. I invited Mia too."

I maneuvered around him to check my phone on the dresser, but it remained devoid of any messages from Justin.

Kiran sauntered over to my bed and flopped onto it with a casual grace, folding his hands behind his head. I couldn't help but admire how utterly beautiful he looked, his wavy blonde hair spilling across the pillow, his eyes striking against his tanned skin. One side of his lips ticked up as my eyes roamed over him. "Am I dressed appropriately?" he asked.

"What? I mean, yes, you look beautiful...I mean, you look..." I stammered, flustered.

Propping himself up on his elbows, he clarified. "I mean for going out. Do I look like any other normal teenager?"

"There is nothing about you that is normal." I deadpanned. "Are you saying you're going to let everyone see you?"

"I am." He flopped back down as I sat beside him. "I took care of the house down the street."

My eyebrows shot up in surprise. "So you're a homeowner now?"

"Something like that."

"How are you going to make this work?" I asked. "I mean, you don't lie, so what are you going to tell people about how you came to live in Mr. Hollander's house?" I leaned in closer, the space between us crackling with energy.

He turned on his side, propping himself up on one elbow. "I don't plan on saying anything except that I'm new in town, which is technically true, and that is where I live." He let one long finger slide along my hand, sending a rush of electricity through me.

I lifted my gaze from his mesmerizing touch to meet his steady eyes. "Humans are curious. People are going to ask questions."

He shrugged, his muscled shoulders shifting beneath his shirt. "I'll figure it out. It's not like I'll be reprimanded by anyone. I'm Fallen."

His words made my heart tighten with a mix of sorrow and guilt, a reminder of the sacrifice he had made. "So, no rules now?" I asked hesitantly, unsure of the boundaries that now defined his existence.

"Not really," he admitted, a hint of resignation in his voice. "I have free will and can choose my actions. I don't wish to be disobedient, but it doesn't really matter anymore. There isn't much more the powers that be can do to me now that I'm bound to Earth for eternity."

Despite his attempt to mask it, I could see the sadness in his eyes, a deep, lingering sorrow that he struggled to hide.

"I'm sorry," I whispered.

"No, you're not doing that," he said, pressing his fingers gently against my lips, silencing my apology. "I will not let you take responsibility for my actions. I chose to save Justin."

I let the subject drop for now, but I had promised myself I would find a way to help Kiran through this.

"Have you been in the house yet?"

He shook his head. "No, and I don't really care to go through it. It's just an address to attach my human identity to." He suddenly sat up with a spark of energy. "I did register myself at school, and we share all the same classes."

I couldn't help but giggle, "You've been busy."

He smiled down at me, a glimmer of excitement in his eyes. "I think I'll like experiencing school."

I laughed, "You say that now."

Kiran abruptly sat up straight. "Your cousins just pulled up. I'll head to Mia's and have her introduce me to them."

Before I could respond, he vanished into thin air.

I skipped down the stairs, eagerly throwing open the door. Steve and Kacey were halfway up the steps. "I'm ready. Just let me say goodbye to Nan," I said, turning back into the house.

I found her in my grandfather's office, her hands deep in a box, rummaging through its contents. "Nan, I'm heading out."

She jerked upright, startled. "Rhi, you scared me."

"I'm sorry, Nan. I just wanted to let you know I was heading out with Kacey and Steve."

She quickly moved in front of the box, trying to shield its contents from my view. I wondered what she didn't want me to see.

She shuffled towards me, gently nudging me out of the room. "Have fun, dear. Try not to be too late."

"What were you looking for, Nan?"

"Oh, just some old photos," she replied with an unconvincing wave of her hand.

I had never doubted my grandmother before, but now I had a distinct feeling she wasn't telling me the whole truth.

Chapter Three

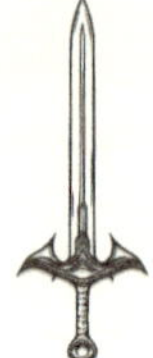

Kiran

I knocked lightly on Mia's bedroom door.

"Enter." She called. "Whoa!" she exclaimed, her eyes widening in surprise as I suddenly popped into her room.

"What? I did knock," I said, flashing a crooked grin as I lounged against the wall, hands buried deep in my pockets.

"True, but you could just walk through the door," she teased, expertly gliding a glimmering gloss across her lips. Her vanity overflowed with makeup and tangled jewelry. She winked at me, her reflection grinning in the mirror.

"I'm planning on allowing Rhi's cousins to see me tonight. I'd really appreciate it if you could introduce me to them."

Her dark eyes glimmered with mischief, a scheming smile tugging at her lips. *Witches,* I thought, watching her, *always up to something.*

"Sure, blondie," she shot back. "Shall I spin some grand tale about how you were abandoned as a child, met your father only to discover he's a monster, have a twin brother—a hot one, by the way—and you're secretly in love with his girlfriend?" Her smile turned downright wicked, lighting up her face with mischief.

"First of all..." I began, but she quickly shushed me.

"Don't worry. I won't give away your deep, dark secret, Kiran. How about I tell them you're new to town, and I snatched you up to be all mine?"

I rolled my eyes again. "New in town, great. Snatched me up? I don't think so."

"It was worth a try," she said, laughing as she grabbed her purse off the dresser. "If you ever get over my Lady Bug, I'm more than happy to snatch you up."

"Why do you call Rhi that? Lady Bug?"

"I was taught that ladybugs are harbingers of good fortune and bring luck. Plus, they are undeniably beautiful. When Rhi came back, she remembered my fascination with bugs. She's stunning, both inside and out, and I feel incredibly fortunate to have her as my friend and neighbor."

I felt a genuine warmth spread across my face as I smiled, "Those are actually really good reasons."

She huffed, throwing her bag over her shoulder. "Of course they are!"

Witch or not, Mia was a genuinely kind person, and I was grateful Rhi had someone like her in her life.

As we stepped out of Mia's cozy, herb-scented house, I spotted Rhi's cousins gathered near the foot of the stairs. "Hey guys!" Mia called out, waving enthusiastically.

We met them just as Rhi came bouncing through the door, her long, dark hair catching the last streams of the evening light in a cascade of shimmering waves. My heart skipped a beat every time I saw her. She was my Ahavah, my love. The feelings I harbored for her were as endless as the sky above. I would do anything for her.

Anything.

I was now a Fallen because of those feelings. I could not take the pain in her eyes as she begged me to save my twin. The thought of her hating me for letting the Angel of Death take him was unbearable. My priorities had shifted; the once unshakeable loyalty to the Creator now overshadowed. My life, my very existence, was devoted to her and her alone.

"Hey," Rhi said. "Who's your friend, Mia?"

"I was about to ask the same thing." Rhi's cousin Kacey chimed in with a bright smile that revealed a row of straight teeth, her chocolate brown eyes gleaming with interest.

Mia squeezed my arm. "This is Kiran. He just moved in down the street. I invited him to go out with us tonight. I hope that's okay?"

"Nice to meet you, Kiran," Rhi said, extending her delicate hand towards me. Her fingers were slender and graceful, the nails polished in a soft pink hue. Pulling my hands from my pockets, I took her hand in mine, feeling a sudden jolt of electricity that seemed to travel up my arm. It was a sensation I couldn't quite understand, but the closer we were, the more intense it became.

"You as well."

"Hey, man, I'm Steve, and this is Kacey." He motioned his hands between them. Steve had a casual demeanor with an easygoing, genuine smile.

Kacey bounced on her heels, full of energy as she beamed at me. "When did you get here? What house does your family live in? Do you have any siblings? What grade are you in?" Her questions fired rapidly one after the other.

"Kacey, give the guy a second to answer," Steve said, nudging her gently.

"It's okay," I reassured with a smile, meeting the gaze of Rhi's younger cousin. Her wide eyes were fixed intently on me, curiosity etched across her youthful face. "I have brothers and sisters, but they don't live with me," I explained, skirting around the truth. "I just moved into that house over there." I gestured toward the shadowy silhouette of the house I had recently acquired at the end of the street.

"Seriously? Mr. Hollander's house?" Kacey's eyes widened further, almost comically. "Have you seen any ghosts?"

I chuckled, shaking my head. "Not yet."

"That old man, Mr. Hollander, was really strange," Kacey continued, her voice dropping to a conspiratorial whisper. "We hardly ever saw him around. I went to his door once when I was in Girl Scouts. He opened the door just a crack, the chain still latched, and glared at me like I was some kind of intruder." She shivered slightly. "I was so nervous; I couldn't even ask him if he wanted to buy any cookies."

"You, at a loss for words?" Steve teased.

Kacey shot Steve a sharp look and punched him on the arm. "Shut up, I'm telling a story." She turned back to me, "Anyway, I just turned and left. That place gave me the creeps so badly." Her large doe eyes blinked at me. "I'd love to see inside now that you live there, though."

"Sure," I said with a nod, "maybe one day."

"Yay! Ghost hunting." Her enthusiasm was infectious, but I couldn't help glancing at Rhi, who was standing next to her. Rhi's lips were pressed into a thin line as she scowled slightly at her cousin.

As I ran my hand along the smooth, freshly polished hood of Steve's vintage Gran Torino, I couldn't help but admire it. "Nice car," I remarked.

"Thanks," Steve replied, his face lighting up with pride. "I've been restoring her myself."

"Her name is Hottie," Rhi said as she slid into the back seat, a hint of amusement in her voice.

"Fitting," I agreed.

We all piled into the Gran Torino, the leather seats creaking beneath us. Steve revved the engine, its deep growl vibrating through the car. "To the res then," he announced as we set off.

Steve maneuvered the car into the reservation, only to find the parking lot surprisingly empty. "That's weird," he muttered, driving slowly past the vacant spaces. "Where is everyone?"

"Wait, what?" Kacey piped up from the back seat, her voice tinged with confusion. "Supposedly, the party got moved."

"Moved where?" Steve asked.

"You're not going to believe this," Kacey leaned over the seat, showing us a text on her cell phone. "The party got moved to Vince Moretti's mansion."

I heard Rhi's intake of breath.

"I wonder if that is where Justin has been," Steve said.

I could sense the tension rolling off Rhi, her posture rigid.

"We should go!" Kacey said eagerly, her eyes darting between us. "I've always wanted to see inside that place."

What she didn't remember was that she *had* been in Vince's mansion. The memories of her captivity in Vince's mansion had been erased from her mind. She had no recollection of being used as bait to lure me in, or of Sam's intervention that had wiped the entire traumatic episode from her consciousness.

Steve glanced at his sister, uncertainty etched on his face. "I don't know if we should." He looked at Rhi, and I turned to observe her reaction. "How do you feel about it, Rhi?"

Rhi's eyes were wide, dark pools flicking between us. She straightened her spine, resolve hardening her features. "We should go."

"What?!" I whispered in her head. Because she was my ward and I her Guardian, we could communicate telepathically. *"I don't think that's a good idea."*

"Yes, it is." She hissed back. *"I'm going to punch that ass right in the face."*

Chapter Four

Justin

I whittled away at the wood on the bedpost, creating the face of a wolf, but as I continued to manipulate the blade, I still saw *her* face. I huffed loudly, throwing the knife across the room to embed in the door. It creaked open as a dark-haired beauty with a face so like my own peered in.

"I'll try not to take that personally," she said, slipping inside and closing the door behind her. She pulled the knife free from the wood with practiced ease. "Are you going to join us?"

My newly discovered sister, Sorcha, had decided to have a party to celebrate the fact that our DNA donor, Vince, seemed to be gone for good. I didn't believe it. That snake was just hiding out somewhere, waiting to strike. She seemed to invite every teen and young adult in this neighborhood.

She sashayed across the room, her outfit blurring the line between dress and lingerie— a lacy bodysuit beneath a sheer mini-skirt, paired with deliberately torn fishnets that left little to the imagination.

Handing me back my knife, her gaze roamed over me.

I shot her an irritated look, "What?"

"Sam says she keeps asking for you. Why are you just sitting up here feeling sorry for yourself? Just go see her."

Her.

Rhiannon. The one girl I had ever given my heart to, only to find out she had known all this insane truth about me and kept it buried. I was a Nephilim — a child of a human and an angel. That snake Vince had manipulated my mother into believing she was destined to bring a divine child into the world. Right. I was the farthest thing from divine there could be. Well — maybe not the farthest, considering I was staring at my half-sister, who was half demon and half angel.

What kind of angel slept with a demon? My scum of a DNA donor, that's who. Sorcha was a Cambion. She seemed normal enough except for the red and silver in her eyes. She said I could *"see"* other beings now because the cross I had always worn since I was a baby had cloaked them from me and me from them. She said humans couldn't see the aura in our eyes.

The first time I looked at myself in the mirror since taking off the cross, I saw a swirl of silver in my eyes. The same silver as Kiran.

My anger boiled over thinking about him — that so-called brother of mine. He had Rhi all to himself. He was her Guardian, but Vince had said he loved her. Really loved her. And I had seen it with my own eyes. The way Kiran looked at her, with that raw, aching longing — it made me want to tear his blonde head clean off his shoulders.

I stood moving to the table in the corner of the room. I chose this room because it was the farthest away from anyone else in the house. It had a large four-poster bed with a thick velvet comforter. There was a whole wall of books and a large bay window that looked over the grounds at the back of the house. I grabbed the bottle of whiskey and took a swig of it. It was almost gone.

When I had explored the mansion, I found a wine cellar with some of the most expensive liquor I had ever seen. This was the fourth one that I had gone through since coming to stay here.

Sorcha had blocked the door that led to the basement and that...dungeon. She also used some kind of otherworldly magic to fix the gaping hole that looked down into that dungeon. What kind of insane person had a dungeon in their house?

"Justin?" Sorcha hedged.

"I don't want to see her." I spat.

"Sure. Keep lying to yourself."

I turned on her. "Get out, Sorcha!"

She turned on her heel, stopping with her hand on the handle of the door. "You can't hide from everyone forever."

She left, the door silently clicking behind her. I growled, my chest heaving as I threw the bottle across the room. It careened into the bookshelf, shattering into tiny pieces.

Several books fell from the shelf. I balled my fists, pushing them against my eyes. I walked to the mess and knelt down to gather the fallen books. I would have to sneak through the party to get some more alcohol. I gathered the books in my arms and began to place them back onto the shelf. As my hand got close to the shelf, I felt a breeze.

That was odd.

I ran my hand along the back of the shelf, the dark wood cool beneath my fingertips. There was a gap at the back of the shelf. I placed the books back on the floor and pushed at the gap, hearing a click.

"What the?"

The whole bookcase swung open. A damp breeze moved over me. I looked back over my shoulder, deciding to lock my door in case Sorcha came back. I still didn't trust her, even though she had been nothing but accepting and kind to me. The girl was more like me than my other siblings, Scott and...Kiran.

I slipped between the bookshelf into a tunnel as tiny goose bumps erupted across my skin. The tunnel was stone. Much like the one that led to the dungeon. The rocks were dark, and I pulled out a lighter, squinting into the darkness.

I noticed a sconce on the wall and lit it with the lighter. As soon as I lit the first, dozens more erupted with flame. I gasped as the tunnel lit up and the dampness seemed to dissipate. I walked along the stone floor. My boots echoed with every step I took. The tunnel wasn't very long until it came to a dead end with a ladder against the wall. I stared up into the darkness above the ladder.

"Oh, what the hell?" I mumbled to myself and began to climb up into the darkness.

It opened into a small circular room with a glass ceiling. This must be the turret I could see from the outside, but never knew how to access.

I gazed up at the starlit sky. It was quiet here, quiet and peaceful. I couldn't hear the ruckus of the party below. I sighed, feeling a bit of relief at the solitude. My gaze drifted around the circular room. There wasn't much here. A chaise sat against one wall. It looked old. Older than the other things I had seen in the mansion.

I walked towards it, running my fingers over the lush material. I sat down heavily, hanging my head into my hands. I sighed, turning my head to see a chest pushed against the back of the chaise. I stood, pushing the chaise to reach the chest.

I grabbed the handle and pulled. It was heavy. Almost too heavy to move, but I managed. I swung the lid back, taking my lighter out once again to look inside. "More books?" Seriously?"

Something caught my eye. The wording on the leather cover of the top book. It seemed to move before my eyes. I shoved my lighter back into my pocket and grabbed the book, bringing it into the moonlight to look at it more closely.

The letters and symbols on the cover were definitely moving — writhing, almost alive. I dropped the book, my heart slamming against my ribs. It fell open where it landed, catching a sliver of moonlight. The words curled and shifted like smoke across the page. Then, as suddenly as it had started, the movement stilled — and the text resolved into plain English.

I kneeled by it, my hand shaking as I touched the page. Squinting in the low light, I read the paragraph on the page.

"And the scribes shall write all the judgments of the angels, and they shall remember them from generation to generation. And their names shall be written before the glory of the Lord of Spirits."

I flipped the page, and more shadows evaporated into words I could understand. "This looks like a book on angels and demons," I said aloud, my voice echoing in the chamber. I picked up the book and headed back to my room. I shut the bookcase, keeping that secret room to myself.

Chapter Five

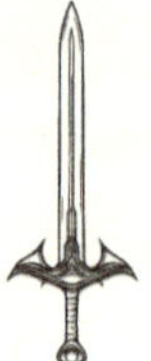

Rhiannon

My blood was boiling as we pulled up to Vince's mansion. Cars overflowed from the long driveway up and down the street. I flew out of the door even before the car came to a complete stop.

Mia and Kiran were on my heels immediately, Kacey and Steve calling out to us.

"Lady Bug!" Mia said, grabbing my hand and twirling me around, "Girl, take a breath."

"I agree," Kiran stated flatly.

Kacey and Steve met us at the base of the stairs. I did as Mia asked and breathed deeply. "Rhi, we don't have to go in if seeing Justin is too much for you," Steve said, squeezing my shoulder.

I stared up the grand staircase. Several people were lounging on the steps, laughing among themselves.

My last visit to this place left me with scars both seen and unseen. Vince used me to lure Kiran, hoping to steal the grace that could free him from his earthbound prison. In the end, Vince's plan crumbled, but not without cost. Though Kiran's grace remained beyond Vince's grasp, it was lost all the same when Kiran himself fell from grace, becoming what Vince had been—Fallen.

I sighed, "I'm fine." My eyes scanned all of my companions. "Really. I promise."

We all ascended the stairs together. The door at the top was open. The house was crowded with people. Music was pumping from somewhere. I scanned the faces for him…for Justin. How could he have a party and at Vince's of all places? We all moved through the house as I spotted Sam dancing seductively with Sorcha.

"Sam!" Mia called out. His head snapped in our direction.

"Sam, what the hell?" Mia smacked him on his arm. "Why didn't you tell me you were going to be here? Or about this party at all?"

Sam smiled broadly at her as his eyes slid to me. I knew why. He didn't want me here. "I didn't really think this was your crowd."

Mia put her hands on her hips. "All crowds are my crowds." She said.

"This place is crawling with demons and all other sorts of supernatural beings," Kiran said in my mind.

"Of course it is." I mind spoke back to him.

"Rhi," Sam nodded to me.

"I know you know where he is," I said accusingly.

Sorcha looked between us, "I'll take you to him."

Sam's head snapped to her, "I don't think…"

Sorcha grabbed my hand, "Yes, Sam, you don't think." She said with a glint in her eye.

"I can go with you, Rhi," Steve said, starting to follow Sorcha and me.

"It's okay, enjoy yourself. I'll be fine."

He didn't look convinced. Kiran took a step towards us, but Sam intercepted him. A worried look crossed his features as Sorcha pulled me through the crowd.

Her hand was warm and soft, very human feeling. Her dark hair was down, flowing like black silk. So much like Justin's.

"Hey girls, can I join you?"

"You wish, Phen," Sorcha said playfully over her shoulder. Phen was tall and slender with copper hair and brown eyes.

"You're right, I do." He smirked and I scowled at him. His eyes widened briefly, and he nodded to me, almost reverently. I felt his gaze on us as we continued walking up the spiraling staircase.

"Ignore him," Sorcha said. I turned and looked at him over my shoulder. His eyes locked onto mine, and he raised the beer he was holding as in salute.

"Ugh, demon princes. They're so entitled." Sorcha huffed.

"Demon prince?"

"Yeah, Phen. He's a demon prince. He's in a band. He has a poetic way with words and has girls falling at his feet when he sings or recites his poetry." We turned right and headed up another flight of stairs. There were large paintings on the walls. They looked so much like the stained glass in Our Lady of Swords church, all religious themed. "He'll sweet-talk you right into his bed."

We finally got to the top of the stairs and headed down a long hallway. "His room is the last door on the left."

I followed her gaze down the hallway. "His room? So, he's moved in here?"

Sorcha shrugged one slender shoulder. "I wouldn't say he's moved in, but he's staying here for now."

"What about Vince? Do you think he's coming back?"

Her eyes grew hard. "If he does, I'll destroy him."

I saw the demon side of her then. No remorse, no fear, just a promise of demise.

I smiled meekly at her, "Thank you for bringing me and I'm sorry Vince treated you so badly."

A glimmer of sadness passed over her features. "Well, it's not all bad. Now that he's gone, that leaves Justin and me to run his empire."

"I thought he said he had lots of heirs?"

"I've never met one. They either are long gone or don't know what they are. Kind of like Justin. He would have gone through life not knowing he was a Nephilim if everything that transpired hadn't happened."

I took a deep breath. "Yeah, if I had never come here and gotten involved with him." A thought struck me. "What about Kiran? He's also your brother."

She laughed without humor. "I'm sure he doesn't want anything to do with any of Vince's businesses or associates, but if he wants in, I'm not opposed to it. Justin on the other hand..."

"You're right. I'm sure he wouldn't want any part of it." I stared down the hallway. "Has he said anything to you about me?"

She shook her head. "I told him he needed to see you." She laughed lightly, "He's stubborn, but I'm sure you already know that."

"I do."

She squeezed my hand. "Good luck. I'll try to keep your Guardian busy to give you some privacy." She grinned conspiratorially, "He's a Fallen now, he doesn't have to be so uptight." She skipped down the stairs, leaving me alone in the hall.

I padded down the soft carpeted floor until I came to the door Sorcha had pointed out. I listened and heard nothing. My hand shook as I raised it and knocked lightly.

Heavy footsteps pounded the floor, and then the door flew open. First, his eyes registered shock, and just as quickly, his brows slammed down on his forehead. "How did you know where I was?"

"No, you don't get to do that," I scowled at him.

"Do what?"

"You don't get to ask me how or why. Why haven't *you* texted or called me? Or how about Scott or your parents?"

Justin crossed his arms across his chest. His eyes scanned me from my toes up my body, sending chills dancing down my spine. He stopped and met my gaze. "Nice outfit. I seem to remember you wearing it when you went out with Sam and not telling me."

I felt heat crawl up the back of my neck. "And I seem to remember telling you that you don't own me."

He laughed without any humor. "Yeah, obviously."

I took a deep breath, then another, trying to calm my racing heart. He was so cold. I couldn't think of a time when he ever acted so indifferent to me. "We should talk about what happened."

He ignored me, looking past me down the hall. "Where's your shadow?"

I growled, "His name is Kiran, and he's your bro—"

His eyes snapped to mine with fire in the green depths. "Do not call him my brother."

I pushed past him, entering his room without invitation.

He turned, a look of shock on his face, and then scowled again. It was my turn to cross my arms over my chest and stare him down. "You're being a pig-headed, uptight, ass..."

He kicked the door with his foot with a loud smack. He crossed the distance between us in two strides. "You knew, you knew about all of this," he waved his hands around him. "About Vince, about my...my heritage, and most importantly, you knew about this brother of mine and never said a word to me."

I opened my mouth to respond, but he cut me off. "How could you, Rhi? How could you lie to me after I laid my heart and soul at your feet?"

That took me by surprise. Some of my anger dissolved as I looked closer at his features. I thought he was just angry and he definitely was, but underneath that anger was sorrow. "If you would let me explain," I said quietly.

"Explain then."

I took a step back, feeling small under his unrelenting gaze. My eyes glided over the room. There was a large floor-length bay window with dark velvet curtains. There were bookshelves overflowing with books. A small desk sat in the corner with an open book upon it, and the bed...well, the bed was massive with luxurious-looking bedding and large fluffy pillows. And the bed posts. He had been carving on them just like his bed at home.

I had to look anywhere but at him. At his long, lean body covered in tight black jeans and a black t-shirt that totally emphasized his hard abs and arms. His thick black hair was pulled back, emphasizing his sharp cheekbones. He was sexy as hell even with that obnoxious scowl on his face.

He interrupted my contemplation. "Well?"

"Kiran and I met not long after I got here. I didn't tell anyone. Mostly because who would believe me? They would think I was crazy if I said I had a Guardian Angel. I had a hard time believing it myself." I walked towards the window and glanced out at the night sky. "I didn't find out about you until the night I went out with Sam." I looked over my shoulder at him. He was still scowling. "It's kind of a long story, but basically, Sam knew about the plans Vince had for me. He sent Kiran on a mission before he would let us know what danger I was in. In reality, he was helping us. He sent Kiran to find a rune to help him defeat Vince."

I turned to face him fully. His features had softened, only slightly. "Would you have believed me if I told you any of this? You weren't even convinced when we were in that...that dungeon."

He let out a deep sigh. "No, I, you're right. I didn't fully believe it myself until I took off my cross. I can see things I never thought existed."

I smiled slightly, "I didn't mean to hurt you, Justin." I said quietly.

He took a step towards me, then halted like he thought twice about getting too close. "I can understand that. I know how crazy it seems because, honestly, I still sometimes think I'm dreaming. What I can't understand, though, is how you let...Kiran," he growled his name. "How do you let him be around you all the time, knowing how he feels about you?"

My chest tightened, and I found it hard to breathe. He took another step closer and then another until his chest touched mine and our breath mingled.

"He's always with you, and he is in love with you."

"He's...my...Guardian." I choked out.

"And I'm a man, Rhi." Then his mouth crushed into mine. The hardness of his arms melted around me as his teeth caught my bottom lip and oh God...

My lips parted beneath his, and all I could feel was the wicked pleasure that coursed through me, and still my body wanted more.

His hands slid down my sides, skimming over my ribs, setting my flesh on fire. He moaned deeply into my mouth, and then his hands were on my thighs, lifting me so my legs wrapped around his body. I pulled at the tie holding his hair back, letting the midnight-black strands flow like silk around us both. He lifted me higher, and I gasped as the thin material of my underwear touched his rough jeans.

Then he pushed my back against the bookcase so hard that books cascaded around us. He pushed his body even tighter against me, and every soft part of me felt every hard part of him. I gasped at the sensation, and his mouth went crazy on mine, in a chaotic mixture of our lips, teeth, and tongues. Desperate need wrapped around me as he obliterated my senses.

I pulled my lips away from his and searched his eyes. He was breathing heavily, almost as heavily as I was. "Is this a yes?" He exhaled sharply.

I stared at the green depths of his eyes, which seemed to blaze with fire. There was a brilliant flash of silver there, too. I blinked, and it was gone. This could be it. I could give myself fully to Justin. Lord knew my body wanted him. I brushed my lips against his lightly. My lips felt tender and swollen as I delicately kissed him. I pulled back slightly, pressing my forehead against his.

"I'm so confused, Justin," I whispered.

His fingers dug into my thighs like a brand. He walked us to the bed, his intense stare never leaving mine. His body hovered over mine, blocking out the light. "I can take you right now."

He pressed against me, skimming a hand up my leg and hitching it over his waist. I felt exposed again, and barely anything separated him from me. He ran his nose along my cheek until his lips caressed the shell of my ear. "Joining our bodies like we did our hearts." He breathed against my ear, sending shivers cascading down my spine. "And you would forget him. You would forget everything except you and me."

He raised himself slightly to meet my stare once again, and what I saw there terrified me. Because I knew what he said was true. My body ached for that. To lose myself in him, and he knew it.

His lips quirked up on one side, "You know it too don't you?"

I did. At least I thought I did. I couldn't think straight with us like this. With the heat of his body setting my skin aflame. I loved this reckless, dangerous boy, but...

His fingers kept caressing my leg where it wrapped around his waist. My heart twisted in my chest. I took a deep breath because this wasn't fair to any of us.

Stupid common sense. My body objected, wanting...needing. I was drowning, I was burning. I was a complete wreck and didn't know how to save myself.

There was a loud banging against the door, and Justin's head snapped up.

"Rhi!"

It was Kiran.

Chapter Six

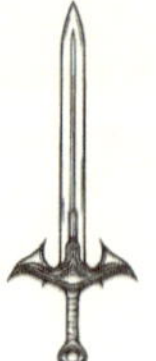

Rhiannon

The sound Justin made was like that of a feral beast. He pushed himself off the bed, storming towards the door as Kiran continued banging on it.

"I'm going to kill him," Justin growled.

I hurried off the bed, adjusting my skirt as I ran to intercept him. I came up short behind him as he ripped the door open so ferociously I thought it would come off the hinges.

Kiran looked like the Angel of Death. His eyes bore into Justin's as his chest heaved. "What are you doing to her?"

I looked beyond Justin and Kiran to see Sorcha leaning against the wall. She shrugged her shoulders as if to say she tried.

Justin steadied himself. "I thought you could sense her feelings," Justin said. "She's enjoying herself."

Kiran's nostrils flared. "Enjoying? No, not enjoyment. Lust, confusion, fear. That is what I felt." Kiran reached for me, but Justin's arm shot out and pushed him back. "You really want to do this?" Kiran asked, his voice low and controlled.

"More than you know," Justin said through gritted teeth. He lunged for Kiran, fist clenched and ready to strike. Kiran's hand shot up in a blur of motion, catching Justin's wrist effortlessly.

"Get your hands off me," Justin hissed as he swung his other arm wildly. But Kiran blocked every blow with ease.

I pushed my way between them before things got worse and turned on both of them angrily. "Stop it! Just stop!"

Kiran's eyes softened slightly but stayed fixed on me; Justin backed away reluctantly, glaring at his brother like a caged animal thirsting for blood.

"You shouldn't have barged in here," I pointed accusingly at Kiran.

"And you—you didn't need to provoke him," I snapped back toward Justin.

"Provoke?" Justin seethed. He shoved me aside and lunged at Kiran with a furious swing.

"Justin!" I screamed as they both burst down the hallway, grappling like wild animals.

Kiran moved like liquid silver—dodging every strike while barely lifting a finger against Justin's assault until finally shoving him hard against the wall where Sorcha stood waiting silently; she didn't even flinch when it cracked under the impact. Kiran grabbed Justin's wrist and pulled it behind his back, locking it in place. "End this now."

"You guys are unbelievable!" My voice cracked somewhere between anger and tears.

Kiran turned towards me. His face fell at what he saw there. He let go of Justin, taking a step away from him.

The air crackled around us as Sam appeared. "I see we're having a party," Sam said, cool as midnight. "Didn't expect you to start the fun without me."

"What do you want?" Justin spat, rubbing his shoulder.

Sam leaned casually against the wall next to Sorcha. "I was looking for Sorcha," he drawled. "But it looks like I stumbled onto something way more entertaining." He glanced between Kiran and Justin knowingly.

Kiran straightened but didn't take his eyes off me or the hurt expression on my face. "We're trying to resolve things."

Sam's gaze flicked to me, then back at Kiran and Justin with an exaggerated understanding dawning across his face. "Both acting all territorial over her? That's cute," Sam continued smoothly. "But seriously guys—how about letting Rhi decide who she wants?" Sam said, shoving his hands in the pockets of his faded jeans.

Rage rippled across Justin's face while even Kiran looked stung by Sam's words; neither spoke, though.

The pressure of Sam's words pressed in on all sides, making the hallway feel impossibly tight. "I—" I stammered, looking helplessly between Justin and Kiran.

"You don't have to do it right now, sweet cheeks. How about we all chill and go back to the party? The band has started playing downstairs," Sam said casually.

Justin pushed past Kiran roughly, rage still simmering beneath his skin as he retreated towards his room. I started after him but stopped when his door slammed shut behind him so hard it shook the wall.

Kiran took a tentative step towards me; his fingers reached gently for mine, but I pulled away, fighting stinging tears as frustration boiled over inside me.

"Rhi!" he called after me softly when I turned and fled down the hall.

I stopped at the top of the staircase, glancing behind me. Sam was talking to Kiran. As if he felt my eyes upon him, Kiran looked up, his silver eyes full of what looked like remorse.

I quickly ran down the stairs, pushing past people lounging on the stairs and against the wall.

Music swallowed me whole the moment I hit the main floor of the mansion. I pushed through the crowd looking for Mia, Kacey, and Steve—and stopped dead when I saw him. The demon prince, Phen. His voice smoldered into the microphone he held between long, lean fingers, his shirt long gone. Intricate tattoos swept from his shoulder down his side, twisting along impossibly defined abs before disappearing beneath the low waistband of his pants.

I heard unbridled screams of admiration from the crowd and turned to see Kacey yelling up at him, her body shaking to the music. Mia was next to her, dancing along with her. Phen reached towards Kacey, cupping her cheek in his hand, and winked at her. She screamed again like an obsessed fan girl.

Phen looked away from Kacey, his eyes burning as he raised the microphone back to his lips and locked eyes with me. His voice simmered through the room with a haunting edge.

"I once flew high," he sang while fingers flirted along the mic. *"Fell far and wide."* The words threaded through the crowd, pulling everyone in closer as more girls joined Kacey in a frenzied scream. *"Love bound me low—unwanted by her side."*

I heard Kacey laugh deliriously over the music that seemed louder now; she danced even harder when Phen's gaze found hers again and lingered there pointedly throughout another verse. *"Shattered wings never heal..."* He leaned down, reaching out to stroke wispy strawberry blonde tendrils off Kacey's forehead gently before releasing them back into wild disarray with an amused grin playing on his sculpted lips.

I pushed forward towards Mia and my cousin. There was no way a demon prince was going to seduce my cousin. Mia noticed me and waved me towards them. She stopped dancing long enough to grab my hand, yanking me beside her just as the band launched furiously into a fast riff.

"Ohmygod can you believe this!" Mia shouted gleefully above the noise crashing around us.

Kacey saw that I'd made it next to them and shrieked, "He is soooo amazing!"

"Is this what you want?" Phen asked, voice smoldering over the mic as his hand slipped over his chest suggestively.

I thought Kacey was going to faint.

"Yeah, we do!" Mia screamed, reaching for his sweat-covered chest.

I yanked her hand back, "Mia!"

Her dark brows furrowed, "Relax, Lady Bug." She grabbed my hips with her slim hands to get me to dance with her.

Kacey screeched again as Phen turned his gaze on us, dark eyes simmering. I felt every beat pounding through me while Phen's haunting lyrics filled the room. His voice was molten honey dripping over each word. *"I reached for Heaven. Touched only air. Looking for something that wasn't there..."*

Phen pulled Kacey into him, wrapping an arm around her tiny frame. He sang to her as his hips swayed suggestively. Kacey seemed to melt into him.

I reached for her arm, but she swatted me away. Mia pulled me back against her, "Let her have some fun, Lady Bug."

"We fell forever...Love never came."

Phen twirled Kacey effortlessly—not missing a single heartbeat as an eruption of cheers echoed throughout the room. He smiled wickedly and pulled the mic back to his lips, voice low like a dark promise. *"Fell from grace for you- Broke my wings in two- Longing but never yours,"* he sang, each word pulling shouts of adoration from the crowd. Kacey practically melted as he pulled her against him once more.

"Touch me if you dare." His voice was deep and rough.

Kacey did. Her hands slid down his chest, following the ornate tattoo.

"Oh, you go, girl!" Mia screamed.

A smug grin appeared on Phen's face as he pulled away from Kacey and winked.

Music pulsed as I felt him—Kiran. My shoulders tensed, and I turned back to see him at the edge of the crowd, watching me. Sam stood next to him with an amused expression on his face.

The entire room fell away. It was only me and Kiran, and the weight of his piercing gaze. I had come so close tonight to giving myself to Justin. I loved him—but I loved Kiran too, and the two truths sat inside me like broken glass. After tonight, I wasn't sure Justin would ever look at me the same way again.

The lyrics snapped my attention back to Phen: *"I've taken all your lies- Worn them like disguise-"* Phen's eyes locked on mine again, even as his fingers slid down across Kacey's hip. I swore those lyrics were aimed at me.

"Getting hotter, isn't it?" Phen taunted into the mic while pushing copper hair off his damp forehead. "Anyone ready for more?"

Girls shrieked frantically around me, demanding another song. Mia pleaded beside me, jumping up and down, "Yes, please! Please!"

I caught Steve out of the corner of my eye, cutting through the crowd towards us. "Kace!" He yelled, trying to make himself heard above the enthusiastic crowd. "What are you doing?"

Kacey didn't even bother looking at him; too busy watching every move that Phen made. She seemed completely spellbound by him.

"Seriously? A rock singer?" He practically growled, tugging on her arm.

"What?" She batted innocently long lashes up at him, trying not to look too pleased about the attention the shirtless singer had given her.

Steve scowled as she pulled her arm free from his grasp.

Phen swaggered closer to us. His voice was smooth as he turned his attention to Steve. "We're just having a bit of fun."

Steve's annoyance clouded his face before concentrating into a hard glare focused on the singer.

Kacey continued to cling to Phen's side unrepentant.

Mia threw an arm across Steve's shoulders. "Lighten up!" She smiled mischievously, yanking Steve closer to her while he continued to glare at Phen. She batted her eyes playfully, bumping against him with slim hips before dropping her arms to his waist, pulling him against her. "Come on, let's go explore this place!"

"You're kidding, right?" Disbelief crossed his face, but Mia pushed up on her tiptoes, whispering something in his ear. His eyebrows rose, and then resignation softened his features enough that she knew she'd won him over.

I watched Mia pull Steve along with her until they disappeared into a churning ocean of bodies, leaving me standing next to Kacey, who looked like she'd just won the lottery—with the prize being a demon prince rock singer smiling wickedly down upon both of us.

"Come with me?" Phen asked, slipping his free arm around mine, drawing me close alongside a giggling Kacey.

"Rhi, don't." Kiran hissed in my head.

"I know what he is, Kiran, and I'm not leaving my cousin alone with him. Besides, I'm still angry with you, so go find someone else to hover over."

As if he knew I was speaking to Kiran, Phen nodded in Kiran's direction, then led Kacey and me into the hallway and another room.

He closed and locked the door behind him. It was a large room with a sprawling couch and two large cushioned chairs. Floor-to-ceiling windows showcased the sprawling lawn outside. It was dark, but tiny white lights lit up a seating area and a pool in the distance.

Phen leaned against the wall, dark eyes amused. "You girls want a drink?"

"Sure!" Kacey said breathlessly.

"Kace!" I shook my head at her. "No, we don't."

Kacey scowled at me, "Yes, I DO." She said.

I glared at her. "You literally are dating someone, Kace. This is not the type of drink you want to accept. Trust me."

She rolled her eyes. "Oh my God, Rhi, you are so—"She broke off, lips curling. "Whatever. I'll take that beer, Phen."

He tossed her a cold beer, then sprawled on the couch with practiced ease. He crooked his finger at Kacey, and she practically glowed as she settled onto his lap, nestling against him.

"Aren't you going to join us?" Phen's dark eyes, with impossibly long lashes, fixed on me, but I stood firmly where I was.

He nuzzled Kacey's neck until she practically purred.

"What are you doing?" I said fiercely.

Phen grinned wide enough that sinful dimples carved into either side of his sculpted cheeks. "What does it look like?"

"I know exactly what it looks like,"I snapped.

Phen grinned lazily up at me while gently stroking strawberry blonde hair away from Kacey's shoulder, exposing pale skin beneath. He took a quick swig of his beer, settling dangerously seductive eyes on mine, amusement twinkling in the dark depths. "You're no fun," he taunted. "I promise there is enough of me for both of you." He winked, and Kacey giggled.

"What the hell is wrong with you?" I kept my voice steady over the frantic pounding in my chest. "We need to go, Kace," I demanded, grabbing her arm, trying to pull her off Phen.

She huffed at me, swatting my hand away just like before. "I'm staying."

Phen laid a gentle hand on her cheek, whispered something like a lullaby, and she slumped against him, fast asleep.

"You ass of a demon!" I reached for Kacey.

"Relax," he said, carefully laying Kacey onto the couch so she sprawled out comfortably. "Your cousin will wake up with nothing more than fuzzy memories and a wicked crush on me."

He stood walking towards me. I glanced at Kacey sleeping soundly. He cocked an eyebrow at me, with a mixture of suspicion and curiosity. I tensed, but he only studied my face, close enough I could see the gold flecks inside his irises.

"You're not even scared," he said. "Most people would be."

"You're not even the top three weirdest or scariest things I've seen."

His voice dropped. "Still, your heart rate is steady, your eyes aren't dilated, and you didn't even flinch when I put Kacey under."

I crossed my arms over my chest, "No, I didn't. I've seen it done before."

"Have you now?"

He turned and placed his beer on a small table. I noticed the tattoo that had run down his chest was also on his back. The design on his back was of a giant Phoenix rising from flames. Its tail wrapped upward and over the front of his body.

"Is Phen short for Phoenix?" I asked.

He looked over his shoulder at me. "Admiring my body, are you?"

I rolled my eyes, "Just noticed what the tattoo was."

He faced me again, "It is. Some call me Phoenix; however, my real name is Phenix."

"A demon prince."

He laughed. It was light and lyrical, almost like a song. An amused glint lit his dark eyes, but I caught the brief surprise that flashed across his face. "That little dark-haired vixen must've told you about me."

"Little vixen?"

"Sorcha likes to talk." He grinned, lounging easily against the wall. He watched me closely. "I'm an angel, actually," he finally said. "Not everyone loves Heaven as much as your Guardian Kiran does. Some of us...relocate."

"Relocate? You mean you gave up being an angel to become a demon" I arched an eyebrow in disbelief. "And how do you know Kiran is my Guardian?"

"Honey," He drawled. "It's obvious to those of us of the supernatural nature." His dark brown eyes studied me. "And the other one. Justin right? You two are a thing?"

"It's none of your business!" I bristled.

He moved closer, and my heart sped up despite myself. "So that's a yes. And to answer your first question, I was once a Throne Angel and am now a Fallen."

"What do you mean? I thought you were a demon." I tried to keep my expression blank, but I was sure I failed since Phen's lips curled into a dark smile. He pushed off from the wall and circled around me so closely that I could feel the heat from his bare skin radiating outwards.

"You don't think we can be both? I assure you we can. You see, I have the ability to coerce beings—all beings with my poetry." His smile grew mischievous. "It's a power, The Morningstar...Lucifer would do almost anything to have on his side. So he made me a prince."

He shrugged, as if this were something everyone should understand.

"So, let me get this straight. You gave up your grace to serve Hell?"

He laughed that mystical laugh again, "I am still an angel, albeit a fallen one simultaneously, I am a demon prince."

I shook my head. I thought it was just one or another.

"I see you're confused." He held my gaze, sincerity lacing his next words. "I will make it back to Heaven."

I was silent as his declaration settled in. It sounded a bit too familiar. A Fallen making his way back, that's what Vince wanted to use Kiran for. Phen must have read my face because he laughed again.

"You're just like Vince," I said bitterly.

"Vince and I have history, yes." He replied, slipping his hands into the pockets of his low-slung pants. "He's a fool...where I am not."

I suddenly felt hot as panic sank its claws into me.

"Don't worry," he said. "I have no need for your Guardian or your boyfriend Justin.

"You're lying." I stepped into his space because I know he wants me to flinch, and if I let him see my fear, he'll use it. "You obviously want something. What is it?"

"Clever girl," he murmured. "But you should know, sometimes the thing I want is simply to understand. Or—" he dropped his hand, and his smile sharpened, "sometimes the thing I want is simply the thing everyone else seems to want. You."

"You can get in line."

He leaned in. "I don't join lines, Rhiannon. I make them. You have no idea what you are to people like us."

Panic buzzed in my ears. "Enlighten me."

His voice dropped lower, seduction laced with the threat of a wolf's hunger. "Let's say..." he drawls, "I take a rather personal interest in the oddities of your bloodline."

My mouth went dry. I glance again at Kacey, who is stirring, a frown crossing her sleeping face, but she doesn't wake.

"You're talking about my family." I press, "What about us?" I don't move as he steps closer, so near that I smell salt and smoke on him. "Stop playing with me."

His eyes flicker, searching my face. For a beat, his bravado slips, replaced by a flash of confusion, almost awe, but then his arrogance slides back into place. He lets out a snort, shaking off whatever he saw. "Trust me, if I were playing with you, you'd be having a much better time than this." He grinned and swiped his tongue along one canine. "But, damn, if you don't make it interesting. I can see why the twins are obsessed."

I rolled my eyes, but my face felt hot. "You're not half as charming as you think you are. Wake Kacey up, we're done here."

Phen laughed softly with a playful aloofness, "Now? We were having so much fun."

"Wake her up!" I said fiercely.

"Of course, whatever you desire." He picked up his beer, finishing the bottle. "So you know, once I have my eye on something, I get it. Watch," he said, motioning towards Kacey.

He bent down, whispering softly and tenderly brushing her hair off her cheek; she stirred, blinked once, and sat up with a dazed smile.

"Hello, beautiful," Phen said, cupping Kacey's cheek in his palm. His dark eyes danced when they met mine.

"Mmmmm oh! I thought that was a dream!" Her crush on him seemed undampened.

I caught her arm before she could attach herself to his side again. "We're going back to the party."

Phen stood motioning to the door. I turned the knob and found it unlocked. He came closer and whispered so only I heard him. "You should really look into your family history." He said, searing me with an intense look. He straightened as Kacey approached us. "Come see us play next weekend."

"Oh, we will be there!" Kacey said enthusiastically.

He slipped an arm around both of us, leading the way back through the door into the hallway. "I'm staying here for the time being if you want to visit." He added, letting his hands fall from our shoulders and disappearing back into the room.

Chapter Seven

Justin

I paced back and forth like a caged animal. I felt like an animal too, wanting nothing more than to hunt down my prey. That is how Rhi made me feel. I wanted to consume her in every way possible. I wanted my lips on every part of her body, I wanted to feel...

Damn. I was obsessed with her — and I would take that to my grave before I admitted it out loud. I didn't understand it. I had walked away from girls without a second thought, without a flicker of guilt. That was where my reputation came from. Player. Cheat. Womanizer. But Rhi? Rhi had somehow gotten her hands around my heart and I still hadn't figured out how to take it back.

It was better when she wasn't around. The need to have her, to claim her, dulled to something manageable when she was out of sight. But then she had to walk in wearing that shirt and skirt. She looked obscenely hot — but that wasn't what had my blood boiling. She'd worn those same clothes the night she went out with Sam.

Freaking Sam.

My newly found sister was completely enthralled with him. Which meant he was here all the time. Thank God my room wasn't next to hers. It was bad enough seeing them all over each other when I ventured out of this room. I would crack my skull if I had to hear it too.

I didn't particularly like Sam. I still had no idea what had possessed my then-sweet girlfriend to climb onto the back of his motorcycle and ride off like she hadn't a care in the world. That wasn't the Rhi I knew — but then again, maybe I had never really known her at all.

She had known what I was...a Nephilim. Honestly, I kept thinking I would wake up and it would all be a dream. But I knew it wasn't. The moment that necklace my mother had given me came off, the world looked completely different. I could see the supernatural. They were literally everywhere. The first thing I noticed was the eyes.

Mine showed it too. The essence, or power, or whatever it was, caused both angels' and demons' eyes to glow. It also caused us mixed-breed supernaturals to have rims that glowed. I figured out pretty quickly that if you had angel blood, your eyes were silver or lined in silver. Demons had the same except for the color. It was blood red. My half-sister was unique. She was a cambion- half angel, half demon. Her eyes were red with silver surrounding the iris.

Freaky.

Humans couldn't see it, and neither could I with that necklace on. Sam had said it hid what I was from those who would use me. Including my no-good *father*...

Just the thought of him made me want to hunt him down and slaughter him. I thought I could do it too.

The thought reminded me of the book I had found. I glanced around the room. There were books on the floor where I had—my blood started boiling for a whole other reason. In a whole other way. That girl drove me mad with desire, and she had almost given in to it. I know she would have if...

I couldn't think of it. That half-brother of mine. I didn't claim him, I wouldn't. I had a brother, Scott. Scott had always stood by me. But, Kiran? He had known about me, too, and still thought it was okay to fall in love with my girlfriend? No, he had to go.

I started picking up the books on the floor and placing them back onto the shelf. I would have to look through them all to see if they held any hidden knowledge. I was sure the book I found in the secret room did.

I sat at the desk and ran my hand over the cover. Just like before, the symbols moved like smoke until I could read the title: The Book of Michael the Archangel.

I watched as the words appeared in the language I understood.

I was there when the decree was given, when the order was spoken into the fabric of existence. The Watchers were to descend, not as Fallen, not as forsaken, but as sentinels. They were to observe, but how does one only witness and not act? How does one watch suffering and not try to help when it is within their power to do so?

I knew their names. I knew their hearts. They were not rebels. They were our brothers. And when they chose to help humanity, it was not out of malice but out of love.

I stopped breathing. Sam was a Watcher. This was about him.

Love is a dangerous thing when it defies Heaven.

Now their children walk the Earth, marked as unholy, but they are not demons. They are Nephilim. Created from love between the divine and humanity. Despite the fact that I was one of the Archangels sent to destroy them, I could not bring myself to do so. I went against the Creator because I believe in my heart that the Nephilim are not abominations. They are not mistakes. They are not inherently evil. They are proof that angels, too, can fall in love. That even we, sculpted by the Creator himself, are not immune to the pull of the mortal world.

I am forbidden to speak this. But I can write it. And if these words ever find any Nephilim, let them know—judgment is not as simple as Heaven would have it seem. For even I gave in to the draw of falling in love.

"Oh my God," I breathed. This wasn't just a book. It was a diary — the diary of an Archangel.

I sat back in the chair, staring down at the words. Why did Vince have this book of Michael's? And why was it hidden in a secret room? There could be no good reason. I decided to take it back to the hidden room, but then thought better of it. If Vince came back and it was so precious to him to hide, then I wouldn't let him find it.

I moved the desk and pulled at the carpet in the corner. I pulled out my knife and slipped it under a wooden plank. It gave way, and I stuffed the book inside, covered it with carpet, and moved the desk over it.

I heard the music start up again downstairs. Maybe I should go find Rhi, although I didn't know how long I could keep my temper in check if Kiran was hovering around her.

I turned to leave when I saw two familiar faces on the lawn outside. Mia and Steve. They were laughing when Mia grabbed Steve by the neck and kissed him.

The world had officially lost its mind. And somehow, I was right in the middle of it.

Chapter Eight

Kiran

I swear, Rhi was going to be the death of me. It was my fault, really. If I had not shown myself to her, then I could have just followed her into that room with that demon prince, and she would not have known.

A demon prince!

What was she thinking? I knew. I could feel her emotions, and she was angry. I chuckled to myself. Leave it to my Ahavah. Only she wouldn't be intimidated by a demon, a demon prince no less, and instead get pissed off.

"Would you like me to go retrieve her?" Sam asked as he casually stood by my side, staring at the same door I was.

I shook my head, "Not yet. She's angry at him and not fearful at all."

Sam laughed, "Ah, well, the child of the warrior wouldn't be."

My head snapped in his direction. "I know who the warrior is, and she has shown no signs of having any angelic blood."

"I cannot confirm or deny," Sam said, taking a sip of some cocktail.

Two half-demons walked by us, both in overly alluring clothing. The idea of Sam casually spending time with demons made my skin crawl — and the thought of him being physical with them? That was something my mind refused to fully process.

Sam whistled, and the two turned their heads towards us.

"Wish to join us?" A thin girl with short curly hair purred.

"Ohh, I'll take the handsome Fallen." Her friend said.

"I would love to," Sam said smoothly. "But, we're both spoken for at the moment."

I crooked an eyebrow at him as the two shrugged like we weren't worth their time and continued on their way.

"I didn't think you and Sorcha were so serious."

"How serious can you be with anyone when you have eternity to walk this Earth?" Sam eyed the girls as they turned a corner and out of sight. "Besides, I couldn't very well hand you over to one of them. A virgin Fallen? Ha! They would eat you alive...literally."

I felt sick at the thought. There was no one for me but Rhi. My love, my everything. I shouldn't think of her that way. It was forbidden for me to do so when she was my ward and I her Guardian.

However, I was a Fallen now, and Fallen didn't play by the rules. Not that I did before I fell. That was the whole reason I did fall.

I sighed heavily, staring at the door and willing her and her cousin to come out.

"You have it bad," Sam said nudging me in the shoulder. "I don't know that I've ever seen an angel pine over someone as severely as you."

I scowled at him, "I'm not pining."

He chuckled, "Whatever you say."

It must be written all over my face. How much I loved her, how *in* love with her I was. I missed her every second she wasn't with me. I could barely stop myself from touching her. I made any excuse to. Just to feel her skin. Then there were the times that I knew she felt the desire as much as I did—I felt it. She had pushed me to tell her how she made me weak a few weeks ago. If we had not been interrupted, I was sure we would have kissed.

Sam was right. I was pining for her. I wanted her lips on mine so badly it hurt. Like physically hurt. Then there was that electricity that ran through us when we were close like that. It overwhelmed me to the point of insanity with the need to have every part of me seared to every part of her.

The door opened and out they came. A growl erupted from my throat seeing that half naked demon with his arms draped over my Ahavah. Kacey was looking up at him like he was the most amazing thing she had ever seen. He looked at Kacey like he would devour her. Where was her Guardian to keep her out of that demon's hands? I never saw a Guardian around her cousins or her grandmother.

Weird.

Phen withdrew his arms from around the girls, and his red eyes with specks of silver met mine. And he winked.

I snarled.

"Easy there, big boy," Sam said, putting a hand on my shoulder. "You're beginning to act like your brother."

"Seriously, Sam? I'm nothing like Justin."

"You, my friend, are in complete denial about everything."

I shoved his hand off of me.

Rhi and Kacey made their way over to us, Kacey talking a mile a minute while Rhi looked...thoughtful. My heart nearly stopped as she came near.

"Hey, you," I whispered into her head, *"Are you okay?"*

She nodded, running a hand through her hair. *"We need to talk."* Was her reply.

"So how was your little chat with His Majesty?" Sam asked.

My head snapped in Sam's direction.

"What?" He asked. "Phen has a huge ego."

"He invited us to his concert next weekend!" Kacey practically bounced on her feet. "You're going, right? You have to go!" Her large brown eyes bounced between us hopefully. "We're on the list. He said just give our names at the door!"

"I'm in," Sam said, chuckling at Kacey's enthusiasm. "How about you two?"

"You don't think I'm letting you go alone, do you?" Rhi said to Kacey.

"Hey," Sam bristled. "I just said I would be there."

"I don't know if you're any better than him," Rhi waved to the door they just came out of.

"Ugh, you wound me," Sam said, clutching his hand to his chest.

Rhi reached out and pulled me away from the wall. She had no idea what that small touch did to me.

"I could use some air," she said, "Will you go for a walk with me, Kiran?"

Sam and Kacey exchanged glances. "Uh-oh!" Kacey giggled, pulling Rhi's arm dramatically. "Looks like my cousin has a hot date! Don't do anything I wouldn't do!"

Rhi rolled her eyes, "It's just a walk, Kace. Relax."

Rhi led the way outside, her scent surrounding me in a sweet cloud as we moved through the house and onto the patio. A few couples loitered about before falling back into the shadows, and I barely noticed them, too focused on the way Rhi's hair bounced down her back. How was it that even when she ignored me, I felt consumed by her? She moved with determination, cutting through the rows of lights someone had zigzagged over the yard until we reached a secluded corner. The noise and colors from inside faded, leaving only us.

She touched my arm, her warmth burning through my skin like fire, "I'm still angry." Her voice was tight.

"Rhi..." Her name fell as a whisper off my lips. It took everything I had not to reach out and touch her face.

"Don't Rhi me with those big puppy dog eyes."

I frowned slightly, "I didn't actually fight Justin. He attacked me."

"Kiran..." Her eyes were hard on mine.

"You don't trust me."

"I do trust you!" She said, pushing her hair off her shoulder.

"Rhi, Justin is strong because of who our father is — but he can't control it. He's powerful and doesn't know how to use it. Not like I do." I could see her softening just a bit.

She stepped away from me, pain filling her eyes, "Kiran, this is tearing me apart." The defeat in her voice punched through my chest.

"I know, sweetheart."

Her eyes seemed to search for something in mine. "I feel like it's my fault you two hate each other."

"I don't hate him. I wouldn't have saved him if I hated him."

She flinched slightly at that. "Thank you. For saving him."

I nodded.

"He's a lot to handle," she said softly. "I'm sorry he attacked you. He has a temper." She hesitated, looking at me carefully. "I tried to explain everything to him, and he was hurt...he thinks we were intentionally keeping things from him." A fresh wave of pain washed over her features.

I looked down, ashamed for letting her take the fall for all of this, as if I'd dealt with everything so perfectly. "I'll continue to reach out to him, to try to get him to understand."

"I'm frustrated at this whole situation," she said, stepping toward me. My heart surged at her nearness.

"Were you trying to punish me then? Running off with a demon prince?" Her closeness made me reckless—I grabbed for her fingertips before she could pull back, holding them tight. "You have no idea how crazy that drove me. I almost tore through the walls trying to get to you."

Rhi snatched her hand away from mine, anger breaking across her face. "You really are just as bad as him."

Her words cut into me like knives. "I—no, I'm not," I stammered.

"Stop trying to control me, Kiran. I know you're my Guardian, but I'm not your prisoner."

Ouch.

"Rhi, please," I whispered, nearly begging. "Forgive me. I'm...I'm trying."

I took a deep breath, hearing Sam's voice echo in my head about being like Justin, his jealousy getting the better of him. A fresh pain came over me at how right they all were. My mind screamed at me to get it together, to be the angel she needed me to be. This wasn't like me—it wasn't how I used to be.

I saw the twin flames of Rhiannon's anger and heartbreak flicker as she studied me. For a moment, her expression was unreadable, but then her shoulders slumped, and she exhaled. "I thought angels were supposed to be the ones with all the answers, Kiran."

"To some things, yes," I admitted. "But the more time I spend down here, the more I realize I'm as lost as anyone."

I stepped closer, almost unconsciously. She didn't back away, and it was all the invitation I needed to close the distance between us. I hesitated before reaching for her hand. Testing the waters. Testing her.

She took a breath and let me take it.

The spark between us was instantaneous and bright. I pulled her slightly closer.

Her shoulders softened a fraction, "I can't stay mad at you for long," she acknowledged quietly, eyes softer now.

We stood together in the shadows, the party behind us a distant hum.

"When we were inside, Phen said something weird."

"What did he say?" My voice came out harsher than I meant.

She looked down at our joined hands before she answered. "He said I should look into my family's history."

"What?" I searched her face, bewildered. "Why?"

"I don't know. I told him I knew what and who he was. Then he put Kaccy to sleep. He told me he is an angel but also a demon."

I nodded. "That is true."

"Is it? Because I didn't believe him. He says he has a gift of coercion and Lucifer prized it, which is why he is a prince of Hell."

"Also true." What did that demon want by telling her all of this?

"He told me he would make it back to Heaven, and I exploded, telling him he was just like Vince."

"I felt your anger."

"When he walked us out, that is when he told me to ask you about exploring my family history."

I released a breath. Her eyes studied mine, wide and intent.

"Why would Phen want me to ask you?"

"I don't know." A strange uncertainty unfurled within me.

My thoughts twisted into knots as I tried to understand what an angel-demon wanted with Rhi.

"Why that look?" Rhi asked, squeezing my hand.

"I just don't understand his endgame," I admitted. "I'll figure out what he is up to."

"It can't be anything good and Kacey...Kacey is enthralled with him."

I pulled her closer in response to the concern in her eyes. It was the simplest and most complicated gesture in the world. She leaned into it, leaned into me, and I closed my eyes tightly, allowing myself to take it all in.

A noise from back toward the woods interrupted us. Voices whispering and giggling.

I opened my eyes, tuning in to the sounds cutting through the air. I knew those voices.

"Is that Mia and Steve?" Her brows knitted together in confusion.

"I think—" I started, but she grabbed my hand and dragged me toward the voices. As we got closer, I could hear them clearly now, whispering fast and low.

"This is insane!" came Mia's voice.

Steve followed right after, "We need to get back before anyone notices."

Rhi pulled up short, finding them tucked behind the trees, shirts wrinkled and hair mussed. Rhi clamped a hand over her mouth to stifle a laugh as their eyes found hers. Both froze like deer caught in headlights. "Oh my..." she gasped. "You two?"

"Rhi!" Steve's face burned crimson.

"Hey, girl," Mia didn't seem bothered at all.

"Mia! My cousin?"

Mia rolled her eyes dramatically while adjusting her shirt. "It's not like it's the first time." She elbowed Steve in the arm. "Well, not the first time we've kissed, but the first time for..."

"Mia," Steve grumbled.

Mia frowned, then pointed an accusatory finger at Rhi and me. "And you're here with him" — she motioned at me — "while Justin..."

"Is pouting," Rhi finished for her.

"Well, well. What do we have here?" Justin strode out of the shadows like he had been biding his time. "And I was not pouting." He looked pointedly at Rhi.

"Justin?" Rhi gasped, taking a step away from me.

"Dude, what the hell?" Steve asked.

"What? I saw you two from the window." Justin said, gesturing towards Mia and Steve.

"Maybe you need to worry more about your business and not ours," Mia said as she placed her hands on her hips.

"Oh, we're all one big happy family," sarcasm dripped from Justin's lips as he swung an arm around my shoulders.

Mia and Steve exchanged looks, clearly not understanding what was happening.

I bristled and took a deep breath. I didn't want to upset Rhi again, but I wouldn't let him use me as a punching bag.

"Stop it, Justin," Rhi said quietly.

"Touchy, touchy." He moved closer to her. "Relax, Rhi. We're good, right, Kiran?"

"Sure," I said, trying to keep control over my emotions.

Justin smirked, shifting his gaze to Steve. "You and Mia, huh? Finally done with Trina?

"Watch it, Justin," Steve snapped, running his hand through his hair.

"Wow, Rizzo. Maybe you should stop worrying about everyone else and get your relationship with Rhi on track."

Justin frowned.

"Look, not that it is any of your business, but Steve and I have hooked up before. We just took it a step further in that little guest house."

"There's a guest house?" Justin looked genuinely surprised.

"Yeah, back behind those trees. It's surrounded by some high bushes."

"Huh." Justin said, "I had no idea."

"You should check it out then," Steve said. "I'm going back to the party to find Kacey."

Mia wrapped her arm through Rhi's, "Come on, I'll show you where it is."

Steve turned on his heel back towards the party. Mia skipped through the trees with Rhi, Justin on their heels.

I shifted uncomfortably, watching them. Then Rhi called to me over her shoulder, "Come on, Kiran."

Chapter Nine

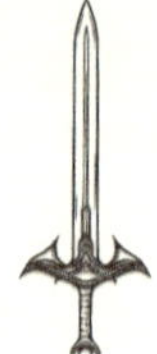

Justin

Great, I came out here to try to smooth things over with Rhi. Instead, I find her all alone with *him*. And what do I do? Come across like a complete jerk because every time I'm near her, Kiran's there too, like her shadow. It makes me crazy. He doesn't see her as I do. He can't. I didn't even think I had the capacity to love anymore. Then she came into my life and cracked my heart wide open.

I can't let my temper mess things up again. Rhi doesn't respond well when I get heated. I'll just end up making it worse, pushing her closer to him. I already pissed off Steve and Mia. I don't know why I feel like I have to lash out at everyone around me.

Footsteps come closer behind me. Kiran. My muscles tense—wanting to fight. I force a breath out through gritted teeth. Instead, I turn my attention to Rhi and Mia walking ahead of me. I know I won't be able to keep it cool if I don't focus, so I move forward into the woods, letting my thoughts swim with images of earlier tonight. Her body warm and close beneath mine. Her mouth on mine.

We should still be there in my bed. My arms around her. Instead, I'm out here stalking through the woods like a jealous idiot with her Guardian freak of an angel.

Mia chatters and laughs with Rhi. I can sense Kiran's steady gaze on me, but don't trust myself to look back. Trees twist together above us like skeletal arms as we walk deeper through the property until we reach a towering hedge.

Mia waves us around the hedge, "It's just around the corner."

A small cottage sits in the center of the wall of hedges. I push past everyone and open the door, feeling along the wall for a light switch and finding nothing.

Mia walks in behind me. "There should be a lamp on that table."

I knock my knee on a low chair and curse under my breath. I grope for the lamp, find a small chain, and click it on. Warm light spreads dimly across the room, casting long shadows over a cramped sitting area of mismatched chairs and a couch that's seen better days. I look around, jaw clenching, when Rhi walks in with Kiran close behind her.

The place looks about ready to collapse in on itself. Exposed beams hang like sun-bleached bones across the ceiling, and a layer of dust coats everything.

"Are you sure this is even Vince's place?" Rhi's voice is uncertain as she hovers near the doorway.

"Yeah," I say. "This whole property is surrounded by a brick wall. This is on our side of the property."

I scan the rest of the room. A dingy rug covers part of the hardwood floor. There are a couple of closed doors I move to examine.

A small door opens onto a grimy bathroom. I push further back to what looks like a bedroom door and smirk. "Not going in there after Steve and Mia used it."

Mia rolls her eyes at me and plops down on the sagging couch. I stop at another door. It creaks loudly when I open it, revealing a closet cluttered with boxes. A cool draft hits me in the face. "Why do I feel a breeze coming from inside here?"

Mia jumps up and peers around me into the closet. "Let's find out!"

"Do you think there's a secret passage?" Rhi asks as she steps up beside Mia.

Kiran hangs back, studying everything with those silver eyes of his like he can see straight through the walls. "Are you sure it's smart to explore?" His voice is calm, controlled. "Knowing who this belongs to, we might not like what we find."

I move the boxes, shoving them aside until I reach the back wall. I press against it, and the wall rattles before shifting open to reveal a narrow staircase leading down into darkness.

Mia pokes her head in next to mine. "That is so cool!"

"Maybe I should check it out first." I hesitate—thinking that if there's something useful for me, like the book I found earlier, maybe I should keep it to myself—but Mia slips past me with a bright grin.

"Ohh, an adventure!"

I follow after Mia, careful not to step on any loose boards. Rhi hesitates, then hurries behind us, with Kiran at her heels.

It's even colder at the bottom of the staircase, and much darker. Dust floats through the air, disturbed by our steps.

Kiran snaps his fingers, and a flashlight appears. Of course, he can make things appear out of thin air.

The flashlight illuminates strange symbols scrawled across sections of the wall. The hair on my arms stand on end.

Mia whistles. "This is creepy."

Rhi steps closer to the wall, her brow furrowed as she studies the markings. "I've seen some of these before..."

"They're like the ones in that dungeon Vince kept us in," I say, scanning the markings.

Rhi shivers and wraps her arms around herself. Kiran moves closer to her. "It must be another tunnel — like the one we escaped through."

The dark walls surrounding us press in with a suffocating weight. I can see Rhi is scared. I want to comfort her. Instead, she stands near him. A low growl comes from my throat. I want to pull her to my side. Away from him.

Kiran nods in front of us, "I see a light up there."

We move cautiously toward it, dread pooling in my gut until we reach another door.

With one quick movement, I press against it, and it swings open with an eerie creak. Everyone stops. The door opens up into the underground room where Vince kept us locked up.

My jaw clenches, and I glance at Rhi. She looks as shaky as I feel. Her eyes dart from the door to me, "This must be how he escaped." She whispers.

The room is empty, as cold and silent as an abandoned tomb. Memories blast through me. Vince chaining me to the wall, laughing while he tortured Rhi. The air once filled with her screams is empty now, but her screams still haunt me.

"Sorcha fixed the ceiling," I say out loud, trying to steady my voice. I point at where it had collapsed when we fought him and the staircase that snaked down to here. "She blocked the door above. We didn't want anyone down here."

Mia walks further in, peeking around cautiously. "This is where I found you guys!" Her voice echoes off the stone walls. "I remember it being bad, but whoa! This is way worse up close."

"He's still out there somewhere." Rhi's voice catches.

Everything inside me snaps. She can't be afraid like that again. I close the gap between us, my hands finding her shoulders. "Rhi, I'm sorry," I say, my voice low.

She looks at me with wide eyes as if not knowing whether to move away, but then she's in my arms. A rush of warmth spreads through my chest. When she buries her face against me, holding tight, I feel it again.

My heart.

All the fear floods back. The fear that crushed me when I was helpless to save her from Vince. Fear of losing her forever. My head spins. Skeletal fingers claw at my skin, dragging me down into a void where whispers freeze the air. Debris rains as the world disintegrates — dust choking my lungs, breath that won't come — and Rhi's terrified cry cuts through the chaos as blackness crashes over me, swallowing me whole.

Rhi's breathing is uneven against my shirt as I stare blankly ahead until something shifts in my mind like a puzzle piece snapping into place.

Silver eyes burning bright above me—Kiran's hand reaching as far as it can go and bringing me back to life when I'd already been claimed by all that darkness.

I jerk away from Rhi, staring at him. "You brought me back."

Kiran doesn't answer right away but holds my gaze. When he does speak, it's a quiet confirmation, "Yes, I did."

"You knew." My voice cracks with disbelief. I step back as everything pieces together, ripping wounds wide open. "I was dying."

More memories slam into me like a train. Rhi begging Kiran not to let me die. Her tears wetting my face as she cried for me.

"I remember now," I breathe, and it feels like poison filling my lungs.

Kiran's calm expression sears through me.

"You only did it for her," I spat at him. "How very noble of you to save me so that she would feel indebted to you."

"That's not true," Rhi protests, grabbing my arm.

"Isn't it?" My voice is harsh as I tear my arm away.

"I did it for both of you," Kiran says, unmoved by the accusation in my words and the venom in my stare.

The memory blurs through me again — so cold, so dark — and her voice echoes: *Don't let him die!* Rhi steps between us as if she's afraid the words might turn into something worse. Her cheeks are wet with tears. "Yes, I begged him to save you. He isn't supposed to change the course of events." She steps closer to me. "But he did it — and not just for me. He told me it's because you're his brother."

An old rage fills my lungs like smoke from a fire that's never stopped burning.

"Justin, look at me." Rhi's voice is stern. "Kiran fell because he saved you. That was his punishment — to become a Fallen Angel."

"What?!" I snarl.

"He's a Fallen."

Kiran's gaze never leaves mine, and he nods slightly.

"Then you're not her Guardian anymore." My voice is raw and sharp.

Kiran looks at Rhi then back at me. "It's complicated," he says softly. "And this is not the place to discuss it."

"Why not? We have the same parents. Why can't I be her Guardian now?

Rhi turns toward me. "It didn't change anything." Her voice is strong even with tears still filling her eyes. "Our connection is just as strong as ever."

"I don't believe that for a second," I mutter, clenching my fists at my side.

"Maybe we need to get out of this creepy dungeon before talking," Mia suggests, rubbing her arms like she's cold.

Kiran nods. "Agreed."

I hold my ground, lifting my chin defiantly. But one look at Rhi, pale and shaken, makes something in my chest twist hard. Her eyes lock onto mine again, and I nod reluctantly toward the door. She heads out quickly with Kiran following closely behind.

Mia speeds after them, her voice echoing through the narrow passageway as she talks a mile a minute to fill the silence. We retrace our steps up through the dark passage until we're back in the cottage.

I watch Rhi closely, trying to read beyond what she says, looking for any cracks in her certainty about him still being her Guardian Angel.

My jaw tenses as Kiran comes up beside her, closer than I can stand without feeling an urge to rip them apart. "I want to go home," she says.

"I'll take you," Kiran says.

"No, we should find Kacey and Steve. They won't understand why I left with you."

She turns her chocolate brown eyes on me, "We can talk about this when you've calmed down. I want to get this resolved. It's tearing me apart."

I let out a breath and reluctantly agree that I'll text her when I'm ready. Deep inside, though, I know I will never accept the fact that Kiran needs to always be with her, that he is still a Guardian.

Chapter Ten

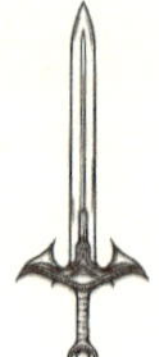

Kiran

Finally, we sat in Steve's car away from that awful place. Everyone was quiet, even Mia, as we drove back to Rhi's house.

Kacey was pouting, or else she would surely have been chatty. She was angry that Steve had pulled her away from the party and from Phen. I had no idea what that demon was up to, openly flirting with Kacey.

I again searched for any sign of celestial beings—for Guardians. Surely her cousins had them. Right? Mia didn't. She was a descendant of witches and Lenape. Sam was basically her Guardian as he has been with her family for generations.

Kacey's phone pinged, and a smile grew as she read the message. Then her fingers glided over the phone as her smile grew bigger. I sat between her and Rhi and glanced at who it was from. Hot singer Phen. Yikes.

"Were your cousins baptized?" I spoke into Rhi's head.

"I think so. Why are you asking?"

"I'll explain later. Right now, Kacey is texting with Phen."

"Kace? Who are you texting with?" Rhi asked curiously.

Distracting Rhi worked. I didn't want to get into this with her until I was sure they either did or didn't have Guardians. It was possible they just didn't hover around them. Most Guardians didn't. They preferred to stay in Heaven or explore Earth until they felt something from their wards that would make them go to them and help. I wasn't like most. Maybe if I had been, I wouldn't have fallen in love with Rhi.

Steve pulled up in front of Rhi's. She and Kacey were bickering about her texting with Phen. Rhi opened the door and slid out. "Seriously, Kacey," she said, poking her head back in. "We need to talk about him."

Steve twisted around in his seat. "What about him?"

Mia snickered. "Calm down, or I'll take you for another walk in the woods." She winked, and Steve turned bright red. She blew him a kiss as she hopped out of the car as well. Mia was staring at the car's rear lights until they disappeared around the corner, a sigh escaping her lips.

Rhi waved her hand in front of her friend's face, "Earth to Mia."

Mia swatted her away.

"You like him." Rhi's smile spread. "Like, *like like* him!"

"Hush, Lady Bug. I told you I was going into my senior year single. Mia motioned at her body with a dramatic flourish. "All this wonderfulness was meant to be shared." She gave an exaggerated shrug. "Wouldn't be fair otherwise."

"So generous," Rhi teased. "Does Steve know he's sharing?"

"Mmm," Mia smirked. "He'll figure it out." She jabbed a finger at Rhi's chest. "Like you're gonna figure out your feelings."

"Feelings? About what?"

"Let me think...hot blondie over here or that dark, brooding Rizzo, maybe?" Mia twirled out of reach when Rhi tried to grab her. "And remember, don't do anything I wouldn't do."

Mia laughed and skipped up the steps to her house. Rhi stood frozen for a moment; her cheeks flushed the prettiest red. "In other words? Do everything." Rhi called after her.

Mia opened the screen door before blowing a kiss to us and saying, "Of course."

Back in Rhi's room, we talked a bit about everything that happened, and I wrapped my body and wings around her until she was asleep.

Having Rhi in my arms was the best kind of torture. The kind that made me want more than I deserved to have, that tempted me to cross every line because my heart belonged to her. I ached with how much I wanted more. My duty had been to protect her, but since I'd fallen, the rules had changed. She sighed in her sleep and snuggled against me, pouring sweet agony into every part of me. Smiling softly in the dark, her lips parted slightly as she wrapped an arm over my chest.

I eased away from her, careful not to wake her. My gaze swept over her in the moonlight, my heart pounding with how much I loved her. She was everything. I didn't deserve her, but I wanted her more than anything in this world or beyond it. I wanted forever.

I teleported from her cozy room to the empty house several doors down. Everything inside was still. Furniture shrouded in white sheets stood like forgotten ghosts throughout the rooms. I pulled at one; dust coughed out, revealing a faded couch with clawed feet.

The place felt untouched by time. My fingers skimmed over the musty covers of books stacked precariously on an old wooden shelf and paused over photographs, faded memories of a family that wasn't mine: children with wide smiles, parents holding them close, moments of earthly happiness trapped forever. The man who lived here, who had died here, had left everything to his only remaining family. A nephew who lived in New York City and couldn't care less about what was in the home. He sold it with everything in it.

My footsteps echoed off the hardwood as I moved through the hushed house, exploring each room until I reached what must have been the master bedroom. It was bigger than I'd expected and filled with pieces that were elegant once but seemed brittle and tired now.

As I entered, something crackled in the atmosphere around me—wards flickering to life like startled fireflies before sputtering back into silence. Shock slid through me. Wards meant protection, power—access to the otherworldly.

Who was the previous owner who felt that he needed wards? I backed up, not trusting that there wasn't some sort of angel trap in the room. I would ask Mia in the morning to see if she knew what the wards were for.

I moved through the house, keeping my senses on high alert for any more wards. Nothing disturbed me as I made my way cautiously to the back of the house. A set of French doors led to a sprawling lawn, overrun with weeds and wildness. It must have been beautiful once. I stepped outside, the air fresh against my skin. My heart quickened at the sight. What looked like a pool was half-covered with a tarp. I waved a hand to remove the covering and paused. It was a pool, but unlike any I'd seen before. The shape was irregular, almost natural, the steps into it crafted from smooth stone. It shimmered like an abandoned pond. It must have cost a fortune to create.

With another wave of my hand, flowers burst forth where the weeds had been, and the pool turned crystal clear. Colors blossomed around me—a garden springing to life with vibrant blooms. I leaned against the doorframe, surveying my work and savoring this corner of beauty I'd brought back from neglect and emptiness by breathing new life into it. Rhi would love it.

Someone cleared their throat next to me.

"Samyaza!"

"Just Sam," his hair ruffled in the night breeze. "I didn't mean to scare you."

"You didn't. Just surprised me."

He glanced around at what I'd done to the yard and nodded approvingly. "Do you plan to restore it to its original beauty?"

"A little at a time. I figured the back yard was safe to start and not draw too much attention." I picked up a loose stone and tossed it into the pool, watching it sink beneath the perfectly clear water. "Did you know the man, Mr. Hollander, who owned it?"

Sam shook his head, "No, I'm afraid not."

I chuckled, "I thought you knew everything since you've been around from the beginning of time."

"Don't poke fun, Guardian. You'll see how it is soon enough, being bound to this plane for eternity."

He was right. I would never see Heaven again. My soul collapsed under the weight of it. I was a Fallen; Guardian no more. Justin had said as much.

My heart clenched around the thought, and I reached for the bond between Rhi and me. The quiet music that connected our souls, it was there—intact, alive, and wrapped around me stronger than ever. But would it last?

"It gets better," Sam said.

"Maybe," I whispered. "There are wards in the master bedroom," I said, looking for a distraction.

Sam raised an eyebrow. "That so?"

"Yes."

"Interesting." His gaze trailed back to the garden. "Never really saw much of him while he lived here."

"Hollander?"

"Mmm," Sam hummed thoughtfully. "Just now and then, tending this very garden."

I nodded, but something unsettled lingered beneath my skin. "Why are you here, Sam?"

A grin tugged at his lips. "Needed out of that house. I can only take so much partying."

I raised an eyebrow. "Thought you liked that sort of thing."

"I have my limits," he said with a smirk.

"Plus, Sorcha can wear me out. If you know what I mean."

"You know I don't."

Sam laughed.

"We found a cottage," I said. "It led to tunnels beneath the house and back to that dungeon."

"More tunnels? Not surprising."

I nodded, returning my gaze to the pool, a thousand thoughts whispering through my mind like secrets. "I'm sure that's how he escaped."

"Indeed." Sam mused. "I've been trying to discreetly snoop through his house." He glanced at me with a knowing look. "Quite confident he has some interesting things in there."

"I bet he does, considering he was obsessed with power, even more so with returning to Heaven."

"Do you know where he is now?"

Sam shrugged. "He's good at disappearing when he needs to. I'll find him eventually."

His confidence should have comforted me, but it didn't quite reach my sense of dread. I raised my eyes to him. "Phen...Rhi told me he said he would get back into Heaven one day."

"He's nothing but a trickster."

"He's a prince of Hell!"

"Kiran, just because he is a prince of Hell does not mean he's all bad. He was a Throne Angel and, at one time, one of the best. He's really not so bad."

"Not so bad?!"

"Look, Lucifer, the Morningstar, covets his power. That is why he gave him such a cushy position. He would give Phen just about anything to keep him under his thumb."

"So you trust him because he used to be a Throne?"

"Oh, no! I don't trust him. He is the best demon prince to have around, though. He isn't evil, he likes excess and freedom."

"He won't touch Rhi," I swore.

"I don't think it is sweet cheeks that you need to worry about."

"Don't call her that."

"I don't think it is *Rhi* he wants...it's her little cousin."

"What about Kacey's Guardian?" I asked quickly.

"Guardian?" Sam's eyebrows shot up. "She doesn't have one. None of the cousins do."

A chill swept through me, colder than the night air around us. "How is that possible? I've seen Rhi's grandmother's Guardian here, just now and then, lounging in the backyard."

"How do you know he's a Guardian?"

"What else would he be? He has the signs."

Sam cut in smoothly, "There is much more to the Crandall family than you know."

"What's that supposed to mean?" Frustration edged my voice. Sam knew something.

He grinned cryptically. "You should do some snooping of your own." His gaze was intent. "Try her grandfather's office."

"What do you know, Sam?"

"I know," he said carefully, "that you still have not figured out that there is not just one side or one story. Guardians were made eons after the first angels. Humanity has had Guardians for only about two thousand years. Before there were Guardians, there were....others."

"Guardians don't just abandon—"

"Her cousins weren't abandoned." His voice was sure. "And what you think you know of her Grandmother's...*companion*...is not correct.

He shrugged and turned as if he was going to leave, then stopped halfway before flashing another grin. "You know, you should have given a lesson to your hot-headed brother. He wouldn't think twice of beating you to the ground if he had the power to do so."

Then he disappeared.

Two supernatural beings, both fixated on Rhi's bloodline in the span of a day? The universe wasn't that random. Something was happening, and she seemed to be at the center of it.

Chapter Eleven

Rhiannon

A groan escaped my lips as I turned over, my mattress creaking beneath me. When my heavy eyelids finally lifted, I found him there—cross-legged on the floor, golden hair catching the morning light. My angel.

"Good morning sweetheart." He said quietly.

"Blah."

"Every day is a gift…"

I pulled the pillow over my head and groaned into the mattress. "I know Kiran but too much happened last night. Phen, my cousin's bizarre behavior, seeing that dungeon again, and…"

I couldn't finish. Justin. I had almost slept with him. I had almost given my body to him completely. My lips still felt bruised from his kissing and nipping and oh my…

Kiran cleared his throat, "And what happened between you and Justin."

I flipped the pillow off my head, my hair a mess of tangled waves falling into my eyes. "How much do you know?"

He shrugged his large shoulders, his cheeks stained pink, "Only what you were feeling. I don't know the exact um, things that caused those feelings."

"Oh God," I said, flinging myself off the bed. "I need a shower."

A cold one.

When I returned, my hair damp and goose bumps covering my skin, Kiran was changed into dark jeans and a snug grey shirt that made him look stupidly hot.

I might need another cold shower. My hormones were taking over my common sense.

"I think you should introduce me to your grandmother today," he said, "So she knows I'm the new neighbor."

I bit down on my lip, combing my hair with my fingers as best as I could. "Fine, get out so I can get dressed."

He disappeared and I rummaged through my clothes until I found a light blue dress. "You can come back." I said aloud. He didn't reappear. Instead I heard a knock on the front door downstairs.

"Rhiannon, honey!" my grandmother's voice rang up to my room. "You have company!"

I nearly tripped over my shoes, tying back my hair as I moved. "Coming!" I yelled, looking down at myself and smoothing out the wrinkles in my dress.

Making my way to the stairs, I paused at the landing, hearing Kiran's deep and confident voice drifting up.

"I met Rhiannon with her cousins last night," he explained warmly. "I was hoping I could take her out today. If that's alright with you."

"Maybe you should ask me," I interrupted playfully, a grin stretching across my face as I descended the last few stairs.

My grandmother chuckled, her gaze sweeping over both of us knowingly. "Well, I think it's wonderful that you young people are making friends so quickly," she said. "So you moved into the big house, Mr. Hollander's place?"

"I didn't know the name of the man who lived there. His nephew sold the property."

"Ah, I guess he really didn't have any family. None I ever saw anyway." Nan shuffled towards the kitchen calling over her shoulder. "Have fun kids."

Kiran turned to me, smiling like nothing in this world or any other could dampen his spirits. "So where are we going?" I was intrigued. This was not what I expected this morning.

"It's a surprise." He moved closer to me, the soft cotton of his shirt shifting with his muscles in a way that made my pulse flutter.

"Ohhh, a surprise huh? Let me just get my phone."

I ran back up the stairs and returned with my phone. His eyes softened with warmth as he took my hand, leading me outside into the bright morning sun.

We walked down the street to the house he had purchased. He swung the metal fence open. We trampled through the weeds until we got to the backyard. I was speechless at what I saw.

The yard stretched out like a hidden paradise, a sparkling pool nestled amid lush flowers and neatly trimmed hedges.

"Kiran, this is...amazing," I breathed, turning in circles to take it all in.

He looked sheepish. "You like it?"

"Are you crazy? This is gorgeous! I love it!"

"I worked on it last night to turn it into something you would enjoy," Kiran grinned.

I slipped off my sandals, the grass soft beneath my feet as I raced towards the shimmering water of the pool. I dipped one toe in and yelped. "It's freezing!"

Kiran knelt next to me, touching his finger to the surface. Shimmering warmth rippled outwards, until soft steam rose up.

"Why are you more eager to use your powers for these little things than you used to be?" I asked, slipping both feet back into now perfectly heated water.

He looked at me tenderly, his gaze open and honest. "Because they make you smile," he said softly.

He settled next to me, slipping off his shoes and rolling up his pant legs. I nudged him with my shoulder, feeling warmth spread through me in a way that had nothing to do with the heated water.

"What's your favorite flower?" he asked casually, his eyes glinting with curiosity.

I glanced at him. "Honestly? Red roses."

Kiran smiled, swirling his feet in the pool. "Why roses?"

"I know, it's totally cliché." I looked down at the water and shrugged. "But my mom was always watching this movie about a rock star. It was kinda dark and depressing. I think it was based on Janis Joplin."

Kiran let his toes touch mine under the water.

"The only part I really liked was this song at the end. The lyrics were so beautiful. They compared love to a rose."

"You remember the lyrics?" he asked softly.

"Kind of." My cheeks flushed with warmth.

"I have a vague memory of the movie. Your mom did watch it every time it was on." He scooted closer, our shoulders almost touching.

Kiran was silent for a moment, watching me carefully. "Look behind you," he said with a knowing smile.

I turned, my breath catching as rows of red roses appeared, stretching across the back of the yard in a sea of vibrant color. They seemed to go on forever, perfect and impossibly beautiful. I was speechless, my hand clapping over my mouth as I took it all in.

"Kiran..."

"I'll do anything to make you happy, Rhi."

For a moment, all I could do was stare at him—the angel who gave me so much without hesitation. Love swirled around him like an aura I could almost reach out and touch. He was devoted to me completely, overwhelmingly.

So what was wrong with me? Why did flashes of Justin still tug at the edges of my mind? Justin and his relentless intensity that seared whenever he was close, whenever he touched me. I felt powerless against it, against him—like I couldn't control myself when he was near. But looking at Kiran now, seeing how much he loved me...maybe if he tried to kiss me just once...

"Rhi?"

I blinked up at him through the blur of thoughts. "You're amazing," I finally managed.

I shrieked as he pulled me into the pool. Water splashed everywhere but was deliciously warm against my skin. Kiran surfaced beside me, shaking droplets from his hair.

"You are so going to pay for that!" I sputtered, trying to splash him back all of which he avoided.

Kiran dove beneath the surface, disappearing in a flurry of bubbles. Just as I turned to look for him, his strong arms wrapped around my waist, and he swung me effortlessly around to face him. Our bodies met with a warm sensation that sent my heart racing.

My cheeks burned; my skin was alive with electricity wherever our bodies touched. And it felt like we were touching everywhere—his grip strong and un-yielding around my waist, like I belonged here with him.

I stared at the angel who held me so completely. My breath caught again at the sight of him, water streaming down his honeyed hair and droplets catching in the thick lashes framing his ethereal silver eyes.

How was it possible for someone to be so beautiful?

Desire tugged sharply at me, and I leaned closer. It would be so easy to kiss him. His lips were right there. A breath away. My heart raced faster as I leaned closer, ready to close that space between us...

Suddenly his hold loosened, and the chill of air swirled between us once more. "Do you want to see the rest of the house?" Kiran asked breathlessly.

"Uh...yeah," I said finally, brushing hair from my face.

Kiran swept me up again, lifting us both out of the pool with ease placing me on the warm grass. I shivered despite the early autumn warmth. Kiran waved his hand over me and then himself drying us completely.

"Not much done to the inside yet," he admitted. "Don't expect too much."

"I won't," I promised, trying to catch my breath.

Just then, a soft meow floated through the air. We both turned as a fluffy orange and white cat slinked across the yard, weaving through the grass until it rubbed against our legs.

Kiran knelt down. "Who are you?"

"Do you think it was Mr. Hollander's?" I scooped up the cat, its purr resonating through my chest.

"Maybe," Kiran said thoughtfully. "But he seems to have found someone he likes better now." His hand grazed down the cat's back.

"He must have been surviving outside," I murmured. "We should feed him."

"We should name him first," Kiran suggested as we made our way to the house, the cat still cradled in my arms.

"He looks like an Ernie."

Kiran chuckled, his grin stretching wide. "Ernie it is then."

I put the cat down as we stepped inside. He padded confidently over to a small dish labeled Stanley. "I guess he's not an Ernie," I said with a laugh.

Kiran snapped his fingers and Stanley's empty plate filled with food. I watched the cat dig in happily.

Kiran took my hand, leading me inside. The front room was dim and dusty; old sheets covered the furniture.

"Wow," I said, glancing around. "This place is so...sad."

"It is in rough shape," Kiran agreed.

"Looks like Mr. Hollander was pretty lonely." I ran my fingers across a mantle, leaving a trail in the thick dust.

"I think he was," Kiran nodded, his expression thoughtful. He lifted a hand, and suddenly the dust was gone, along with the sheets and any trace of neglect.

He motioned me toward an old but elegant Victorian couch. Stanley followed us into the room and curled up in a patch of sunlight streaming through the window.

Kiran sat beside me, "So Sam came by last night."

"Sam was here?" I asked, surprised.

Kiran paused, his eyes carefully searching mine. "I've noticed something, Rhi," he said slowly. "None of your cousins have Guardian Angels."

"What?" I drew a shaky breath, "What about Nan?"

"I see her Guardian sometimes," Kiran said gently. "Actually, that's another thing. Sam said her Guardian might be something else."

"Something else? What is that supposed to mean?"

"Guardians were not created when the first angels were. We've only been around a couple of thousand years compared to other angels."

I slumped back against the couch, trying to process what he was saying.

"Sam said we should check out your grandfather's office."

"Pops? But, he's passed on for several years now. I don't understand." My voice was sharp with disbelief.

"I don't really either. I asked him what he knew and that is what he told me. Check out the office."

"We should do it," I said suddenly. "But we should wait until after school tomorrow when Nan is at work."

Kiran nodded, lacing his fingers through mine.

School. Ugh. My stomach clenched at the thought of starting somewhere new.

"How do you feel about going to school for the first time?" I asked, hoping he didn't notice the edge in my voice.

"Pretty excited," he said his enthusiasm almost innocent. "I can experience another human right of passage."

"I don't know if it's that great," I muttered. "Aren't you nervous?"

He shook his head, wrapping an arm around my shoulder and pulling me closer. "Never when I'm with you."

The reassurance calmed me a little. He must have felt tension still running through me because he pressed a soft kiss to my forehead.

"It'll be okay," Kiran murmured against my skin.

Electricity sparked where his lips touched my skin. His warmth surrounded me, and his sweet vanilla scent filled the air. I let go of his hand, my fingers trembling as they slid up his arm, over the hard curve of his bicep, and into his hair. His body tensed under my touch, and for a second, he went completely still.

"Kiran?" I whispered.

He pulled back just enough to search my eyes, the heat in his gaze making me dizzy. Maybe this time he really would...

Spirals of anticipation curled through me, every part of me alive and wanting.

I pushed myself against him, feeling the racing of his heart through our joined bodies. It left me breathless. Kiran groaned softly as his arm closed around me.

"Rhi," he said hoarsely. "Do you know what you do to me?"

Hope flared bright within me. I lifted my face to his, seeing the intensity there—and something else, something desperate and beautiful.

If he wouldn't kiss me...I leaned closer with every intention of doing it myself.

A loud chime suddenly echoed through the house.

We broke apart, each of us breathing heavily.

Stanley scurried out of the room with a flick of his orange tail.

Kiran stood and walked towards the front hallway. He hesitated at the doorway, turning back to look at me.

"We should see who it is," I said quickly, standing and brushing past him into the hallway.

He followed, quiet but close as we crossed toward the big oak door. The late morning light streamed through tall windows, casting long shadows down the empty corridor. My pulse still raced from what almost happened.

Kiran peeked through the sidelight window. The sunlight caught streaks of gold in his hair. It was absolutely beautiful like all of him was. "It's Mia."

Chapter Twelve

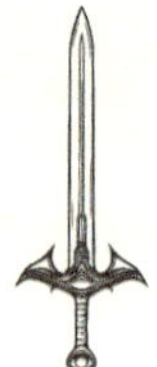

Kiran

That witch had impeccable timing. I groaned. Swinging the large door open, I invited her in.

Mia looked between us both, and then gasped dramatically. "Were you two?"

"No," Rhi and I blurted at the same time.

Mia eyed me with amusement. "You don't lie, blondie."

I frowned. "I'm not. We were not doing what you imply."

"Mmm hmm," Mia smirked. "But you two are blushing like..." She laughed and waved her hand. "Never mind. I'll get it out of Rhi later."

Kiran and I exchanged looks.

"Anyway," Mia drawled out the word. "Sam mentioned you have some wards in here I should check out?"

"Wards?" Rhi said, confused.

"In the master bedroom." I kept my voice steady as I shut the door behind her.

"Sweet." Her curiosity still hanging in the air, she sauntered down the hall. "This place is like a museum. It's weird," she called back, inspecting the walls.

We hurried after her into the room Rhi, and I had just been. She gawked at everything around her like a kid in a candy store. "It's to the right," I said, gesturing towards the open doorway.

As we passed the couch that Rhi and I had just been on, I swore I saw her blush. Heat surged through me. I wanted to kick Mia out, pull Rhi close, and lose myself in her.

"World to Kiran." Mia snapped her fingers.

"Yeah, follow me." I huffed.

I paused at the entrance to the room and let her step in front of me. She cautiously entered and trailed her fingers along the doorframe.

"Ohh yeah," she said with a satisfied smirk. "I feel it." Her eyes flicked over to me, curious. "What do you feel?"

"Like there's a trap," I admitted, hanging back slightly. "An angel trap, maybe...or just warded against any supernatural. Either way, Mr. Hollander didn't want anyone like me in there."

"Or maybe it wasn't him," she suggested thoughtfully. "Maybe it was someone who owned the house before."

"I know whoever set it didn't want angels around," I said.

"This room feels old," Mia said, rubbing her fingers slowly across a wooden board. "Like...really old. The walls are different in here than out there."

I watched her closely as she seemed to be piecing together an idea.

"Colonists?" Rhi asked.

"Possibly or Revolutionary War, maybe. There was a trading post here back in the day." She flicked a quick smile. "My tribe helped them. Look where that got us."

"You really think these wards are that old?" Rhi asked, running her fingers tentatively along the door frame.

"I bet as new people owned it, they just built around it." Mia sat cross-legged on the floor and closed her eyes. "Think I'll have a meditative moment."

I gave her an incredulous look. "A what?"

She peeked through one eye at me and laughed lightly. "Chill out, angel boy. I'm just tuning in to these old walls."

Rhi and I exchanged silent glances as Mia lapsed into concentration. After a moment, she spoke again, chewing thoughtfully on her lip. "It's weird," she said. "I can feel the spirits here, but I can't hear them. My Gran probably can." She jumped up, shaking out her limbs. "Religion and superstition went hand in hand in Colonial America. Their belief in God confirmed the validity of believing in ghosts and spirits as well. The colonists were obsessed with religion. Their outlook on everything—good or bad—was totally shaped by it."

"So you think they left these wards?" Rhi asked.

It makes sense," Mia replied. "The colonists accepted the unseen world of angels and devils completely."

Rhi glanced at me, her eyes full of curiosity. "So that means Kiran wouldn't just be possible to them, but probable?"

Mia nodded and then gave me a pointed look. "Makes you wonder what they were worried about."

"Or what they needed protection from," I said.

"Anyhoos, do you want me to ask my Gran to come over and see what the spirits are saying?"

I shook my head. I didn't need such a powerful witch in here. Mia, I trusted. Mostly. But I couldn't say the same for other witches. "For now, I'll just stay away from the room."

"Suit yourself," Mia shrugged. "Let me just see if there is anything in here I can find that may be of help.

Mia opened a dresser and pulled out some old clothes with a disappointed grunt. "Unless you need antique outfits, nothing special here."

Rhi laughed. "I think we're good."

Mia headed to the closet, rummaging through it. "Same in here," she called out. "Gotta say, it doesn't look like anyone's been here for a long time."

Rhi's shoulders relaxed slightly. "So you don't see anything unusual?"

"Nope," Mia said, popping back into the hall with us. "We should check out the rest of the house. Maybe there's something in another room."

I moved back into the hallway, grateful to put distance between myself and the warded space.

"Where do you want to start?" Rhi asked, looking between us.

"Attic?" I suggested. "Old houses always have something hidden in the attic."

Mia nodded enthusiastically. "Or haunted up there." She clapped as we turned a corner, heading towards a narrow staircase.

Rhi giggled and sped up to walk alongside me, her hand brushing against mine briefly.

"If nothing turns up in the attic," Mia glanced back at us over her shoulder, drumming her fingers on the banister, "we should ask around town about the place. People love gossiping and telling stories. There is usually a grain of truth to them."

An old wooden ladder led up to the narrow hatch in the ceiling. I reached to tug it open. With a loud creak, the opening gave way into darkness above us.

Mia squeezed past and practically bounded up. We heard her sigh of disappointment immediately after she stepped off the ladder. "Not even a ghost."

Rhi joined her, peering around. Her eyes met mine as I came up to her. "It's empty," she said, frowning.

"Yeah, maybe stuff is hidden in the basement," Mia suggested grudgingly.

"Or one of the other bedrooms," Rhi said, grimacing at the bare rafters.

I laughed under my breath and pulled Rhi close enough for our shoulders to touch. She leaned into me as Mia slunk over to a far corner.

"A totally empty attic is just wrong," Mia said dejectedly. "I'm not giving up until we find something good."

"I think I would have known if there was a ghost in here," I said. "Celestial, remember?"

Mia stomped over to the ladder and started climbing down. "Basement, here we come."

"Come on," Mia called as we hurried back down. "There has to be something in this ginormous place."

We passed door after door along the second-floor hall, opening each one. Mia stuck her head into every empty room, giving an exaggerated groan when nobody jumped out to scare her. Rhi and I exchanged amused looks.

"This house sucks," Mia said, folding her arms as we hit the first level again. "Thought for sure there'd at least be some spooky ghouls."

We walked until we circled back to the main room, opening doors but finding nothing other than old furniture.

"We've seen this one," Mia continued toward the kitchen. "Did you check that door?"

A heavy wooden door sat at the back of the kitchen.

"No," I said.

Mia wiggled her eyebrows mischievously and pulled it open, revealing a set of steep stairs.

We crowded around the entrance, but she didn't wait for us to say anything before she rushed down into the dark.

It was damp and cold with a bare bulb swinging from above as she clicked it on.

Rhi shivered beside me; I longed to pull her close and forget all this.

Lots of boxes lined the walls, and another door stood at the back. I examined how old some of the boxes looked, and then noticed Rhi doing the same.

"Where do you want to start looking?" I asked.

"We should look through some of these," Rhi said, running her hands over a stack of boxes.

"Look at this guys," Mia called over her shoulder. "Another door." She pulled it open with a loud creak, staggering back as a musty wind gusted over her.

"Oh!" Her eyes widened in shock before they settled into excitement again. "There's a tunnel!"

Rhi bounded to her side and ducked her head through the doorway to see for herself.

"This is insane," she breathed as I came up behind them.

I studied the rough walls and uneven floor leading away from us. "Why are there tunnels everywhere in this town?"

"Tunnels," Rhi's eyes were wide as she glanced back at me. "Sam told me there are a bunch of them and that some were used by the natives, but that the mob were the ones that really used them for illegal stuff."

I thought I saw something else in her eyes.

Fear.

"During the Revolutionary War, people hid out in tunnels like this, too." Mia mused, her gaze darting between us, "They got used for spying. There's a church off Main Street that has a plaque with a story that the British kept surveillance via these tunnels."

"Do either of you find it strange that this tunnel goes towards Rhi's house and not in the opposite direction?"

"Not really," said Mia, squinting into the darkness. "What if there used to be a barn or some other structure over there that they used it to get to?" Her head snapped up, eyes dancing. "I'm going to check it out."

"Be careful," I said, taking Rhi's hand and following.

We walked hunched through the passageway, our footsteps echoing around us.

Mia halted abruptly and crouched down. "Whoa."

"What is it?" Rhi asked breathlessly, peeking ahead.

"It just ends, but there's a trapdoor under here." Mia ran her fingers over the floor.

Anxiety prickled at my senses. "Is it connected to anything?"

She brushed away some dirt, revealing an old iron handle set into the wood. "Only one way to find out."

We worked together to pull it open; the heavy door fell back with a rusty thud, and a ladder extended down to yet another level below.

"This is insane," Rhi whispered.

Mia looked between us, her expression triumphant. "Who wants to be a pioneer?"

I hesitated a moment too long; Rhi dropped my hand and climbed down first.

I jumped after Rhi, landing beside her with ease. "Show off," she teased.

Mia clattered down the ladder and joined us. "I think we walked at least two houses from that basement by now," she said, shaking some dirt out of her hair. "One more and it should be Rhi's."

We continued through the darker passage, goose bumps rising on my skin. I willed a flashlight into existence, its beam cutting cleanly through shadow.

"Convenient," Rhi said.

"Looks like it ends," I said as we stumbled to a stop.

"And right where your house is, Rhi," Mia added.

"So it seems," Rhi said, frowning at the rough rock and dirt wall.

We all looked up. The flashlight illuminated another hatch.

"Hey," said Mia, glancing around until she found an old wooden ladder. She lifted it toward me, and I climbed up, pushing at the hatch. It didn't budge.

"Now what?" asked Rhi, watching me slide down the ladder.

"I can teleport myself wherever it opens up to."

"And if someone sees you materialize in thin air?" Rhi put her hands on her hips.

"I can mask myself," I said, gently squeezing her hand. "Become invisible."

She hesitated, biting her lip in that way that drove me crazy. "Okay, but only if you promise to come right back."

"I'll call you up the second when I know it's safe."

I focused until everything else disappeared. In a blink, I was in the house. It was Rhi's house in a room I hadn't been in before. I could hear the TV in the living room. I glanced around, trying to find the hatch, and saw a large, old wooden desk that sat at the back of the room. My guess was that it was under there.

This must be Rhi's grandfather's office.

"Well, what's up there?" Mia looked at me expectantly when I rematerialized.

I met Rhi's anxious eyes. "I didn't see the hatch. Maybe it's under something or was covered years ago by flooring."

"And..." Mia pressed. "Is it Rhi's house?"

I nodded. "It's in what I assume is your grandfather's office."

"Why can't I have an underground tunnel that leads to everyone's houses?" Mia pouted, kicking lightly at some loose dirt.

"Who says you don't?"

"Now we have to get into the office," Rhi muttered, pacing. "Between the tunnel beneath it and what Sam told you..."

"What did Sam tell you?" asked Mia.

I glanced at Rhi before answering. "That her grandfather might be hiding something about..."

"My family," Rhi cut in, her voice tense.

"Tomorrow then," I insisted softly, choosing my words more mindfully than usual with Rhi so frazzled. "We'll go in after our classes."

Chapter Thirteen

Justin

What was that banging? I forced my eyes open, rolling toward the sound. It came again, this time with a voice. "It's almost noon. Time to get up."

Who the hell was that? I groaned, swinging my legs off the bed. The book I had been studying all night slipped to the floor. I picked it up and slid it under the blankets.

I forced myself across the room to the door. Opening it, a tall slender guy leaned against the doorframe. His messy copper hair hung over his dark eyes. "What do you want?"

"Now, now. Is that any way to treat a guest?" Phen said.

"You're not my guest. You're Sorcha's." I went to slam the door in his face, but he put a hand up to stop me.

"C'mon, Justin. Don't be that way." Phen tilted his head and grinned. "Heard about your scuffle with Kiran."

I glared at him, refusing to take the bait.

"That must be some girl," he went on, unfazed. "Taking on your brother, an Arch-Nephilim like that. To say nothing of his true-born angel status."

"Shut up, Phen," I snapped.

His voice was syrupy, mocking. He leaned in closer. "You must be head over heels."

I went to slam the door in his face again, but he slammed a hand against it to stop me.

"Wow! Touchy subject?" He pushed on the door, sliding past me. "What if I told you I could help you with that?"

I stood there for a moment, annoyed he got under my skin—and even more annoyed that he was right about everything else.

He looked around the room before turning back to me, "For real," he said smoothly. "I can help you get her away from Kiran."

"And how the hell do you plan on doing that? You can't kill an angel."

Phen shrugged casually, a devil-may-care gleam in his eyes. "Let's just say I've got some insider knowledge."

I crossed my arms, trying to play it cool even though I felt a twinge of curiosity. "Knowledge on how to kill an angel?"

"You're correct in that Kiran can't be killed. At least not by us." Phen said with a sly smirk.

"What do you mean?"

"Angels," Phen said, dragging out the word. "To bring them down takes divine intervention. Only the one who created them can really put a nail in their celestial coffins. Or the big guy, of course."

"You mean my fath...," Justin said slowly, "I mean Vince?"

Phen sat down on the edge of the bed, stretching his lanky arms. "I mean the one who plucked his little baby soul and made him an angel."

"So who would that be?"

He raised an eyebrow at me, "The Archangel Michael."

I had just been reading about Michael in the book I found last night. It read mostly like a diary however I had found some useful things in it. I tried to keep my face blank before I spoke again. "Even still, why help me?"

"Why not?" Phen grinned lazily. "You're my dear friend Sorcha's brother."

I clenched my jaw. "So is Kiran."

"Yes, yes," Phen waved a dismissive hand. "But it's obvious he's the black sheep of the family."

I snorted, leaning against the wall. "There has got to be something in it for you."

Phen steepled his fingers, tilting his head in mock thought. "Justin, you have no idea how delighted upper management is when a player from the light side crosses over. There's so little sport if you're just born with a taste for sin, you know? But turning—really turning—an angel, that's how you make an impression."

Part of me ached to have Rhi all to myself, but helping Phen turn Kiran evil? No. I couldn't do that. Rhi would never forgive me. Despite everything, there was no denying my curiosity. "Say you can't turn him, then how do you think you can get him out of the way for Rhi and me?"

Phen leaned back on his elbows with a lazy smirk, getting too close to where I hid the book. "There are other ways to bring an angel to its knees."

"What does that mean?"

"He's a Guardian Angel. His devotion is his strongest weakness."

I shook my head, forcing a laugh. "You think he'll just give up his guardianship? The girl he's devoted to? You don't know Kiran, and more importantly, I'm not using Rhi to get to him."

"So maybe we do it another way. Harder, yes—but still can work."

"How?"

He gave me a wicked look. "He can be trapped in Hell."

I stared at him, shocked into silence. I didn't want Kiran out of the picture that much. Rhi would hate me forever. "That's insane," I managed to say.

"Is it?" Phen stretched out cat-like on the bed.

It was too much, but the idea gnawed at me, and Phen knew it. "How would you even do something like that?"

He clicked his tongue like a sly fox with all the answers. "Ah, that's the question, isn't it? I can't force him there, but if he gets there voluntarily..." he paused for effect, eyes gleaming, "I can cage him."

The words exploded in my mind like a gunshot. I rocked back, my voice low and incredulous. "That's...too much."

"Think about it," he encouraged softly. "But don't take too long." He laughed lightly and went for the door. When Phen reached it, he turned dramatically and gave me one last look as a smile crept up his lips.

Creepy.

I stood there long after he was gone; staring at the open door and feeling the sharp pull of everything I ever wanted just out of reach.

Again.

I shut the door at last, locking it. What Phen was suggesting...I couldn't do it. Not even to Kiran.

It killed me to consider it, but I would go to Sam and tell him about Phen's plan. In the meantime, I'd finish the book. There was a whole section on *"Ossaris"* that caught my attention. I could play along until I found out what Phen was really up to. Keep your friends close and your enemies closer. Vince used to say that. For once, he was right.

I dug out the book, flipping through worn pages covered in heavy scrawl until I got back to where I left off.

According to the book, Michael and Gabriel hadn't agreed with what God commanded—cast the Watchers into the Abyss for eternity. Was Hell the Abyss? They had thought of the Watchers as brothers. So they devised a plan: they gave the Watchers shields. Not physical shields, but some kind of brand or tattoo etched into their skin. Supposedly, it hid them from God's sight.

Then there was all this stuff about Ossaris. Ossaris were apparently humans with traces of angelic blood who safeguarded supernatural boundaries. Michael and Gabriel gave the humans their blood, which left a scar. Apparently, each generation would be born with a scar, also indicating they were an Ossaris.

It was their jobs to keep a balance between the mortal world and the divine, demonic, and spiritual realms. Not doing so could result in souls getting lost or dark forces gaining more influence.

Couldn't have that. I'd been around enough demons since learning about my heritage to know they were a bad influence on everything they touched.

The Ossaris had to make sure the Watchers obeyed celestial law in return for sparing them. That conveniently kept the Archangel's hands clean while still maintaining some sort of order. I was beginning to understand why this book had been hidden.

Reading on it said that Ossaris all were given specific abilities. Some could use the ability to control and manipulate the elements and the natural forces of the earth. That would come in handy.

Some had heightened senses. Not quite as cool as controlling the elements.

Some were mediums and had the gift of coercion. They could perceive and communicate with spirits and make people do their bidding. There were mediums everywhere these days, real or not. But being able to coerce people, now that was cool.

Some could channel the energy from other living beings. Could you imagine being able to channel the strength of an elephant or the speed of a cheetah? I think this is the coolest one yet.

I wondered if there were still Ossaris around. Could supernatural beings see them the way we saw each other? If I could find out who the Ossaris were, maybe it could help me figure things out with Kiran and Phen.

Folding the book up, I put it back under the floorboards. Heading out to take a shower, I knew I had to find Sam once I was done.

I finished showering and headed downstairs. Voices floated up from the first floor, and I paused, listening in. Sorcha's laughter mixed with Sam's and Phen chimed in with some comment I couldn't understand.

I followed the sound to the kitchen and found them all there, gathered around the island, sitting on stools.

"Hey," I said, opening the fridge for a soda.

Sorcha flashed a smile at me while Phen lounged back in his chair like he owned the place.

I pulled out the soda, pointing to Sam with my chin as I cracked it open. "Hey. I found another tunnel last night."

Sam sat up straighter, "Did you?"

Phen watched with sharp eyes as I took a deliberate sip. "Yeah," I said, pinning him with a look before returning my gaze to Sam. "To the dungeon."

His face remained impassive.

"You want to take a look with me?" I asked Sam, trying to draw him out and away from Phen's watchful eyes.

He considered for a moment, then nodded. "Sure."

"Let's go then."

Sam followed, casting a quick look at my sister and Phen.

We stepped outside; the warm, humid wind blew around us as we crossed the lawn. I glanced over my shoulder to make sure no one else followed. Falling into step beside me, Sam shoved his hands into his pockets. "So what's up? You looked like you had more to say without the others hearing."

I waited until we were past earshot of the house. "That demon prince you're so chummy with?" I finally said.

"What about him?" Sam eyed me suspiciously.

"He offered me a deal."

"Phen?" Sam stopped in his tracks. "What kind of deal?"

"To get Kiran out of the picture—out of Rhi's life." I shook my head, "Said he could trap him."

Sam swore under his breath. "Normally he plays it casual—charming, even—but a demon prince doesn't offer favors without a price. He's definitely up to something."

"That's what I thought." I held back a branch so Sam could pass through. "Any idea why?"

"I got nothing, but I will find out."

No matter the reason, it didn't make sense for a demon prince to suddenly play Cupid for Rhi and me. At least not without something big in it for himself.

The old guest house appeared through the trees. It loomed quiet and untouched, as if waiting for us. "This is the place," I said.

"So where's this tunnel?"

"In here," I said. I led him through a dust-filled hallway to the closet. I shouldered the hidden door open and stepped inside.

Our footsteps echoed through the tunnel. Dust dislodged from the ceiling in thin clouds as we made our way deeper inside. "You need to be careful," Sam warned, straightening up as we continued down the tunnel. "There's always a dark side with demons."

"You think?" I laughed shortly, sound echoing off stone walls. "I know better than to take him up on it."

"It's dangerous even messing around with it. Don't sign—don't swear to anything."

"I figured I'd go along for a while," I said, kicking at some debris on the path. "See what else he says without actually committing."

"You're way too casual about this," Sam said as he made a flashlight appear in his hand and turned it on.

"I can handle Phen," I told him.

He gave me a skeptical glance.

Flashlight beams bounced ahead of us, illuminating walls that gleamed darkly with dampness. Water dripped slowly somewhere in the distance. My curiosity got the better of me, and my voice broke the silence again.

"What do you know about Ossaris?" I asked.

He stopped abruptly, staring at me. "Where did you hear that term?" he asked, a steely edge to his voice.

I shrugged, glancing away. "Overheard it at the party last night."

"Liar," he said, expression set like stone.

"What? Someone was talking about them." I tried to sound convincing, but there was a tightness in my throat I couldn't quite swallow.

"Lie," Sam cut in, stepping closer as his eyes bore into mine. A flicker of something ancient blazed behind them. I felt a chill run through me.

"I know you're lying," he went on. "That word is only known by certain people, and none were there last night."

His stare felt like it was cutting straight to my soul. "Except myself," he added, "And I did not—or will not—mention Ossaris."

"So what if I did know something?" I said at last. "What difference does it make?"

Sam studied me for a long time before speaking again. "You found something," he said, his voice a mix of surprise and suspicion.

"Maybe," I replied, trying to sound casual.

Sam inclined his head, expression shrewd. "I know Vince was a collector of sorts. You found something that mentions them, didn't you?"

"What are they?" I pressed.

"I've been through his library," Sam said, ignoring my question. "Nothing of interest was there. So there must be other rooms, secret rooms that house his collections."

"Okay, you're right. I found some things." I took a breath, "Like how Gabriel and Michael helped you..."

His expression went dark.

"I mean the Watchers," I corrected, "And had some people called Ossaris to help you as well."

"You shouldn't know any of this—Vince shouldn't have either," Sam's eyes flashed.

I tried to slow the flood of questions racing my mind. Clearly, there was more going on here than I thought. "Why? What aren't you telling me?"

I leaned against the stone wall, watching him process everything.

He stopped pacing for a second, grabbing my arm with a look that was part anger, part fear. "Did you tell the others?"

"No."

"Good," Sam breathed. "I need to see what you've found, Justin."

"I don't think that's—"

With a speed I didn't expect, he reached out and grabbed me by the throat. I shoved back at him instinctively, eyes narrowing. He barely budged, and his grip tightened—an iron reminder that he could overpower me as easily as if I were a bug under his shoe.

"Why should I trust you?" I seethed, fury edging my words.

"I don't care if you trust me or not," Sam retorted, eyes blazing. "But if you care as much for Rhi as you say you do, you'll show me what you've found." He finally let go, and I sucked in air while watching him warily.

Rubbing my throat, I scowled at him. "What does this have to do with her?"

He stepped back, a calculating look on his face. "The less you know, the better—for now. But trust me; this does have everything to do with her." His words hung in the air, and I stared him down, wrestling with my pride.

Sam had always known more than he let on; he had known since the day I was born that I was a Nephilim. As much as I hated to admit it, Sam had kept secrets, but he'd also helped me. Right now he thought this was something dangerous to Rhi and I couldn't—no wouldn't let anything happen to her. "Fine," I said at last, running a hand through my hair with a sigh. "I'll take you there."

A flood of relief swept through Sam's eyes. He pulled out his phone, tapping a quick message before looking up. "I'll have Sorcha take care of Phen," he said. "Get him out of the house for a while."

"We should use this time to take a closer look around here." Sam gestured for me to follow him further into the tunnel's depths. "Don't underestimate how much Vince may have hidden." A network of questions tangled in my mind as we moved through the tunnel. What other secrets had been collecting dust beneath our feet? And if Vince had such a valuable book to the Watchers, what else did he know—did he plan for—before we got rid of him?

The door appeared ahead, and I shoved it open.

Dark images clawed at me—memories I'd buried, suddenly exploding to the surface. Vince looming over me, taunting, beating, chaining me. Rhi's scream cutting through everything. Agony ripping through my body as the ceiling came down. Kiran's voice in my mind—begging, fighting to keep me alive. I had grabbed his hand and seen the terror in his eyes. I thought I had died. Maybe I had, for those few haunting seconds before Kiran pulled me back.

Sam was roaming the room. Feeling the walls and examining the strange markings on them.

"You said you couldn't kill Vince or any angel, right?" I asked.

Sam nodded. "Angels can't be killed in the traditional sense. Only the one who brought them into existence holds that power, and of course, the Creator does. But," he lowered his voice, "they can be wounded severely enough to render them powerless for decades. And there's something most don't realize— Lucifer himself possesses the ability to permanently destroy other angels."

"Like what Phen said he'd do to Kiran?"

Sam considered, looking hard at me. "Yes, but they don't have to be in Hell to be imprisoned. Sorcha and I planned to do it to Vince and keep him here—in this dungeon."

My eyes swept the space again. "Do you think he'll return?"

"I've warded the place so he can't get in," Sam said carefully. "But if there are other tunnels I don't know about, then yes. He can get through them. I'll ward this one, and we should look for others."

His phone buzzed. He looked at it briefly before meeting my gaze with urgency humming behind his eyes. "It's clear from Sorcha," he said. "Come on, Justin. We can check out the dungeon later," He reached for my wrist. "I'll teleport us there."

"My room then."

The room surged into view. I'd never get used to the teleporting thing. It was like being ripped apart and shoved back together again. Nausea raked my body, and I leaned against the door.

"Where is it?" Sam demanded, eyes scanning my room.

"In here," I said, brushing past him to the corner of the room where I'd hidden the book beneath a floorboard. My heart pounded as I pulled it out.

"It's like a diary or something," I said, handing it to him.

Sam took it slowly, his hands shaking. "The Book of Michael," he whispered, awe touching his voice.

"So it's important, then?"

Sam sank onto the edge of the bed, staring at it as if he'd just found the Holy Grail. "More than you know."

Sam opened the first page, skimming over words as if they were pure gold inked on parchment. His eyes snapped to mine, "You can tell no one about this."

"So what is so important about these Ossaris? They seem to just be glorified babysitters for you Watchers."

Sam looked irritated at my words. "The Ossaris are not known to any other supernaturals besides the Watchers and a handful of Principalities..."

"Prince what?"

"Principalities. They are another sector of angels and demons. There are not many of them, like there are other types of angels and demons." Sam's eyes seemed lost in memory, "They oversee nations, rulers, and groups of specific people...like clans or tribes. They are enforcers of spiritual order. If the balance of good and evil is not maintained, a Principality will guide either side depending on where the deficit is to bring balance to all realms again." His jaw worked in distaste.

"You don't sound like you like them."

"You have no idea," Sam said. "Principalities guide Ossaris. However, they can both trick and support an Ossaris. They're slippery beings, but necessary because of the knowledge they carry." His eyes slid to mine. "You tell no one, and I mean no one, what we've discussed."

I wasn't about to take orders from him, but I nodded anyway. I would decide what to say and to whom about any of this.

"Where did you find this book?"

I motioned with my hand around the room. I wasn't telling him or anyone until I was good and ready about that secret room. "Right here."

Sam scrutinized me, his eyes narrowing. He got up and began to examine the rest of the books on the shelves. "There is nothing else here like it." He turned to me. "I'm going to keep this safe."

"No, you're not," I demanded.

He was in front of me faster than I could track him. "You would do well to remember who I am, boy."

I scowled at him, not backing down. "I found it, and I am part of your world too."

"You are a Nephilim. You are not a full angel and certainly not an ancient one like me. I'm keeping it. No argument from you because if you push me, I will just wipe your memory of it and take it anyway."

Heat rose in my chest. I hated being told what to do—hated being threatened even more. That was exactly why I'd wanted the book in the first place: leverage in a world I'd been thrown into without a map. I had read it all, though. I just hadn't had time to work out the angelic alphabet.

"Fine," I finally huffed.

Sam's face lightened to its normal jovial expression. "Great, now let's explore the rest of this mansion and see what else dear old Vincent has stashed here."

Chapter Fourteen

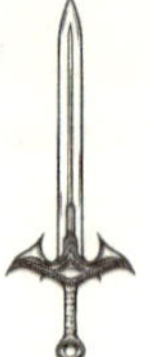

Rhiannon

I'd faced angels, demons, and a crazed Fallen Angel who'd tortured me in a dungeon — yet here I was, standing in front of my new high school with clammy hands and a pounding heart.

Kiran was next to me, his presence calming as he leaned in close. "We're in this together. It's my first day, too, remember," he whispered, silver eyes soft with promise.

Mia rolled her eyes from my other side and huffed dramatically. "Pshh, you've got me, too. You're golden."

"Yes, but we don't have any classes together."

"So tragic," she sighed dramatically. "But no worries—I'm here in spirit."

"Rhi, there you are!" Steve's voice cut through the crowd as he and Kacey approached.

Kacey waved energetically, glancing from group to group like a social butterfly touching down on every flower. "Hey!" she called out, grinning at us.

Steve bumped my shoulder. "You look terrified," he said with a playful grin. "It's just school."

I shrugged as students rushed past in a blur of backpacks and noise — laughter, shouted names, the chaos of everyone catching up after summer. Kiran's eyes followed mine as I scanned the crowd.

"Come on, Lady Bug," Mia said, grabbing my hand and leading our group to the doors. I caught Steve out of the corner of my eye watching Mia, who seemed oblivious.

Kacey dropped to step in line with us with a bright smile on her pretty face. "You're going to love it here," she said confidently.

"It's huge," I said absently, taking in the high ceilings and long corridors.

The students' energy swept us along, filling the halls with a tidal wave of chatter. I could feel my nerves flutter as we were jostled through the masses.

Steve dropped back beside Kiran. "How's it going, man?"

"I'm well," Kiran replied smoothly.

A familiar voice called from behind us. "Hey! Wait up!"

We turned to see Sam weaving through the crowd. He slid an arm around me, eyes bright. "Are you doing okay, sweet cheeks?"

"Sweet cheeks?" Steve raised an eyebrow.

"It's...just a nickname," I sighed.

Sam smirked and gave Kiran a nod just as the first warning bell clanged loudly above our heads.

"Can anyone point me to Trigonometry?" I asked helplessly.

Kacey laughed. "Follow me! It's on my way."

"I actually have that class too," Kiran said.

"Me too," Sam said casually.

I fell into step with her as Kiran and Sam trailed behind us. I noticed how many girls batted their eyelashes and tossed smiles at them. Kacey glanced back, raising her eyebrows with a knowing look.

"Looks like you've got some fans," she said with a smirk.

A tall boy with short dark hair passed us. He glared angrily at Kacey. I recognized him. It was the boy she had been dating, Jake.

"What's his problem?" I whispered to Kacey.

"He's mad because I broke up with him."

I looked at her, confused. "When? You didn't tell me."

She flipped her long hair over one shoulder, "Yesterday. I really like Phen, and I can't pursue that with Jake in the picture."

Ice poured through my veins. "Isn't he a bit old for you?" I did not want my little cousin anywhere near that demon prince.

Kacey stopped short, "I supported you with Justin. Why can't you support me with Phen? I like him, Rhi! He's only three years older than me."

"More like three thousand years," Kiran said into my head.

"Anyway, there's your class." She pointed to a door a few down from where we stood. Then she turned on her heel and strode away.

The second bell rang. "Oh no," I muttered. The halls had emptied. Late. On my first day. I caught a few heads turning when we stumbled into the classroom, and Kiran met them with a level gaze.

"You must be our two new students," the teacher said.

I nodded as I felt heat flush my cheeks.

"I will excuse your tardiness this time because you're new to the school." She turned a pointed look at Sam, "You, however, are familiar with our school, Sam." She slid her glasses down and peered over the tops of them at him.

"I won't be late again, Ms. Calhoun," Sam said with a flirtatious smile.

She didn't seem to notice, just waved us to the back of the room, where some empty seats were. Miss Calhoun droned on about functions as I tried to melt into my chair and focus at least one ear on what she was saying.

"Nothing like making an entrance," Sam teased from the seat beside me.

Later that day, when I was with Mia, we spotted Kiran and Sam in deep conversation. "Ooooo, what's up with those two?"

"I don't know," I admitted.

"Let's find out!" She grabbed my arm, already dragging me along.

Before I knew it, we were cutting across the grass toward them.

Sam glanced up from where he leaned against the tree when we got closer. He actually looked...worried.

"What's going on with you two?" Mia asked.

"It's nothing for you to worry about right now," Kiran said, glancing quickly at me before shifting the subject. "Are you ready to go find out what's in your grandfather's office?"

"So you took my advice?" Sam asked with a raised eyebrow.

Mia answered before I could. "Actually, we found a tunnel from Kiran's new place that goes straight to Rhi's grandfather's office."

"You want company?" Sam offered.

"Actually," Kiran said, "I think just Rhi and I should go."

Mia pouted. "Aww! I want in on the fun!"

"Don't you have a class after this?" I asked her.

"Yes, but Sam can do his glamour thing for me," Mia replied impatiently, staring hopefully at Sam.

Sam hauled a protesting Mia back towards the school. "We'll meet up with you later!" he called over his shoulder.

Kiran watched them. He slipped his hand into mine as we crossed the campus and headed towards my house.

Walking into the empty house, Kiran closed the door softly behind us as I tossed my backpack on a chair. I pulled him towards the office at the end of the hall and turned the knob. "It's locked." My eyebrows pulled together. "That's weird. Why would Nan lock the door?"

"I'll snap us inside," Kiran said and wrapped his arms around me. The world blurred and shifted, the familiar room tilting into focus around us.

"It looks just like I remember," I said softly, eyes moving over everything at once. "I used to play in here while my grandfather worked." I settled into the large desk chair. "Even after everything he went through in the war, he was so kind and funny. I can still smell his aftershave."

Kiran smiled gently.

"Did you know he did our astrological life charts?" I asked, looking up with a grin. "Nan's, my mom's, and uncle's, my cousins', and mine. I know it's weird, him being Catholic, but he was also Irish. Very superstitious. So what are we looking for?" I asked as I opened one of the drawers.

"I'm not sure exactly," Kiran admitted, rifling through some old papers.

We started opening drawers and old cabinets filled with papers, files, and books. A large cardboard box sat on the floor next to the desk chair. Untouched. I reached down and swiped off some dust, picking it up.

"Looks like this is for you," Kiran said, nodding toward my name written along the edge in my grandmother's curly script.

I flipped it open to see notebooks, papers, and pages of notes and charts.

"What is it?" Kiran asked.

"Looks like they really kept track of me." I laughed softly.

He moved behind me, looking over my shoulder as I turned the pages. The warmth of him so close made my breath catch. Then the last page stopped us both cold.

"She was born to become the Veilbreaker; she is the Seventh Flame." Was written in my grandfather's neat handwriting.

"What does that mean?" I asked Kiran in a shaky voice.

He hesitated. "I—"

The creak of the front door interrupted us as my grandmother's voice rang out, "Rhiannon?"

Kiran wrapped his arms around me. The room blurred, and we landed on my bed. Quickly, I shoved the notebook beneath my pillow and yelled, "I'm in here, Nan!"

"We have to see everything in that box," I whispered, eyes wide with urgency.

"We will," he promised. "Later."

"Are you okay, sweetheart?"

"Yes," I answered too quickly. "I just got home."

"Just wanted to see how your first day of school went!" I could hear her setting down her things.

I left Kiran in my room and headed downstairs to see her.

"I wanted to hear all about your first day," she said with a warm smile, pulling me into a hug.

I returned her embrace. "It was school. I'm just glad I have my cousins and Mia there." I admitted. "And Kiran. We're in trigonometry together."

She squeezed my hand, eyes full of relief. "I know how anxious you get in new places. I was worried."

"I'm okay, really," I reassured her. "I was actually just going to check out the online classes and assignments."

"Back to work for me then," she said with a smile. "How about I bring us some food from the Pier on my way home today?"

"That'd be great! Maybe bring some extra?" A story formed fast in my mind. "Kiran mentioned his parents travel a lot for work, so he's alone a lot. Maybe he could have dinner with us some nights?"

She gave me a sweet look of understanding. "Of course."

She grabbed her purse and keys. "I'll be home around six."

I watched from the window as she backed out of the driveway and sprinted upstairs, shutting my bedroom door behind me.

The notebook was already in Kiran's hands. He frowned at it, brows knitted together.

"You look angry," I said.

His eyes snapped to mine, and his expression softened at once. "Come sit with me." He moved over so there was space for both of us on the edge of the bed. "We should talk about some things."

Chapter Fifteen

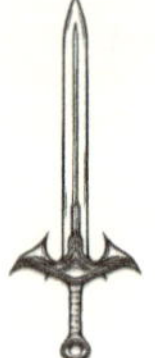

Kiran

I wasn't sure exactly what I was looking at. What was the Veilbreaker? Or the Seventh Flame? I know there are seven flames of the Spirit.

The Creator's Spirit.

This can't mean she is one of them. But, what if she is? How would her grandfather even know that? Which one would she be if she were one? Wisdom, Understanding, Counsel, Might, Power, Knowledge, or Fear?

It can't mean that Rhi is somehow...celestial. I cling to the thoughts, pushing through each gnarled possibility, wondering how it could be true.

Sam's earlier warning at school about these things called Ossaris and Rhi's family being involved—I refused to believe it. They had secrets, he said, deeper than the ocean. Why didn't I know any of this? Sam had never been so directly concerned before, though. He must believe it. And did Phen know? Is that why he told Rhi to look into her family history?

The letters before me blurred into each other, possibilities folding and unfolding in dizzying layers. I fought against what they seemed to be spelling out—the impossible magnitude of it petrified me.

Would she need protecting from it? From herself? Some new part of me wants to run, pull her so close that nothing can find or touch her.

"You look angry again." Her soft voice interrupts my thoughts.

Her eyes, those liquid chocolate pools, pierce through a place in me so deep I almost forget how to speak. The thought of losing her, even to some prophecy, even to herself...

When she lowers herself next to me, so close our shoulders touch, heat and electricity ricochets through me. Rhi glances at the notebook on my lap, curls straying down her cheeks. "Do you know what it means?" she asks.

Innocent. That's what she is—perfectly innocent in all of this madness I caused by revealing myself to her. And that innocent beauty—I would do anything to keep it from harm.

"I don't know exactly," I admit slowly.

"I've heard of seven flames before. I'm not sure if that's what your grandfather was referencing."

Her eyes widen, catching fire with curiosity. "Tell me."

So I do. I tell her everything I can remember about them. "It doesn't really make sense, but that's all I can equate it to," I say, "The Veil, though—you know what that is. But why you're being called a Veilbreaker..."

"What if we look it up?" She springs from the bed. "Someone out there on the internet probably knows."

"Wait." I reach and rest my hand lightly on her arm.

She stills under my touch, waiting.

"There's something else." I nod toward the bed, guiding her gently back down. That desire grips me again—to take her away from all this.

My words tumble like heavy stones. "Your grandfather's notes and what Sam warned me about earlier...Your family might know more. Be more."

"What did Sam say?" Her tone is sharp now, urgent.

I run a hand through my hair, wishing I didn't have to say any of this, wishing I could shield her from everything. "He asked if I knew what an Ossaris is."

Her eyes search mine, desperate and bewildered. "An Ossaris?"

"I told him I didn't," I say slowly, "so he told me. They were created by the Archangels Michael and Gabriel."

Rhi stays silent, absorbing it all in a way that chills me. "Do you think that my grandfather..." she starts, her eyes nervously scanning mine for answers, "that he was one of these Ossaris?"

"I don't know," I say softly. "It might come from him or your grandmother. Maybe both."

"Nan?" She shakes her head.

"Let me go back," I say. "The Watchers. You know they were sent to watch humanity, right? Sam said that Gabriel and Michael were sent to destroy the Watchers when they were caught teaching humans about angelic magic and taking human wives."

"I know all this. What does this have to do with my family?"

"Gabriel and Michael couldn't bear to condemn their own brothers, the Watchers, but neither could they allow them complete freedom. Instead, they crafted protective shields to conceal the Watchers from the Creator's sight. Then they chose humans, humans they believed to be pure of heart, and bestowed upon them the essence of angels."

Rhi began to turn white, her beautiful face becoming ghostly. "The essence of angels? What does that even mean?"

"It's called an angel's kiss. The Archangels infused part of their power directly into these chosen ones—the Ossaris."

"The Ossaris had to make sure the Watchers stayed in line. The angelic essence flowing through their veins granted them the strength to do so." I took her hand in mine. It was clammy, and I brought it to my lips and kissed her palm. She stared at where my lips had just been.

"Ossaris have unique abilities. Sam said some controlled and manipulated the elements, and others had heightened senses. Some could communicate with spirits, and the last could channel energy from other living beings."

A small shudder runs through Rhi's body, almost imperceptible. My wings spring from my back, instinct guiding them around her, enveloping her in the radiant glow of my angel light. She gasped at their suddenness, but I feel her melting against me as they hold her safe in glowing whiteness.

I close my eyes, wishing she could stay like this forever—warm in my light. "Rhi." I breathe the name of everything that binds me to this world. I'm a Fallen, tethered by love or desire or whatever mix of those reckless feelings that stir inside me, to this beautiful girl. "My Avahah."

Her eyes are wide as she looks up at me. "There is more," I say gently, my voice a hush against the rush of light between us. "Sam believes your family is descendants of Ossaris."

"Descendants?" she breathes.

"He said that an Ossaris with angelic blood—" I pause, hating to voice the final revelation. "...will have a scar."

"A scar?" Her hand still held in mine pulls away. She stares at her palm that I just kissed. Her fingers trembled over the delicate skin where the star-like scar has been for as long as she can remember—a mark that was always just a part of her.

"Rhi," I say urgently, taking her hand again.

"You knew?" Her voice quakes with something between fear and accusation.

"I didn't know," I insist, pulling her back into my embrace so she can feel how true it is through our soul connection. "Not until now." I draw her against me more and hold tight as she quivers beneath my embrace, feeling so fragile it scares me.

A sudden cough slices the air. I turn, releasing Rhi, my wings disappearing, and see Sam peering through the open doorway, eyebrows arched. "Am I interrupting?" he asked with a smirk. "You sure look cozy."

Rhi sprung to her feet, heat flashing across her cheeks. "You!" Her accusation is like an unsheathed blade. "You knew all about this! About me!"

Sam raises his hands in defense. "Easy now." He tilts his head at me. "Kiran, control your girl."

"How long?" Rhi's voice is high and breaking. "How long have you known?"

He regards her calmly. "That is why I am here now. I was hoping to wait until your birthday..."

Rhi's fingers bunch into tight fists at her sides, every part of her seeming to tremble.

"Her birthday?" I ask, confused.

"Yes, Guardian." Sam inches away from Rhi, "An Ossaris's power is always there, but it comes to its full potential on their eighteenth birthday. Now, if you will calm down," he continues, turning to face Rhi directly, "I will explain as best I can."

"You knew my family is descendents. That they're...Ossaris?" She stares at him, almost daring him to deny it.

"Yes." Sam nods. "It comes down from both your grandparents, so you and your cousins will be extra strong. Sometimes it skips a generation or two, depending on how great the need is for more Ossaris."

Rhi's questions fall from her rapidly. "Is my mother one? My uncle?"

Sam shakes his head. "No. But I know you are one, and I sense it in your cousins as well."

I glance at Rhi, worried about how much more she can handle. "Do they have scars," I ask gently, "like the one on your palm?"

She seems to think about it, slowly sinking back into herself. Memories flicker in her expression; I see them reflected across her eyes. "They do," she says softly, more to herself.

"Why did you keep this from us?" I demand. "And why now?"

Sam rubs the back of his neck with one hand, hesitating. He seems to measure his words and how far he can trust us with them. "You and your cousins could be in danger if your heritage becomes known to certain...parties." He looks directly at Rhi. "Especially before your eighteenth birthday."

"My cousin Taylor is already over eighteen. Does she know too? Did she keep it from me?"

Sam doesn't meet Rhi's eyes, muttering something under his breath before he looks up again at last. "No," he assures her. "I suspect that's what your grandfather left behind—instructions for all of you."

Rhi seems to let that sink in.

"I'm sorry, Rhiannon," Sam says earnestly, "I'm bound by my oath to an Archangel. There is only so much I can say."

My mind races to the notebook. The neat, handwritten letters that read "Seventh Flame" and "Veilbreaker."

"My grandfather called me the Veilbreaker and a Seventh Flame?" Rhi interrupts, seeming to read my mind. Her wide eyes flicker with hope and fear.   Sam looks steadily at me before turning his gaze toward her, genuinely puzzled. "He says you're what?"

"Why would he write that?" I press, studying Sam with suspicion riding high in my chest. He seems sincere in his confusion, but I'm not completely convinced. He's holding something back.

"I—don't know," he admits. "However, there is someone who might."

It hits me when he says that. The angel of secrets—Raziel. "You can't mean..."

"Raziel," Sam confirms.

"I, as you know, am forbidden to go to the Veil. But you," he looks at me intently, "as a Fallen, you are not. You're only forbidden back into Heaven. The other realms...they are open to you."

"The only reason I found him last time was because of your daughter," I point out.

"So ask her again."

"And you're going to guard Rhi again?" I cut back at him, my words sharp as glass. "Look how it turned out last time."

"Hey now." Sam holds up his hands defensively. "If I didn't send you, we wouldn't have gotten that rune around your neck, and we might not have beaten Vince."

"Who," Rhi interrupts, "is still out there somewhere."

"Yes." Sam draws the word out slowly. "But I've warded his house to keep Justin and Sorcha safe. I've also warded the garage."

He waves a hand towards me, "And you have your shadow here to protect you."

My stomach lurches at the thought—Rhi without me. There was no way I was leaving her again. The image of her in that dungeon flashes through me like a blade. "I'm not leaving her."

Sam narrows his eyes, contemplating. "There is another way, possibly."

"How?" Rhi asks.

"We could summon him. Well, not us, but a witch can."

"Mia?" Rhi asks.

Sam shakes his head, "No, she is not experienced enough."

"What about her grandmother? She knows what you are." Rhi pushes.

"The tricky part," Sam admits reluctantly, "is that another might hear the summons and answer instead."

"We should chance it," Rhi blurts in a rush. We all fell silent until Rhi insisted more quietly, "I need to know who I am."

I know how she feels. I remember that same twisting inside of me when I found out I was not just created an angel, but was made from a human soul. When Michael's hand reached out and took my soul, not my twin's, to become a Guardian.

Michael told me that when Nephilim are born, they break the rules. I feel like a fool. I was so obediently blind. Michael chose souls with promise he had told me—claiming it was the only way to keep balance in the universe. None of this felt like balance. It feels like chaos.

I wanted to pull her in my arms again and tell her she'll find the strength to get through this. That I found strength I never even knew I had because of her. "We need to think carefully before doing anything," I say finally.

"I'll go ask about the summoning. I'm sure she will. That woman adores me—who doesn't?" Then Sam vanishes.

I let out a breath and shake my head slowly. "You're not giving up on this, are you?"

"No."

"Stubborn girl." I smile in spite of the worry braiding tightly through me.

Rhi comes close, winding her arms around me, melting against me. "Why is my life so crazy?" she asks, half sighing.

"I don't know, sweetheart." I hold her tighter still, trying to touch every part of her with everything that I can give. "I don't know."

Chapter Sixteen

Rhiannon

I needed to calm down. My heart was hammering in my chest. Why was I caught up in this web of the supernatural and lies? Why hadn't my grandfather told me? I clutched at the memory of his jovial smile, his warm hugs, and his teasing nature.

Kiran watched me, his silver eyes quiet and kind. "Maybe we could look through the notebook some more while we wait for Sam."

"Okay," I said finally.

He sat on the bed next to me, my knees leaning against his thigh. I curled my legs beneath me and opened the notebook. I could go through it more carefully later. For now, I skimmed, fingers grazing across pages for any words that glowed with recognition. The familiar loops of my grandfather's handwriting caused an ache in my heart. I missed him.

My eyes glanced over the pages for anything about a Seventh Flame or Veilbreaker, or about scars, anything to tell me—

Scar.

My breath snagged in my throat, and Kiran leaned closer. "What is it?"

I read aloud: "The angel's kiss leaves a scar."

His eyes danced with something I couldn't name—surprise? Excitement? Fear?

"It is the only indication Ossaris have angelic blood," I continued. "The scars sometimes look like certain shapes."

"And...?"

"The shape will identify what their power will be." My voice faltered to a whisper.

I opened my hand. The scar in my palm seemed to glare at me. It was unmistakably the shape of a star. "Kiran?" I looked up at him, words faltering on my lips.

"A star," he said, disbelief sharpening his voice. He stared back at the page, then into my eyes, searching for something. "It explains," Kiran glanced back down at the notebook in my lap, and then looked back to me with a flush creeping along his face, "a lot."

I was baffled, "I don't understand? Do you know what a star means?"

"I—I don't know." He ran his fingers through his hair, the locks falling in disarray across his eyes.

His hand covered mine, slowly turning it so the scar faced outwards. He guided it to his cheek, cool and smooth against my skin. Instantly, a current shot through me like lightning

"I need to try something," he said. Without letting go of my hand, he moved it down to his neck and then pressed it gently against his chest. I could feel the beating under my palm—his heart—but more than that.

We both gasped—a single breath drawn together. A familiar pull rippled through me, a yearning to be as close to him as possible. The notebook slipped from my lap and thudded softly on the floor.

"You felt that?" he whispered breathless, as if any louder word would break the fragile air around us.

There was no way to answer except to nod. I found myself inching nearer, every movement deliberate, until there was hardly space left between us, and all I could see were his silver eyes.

"You've felt this before, haven't you?" Kiran's voice wavered. "This pull, this need..."

"Yes," I exhaled, barely able to breathe. "I think I know what it is."

"What?" I whispered.

His lips were so close. My fingertips brushed the edges of his hair. This should be it; he should kiss me, or I should kiss him.

"It's the angelic blood in you connecting with mine." The words spilled out with a pained edge, as if they wounded him with their truth. "You feel this with Justin, too, don't you?"

I drew back to see Kiran's face.

"Don't deny it, Rhi," he said softly. "I've felt it. I didn't know what it was, but if you are indeed an Ossaris, which seems like you are—then you have angelic blood in you. You unknowingly are drawn to others with it, too."

My memories of Justin flooded through me like a storm—the dark hair curtaining his face, the intensity of his voice when he spoke my name—and I understood then why I'd been unable to resist him. Why he could consume me so entirely just by being near. And Kiran too...?

That couldn't be right. Did it mean what I felt wasn't real? How could something so deeply tied to me be a mere instinct? No, my heart countered. You love Kiran. And oh God, you love Justin too.

"Rhi," Kiran said, his own voice a storm cloud.

My head was shaking before I realized it. "The time before I left to go out with Justin," I said, "and I begged you to tell me what you were feeling—are you telling me that was just some connection of our blood?"

His brows pulled together like magnets. "I didn't understand..."

"I don't believe it!" The words shot out like arrows. "I won't!"

I stabbed him in the chest with my finger, defiant and insistent. He sat still and blinked at me as if bracing himself for a hurricane. "You have feelings, Kiran, and they're real! As real as mine! It isn't something that just happens, or wouldn't you feel this with my cousins or other angels? Wouldn't I have felt it with Sam?"

He fell silent. His fingers brushed over my cheek like butterfly wings and then fell away. I watched the way his breath caught and held for a long, quiet second. The closeness, the longing, the spark jumping between us—it was real. Deep in my soul, I knew it. It wasn't just blood and instinct. Not with Kiran. Not with Justin either. The love, the heat, the anger, the sadness—all of it was mine to claim.

"You can't pull away from this," I forced the words from my throat.

Kiran sighed, the sound filled with doubts. "Rhi."

"Don't you dare! Do not question my heart!"

I clamped my hands on either side of his face. He gasped in surprise, and then I kissed him.

Everything about him caved in around me; delicate strains of something barely held back shuddered through both of us. His fingers folded into my hair as he moaned. The universe seemed to shift. He pulled away briefly, breathing hard. His lips hovered uncertainly against mine, still questioning. I pressed harder, proving even my soul wanted him as much as my body did.

I grabbed his shirt and pulled him to me. The force tumbled us back against the bed, and with another surge of daring I hadn't known I had, I trailed kisses along his jawline, down the smooth curve of his neck, before finding my way back to his lips.

The kiss was raw, desperate, an earthquake of need that sent shockwaves through every nerve in my body. His fingers tangled in my hair, tugging hard, pulling me closer as if he couldn't get enough of me. His moan vibrated against my lips, low and guttural.

"Tell me," I said between each gasp. "Tell me this is just my blood connecting with yours."

His mouth trembled against my lips. "No. It is too strong. I have never felt anything like what I feel for you."

He shifted slightly to keep from crushing me, but I couldn't bear the space between us. I wrapped my arms around him and pulled him flush against me.

"Was that your first kiss?" I asked, breathless.

"Yes."

I kissed him harder at that, and he didn't retreat—his mouth opened deeper around mine.

Kiran's hesitant fingers moved along my ribs to rest on my hips. "I've waited so long for this," he said, his voice tight, full of wonder.

"Me too," I said, feeling everything inside me crack open. "All this time...I thought I was horrible for having these kinds of...of thoughts about an angel."

His lips moved to my cheek. He kissed there and down the line of my jaw. I grabbed at him, losing myself, arching into each tiny shock he left along my skin.

He paused only for a moment, catching his breath. "Same," he confessed urgently. "I fought it for so long, Rhi." Then his words trailed to a whisper against my neck, a promise that melted over me. "But I love you...more than anything in this world or the next." His voice caught lightly in his throat. "I've never wanted something so much. I would fight Heaven and Hell for you." Kiran's eyes locked onto mine as if sealing a vow that ran deeper than blood.

His mouth brushed over mine again—gentle this time, reverent. "My heart, my soul...It's all yours."

Light exploded around us, and I sighed into his mouth. His wings, beautiful and blinding, unfurled from Kiran's back. My touch traveled the outline of those wings. Soft, ethereal, beautiful. A trickle of what felt like magic tingled through me. His mouth fell away from mine, and a groan escaped him.

"Your touch," he panted, breathless with awe. "My wings..." He couldn't seem to get the words out. "You can't imagine how good it feels." His eyes closed in surrender.

I loved hearing that. My fingernails grazed over them again, and he hissed through gritted teeth, trembling.

Between us, the melody began to rise—that ethereal tune only he and I could hear, binding us as soul mates, marking him forever as my Guardian. "Your soul responds to mine," he said, voice shaky.

A sharp rap at my door preceded it swinging wide open. "I hope I am interrupting." Sam's voice cut in.

Kiran's wings vanished instantly. Sam leaned against the doorframe, amusement in his eyes.

Kiran pulled away from me, and I sat up quickly. "Maybe you should call or text before just popping in." I fumed.

Sam laughed. "It's so much funnier this way, though."

"It's not funny," Kiran snarled.

"Dear boy, did I not tell you being a Fallen isn't that bad? You can let go of some of that holier-than-thou stuff."

Kiran's jaw tensed. Sam moved from the doorway and leaned against the dresser. "Besides," Sam said with a gleam in his eye. "It's about time."

I ran my hands through my unruly waves, trying to untangle my thoughts and calm the heat still running through my body.

"I'm here to let you know we have our witch," Sam said. The light in his dark eyes was mischievous, "Actually, two. The elder Buckram wants Mia there to see how it's done."

"We can do it when she gets home from school, then?" I asked.

"That's the plan," Sam confirmed.

"That's good," Kiran said, stuffing his hands into his pockets.

I couldn't look at him without feeling that magnetic pull, the flutter in my gut. I willed myself not to think about his lips on mine or how hard he had kissed back. Later, I told my heart. We'd figure it all out later. But now…

"Sam?" I asked, pushing myself off the bed and onto unsteady legs. "How much do you know about an angel kiss?"

Sam's eyes glinted under his raised eyebrows. "A lot, actually."

"Like?"

He smiled as if waiting for this moment for a long time. "It's used to transfer angelic powers to someone by blood." He looked between Kiran and me with exaggerated slowness. "It's also a way to mark them as belonging."

"Belonging?" I asked, confused.

"Yes," he said, smiling slyly. "Sometimes marking a family member for protection or to mark their destined mate."

"Who gave me mine?" I asked quietly.

"Wrong question, sweet cheeks."

I growled, frowning at the Watcher.

"You're getting there," Sam said, stepping even nearer to me, "I'm bound by my oath, but if you find information and ask the right questions, I can answer them."

"But, you won't tell me who."

Sam shook his head slowly, "No, that's too specific with the oath I took."

I thought about what he was saying. Was my scar from a family member or a destined mate? A shiver ran through me. Was there another angel I was supposed to be with? There was no way I was accepting that.

"How about is it from someone in my family or a fated mate?"

Sam tapped his fingers to his head. "Now you're getting it." He smiled knowingly. "It's from family."

I was relieved. I didn't want a destined mate. I had had enough with Kiran and Justin. Another question popped into my brain. "Do you know what having a star scar means? I mean, what power do I supposedly have?"

He clasped his hands behind him and paced the room slowly, letting the silence linger like smoke—thick, almost tangible.

Kiran and I watched him until finally his lips twisted into that same unreadable smile. "What does a star do?" Sam mused aloud, glancing over his shoulder.

I didn't know. The sun was a star, stars glowed at night...

Kiran's head snapped up. "You mean something like The Star of Bethlehem?"

Sam smiled and turned toward us. "And what did that star do?" He tilted his head at Kiran expectantly.

"It...guided," he said, quieter this time, "Guided those who followed it..."

"The sun is a star too," I said quickly.

"Indeed it is," Sam's smile widened. "And what does it do?"

My words came in a rush. "Give warmth and light."

Sam nodded, "Ossaris with a star power often guide and lead the way for others."

Sam turned to Kiran, "You are correct about the star of Bethlehem. It was used as divine guidance and a fulfillment of prophecy." Sam turned to me, "You are also correct. The sun gives light, and so an Ossaris with a star scar can summon pure starlight to heal, shield, or burn away shadow creatures. It is the most powerful of all the scar marks."

"And that power?" I asked shakily. "What does it have to do with being a Seventh Flame or Veilbreaker?"

Sam pursed his lips. "That, sweet cheeks, I don't know. But I'm sure once we summon Raziel, we will."

I tried wrapping my mind around everything. This news circled my thoughts, each revelation tangling with the last. Begging clarity where none existed. The idea that things would clear up once Raziel was summoned brought some relief, but what if he didn't answer the summon? Or worse, what if someone we didn't want to summon showed up instead?

Chapter Seventeen

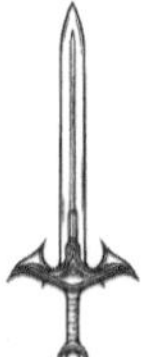

Justin

It was Rhi's first day at school. I had originally planned to surprise her in the morning with flowers, then drive her there and pick her up afterward.

So much for that plan.

Maybe I should text her to ask how her first day went. Then anger bloomed in my chest right next to the love I felt for her.

It shouldn't matter that I hadn't talked to her in a couple of days. I shouldn't be freaking out about it. But I was acting like my entire identity was wrapped up with this girl. Maybe a completely insane notion, but the more crazed my feelings, the more reason there was to believe she felt the same way. I know she did, if how she kissed me was any indication.

I thought of our weekend together all those weeks ago down the shore. Every moment with her made me want to tear off the hard, cold shell I'd spent my whole life building around myself. Before her, I never understood how much being untouchable had left me hollow.

But then Kiran had to show up and be the tragic freaking hero. Now, that image of him hovering over her at the party dogged me like a virus I couldn't get rid of—plaguing every good thought I tried to have. It wormed its way deeper and deeper, just like he was trying to do with her.

But what if not texting her just made everything worse? If this time away made it easier for Kiran—or harder for me?

At least away from her, I wasn't tormented by this soul-crushing urge to possess her.

Just let her go.

The urge to fling the phone across the room gnawed at me. Better that than feeling it burn with silence every time I looked at it. What was it about her that left me this raw?

I dropped the phone on the bed, left it there like we were playing a dangerous game of chicken. I could win this round.

The air in the room felt easier to breathe in with the distance between us. I wasn't suffocating from wanting her here, now, always. Behind closed eyes, she faded just enough for me to exhale without that sharp catch beneath my ribcage. If she loved me even half as much as I loved her, she'd find a way back.

Restless for any distraction from the lurking thoughts I was having, I decided to go explore for more things Vince might have hidden in the house. I knew the secret room I found would be a good place to start.

I pushed at the bookcase that led to the turret above. Sunlight made it easier to see, easier to breathe up here. Book after book crowded the chest where I'd found Michael's journal. They were smaller than his, but their peeling leather spines felt ancient and rough against my palms as I pulled each one out. I stacked them on the floor, dust shaking loose in the light. They could stay neglected for all I cared—most were more mold than book anyway.

My phone buzzed in my pocket.

It was the garage. Blue or Taz probably just needed to pick my brain about a Benz or wanted help with parts.

The cross my mother had insisted I wear for as long as I could remember did its job — hiding me from celestials, and them from me. When I took it off, my whole world cracked open. That's when I found out Taz and Blue were Fallen.

Maybe work would distract me from her better than hunting through musty attics. Sam could have fun plowing through every last moth-eaten book.

"Do you need me to come in?" I asked.

"Nah," Taz's deep voice said. "We do have a lead, though."

"On a car?" I asked.

There was a hesitant pause. "No, on Vince."

My heart seemed to stop. I don't know how long I stood there clutching the phone before I could say anything. Vince had nearly killed me and tortured Rhi. Not to mention kidnapping Kacey.

"What?" The word came out harshly.

"In Florida," Taz rumbled. "Word is he's hiding out with friends there. Just talk at this point, but..."

Friends? Vince always said he had family who lived in Florida. My guess was that they were other Fallen or demons.

"We figured you'd be interested. He's after something," Taz said.

"Likely the same as always. Power." I grumbled.

I looked at the books haphazardly stacked around me. "Sam should be able to keep us a step ahead." I was saying it for my own ears as much as his. Reassurance, maybe, or at least an attempt at it. "He warded up the house and garage pretty well."

"Yeah, Sam's all kinds of powerful." I could almost hear the shrug in Taz's voice. "But so is Vince."

My grip tightened around the phone until my knuckles went white. Anger and fear hit me at the same time, a combination I was getting too familiar with.

"Maybe we should head down there," Taz offered.

I shoved my free hand through my hair, caught between the urge to go and thinking I should wait him out—make him come here. "Sam has it locked down tight," I said again. Convincing myself or him, I wasn't sure.

"If you say so, man." He paused, as if he was going to say something else, but didn't.

"What?" I demanded, my voice ricocheted around the room.

"Nothin'. Maybe just let us know if you change your mind?"

"Yeah, thanks, Taz," I muttered and hung up.

I needed to think. I needed a plan. I scooped up as many books as I could carry and headed downstairs, nudging the secret door shut behind me with my foot. The pile landed on my bed with a heavy thud.

What if Vince went after Rhi again? Or my parents? Or Scott, or...my baby niece?

What if I hunted down Vince myself before he hurt everyone I ever cared about? Taz and Blue would help me. They were glad he was gone.

But then what? Even if I found him, how would I take him down? He was immortal.

Phen's voice echoed in my head, telling me how celestials could be captured in Hell. But how could I get Vince there?

My brain hurt.

I should at least see my parents—convince them to be careful without telling them why.

I grabbed my car keys. I would go see my parents. My mother had called or texted every day that I had been gone. I hurt her, and I knew it. Guilt ate at me. I'd go to see Scott, Taylor, and the baby when I was done at my parents'.

Maybe I couldn't tell them everything, but there had to be something I could do to protect them.

Chapter Eighteen

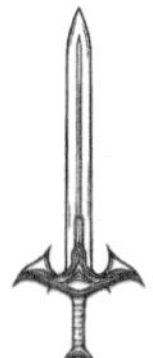

Rhiannon

Mia lost it when we told her we were summoning an angel. She actually screamed. Her grandmother told her to follow every instruction exactly and not to interfere, no matter what happened.

That had sounded ominous to me. Goosebumps erupted over my skin as they drew a circle in salt and placed three candles around it to form a triangle.

Mia's grandmother instructed us to sit close around the circle, row after row of rings stacking her thin fingers. I wondered how any of this was supposed to work. I bit my lip and watched Mia's grandmother set a brass bowl in the center of the triangle. The metal clanged against the floor.

Mia fidgeted beside me, tapping an unlit box of matches against her thigh. Her grandmother shuffled toward us, the bronze bird amulet at the hollow of her throat gleaming in the low light.

"Mia," her grandmother said, pushing up the sleeves of her flowy blouse, "light the candles."

Mia was quick to obey. Once lit, the candles cast dancing shadows across our faces. A faint scent of sage joined the damp chill, curling in puffs.

"Good," declared Mia's grandmother, sweeping around so we were all within her fierce gaze. "Remember what I said—no interference."

I nodded but kept my eyes on Kiran, searching his face. He offered a small smile to me, but I could tell this made him uncomfortable.

Mia's grandmother began to hum — a low vibration that built in her chest and layered itself into the air, strange and deep and steady, rising from her throat in an ancient chant.

A prickling tension filled the room as Kiran shifted closer to me. "Rhi," he said, his voice barely above a whisper, "you don't have to do this."

The old woman's sharp eyes snapped towards him. "Quiet Guardian!" She hissed.

Her humming turned rhythmic, resonating, and expanding through me. She spoke in a language I didn't understand. She motioned to Sam, who placed one of his feathers and one of Kiran's in the brass bowl. They were instructed to give up one each before we started the ceremony.

Before all of our eyes, the feathers erupted into a brilliant blue flame. I felt like I couldn't catch my breath.

The chanting started up again; this time, some of the words were recognizable.

"Zamariel echad, ori'el-nur,

Sha'ar ha'razim, lifnei ha'or.

By the flame behind the Veil,

By the spirit that does not fail."

I spoke into Kiran's mind, *"flame...veil..."* Even in my mind, I stuttered with fear.

"I know." He spoke back to me, squeezing my hand.

"Raziel, whose voice the realms hear,

Whose breath births the wheel of secrets—

He who stood when the stars were flung,

Whose name is written, yet never sung.

Etz chaim yishtalek l'davar,

P'tach ha'sefer, galah s'dar.

Come, Raziel, bearer of the scroll,

With wings of fire and eyes of soul.

By truth unspoken, I draw thee near—

Let secrets bloom, and paths appear."

The flame burst into a blinding light, then disappeared, leaving a shroud of smoke. I looked between all of us. My heart pounded against my ribs, and silence sat between each beat. A pressure like nothing I'd ever felt came from the smoke, making it hard to breathe. Everyone had wide eyes. Sam pressed his lips together, Mia's fingers trembling as she gripped my other hand, and even Kiran, usually so composed, knitted his brows into worry.

"Stay close," Kiran said against my hair.

A low sound emerged from the cloud, curling out with an animal fury. A growl deep and primal flooded the room, pouring into me. The smoke parted like a curtain.

What emerged made my bones rattle.

A woman stood there, glaring with beast-like eyes beneath the head of a snarling wolf. Her jaw snapped, lips curled back in a fierce grimace.

Mia jerked beside me. "What is that?" she gasped.

Her grandmother was silent for a moment, standing firm with her eyes locked on the figure before us. "Hush," she finally said with purpose. "Keep still."

The creature took another step forward, its expression caught somewhere between a snarl and a grin, reveling in having been called forth.

"Mëteìnu," the creature said.

Mia's grandmother only nodded.

The creature spoke again, its voice layered, guttural beneath a woman's whisper. "Tëme," it intoned, sweeping its gaze across the circle. It settled on Mia's grandmother, a wicked humor dancing in its eyes.

Tension coiled around us as she responded in kind, low and deliberate. A strange lilting language passed between them, escalating in speed and intensity.

A gleam of satisfaction crossed the creature's face as it retreated slowly into the smoke. Mia's grandmother bowed her head low where she stood, the weight of her amulet bowing with her.

The smoke swirled violently again, roiling until another figure emerged. Mia shielded her eyes. I gasped. The being was terrifyingly beautiful — too much to look at, yet impossible to turn away from. Multiple sets of eyes adorned a flawless face, each pair unblinking and fierce beyond comprehension. Long strands of hair billowed around him like liquid stars.

And wings! So many wings unfurled behind him—feathers glistening with shifting hues, some gleaming like metals, others stark like sheets of paper marked with letters that twisted over them. He was cloaked in robes that rippled with moons, planets, and stars.

"Raziel," Kiran breathed.

Raziel turned, fixing a full set of eyes on Kiran, and then the rest closed until only two remained on a more human face. His hair was still silver, but now it rested around a dark tattoo shaped like an eye on his forehead. He tilted his head. "You summoned me?" The echoing cadence had sharpened to one voice.

Kiran nodded, looking serious, almost guilty. "I didn't know where you were or how long it would take me to find you."

"I see," Raziel mused with glee that was almost childlike, "What's an angel's favorite type of music?" He paused as we looked at him in confusion.

Not one of us spoke.

Then Raziel laughed. He took stock of each of us with his eyes—metallic where they should have been white. "No one even has a guess?" The ancient angel rolled his eyes, "Soul music!" Raziel laughed harder, the sound peeling through the room like thunder. Sam's choked laughter joined in.

I looked between Kiran and Mia in bewilderment. "Angels tell jokes?" Mia managed to say.

"Of course," Raziel replied as though it were the most obvious thing in the world. "Living for eternity—we need some way to entertain ourselves." He turned his gaze towards me, an extra beat passing as he seemed to process what he was seeing. His eyes widened a fraction before lifting one arm, pointing a long finger in my direction. "You," he declared, sending a shiver along my spine. "You're the Warrior's child. The Veilbreaker."

All eyes lurched towards me. My cheeks flamed.

Raziel studied me, "Curious," he murmured more to himself than anyone else.

The Warrior's child. Another angel, Azrael, had called me that before. What did it mean? A warrior — my father? My father was Jared. I'd never known him, so maybe it was possible.

I took a deep breath, and the words came out in a tumble. "You know my father?" I said towards Raziel.

He looked at me like I had asked him if water was wet. "Of course. But you don't."

An ache settled beneath my ribs. "I—"

"She doesn't," Kiran spoke up beside me. "I don't either." His eyes found Sam, "but Sam apparently does and is bound by an oath."

Raziel turned to Sam, amused. "Are *you* now the angel of secrets?"

"That is not the reason we summoned you," said Sam, squirming where he sat. He refused to meet my eyes. "We need to know what the Veilbreaker is and also the Seventh Flame."

"And I want to know what that thing was," Mia added, "that came in before you."

Raziel looked taken aback, "What thing?"

"That child was one of our ancestors," Mia's grandmother explained, her voice calm. "A spirit of the wolf clan." She flicked a quick glance at Mia as if telling her to stop interrupting. One hand lifted to the bronze bird at her neck. "She was making sure I knew whom I was summoning."

Sam's expression turned serious as he turned back to Raziel. "Will you help us?" he asked.

Raziel exhaled, "So the Warrior isn't ready for you to know who you are." He glanced between Sam and me, "Then it is not up to me to interrupt his plans."

I sank with disappointment. "Would you tell me what a Veilbreaker and Seventh Flame are?"

His form fluctuated, bright as a blaze, and then resolved into the many-winged and eyed angel, cloaked in cosmic robes. "Those mysteries are within my right to say."

He focused all those creepy eyes on me.

"One born of human blood that is woven with celestial threads. The Veilbreaker is tied to the Veil, able to cross all boundaries. When stars fall silent, and the Veil grows thin, a long laid plan will awaken, and the Veilbreaker shall rise—not in glory, but by choice."

I felt sweat roll down my back despite the cool basement we sat in. Raziel's light flared again.

"The Seventh Flame is born to lead the Ossaris and to fight in the longest war. They have the power to banish even the most powerful of beings."

Again, Raziel's light died down, his form flickering until the many eyes melted into two semi-normal ones again. The hippie-looking angel smiled broadly at me. "Does that answer your questions?" he inquired, tilting his head.

"My man, wow, that's not sketchy or anything." Mia drawled. "It's a total riddle—and tells us nothing."

"Some riddles are not meant to be solved all at once," Raziel replied, unfazed. He turned to me again, "Paths must appear before secrets bloom."

"Oh, come on." Mia crossed her arms across her chest. "Plain speech angel, plain...speech."

Raziel laughed, "I like you, little witch!"

"Well, I'm not liking you very much right now, Raz."

"Mia!" Her grandmother interrupted with a hint of warning.

Raziel waved a hand in dismissal at her grandmother, "Raz?! Ohh, I like that!"

I squeezed Kiran's hand tighter. Raziel was funny and terrifying and somehow friendly all at once — and completely, infuriatingly dismissive.

Raziel's eyes exploded into multiple sets, and just as quickly, they contracted again, leaving only two on his face.

"Sorry," he flinched, "sometimes a secret comes across suddenly." He became his jovial self again, "I have to go, unfortunately. Things to do, beings to see...everyone wants a piece of this." He motioned to himself.

"But wait!" I begged as he turned away too quickly. "I need you to tell me what those riddles actually mean."

Raziel looked at me with an indulgent—almost sweet—smile and knelt down beside where I sat.

"My dear, as simple as I can put it...your destiny is to become the leader of the Ossaris. You will have such power, powers to banish both angels and demons." It was so absurd my head spun. Raziel smirked as if he could hear what I was thinking.

"Think on it awhile." He pointed at Kiran and Sam. "Perhaps with the help of these two?"

"Oh, Kiran," Raziel said, pulling one of the feathers from his wings and handing it over. Scrawled across it was a spiraling web of letters. "Use this if you need me. You don't have to go through all this." He gestured around the basement in amusement.

"Catch you later, little witch," he winked at Mia.

"Samyaza," He nodded towards Sam and then bowed at Mia's grandmother, "Elder witch."

Then he evaporated through the smoke.

Chapter Nineteen

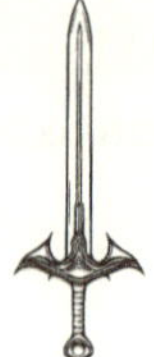

Rhiannon

I was shaking. Every time I thought I had seen it all, something new came along. Kiran had passed his hands over my head and heart, and a wave of calm washed through me like warm water.

We ate dinner with Nan. She had brought home meatloaf and garlic mashed potatoes along with a cheesecake. I was distracted thinking about all I had learned, while Kiran charmed Nan. She seemed to really enjoy his company and invited him to come over and eat anytime.

I thought I should see Taylor. If anyone might know about this, it was her. She was the oldest, and I knew she had a scar on the top of her foot.

"Nan, I was thinking about going to see Taylor for a bit."

"Tonight?" She furrowed her brow. "It's a school night."

"I don't have any homework, and we won't be long. An hour or two." I glanced at Kiran, sitting across the table, wiping cheesecake remnants from his lips. "Kiran can take me."

Nan looked between us, "Okay," she relented with a sigh. "But not too late."

I practically jumped out of my seat. "Thank you! You're the best."

The warm, humid evening closed in around us as we walked down the steps.

"Thank you for dinner," Kiran said over his shoulder. Nan waved from the doorway, her silhouette framed warmly in light before she disappeared inside.

Kiran slipped his hand into mine. "I have a car now, do I?"

"You can teleport us there," I said, squeezing his fingers.

He chuckled softly. "And then tell Taylor what? How do we explain how we got there?"

"I have a better idea." He steered us down the path toward his place. "There is actually an old car in the garage. I told you the nephew didn't want anything in the house when he sold it."

When we reached his home, he unlatched the garage door and it groaned open, rusty hinges shrieking in protest. Inside sat a vintage green Volkswagen Beetle, blanketed in dust and forgotten years.

"Do you think it even runs?" I asked.

"I can make it run," He twirled his fingers in front of me. "Angel magic, remember?"

I laughed, "Do you even know how to drive?"

Kiran grinned, brushing the hood with a swipe of his hand. "Should be fun to find out." A look of mischief crossed Kiran's face, his eyes flickering with silver light. "I can just make this run, or..."

"Or what?" I asked.

"Or I can turn it into any type of vehicle you want."

My eyes grew big. "I don't want you to go out of your way. This is fine."

He tapped the trunk with the back of his knuckles. "It's no trouble."

"I've always wanted a pickup truck," I admitted. "Like an old classic one, cherry red. Or maybe a Mustang." I laughed. "Steve once compared me to a Mustang."

Kiran smiled softly. His expression shifted, eyebrows quirking in focus as he knelt towards the Beetle, hands hovering above the roof. The air around him blurred and shimmered as if alive. Ripples of energy cascaded over the car's surface, the metal humming with transformation. Its color deepened and darkened, twisting into a bright scarlet. Metal retracted and expanded in perfect harmony. A sleek Chevy pickup gleamed in the dim light like a fresh candy-apple.

I gasped. It was beautiful.

"Thought you might like it," he said, brushing off his jeans and standing back to admire his work.

"I love it," I whispered, fingers trailing along its shiny new surface.

"Get in then." He grinned, a hint of pride in his voice.

I swung open the door and slid inside, the smell of leather filling my senses. "Wow," I said, admiring the interior.

Kiran popped into the driver's seat. I heard a jingling sound and a set of keys materialized in his palm. As he turned the ignition, and the engine roared to life, he looked oddly out of place but excited. He clutched the wheel, easing the truck backward slowly.

He seemed a little unsure of what he was doing. "Do you want me to drive?" I offered.

"Maybe." His smile warmed me as he pushed the gear into park and slid over. "I can watch and learn from you."

I ran my hands along the wheel, reveling in the beauty of the truck. Kiran waved his hand, and the garage door shut. I saw movement to the side of the garage and noticed Stanley sitting on a rock observing us. "You've been feeding him, right?" I asked, motioning towards the cat.

"Of course. I wouldn't neglect him."

Stanley's eyes seemed to be focused on me, like he knew me. Suddenly, he jumped down and disappeared into the night.

"This truck is amazing," I said as we glided through traffic and lights.

Kiran watched me intently, eyes scanning over the road and my hands on the wheel. "You're amazing," he murmured.

I felt my cheeks warm and smiled timidly at him. I had forgotten what it was like to be free like this. To drive myself and feel the open road around me.

As we got closer to Taylor's house, a familiar car sat on the street. A Cadillac. Justin's Cadillac.

I felt my nerves bubble up, and I took a long breath.

Kiran glanced at me, his expression unreadable. "Do you want to turn around?"

"No," I said, my voice breaking only a little.

He nodded as I parked across the street from Taylor's place and we walked up to Taylor's door together. I knocked on the door, biting my lip. Just knowing Justin was inside made my hands sweat.

Footsteps padded quickly towards the door. Kiran's voice floated warmly into my mind, *"I feel your nervousness. Take a breath."*

The door swung open, and Taylor stood there, her eyes widening with curiosity. She gave me an exaggerated once-over and then her gaze landed squarely on Kiran's silver eyes and lingered there. "Rhi! What a surprise!"

"Hey, Taylor," I said, trying to sound more relaxed than I felt.

She glanced over her shoulder, then back to me conspiratorially. "Guess who showed up tonight?" She whispered.

My pulse quickened, but I forced a smile. "We saw his car."

She pulled me into a hug and studied Kiran with those sharp eyes of hers. "Who's this?"

"Kiran." He put out his hand, but seemed taken aback when she hugged him, too.

"Nice to meet you, Kiran!" She laughed, grabbing both our arms and pulling us inside.

Justin sat on the edge of the couch, one leg bouncing as if he couldn't quite hold himself still. His hair hung loose across his cheekbones, and his jade eyes locked on mine the second I walked in. That familiar electric pull hit me low in the stomach. His gaze slid to Kiran at my side, and his lips pressed into a hard, flat line. "Rhi," he said flatly.

Scott sat on the couch next to Justin, holding his daughter. He looked up as we came into the living room, smiling. "Hey, Rhi."

The baby gave a small whimper, twisting gently in his arms. Scott cuddled her, making soft hushing sounds. He said something low to Justin that I couldn't catch.

"I'm Scott," he said, holding a hand out to Kiran with baby Eva against his chest.

"Kiran."

"I'll be right back. Just putting this one to bed."

The apartment felt too warm and small. Taylor motioned for us to sit. I took a seat on the oversized recliner, Kiran leaning on it beside me. The room felt smaller still as Justin's gaze didn't leave us.

Taylor looked between all of us, "Do you two know each other?" she asked, motioning between Justin and Kiran.

Justin leaned casually back, "We met over the weekend."

Once Eva was asleep, Scott reappeared. The minute he drew closer to where we were sitting, with his quick steps and easy smile, something clicked, like a neon sign going off in my head. My heart jumped, and I felt dizzy. What was I thinking, bringing Kiran here?

Until they were side by side, it hadn't sunk in, but now it was unmistakable. Scott's hair was lighter and shorter than Kiran's—and his eyes green—but the build and lines of their faces...it was uncanny.

"Something to drink?" Taylor asked, cutting through the awful knot of tension that wrapped around my chest.

"It's okay," Kiran's soft voice wisped into my head.

"I forgot, Kiran, I'm so sorry." I mind spoke back. *"Scott is your brother, too. Half-brother, but still. You guys look so much alike."*

"Hello?" Taylor waved her hand in front of my face.

"Oh, sorry, Tay. Sure, a drink would be nice." I stumbled out.

Taylor got up and headed towards the kitchen. It felt like a thousand boulders were sitting on my chest. Justin bounced his leg with more intensity as Scott took a seat next to him again.

"Can I talk to you?" Justin was up suddenly, running a hand through his hair. "Outside."

"Uh...sure." I followed his long, easy strides towards the door, then outside, shutting the door behind us.

The way we left things at that party—when Kiran showed up and for a moment I thought they would tear each other apart in front of everyone made this night stifling. We had not resolved anything between us.

He didn't look back to see if I was following, just stopped halfway down the porch steps and turned to me, arms crossed over his chest.

"So..." he said, drawing it out slowly.

"So." There was no way I could make this feel as nonchalant as I wanted it to.

Despite everything, that pull was still there—deep and primal and completely unfair—as he leaned against the old railing, eyes dragging over me before cutting away to the street where his Cadillac gleamed darkly under the lamp. The need to be near him, even now, even with everything between us scraped raw and twisted, was agonizing. I hugged myself tightly, as if that would ward it off.

His voice came out low and accusing, "You want to explain what's going on?"

"Justin...it's complicated."

"Didn't seem too complicated in there. Looked pretty cozy, actually."

"Don't," I said too sharply, my anger bubbling over. "I don't have to explain myself to you."

I should tell him what I discovered. What was between us might be more than just a wild attraction. That electricity raging between us could be coming from my blood. Now that I knew about my blood—our blood—and how angelic ties pulled through it, confusion and heat bit into me as I stood there.

My voice pressed out hard and tense against the hot evening air, "You're not the only one with angel blood." My nails dug crescents into my palms as I took a breath.

"What are you talking about?"

So I told him. About the notebook in my grandfather's office, about summoning Raziel, and about my cousins and me having angelic blood. I showed him my scar. "We all have weird scars."

His voice dropped to a ragged whisper. "You think what we have is just some...celestial side effect from angel blood? When I said those three words to you, they came from somewhere real." He thumped his fist over his heart. "It's what's in here." He stepped closer to me, still, green eyes blazing. "Remember? Remember what we said? If we put our broken hearts together, we will feel whole."

I saw the pain behind the anger in his eyes, and my resolve crumbled. "Of course I remember, Justin..."

"You think he's more real than me?" he said bitterly. "Like he really loves you and I don't?"

"No! It's not like that."

"What then? What is it like then?"

My breath caught; there was so much heat, so much anger beneath his words, but also fear—a raw longing that cracked open everything inside me until I felt laid bare before him.

"I don't know," I admitted, "I'm trying to figure it out."

A muscle in his jaw twitched as he spoke through clenched teeth, "Trying to figure out what? If you really love me, if you ever did? Or is it if you love him?"

"I'm sorry," I said softly, stepping towards him, wishing I could erase the hurt from his face.

He ran both hands through his hair and down over his neck, "Vince was right, wasn't he? He's in love with you." He deflated slightly and spoke more softly, "What I didn't know is that you were in love with him too."

My mouth was dry, and I turned away from him, "I love both of you and..."

"Don't," he said, almost pleading. He paused, exhaling sharply through his nose as if releasing some of that tension building inside of him. "Just don't say it's not real." His shoulders sagged slightly, the fight leaving him, replaced by a look that broke me even more.

God, he sounded like me...like when I told Kiran the same words before we kissed. It was not just the angel blood with either of them. I loved Kiran, and I loved Justin.

"I won't." My voice was barely a whisper on the thick night air.

He looked at me with dark intensity, and I thought he would leave. But then, in two quick strides, he was there, wrapping his arms around me so tight I could barely breathe. "Please," he murmured, his voice splintered with pain.

Heat and hurt radiated from him, mingling with my own. I couldn't help it; I wrapped my arms around him. His body shuddered against mine, and then his face was wet against my cheek. I shook against him and pressed into his chest. Soon, I was crying too.

The door swung open behind us. "Hey guys..." It was Scott.

Justin jerked away from me, and I saw them—the tears I had felt, glistening on his skin. "Justin...." I reached for him as he turned away.

He said nothing, stalking towards his car with quick strides.

"Justin!" Scott and I called as he made his way to the curb.

He didn't turn back. His car roared to life, tires screaming against the asphalt as he sped off into the dark. I stood there watching his taillights blur and shrink—two red streaks bleeding into nothing. The night swallowed him whole, leaving only the fading growl of an engine and an aching hollow in my chest where he had been standing just seconds before.

Scott raised an eyebrow at me from the porch, his expression softening when he saw the look on my face. "C'mon, Rhi," he said gently.

I nodded mutely then turned up the steps.

Kiran and Taylor paused mid-conversation as we appeared. I saw the way Kiran watched me, eyebrow quirking with worry.

"Tay, I need to ask you some things," I said quietly.

She cocked her head in curiosity. "Okay..." she drawled slowly.

"It's about that scar on your foot."

Chapter Twenty

Kiran

Taylor looked startled for a moment. She knew where this was leading — she had to. She must have found out about the Ossaris on her eighteenth birthday.

"Scott, maybe you should go after Justin," Taylor said. "If he looks anything like Rhi then he is not doing well."

Scott blinked at Taylor, confusion furrowing his brow. But then something shifted in his eyes, and he gave a quick nod, almost mechanical. "Sure," he said. "I'll go check on him."

As he hurried off, I turned over what I'd just witnessed. Had she coerced him? My pulse quickened. That was one of the powers of an Ossaris — a voice that could bend wills and reshape reality without a single touch. If Taylor carried that gift, then Rhi — my heart hammered painfully in my chest — Rhi most definitely was an Ossaris too.

The engine of Scott's car roared to life, and then Taylor wheeled around, fixing those sharp blue eyes on me. "Okay," she said, her voice sharp, "what are you?" She jabbed a finger in my direction. "And why do you look so much like Scott?"

Rhi's breath caught audibly next to me.

Taylor turned to her. "And why," she pressed, suspicion needling through her voice, "why are you asking about my scar?"

Rhi froze, glancing from Taylor to me. Her mouth opened then closed again in obvious indecision.

"What's happening?" Taylor searched Rhi's eyes, bewilderment settling in her own.

"It's complicated," Rhi said finally, as if testing the limits of what she could reveal.

"Well, uncomplicate it, little cousin."

Rhi flipped her hand over, palm up, revealing the small star-shaped scar. It was pale and distinct against her skin. "Your scar," she said. "If I remember, it looks like a triangle. Right?"

Taylor's eyes narrowed, a crease forming between her brows. "Yes," she said slowly, her gaze darting distrustfully toward me. "What does that have to do with him?" She gestured at me with her chin.

Rhi shifted uncomfortably beside me; I could feel a tremor course through her. "What you did," she started, pausing for air as if weighing each word, "to Scott...It's some sort of power you have, right?"

Taylor straightened, surprise—and something like fear—flickering across her face in quick succession.

"You always sort of had it," Rhi went on carefully, "but it manifested to be more powerful when you turned eighteen."

"How did you know that?" Taylor's voice was breathless, "I never told anyone."

Rhi lowered her gaze. "Because we all have these weird scars. You, me, Kacey, and Steve." She paused, looking for signs of recognition in Taylor's eyes. "Pops knew what they meant." Her voice dropped to a whisper. "Did he ever tell you?"

"No," Taylor whispered.

"This is going to sound crazy," Rhi said, words tumbling out fast. "If I were in your shoes, I'd think the same thing. But I've seen too much to pretend otherwise."

"What are you saying, Rhi?" Taylor glanced towards me again suspiciously.

Rhi bit her lip. "I found a notebook and some other things in Pop's office. He says I'm something called a Veilbreaker and a Seventh Flame." She stumbled slightly over the words. "Does that mean anything to you?"

Taylor shook her head, a bewildered frown creasing her forehead.

I spoke up then, "Did you ever have a person you didn't know tell you about your powers? Or has anyone just said something to you out of the blue about them?"

She let out a small breath. Her eyes were miles away. "I had a dream about a woman I didn't know once. It was weird and convoluted. I don't remember much of it except she told me...told me the scar meant I was blessed and I would become something powerful."

She turned, facing us again, "It kind of freaked me out when it happened, but I haven't really thought of it since. It felt really real at the time." She wiped her palms on her pants. "I just thought I had some gift like Mia's family has. I hardly use it. But when you came in the door." She motioned towards me. "I felt like something was off about you, and you look so much like Scott..."

I exchanged a look with Rhi, *"How much do you want to tell her?"*

"I think we should tell her everything. I trust her." Came her response in my mind.

I nodded. "I look like Scott because we share the same mother."

Taylor looked like she would faint. "No, that's not possible. She couldn't have had another affair."

I shook my head, "No, it's not like that." I scooted closer to her, and she backed away. My voice was low, gentle. "I'm an angel," I said evenly. "Rhi's Guardian Angel."

Taylor stared at me, unblinking for longer than seemed humanly possible; then something flickered in her eyes—amusement. Then she laughed. "What kind of joke are you two trying to play?"

"It's not a joke," Rhi said beside me, a delicate urgency in her tone. "You asked what he was. You can sense there is something different about him. It's because he's my Guardian Angel."

Taylor looked between us as if trying to catch any deception on our faces.

Rhi turned to me, mind speaking again, *"Show her your wings."*

"What?!"

Rhi's thought nudged at mine gently, *"She won't believe otherwise."*

I took a deep breath, allowing silver light to stretch behind me until my wings unfurled around me.

Taylor's eyes went wide, disbelief flooding her face. Her lips moved soundlessly, words failing her completely.

I held her gaze. "I am what I say I am," I told her, folding my angel light back into myself.

"This is...I can't..." She brought a hand to her forehead. "You're serious? You really—"

She shook her head violently as if to clear it; when she spoke again, her voice still carried a hint of hysteria. "Angels? Like from the Bible?"

"It's more complicated than that," Rhi said quickly, searching Taylor's face.

I folded my wings back in until they disappeared completely. Taylor's eyes followed their trail, lingering on the space where they'd been moments before. Even with them gone now, she seemed unable to quite catch her breath.

"Scott!" The name flew from her mouth.

"He isn't...he isn't any type of supernatural being," Rhi said quietly. "But, Justin...he is."

Taylor stood eerily still. "Justin." The name lingered in the air between us all. "I felt something off with Justin tonight. What—what is he?"

For a moment, I didn't know how to answer. Rhi's hand found mine again and squeezed firmly. I lowered my head. "He is...he's my twin. And there's something different about us because our father...I mean, Vince isn't normal." I heard the edge of desperation in my own voice, but went on anyway. "He's a Fallen Angel."

Taylor flinched at the last words, as if they were physically thrown at her. I looked at Rhi and then back at Taylor. "When angels have children with mortals, the offspring are called Nephilim. If more than one child is conceived, an Archangel will take the soul of one of the children to become a full angel." I shook my head. "It's to keep the balance. Or so they say."

Taylor stumbled back, taking it in. We were overwhelming her. She turned to Rhi, panic closing her throat. "I don't know what to...Jesus, Rhi!"

Rhi took a step closer to her. "I came tonight," she said quickly, forehead creased with concern. "To see what, if anything, you knew. You're the oldest. I was hoping you knew more." Her head sank with the words.

Taylor lowered herself onto the sofa. "And Justin...with all of this...he probably doesn't know what he is?"

"He knows," I said. He only found out recently, but he knows."

"That is a whole other story that I promise I will tell you later. I'll tell you everything." Rhi promised her cousin. "Please don't tell anyone," she begged softly, eyes pleading with Taylor's wide ones. "Not until we figure all of this out."

Taylor's eyes flickered back and forth between Rhi and me.

"There are more things in Pop's office that I need to look through."

Taylor pressed her hands to her temples as if trying to hold herself together at the seams. "Oh, my God."

"Tay," Rhi said gently. "The scars mean we have angel blood in us."

Slowly lowering her hands in disbelief, Taylor met Rhi's eyes.

"We're Ossaris," Rhi said quietly. "We're meant to keep the balance, or something like that, between realms."

Taylor didn't say anything for a long while; the street noise hummed faintly outside, feeling intrusive against the thick silence that had fallen in the room. Then she looked up from under blonde lashes, studying Rhi with a new intensity.

"If Pop knew about this," Taylor finally said, a trace of bitterness underlining each word, "Why wouldn't he have told me?"

Taylor's phone buzzed on the coffee table. She grabbed it with trembling hands, throwing a glance at Rhi before lifting it to her ear.

With my angel hearing, I caught his voice clearly on the other end. "I checked my parents, the garage, and now I'm sitting outside Vince's. The gate is locked. Justin isn't answering his phone."

Taylor's eyes darted to me, then back to Rhi before steering themselves to the floor. "Just come home then, honey," she said sweetly.

She dropped the phone into her lap and exhaled sharply, pressing her lips together as if she might break. Her gaze flicked up briefly, unsure of who to land on.

"Are you okay, Taylor?" Rhi asked softly.

"You really believe I'm an Ossaris or whatever you called it?"

Rhi nodded earnestly.

Taylor stayed silent for another long moment, eyes locked on the phone in her lap. She heaved a long sigh. "I believe you," she finally said, her voice low.

We had waited until Scott got home to leave. During the half hour it took for him to get there, Taylor asked a million questions. Rhi and I both tried our best to answer them all. Taylor made Rhi promise she would let her know if she found anything else out. I also told Taylor that she probably had other powers besides coercion and should try to tap into them.

Later, Rhi had asked me to hold her until she fell asleep. She stirred beside me now, her brows drawing together in a soft crease. A murmur escaped her lips — lost somewhere between sleep and waking. I brushed wisps of hair from her forehead, willing the worry out of her dreams. Outside, rain beaded across the windowpane, forming tiny reflective stars before slipping down the glass. Like me, a Fallen.

Rhi's breath took on soft rhythms, the peaceful sounds of sleep; I knew it wouldn't last.

She worried for Justin.

I had not heard or seen them on the outside, but I felt her emotions.

Fear and guilt.

I didn't wish my brother pain; I also didn't want him to hurt Rhi's feelings. I traced the outline of her jaw, allowing my fingers to linger on her lips. This draw I had to her, she insisted it was real. And I believed it was.

Still, was my blood responding to hers? Maybe, but it didn't negate the fact that I loved her. I loved her as my ward, yes, but my whole being loved her, wanted a life with her. A human one with dates, marriage, and babies...

She stirred again, pulling me from the storm inside myself into the turbulence of hers. Her fingers curled instinctively around my arm as if holding on to the remnants of a dream that had already started to fray. Then her fingers caressed the feathers in my wings.

"Rhi," I begged, lightly brushing my lips over the freckles that dotted her forehead.

She settled back against my chest, murmuring something incoherent, but tinged with worry.

I shouldn't be just lying here holding her and wishing...

I should go look through her grandfather's office while she and her grandmother slept. She had wanted to do it when we returned from Taylor's.

"She could catch us," I'd insisted as Rhi paced her room.

"We'll be extra careful." She insisted.

In the end, I convinced her to wait until tomorrow. I, however, would not.

I gently eased out from beneath her warmth, my arms feeling empty.

I teleported myself into the office. I would make this quick and then return. I moved quickly, my movements silent and careful. Across the room was the box where Rhi had found the notebook. There was more in that box about her. I stayed on mission, though, searching specifically for things about Taylor, Kacey, and Steve.

I moved through the office like smoke, from one corner to another, scanning bookshelves and cabinets for anything hidden. When I got to the closet, I pushed aside old coats and jackets until I uncovered an old-fashioned hatbox on an upper shelf.

I brought the hatbox out and perched it on the desk, hesitating for only a moment before lifting the lid.

Inside lay old letters stacked in haphazard piles, each one creased from years of unfolding and refolding — worn thin like paper origami. I picked one up at random, eyes racing over familiar names: Rhiannon, Kacey, Steve, Taylor — all of them blurring together.

And beneath that initial layer of parchment ghosts, as if guarding a deeper secret, was another leather-bound notebook.

I opened its cover reverently; pages flaked at the edges with age and delicate sketches linking constellation diagrams scrawled alongside messy but urgent notes: 'Unleashed potential,' 'Uncontrolled power'...

I held the letters and notebook to my chest. Moving like a shadow, I returned the hatbox to its hiding place. When I finished securing it, I teleported away from the heavy darkness of the office to my house.

Feeling clearheaded now, where silence stretched around me, I began going through each page with patient intensity.

My breath caught when I came to a page listing Rhi and each of her cousins by name. Each was followed by a symbol. Rhi's was a star — just like her scar. Taylor's, a triangle. Steve's, a round sun. Kacey's, a crescent moon.

Beneath Taylor's was written Coercion and Mediumship.

Steve's was written Heightened Senses and Accurate Intuition.

Kacey's said Ability to Control the Elements.

And Rhi — time seemed to slow around me as I read. Rhi could channel energy from any living thing. She could transport the soul of a mortal, angel, or demon through the Veil to the other realms.

Chapter Twenty-One

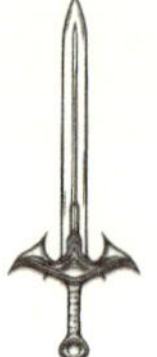

Rhiannon

Fog swirled around me, and coldness seeped into my bones. I looked down at the frozen ground, my bare feet covered in mud. Ugh, I was dreaming again, and of course, not dressed properly for my surroundings.

Cool glass trees jutted up from the ground in front of me. The crystalline forest loomed, calling, glistening in dim violet light. No, nothing but nightmares came from there. The thought of it sent a familiar chill across my shoulders. I turned away from its shimmering trap and ran.

My steps were slow at first, bogged by the wetness of the earth, but the mud grew drier and the path easier. The farther I traveled, the lighter it became; the fog slipping away. Tall fields of grass swayed around me. Below me, several buildings spread out, but one stood solitary and clear.

It was Kiran's house.

But there was no Nan's house or Mia's down the street, no familiar neighborhood, just his home standing starkly alone with a few outbuildings surrounding it.

I ran and landed with that thump peculiar to dreams. Wet grass smacked against my shins as I plodded through a field until it opened to a sprawling, beautiful lawn.

I slowed my pace as I got closer to the house. It was different. Newer, well-maintained, and a...a carriage sat in front of it.

I was hesitant to go further. It was like I was in the past.

I heard voices and moved quickly towards the house. My hand reached for the front door hesitantly, knowing that dreams could change in a moment's breath.

The door opened as if willed by thought alone.

"Kiran?" My voice sounded hollow to my ears.

The floor creaked with every step I took, my own breath loud in the silence. Walking into the home, I noticed the wood floors were polished to a high shine, and the furniture looked new and spotless.

A quiet meow broke the stillness, and I felt soft fur as a cat wound its way around my legs. It stared up at me with big golden eyes. It was Stanley. How was this possible? Oh yeah...dreaming. I picked up the cat, and it purred in my arms.

Voices raised again, their tones urgent and tense, drifting in from outside. I made my way to the master bedroom, moving as quickly and silently through the house as I could. Strange yet familiar symbols covered the doorway. Opening the door, hoping no one would hear, Stanley jumped from my arms and disappeared back down the hallway.

The voices were closer. I moved towards a giant bed and slid beneath it just as booted feet came through the door, slamming it shut.

"You said they were closing in," a deep voice demanded.

"We still have time," another answered calmly yet with a trace of irritation.

I watched shadows shifting under the bed's edge, my muscles tensing like coiled springs.

"This is reckless," the first voice said again, softer now but seething with anger.

A pause hung heavy between them. I held my breath, waiting.

"I'm telling you," a voice said. "Somebody's been here, John."

"And I'm telling you, it does not matter. The binding will hold."

The second voice was deep, smooth, not unlike Kiran's. "They can break the line."

"Eli, your faith is somewhat limited." A pause. "We will know tonight if it's still true."

"I don't like this."

A loud blast shook the house. I clamped my hand over my mouth, stifling a scream as plaster rained from the ceiling.

"It's not possible!" one of them whispered.

Slow footsteps stretched down the hallway, each one an icy tick towards us. An uneasy silence blanketed the room. I barely breathed.

"Knock, knock," a syrupy voice cut through the air.

"Begone, demon!" A man's voice was thin, cracking like dry glass.

Laughter seeped under the door, thick and taunting. The knob twisted. The hinges groaned. Then the door exploded off its frame.

"Oh, I am no demon." A female form filled the room as yellow-orange light flickered through it like wildfire. "I'm the Veilbreaker."

Heat engulfed everything. I felt it burn through my skin as a choked scream billowed through the room. A fleshy thump sounded beside me as hot blood splattered across my face. I turned my head to see the tip of a flaming sword piercing through a man's chest. I screamed as terror filled my lungs and burned like acid, writhing backwards away from his sightless eyes.

"Rhi!" A familiar voice sounded in my mind. My eyes flew open and met a set of silver ones staring at me with terror.

"You were dreaming," Kiran says quietly.

I shook uncontrollably. He pulled me tightly against his chest, whispering soft, calming words.

"K-Kiran." My mouth was too dry to go on. It feels like I can still taste the smoke.

"Shh," he said. "I have you."

"Kiran..." I try again, panic lacing through my voice, but the words stick in my throat before forcing their way out. "It was...I saw...the Veilbreaker."

He's silent and still, so incredibly still compared to how violently I'm trembling.

"It killed them," I said, pressing closer to him and feeling the beat of his heart strong and constant against my ear.

"Killed who?" The breath of the question ghosted through my hair.

I hesitated, thinking, remembering the fiery sword and blood. Eyes staring sightlessly at me.

"Two men. One was called John, the other Eli." A chill spread through me again as I tried to push the gory details from my mind.

"It was just a dream." His hands stroke down my arms, resting on either side of me. "You have so much on your mind and the summoning…"

I breathed in slowly and buried my head into his shoulder. There's more I need to get out. I traced my hands over the hardness of his chest, finding comfort in his strength. "She…the Veilbreaker was in your house, only it wasn't how it is now. It was like I went back in time." My words were spilling out in a ragged tumble. "But Stanley was there."

I felt him stiffen and pulled back to meet those intense silver eyes filled with worry.

"The room in your house that is warded was where it all happened. I saw the symbols on the door, and when she arrived, they called her a demon. That's when she laughed, telling them she's the Veilbreaker before…before killing them." Everything rushed back to me as my voice broke to a whisper. "Kiran, I don't want to be a killer."

"A killer? Rhi." His hand tilted my face up, gently. "You are no killer."

"What's happening to me? Why would I dream of such things?"

"Nothing will happen to you. Not while I am here." His jaw tightened with resolve.

Kiran pulled me close, his wings springing from his back and enveloping us both in their feathered caress. A tranquil, glowing warmth radiated around us as our soul song spiraled, wrapping me in its melody. I melted against him, my heart trying to slow itself to the gentle rhythm of his.

His hands moved up through my hair; waves fell through his fingers like water. He paused, twirling one loose strand around his finger. "Dreams and reality are not the same." His voice was calming and sure. "Please understand that."

I closed my eyes, trying to lose myself in him. As he held me, I saw something strange trailing from where the collar of his shirt touched his neck. Odd scrawls were almost hidden in the hollow of his shirt. I lifted a hesitant hand to move the fabric aside for a better look. Kiran's grip was there before mine even touched it, gently stopping me.

"What is that?" I asked breathlessly, "I've never seen it before."

His lips pressed together as if sealing off something painful, "They're marks of a Fallen."

"Kiran," I whispered. "I'm so sorry."

"It isn't a big deal."

"I want...please let me see."

He didn't answer, staring at a space beyond my shoulder.

"Please," I ask again, reaching.

I moved to the hem of his shirt, hand unsteady as I pulled it up. He inhaled sharply when my fingers grazed his skin. As I moved it farther, the shirt vanished completely with a shimmer of angelic magic.

His muscled torso was breathtaking. My eyes travelled over the harsh scrawl of symbols on his chest.

"Do they hurt?" I asked, running my finger over the strange etchings. Tiny sparks of electric energy cascaded along my fingers where they met his skin. It raised small bumps down my arm and sent shivers down my spine.

"They don't," he said simply and let out a shallow breath as I continued tracing them gently.

My voice was barely audible. "They look...they look like they hurt."

He captured my wandering fingers in his, pulling them up to his lips where he kissed them softly. "Please stop worrying."

He twined our fingers together as light spiraled around us and cloaked everything with a warm glow. I felt tranquility flow through my limbs.

I remembered what he said once about being in his angel light—how sacred it was to him. How we didn't need words when we were like this. My eyes roamed over him, shuddering at the scars on his skin. He was more beautiful than I could have imagined. More human than he understood. His chest rose and fell rapidly as I let my thoughts slow. How sorry I was that he had fallen for me. That guilt weighed heavily inside me, knowing he fell for me. That I longed to kiss every mark it left on him.

There was a pause in him. His eyes found mine. His breath caught on the edge of a gasp. He felt my thoughts; I knew he had.

"Rhi," he said softly.

I wanted to close the distance between his lips and mine, wanted nothing more than to dissolve into him.

Heat surged through me as I angled desperately towards the kiss, chasing itself through my mind, but abruptly he pulled back, pressing our foreheads together instead.

His ragged breath mixed with mine. His entire body trembled against me, as if with some unspeakable effort. "Rhi," he said again, pulling back just far enough to search my face. "We have to talk."

I didn't want to talk.

"Your touch, Rhi," he said, voice low and uneven. "It drives me..." He paused, eyes closing briefly as if trying to center himself. "It drives me..." He drew in a sharp breath as I moved closer, silver eyes clouding with intensity.

I slid my hands through his hair and pulled him to meet me.

"When you touch me and think..." His ragged whisper filled the still air between us. "Think those *things* in my angel light—I can barely restrain myself."

"So don't." I pushed the words free like a dare, like a hope. "Don't hold back."

His mouth captured mine— hard, hungry, and every thought spiraled away from me into pure feeling. Thought didn't exist outside of us; everything was stripped away until nothing remained but raw feeling, intense and pure, our souls fusing together.

I felt him pouring his love into me with blinding brightness—melding with my own raw longing and despair that he should never have fallen for me.

"Kiran..." I felt the softest groan pierce through me.

My name was on his lips again as we both slowed, our breath mingling.

I wrapped myself around him as his kiss deepened, becoming more than anything it had been before; more desperate and overwhelming—more complete.

The patterns on Kiran's chest pulsed where my fingers touched them, vibrant with our mingling souls, then seeped from his skin and coiled around mine—luminous shackles binding us together.

"I want this," he said against my ear, fierce and breathless. "I want this more than anything."

Kiran's eyes burned with a need so intense it enveloped me, pulling me deeper. His body was rigid with wanting—all of him poised on the crux of desire and control. "And you." His voice shook with something at the edge of breaking. "You are my soul mate. In every definition of the word."

In the deepest part of me, I knew he meant it. The shackles between us tightened in their embrace; molten silver heated by our mingling souls. Some distant part of me broke with sorrow for Justin.

Kiran's mouth found mine again, obliterating everything except him—his touch, his breath, his light pouring into me so completely I trembled. A smothered groan rose between us as he shifted me. My legs wrapped tightly around his waist as if anchoring us to the moment.

Another aching, needy sound filled the air; I wasn't even sure whose lips it came from as Kiran's hands traced down my side, leaving spirals of heated electricity in their wake. His hands moved over me like flames—it felt eternal; it felt wild and perfect.

"I've waited eternity for this," he whispered hoarsely.

His first kiss was such a short time ago, but now he was so sure of himself, knowing exactly how to dissolve me completely.

Chapter Twenty-Two

Kiran

Her name, her name was a sacred prayer on my lips. I loved this girl. She felt guilt for me falling and sometimes the pain and longing I felt to be back in Heaven, feeling the Heavenly light surround me...was torture.

This girl, this incredible, kind, strong, beautiful girl in my arms now took it all away. There had been a time, before all this, where I existed for her protection. Her angelic guide, eternal and unchanging. Now, as she smoothed her fingers around the curve of my wings and pulled me closer, I existed for nothing but her.

I wanted nothing else in this world or the next but her and her love. Damned, I knew it—it was certain. But, I didn't care. Maybe that's because I fell. That thought spun out as my sanity and my restraint snapped when she kissed her way down my neck and then lower, lower, over the marks of the Fallen. My soul, my heart was already hers. A gift given freely and fully. Now my body would be too, and hers mine.

I traced my hands down her spine to rest on her hips before they wandered beneath the hem of her t-shirt she had fallen asleep in. I found her bare skin beneath the thin material warm, pure and perfect.

Something nagged at my mind. It was what I found in her grandfather's office, what I learned about her and her cousins. The knowledge swarmed my mind like crows at dusk.

"Rhi," I could hardly speak as her soft lips came up from my chest to meet mine once more.

"Hmm?" She pressed closer to me still.

Why did I have to find anything? I should have stayed with her cradled in my arms instead of investigating. I was halfway through the notebook I found when I felt her fear. I snapped to her side at once. And now she was soft, giving, wanting...

"Ugh, Rhi please." I pulled away slightly as she opened those dark eyes. "I found something."

She stilled in my arms, head tilted in that way that made me feel weightless with love.

"What is it?"

Her hair tumbled around us like a dark curtain, crowding out everything but the closeness of us together. "In your grandfather's office," I said trying to regain my composure.

"It can't wait?"

I shook my head, "As much as I wish it could, and trust me—I really don't want to stop..."

"Tell me," she said softly.

So I did. I drew back in my wings and my angel light so I could concentrate better on telling her even with her t-shirt bunched up around her waist showcasing her soft stomach and...*Concentrate Kiran*! I thought to myself.

"I found more in your grandfather's office. I didn't get a chance to go through it all, but your powers and your cousins' powers. It listed them"

Her large brown eyes grew in interest.

"Taylor's are coercion and mediumship, Steve's are heightened senses and accurate intuition, and Kacey can control the elements."

She swallowed her lip trembling slightly, "And me?"

"You, you can channel energy from any living thing and can transport the soul of mortal, angel, or demon through the Veil."

She just stared at me unblinking.

"Speak to me, Rhi," I said.

"So..." she starts."That explains what a Veilbreaker is." She shook her head. "I don't want it...I don't want this power." Then her eyes grew large again. "The sword, the one the Veilbreaker held in my dream. It was on fire."

My breath hitched. "You're sure?"

She nodded. "Do you think that is the Seventh Flame?"

I shook my head. "I understand the seven flames to be Wisdom, Understanding, Counsel, Might, Power, Knowledge and Fear." I thought back through my knowledge. "There is another mention of a sword of fire."

"What?"

"It guards the gates to paradise."

"Paradise?"

"It is where the souls of the good hearted go when they pass."

"So Heaven?"

"No, that is a common misconception. Souls don't go to Heaven per say, just a plane within Heaven...paradise."

She pulled herself away from me and I felt like I was falling all over again. "Do you think it just appears to me on my eighteenth birthday?"

I didn't know and the thought of losing her to this was suffocating me. It should have been just us, just this, just love and only love forever. "We need to find out more," I said, dismayed by my own helplessness.

She sighed then dropped her head into her hands. "I can't do this Kiran. The whole idea of Veilbreakers freaks me out, and I have no interest in wielding some supernatural power."

So much was unknown, so much hovered over us like storm clouds darkening everything else in our lives. I was determined to find out more for her, if for no other reason than to make sure Rhi had the kind of life she wanted—one I could share with her.

"Let us find out more before we jump to conclusions," I said softly, brushing a stray strand of hair from her cheek.

She buried herself in my arms again. And despite everything lurking beneath the surface of our lives, knowing we can never fully close our eyes to it, I still kissed her.

The past few weeks had unraveled so much that had seemed clean and distinct. Black and white smeared into grey. The chains that held me to a certain standard had broken loose by my fall.

I needed to know exactly what we were up against. For myself. But most importantly for her.

I realized with shock as I held her once more that Fallen Kiran—a more humanized Kiran—even felt more love for him. My brother. And while I still saw him as reckless and irresponsible and selfish and proud...how could I not understand the sheer animal drive behind his actions now? To love this girl was to be driven wild by fear and longing.

"Rhi, my Ahavah" I said. "What do you want?" My voice was just a whisper and I wasn't sure if she knew what I was asking. My heart ached to know if she only wanted me and had given up my brother.

On Justin.

Her gaze held mine in silence—for an eternal moment until she blinked and sighed. "Not this, none of this. I don't want any special powers. I don't want a scar from an angel's kiss. I don't want my cousins wrapped up in this and I don't want to hurt Justin. I just want us. Just us...together."

The words should have made my heart soar, but there was a shadow in them. A darkness looming behind the hope of them that left less promise than I wish they had left. Like maybe, despite my best intentions and my boundless love for her, something neither of us could control would change everything.

Her fingers brushed over my lips drawing me back into the beautiful present moment and breaking all the unwelcome thoughts crashing through me. "You clearly need a better distraction from all of this," she said, draping herself over my lap once more.

Not a second passed before her mouth was on mine again, frantic and fervent, like I might disappear and never return.

"I need to know what we're facing," I said against her lips when I finally pulled away. I sought her eyes, "Sleep, Ahavah," I said more softly. "Morning is almost here. You need your rest."

Her head tipped in protest, but I touched her cheek and kissed her forehead to still the refusal.

She pressed her lips to mine, long and lingering, as if capturing every moment we had. The flutter of her heart beneath my hands. A final breath stuck in my throat as she crawled back under the covers. "Stay until I'm asleep?"

My resolve slipped as I wrapped my arms around her again, my own skin screaming against stopping. Her breathing slowed and calmed—but still, it felt too soon when I finally lifted myself from our tight knot of shared souls to continue searching through the notebook and papers.

Chapter Twenty-Three

Rhiannon

My lips were deliciously sore as I twisted my hair up into a high ponytail. I smiled at my reflection in the mirror. Last night...last night was magical.

It was also scary. How did I become this celestial creature, and why did no one in my family tell my cousins or me? There was no handbook for Ossaris. Then again...maybe there was, and I just hadn't found it yet.

Kiran wasn't here when I woke up. My memories of last night, though...I shook my head. I needed to concentrate. I should text Taylor about what Kiran had found so far. About her abilities and the rest of ours.

I picked up my phone and quickly typed a very condensed version of what Kiran had told me last night. Taylor immediately texted back.

I can help look too. I can come by your house while you're at school to search through the things you found.

I wasn't sure if that was a good idea. I responded to her, saying I would ask Kiran.

Speaking of my Guardian Angel. Where was he? He should be here to walk with me to school. I took one last look at myself in the mirror and headed downstairs to grab some juice. Nan's car wasn't in the driveway. She must have gone to work early.

As I opened the fridge, reaching past the milk to the orange juice, Kiran appeared like a sudden breath of wind. He stood in the doorway, those silver eyes piercing through me.

"Juice?" I asked, raising an eyebrow at his somber expression.

His silver eyes softened as he nodded. I poured some for both of us and slid a glass across the counter to him. "I told Taylor about what you found," I said. "She offered to look through everything while we're at school."

He took a sip and seemed to chew over my words, "If she wants to search at my place, she can." He paused, meeting my eyes again. "And if you're okay with leaving the first notebook we found at my house."

"Okay, I'll grab it, and then we can go."

He stopped me with a light touch on my arm. "I'll get it," he said, vanishing before I could argue.

I grabbed two bagels on my way out and locked the front door behind me. Kiran emerged from his place next door in fresh clothes.

"Ready?" he asked when he reached me.

"I'm all yours," I answered, and a sweet smile crossed his face. He seemed to like those words.

Math, as always, left my brain in scrambles. How was I some powerful Veilbreaker and couldn't wrap my head around trigonometry problems? It didn't help that Sam sat next to me, constantly poking me with his pencil.

I was relieved when the bell rang. I had texted Taylor that the things were at Kiran's. He said he left it unlocked and to just head in. I was eager to join her.

"Where are you two off to in such a hurry?" Sam asked, falling into step with us.

I stopped and shot him a look. "Do you have to jab me all the time? Math is hard enough without you stabbing me with a pencil every five minutes."

"Would you rather I use other ways to distract you?" Sam waggled his eyebrows.

Over my head, I heard Kiran growl low in his throat.

My mouth hung open, searching for something smart to say, when a familiar figure at the end of the hall made her way towards us. The crowded hall seemed to part around her.

Trina.

Glorious as ever in a bright white skirt and a canary yellow blouse. Her long dark hair swished around her shoulders.

My feet rooted themselves to the floor as my mind scrambled for an escape route. Trina didn't slow down; if anything, she picked up speed when she saw she had our attention.

"Rhi!" Trina called out, closing the gap between us. Her eyes flared, at odds with her cheerful outfit.

I gulped as Kiran's hand slid lightly over the small of my back.

Trina stopped in front of the three of us, her eyes raking over Kiran, Sam, and me.

"Oh, hey, I see Jess," Sam said and darted off without further word.

"Hi Trina," I started to say as she cut me off.

"What did you do to Justin?"

I opened my mouth, but nothing came out. How could I possibly have an answer to that? My brain flashed to our last conversation. How hurt he'd been. "Haven't seen him," I finally stammered, the worry seeping in more than I liked. "Why? What happened?"

"Wow. You move on quickly," she scoffed, flicking her eyes towards Kiran, then back at me. "He loved you, you know."

Loved—past tense? My ears rang as Trina's gaze flitted to Kiran, staring him down like a hawk on a mouse.

"You have no idea what you're talking about!" The words exploded from me. "Maybe try concentrating on your own relationship for once!"

"Oh, the one you helped ruin?" She looked seriously hurt, as if all of this was somehow my fault. "I know Steve hooked up with Mia."

I swear I saw tears forming in the corners of her dark eyes. Trina brushed at her eyes before I got a chance to reply. "I thought Mia was my friend." She sniffed, waving towards where Jess stood with Sam. "Look at poor Jess over there. Heartbroken over her."

"I'm sorry you're hurting," I said, trying to catch her eye. I seriously did feel bad for her. She really loved Steve; maybe even too much because Steve wasn't ready for that level of seriousness. "But I have nothing to do with Steve or Mia. And you haven't told me what happened to Justin."

Her voice quivered, "He said he might leave town for a while." Her eyes bore into mine. "He said his heart is broken, and I have never heard Justin say anything like that before about anyone."

Pain prickled through me more than I wanted it to. I knew what pain was like. I knew what it felt like to trust someone only to have them stick a dagger in your heart.

"He said something about going after Vince. Whatever that means." Trina's eyes dug into me like daggers, "He is not in a good way. I have never seen him like this, and I have known him my whole life." Her eyes became softer, "I just don't want him to get hurt." Then she turned on her heel and disappeared in the crowd of students.

Kiran's hand found mine, twining our fingers together. "Are you alright?" His voice was low, concern threading each word.

Was I? I didn't even know anymore. Part of me hoped it wasn't as bad as she made it sound. Trina lived for drama and blowing things totally out of proportion. But a sick feeling settled in my stomach like a stone. "He can't go after Vince," I finally said. "And her saying that means he knows where Vince is." I shivered at the thought of the Fallen Angel.

"I could find Justin for you," Kiran offered.

"He might not take that so well, I should go," I said, hating how shaky my voice was.

Tiny lines formed between Kiran's eyes. "I will go and find out if he's safe. I'll let you know what I find out. I don't want you near Vince if Justin has found him."

I bit my lip and nodded. "Okay," I said, my voice thin. "Just let me know as soon as you find him, please?"

Kiran brushed his lips across my forehead and pulled me against his chest for a half second before leading us through the crowd. I noticed the looks I got from a few girls who must have seen him hug me. Jealousy roared behind their eyes.

We stepped outside and stopped. A few kids were smoking where they thought the teachers couldn't see them. I shrugged off the hollow ache in my chest and kept moving with Kiran up the street towards his house.

"Let's hope Taylor found something useful." Kiran opened the door to his house, ushering me inside.

"Hello?" I called, stepping inside.

"In here!" Taylor yelled from deeper inside.

The living room table was a massive pile of chaos. Papers were spread like a torn apart book; pages strewn everywhere while Eva lay in her carrier next to Taylor, kicking tiny feet into the air, drool-covered fingers in her mouth.

Taylor looked up, her face a mix of wonder and excitement. "You won't believe some of this stuff," she said. "And you said there's more in Pop's office?" She didn't seem fazed by the mess around her.

I nodded, moving papers aside to sit near her on the couch.

Taylor glanced at my expression, "You look upset. Is everything okay?"

"Have you heard from Justin?"

"No...why? What happened? And do I want to know?" Her brow furrowed as she tucked a loose strand of hair behind an ear.

A tightness clamped down on my throat. "Trina said he might leave town."

"I'll text Scott and see if he's talked to him."

"Thanks," I said, hating just how raw I still felt from Trina's words.

I peeked over at Kiran. His jaw was set firm while he spread more pages across the wooden table.

Taylor's phone chimed. She glanced at the screen and frowned. "Scott says he hasn't heard from him, but he'll try calling."

Kiran stood, and I fought not to reach for him, feeling helpless. "I'll find Sam and look for him."

My fingers fidgeted with the hem of my shirt as I swallowed down my worry. Part of me didn't want him to leave at all, but another part wanted him to go right away so that I'd know Justin was safe.

"I'll let you know what we find out," Kiran said, those silver eyes burrowing into mine. He stepped towards me, pulling me up and wrapping me in his arms. I shut my eyes tight as he pressed his cheek against my hair. Seconds later, he vanished from the room.

Taylor stared at me, suspicion lacing her voice. "Okay…what's going on between you two?"

I opened my mouth, but nothing came out.

Kiran was more than I could have ever dreamed of; being with him last night was intense and lovely and made my heart ache to touch him again. But Justin…he drew me in every time I saw him. That reckless hurt in his eyes spoke directly to my own tangled heart.

"Rhi?" Taylor tried again, leaning in closer.

What was going on with us? What was going on with Justin? How did things get so complicated? I didn't know how it happened—falling for both of them—but it made my heart twist painfully because they were brothers and they both deserved better than this.

"I don't want to talk about it right now, Tay."

"Okay, when you do, I'm here," Taylor said, backing off but not convinced. Reaching for a clump of papers, she settled back on the couch. "Let me tell you what I found."

Before she could begin, a small furry shape darted into the room. Stanley sprang onto my lap, purring loudly.

"Where did that cat come from?" Taylor raised an eyebrow, looking amused.

"Not sure," I said, scratching him as he snuggled into my hand. "I think he belonged to Mr. Hollander and just came with the house."

She reached over to stroke him, too, and he sank into her touch.

"Let me show you the most important thing I think I found," Taylor said while digging through more papers.

I flipped through some pages quickly, scanning the neat handwriting. My pulse jumped as notes about Ossaris sprang out at me.

Taylor bit her lip as she watched my expression flicker through disbelief and amazement.

"This is incredible," I whispered, unable to tear my eyes from the scrawled words.

Deep truths were put in mortal hands—the Ossaris—and Principalities are to guide Ossaris.

But the truths they guard are dangerous: How to collapse the Veil between worlds, how to bind or banish celestial beings, and how to define cosmic law itself.

Taylor took the papers from my hand and then handed me a notebook. "I don't know who wrote that, but this is all Pop's writing."

I took the leather notebook from her. She pointed down the page, "Here it lists our names and what our powers are, just like you texted me."

I can transfer souls between realms—I read the words again and again—*of angels, demons, and mortals. And I can channel energy.* My stomach squirmed. I wasn't even sure I knew what that was or what it meant.

Taylor interrupted my thoughts, like she could hear me thinking too hard. "He writes about those Principalities in there, too, just like the other papers." She flipped to the next page while Eva gurgled happily beside her.

I read where she pointed as Stanley batted at my fingers.

Principalities walk the line between holiness and wickedness because they must understand both to teach balance.

Some Ossaris say their Principality taught them mercy. Others say they were taught cruelty first, and had to choose otherwise.

They may tempt as much as they protect—seeing who is truly worthy of truth. The words that stood out said every Ossaris since has heard the warning:

Your Principality will teach you how to burn. But it is you who must decide what to set alight.

"There's so much here," I said, then squeezed my eyes shut, overwhelmed by all of it.

"That's not even all of it." Taylor dug through another pile, pulling more pages from the mess. "Here are the names of the Principalities known to our family."

"Auroriel, Principality of Oaths," she read.

I could feel her eyes on me as my face fell in disbelief.

"Lirien, Principality of Grief," she continued.

My chest hammered. Each word felt truer and heavier.

"Calethe, Principality of Fire," Taylor said.

Panic ignited under my skin as she handed me more papers. I took them with trembling hands.

"Ophaniel, Principality of Mirrors."

Taylor's voice dropped to almost a whisper. "Nirenth, Principality of Silence Between Heartbeats," she finished.

Below the last name scribbled in Pop's handwriting was a footnote: Rhi's Principality may be Lirien.

I sucked in a breath and scanned the pages again. More footnotes accompanied Taylor, Steve, and Kaley's names.

"Show me everything," I said, determined to understand it all.

Chapter Twenty-Four

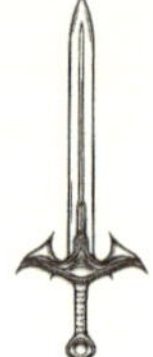

Kiran

I needed to find Justin, but I wasn't looking forward to it. The last person he'd want to see was me — which was exactly why I dragged Sam along. Sam had many more friends and acquaintances than I had, and the sooner we found Justin, the sooner I could get back to Rhi.

The beach stretched around us, the sand a cool ivory underfoot. A breeze, tinged with salt and late summer, tousled my hair as gulls wheeled in lazy arcs above. Sunbathers dotted the coastline, their laughter and radio songs moving with the wind. I imagined taking Rhi somewhere like this — somewhere more private. I wanted to see her smiling in the sunlight, laughing in the frothy waves.

"This is where they last saw him, for sure?" I asked.

Sam squinted into the distance, his hair blowing slightly against the brisk gusts that cut across the surf. I glanced at him as his gaze ran over two attractive women lounging near us. "Definitely."

The last time Vince was spotted here had been several weeks ago. Who knew what trail Justin would be following—if any.

Sam shaded his eyes, scanning for anyone he might know. "Doesn't sound like you're looking forward to finding Justin."

I ducked under a volleyball sent flying by a group of shouting teenagers. "We didn't part on great terms."

"He seemed pretty pissed off last I saw him," Sam said flatly.

"He's more than pissed, he's hurt."

Sam laughed and shook his head. "You've got some serious drama going on here, you know that?"

"It's not something I wanted to happen." I ran a hand through my hair, keeping my voice light despite the knot of guilt tightening inside me. "I loved her long before he ever came into her life."

"Yeah, well," Sam said, nodding toward someone further down the beach who looked suspiciously like Justin. "It's entertaining as hell."

The distant, barely familiar silhouette lingered by some fishing boats pulled up onto higher ground.

It was Justin.

Drawing closer, I studied him. He was absorbed in conversation with a tall girl. The girl looked past Justin, narrowing her eyes at Sam and me. She muttered something, nodding in our direction, and Justin turned abruptly. His face tightened, eyes dark with irritation, the moment he saw it was us.

He drew up to us, scowling. "What are you two doing here? How'd you find me?"

"Trina told Rhi," I said. Beneath the tough front, I felt the ache of betrayal and resentment he aimed our way. "We were worried about—"

"Worried?" he interrupted, laughing harshly as if it was the most absurd thing he'd ever heard.

"You haven't been answering your phone," Sam chimed in, a little edge in his tone.

"I know," Justin snapped, turning to him and then back to me just as quickly. His anger came easily these days; I knew it, saw it, and I was part of the cause. "Stop following me."

"If you do find Vince, what the Hell do you think you'll do?" Sam snapped.

"Get the hell out of my face," Justin said, but the annoyance in his voice sounded less certain now.

"He's immortal, Justin," Sam continued. "You're not."

"I'm not afraid of him." Justin's shoulders heaved slightly under his t-shirt, breath coming in sharp puffs.

"You can't beat him," I added quietly, searching his face for any glimmer of understanding.

Sam sighed, frustration evident in his tone. "You'll end up dead."

I studied my brother — this person who felt at once so deeply familiar and impossibly distant. Somewhere behind the anger was something else: an echo of the boy I'd pulled back from the edge of death, before the darkness had swallowed him whole.

"Is that it, Justin?" I heard myself ask, unable to stop the quake in my voice. "Did you come here to get yourself killed?"

A shift passed over him like a cloud blotting out the sun. His eyes flicked to mine and then away again, "Are we done?"

I held my ground, pretending to be unfazed by how painful it was to see him unraveling. To see how lost he really was. "We're not done. Not done at all."

"Let's go then." Sam glanced around us. "Somewhere not this public."

I watched Justin hesitate, shifting his feet in the sand. "This better not take long." He finally said.

Sam motioned with his head toward a nearby jetty. He led us under its crisscrossing wood beams into where there was more shadow than light.

Sam grabbed both our hands, and everything shifted, air crackling like a static charge. We landed inside an abandoned building, dust swirling around sunlight streaming from broken windows and patched drywall bare as bones. A cracked NO TRESPASSING sign was pasted against splintering boards.

"Now," Sam said, gesturing to keep us from moving any further away from each other. "You two need to sort this out."

Justin launched himself at me, faster than I'd expected. He swung with everything he had, landing his fist squarely on my jaw. I allowed the blow to connect and stumbled back a few steps before straightening. Somehow, he seemed stronger. "Does that make you feel better?" I asked, holding his gaze steady with mine.

"Shut the hell up," Justin shot back. "You took her from me, Kiran! You think this is some joke, but she's everything to me. I've never loved anyone like this before." His voice broke around each word, flying at me like shrapnel.

"You think I don't love her?" My own voice surprised me — raw in a way I hadn't expected. Something cracked in the iron wall I kept around myself. "I've loved her for years, Justin. And I held back. I chose not to act on it."

He stared at me blankly for a moment, and then the heat rose again in his eyes. "Or maybe you just couldn't stand that she picked me. Maybe you showed yourself to her and professed your love because you were jealous and couldn't stand the fact that she loved me."

"You think it is only me that stands between you?" I asked, but some of his words hit truthfully. I wanted Rhi; I was in love with her. But I had held back. I had until Justin came into her life, and I saw what I so desperately wanted.

"You are!" He shoved his hands through his hair, "Rhi said she loved me! You're trying to take that away—you took it away."

"I know you love her, and I know she loves you." My voice cracked with the emotion of meaning it. "But," I said, searching for his understanding and finding none, "I feel her love for me too! I love her too, Justin, and it is more—so much more. I am her Guardian, and we're soul mates."

He scoffed at the words like they were a bad taste in his mouth. "I don't believe that." I felt him readying for another swing, but Sam moved slightly from the side, not stopping enough to end what had just begun, but ready all the same.

"It is the truth!" Each word came out with iron clarity. "Not in the way humans have come to believe, but our souls are literally entwined!" It was so hard saying these things aloud without feeling exposed, fragile as glass in front of him. "I can't leave her. It would not only break me, but it would destroy her as well."

"What he says is partly true," Sam said, his voice calm and steady. "Their souls are entwined, but it doesn't have to be romantic."

Justin's face shifted. Something new blooming over his features—maybe hope. "Then end it," he demanded.

A ragged breath caught in my throat. I couldn't end it — not now that I knew she loved me that way too. Not after we'd kissed, touched, in ways I had only ever dreamed of. When we were close like that, it overwhelmed every sense I had. I didn't just feel my own feelings — I felt hers. And she wanted me just as much.

"And how would you deal with that?" Sam asked Justin, "Could you handle him? Her Guardian. Always connected to her." He took a step closer to both of us, still focused on Justin. "Knowing he feels all she does? Knowing what you know of his feelings for her?"

Justin's eyes met his, "It is better than living with a broken heart and without her." He grabbed at his shirt above his heart.

"Would it be?" Sam pressed, his words relentless but without malice.

Justin closed his mouth around any reply.

"You know I've known Vince for almost his entire existence," Sam said, shifting the subject. "He was once good. I see so much of him in both of you."

Justin let out a mocking laugh.

Sam didn't flinch, only stared at Justin. "You don't believe me?"

Silence hung in the air, filled with the faint creaks of the old building. "He fell in love." Sam's words stretched between all three of us. "You know this, right? You know he became a Fallen because of Rhi's grandmother?"

A flicker of surprise altered the anger etched into Justin's face. I already knew the story. It looked like my story. That did not mean I was anything like Vince.

"It overtook him," Sam said, the words directed at Justin. "Like yours is doing to you."

"It isn't," Justin insisted.

"You are heading in that direction, Justin," Sam said firmly. "You are doing stupid and reckless things because of your feelings for her."

Justin ran a hand through his hair, pushing it back from his face. "What?" he said, glaring at me, then Sam. "Do you expect me to stop caring?"

"We all have choices." Sam kept his eyes on Justin, but his words were aimed at me, too.

Justin's mouth curved into a bitter line. "I've heard enough."

Sam then looked pointedly at me. "And you. You fell from grace to save your brother," nodding toward Justin. "But it was her...she gave you the final push." His words were full of sadness and understanding more than accusation.

"That's not entirely true," I said, feeling the weight of both their stares. "I saw the fear in Justin. I saw our kind. And I saw the *others*."

"Others?" Justin asked.

"Demons," Sam answered.

"You are my brother!" I took a step closer. "When you needed me — I couldn't let you go." Justin's mouth opened and closed. I couldn't bear the thought of seeing him go limp at my feet again, swallowed by shadows. It ripped through me sharper than any blade. "Rhi blames herself," I continued reluctantly. "For the mess between us, for what happened at Vince's. She thinks none of it would have happened if not for her."

The silence stretched between us like a shadow, dipping into every corner of the room. I expected another outburst from him. But instead of screaming at me, Justin punched the wall, splitting it and sending clouds of dust fanning out from the crack. "I want to kill Vince!"

"I want to kill him just as much as you do...but...it's impossible."

"I know he is somewhere here," Justin swept dust from his shoulders, "He'll come back for us."

"He will," Sam said. "But I'm doing everything I can to protect all of you."

"That girl you saw me talking to on the beach? She works at one of the local bars. Said she's seen Vince; he comes in a few times a week." Justin glanced around like Vince might appear from the shadows. "I went there yesterday. Didn't see him."

My temper boiled, hot and red right under my skin. "I want to destroy him," I seethed.

Something passed over Justin's face, some thought or plan blooming behind his eyes. "Maybe...maybe there is a way."

Sam stared hard at him. "What are you talking about?"

"Phen...Phen offered me a deal."

"What kind of deal?" Kiran asked slowly.

Justin held my gaze warily, then let out a breath. "He said that I could have Rhi...if I wanted. Said he'd take care of you for me by chaining you in Hell."

Shock spread through me, cold and fierce, but it was Sam who spoke first. "And you're not considering this now?"

"No!" Justin's voice rose abruptly. "I'm not a murderer or chain your brother in Hell type of person."

"What do you mean *now*?" I said, my temper simmering.

"I never considered doing it," Justin said.

"And you knew about this?" I turned to Sam.

"I did and didn't think he would go through with it."

"It might have been nice of you to tell me," I growled.

"Calm down, Guardian. I had no intention of letting either of them deceive you." Sam scratched at his chin, musing aloud, "He wants something."

I felt a jolt of realization. "Maybe he wants Rhi, maybe he wants to use her."

Sam's head whipped my way. "Why would you think that?"

"He told Rhi to look into her family...as did you."

Sam turned his eyes dark with thought toward me again. "It's possible he knows what she is, but not probable."

"Wait? What she is? Does this have to do with her angel blood?" Justin asked.

Sam and I whipped our heads toward him in unison.

"Rhi confessed about her angel blood to me that night at Taylor's place," he said.

Sam's eyes narrowed. "You kept quiet about the book, right?"

"What book?" I asked.

Sam jerked his chin toward Justin. "Tell him."

Justin ran a hand through his hair, hesitating before he finally spoke. "At the mansion, I discovered something—a kind of ancient diary...the Book of Michael."

My muscles coiled tight. Missing gospels were one thing, but this? "Michael as in...The Archangel? What's in it?"

"I haven't had a chance to go over it in detail yet," Sam said. "But, we must keep it away from Phen. He may use the knowledge and Rhi to go from being a prince of Hell to its king."

"Is that why you think he's been hanging around?" I asked.

"I don't know. It's not like Phen. He's usually pretty easy going."

"You mean for a demon." I huffed.

Sam gave me a sidelong look, "He is a demon prince, yes, but he still is an angel. An old and powerful one. And not just any angel...he's a Throne."

I shook my head, "Why didn't you tell me you found this book?"

"It doesn't matter. You know now. Look, Lucifer gives Phen anything he desires. He covets Phen's gifts of coercion. I don't know why Phen would want to take on Lucifer when he has such a cushy position."

"Wait," Justin interrupted. "You mean Lucifer, *the Lucifer?...*Satan?"

Sam nodded, "The one and only." He took a deep breath, "Phen is still an angel, the way Lucifer is still an angel...Fallen Angels, but angels just the same. I honestly think the Morning Star prefers Fallens to any demon he creates."

"We should get back," I said, tension coiling through me. Every second away from Rhi felt wrong. Her face surfaced in my mind, and with it, the reason I'd come at all. "Justin — Rhi sent me. She's worried about you."

He hung his head. "Let's go then. I drove through, unlike you, I just can't snap my fingers and be somewhere else."

"I can teach you how to do it," Sam said with a slick smile. "But, for now, let's go to your car. I can snap my fingers as you say and be home, your car as well."

Chapter Twenty-Five

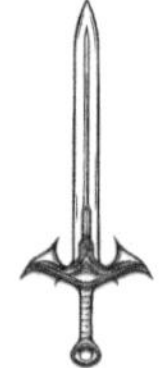

Rhiannon

Kiran returned with news that he and Sam had found Justin. Relief loosened something tight in my chest—he was safe—but the fear of what Justin was planning crept in right behind it.

I sat on the edge of my bed, Kiran hovering near me when he returned from Florida. Every word he said formed anchors in my chest—Justin wanted Vince dead and didn't care if it killed him.

The thought settled like ice in my bones—the horror of losing Justin, of him slipping away while I stood helpless. Then he told me about Phen's offer to Justin—to eliminate Kiran by chaining him and leaving him caged in Hell.

My breath caught sharply, fear suffocating me. The thought of losing Justin was more than I could handle, more than I could even begin to process. But the thought of Kiran locked away—left me chilled to my bones. Thankfully, Justin said he wanted no part in locking away Kiran.

The rest of the week dissolved—school days bleeding into late nights hunched over my grandfather's journals, searching for answers I wasn't sure existed.

It was Friday, and tonight was Phen's band's show. Kacey lounged cross-legged on my floor, a riot of clothes strewn around her. "I'm definitely going with the red one tonight," she declared, tossing the others onto the bed. Her phone buzzed every few seconds, an unsettling reminder of who she was talking to.

I ran the curling iron over my hair slowly. "Is that him again?"

Kacey grinned up at me. "Three guesses."

"So you two are really a thing now?"

"I don't know," she sighed dreamily, "But he's seriously the most romantic—and hot—guy I've ever known. He recites poetry to me, Rhi!"

Part of me wanted to drag her back from what she didn't know was an abyss. Tell her that Phen wasn't just dangerous; he was a demon. "I'm glad Taylor and Scott are coming tonight," I said, trying to keep my voice light.

"They have to witness how insane this band is." Kacey pulled on the red shirt and examined herself in the mirror.

Behind her, I grimaced but quickly erased it when Kacey turned back around, her eyes dancing with mischief.

"What?" she said.

"Nothing, you just look amazing," I kept my face as neutral as possible. I'd told Taylor about Phen, about Kacey's massive crush. *He's not getting my little sister,* she'd fumed.

"Phen won't know what hit him," I said, trying not to choke on the hairspray.

"I really think he likes me! He's been texting all week. You should read what he sends me." She dropped her voice, imitating Phen. "You are the very breath I breathe—" She burst into giggles.

"Smooth talker," I said, turning away so she couldn't see my face twist into a worried frown.

"I know!" Kacey gushed. "Oh shoot," she groaned suddenly, we're going to be late! Where is Kiran?"

She didn't know he had been sitting invisibly in the hall the entire time, but a second after her words, Nan called up to us that he was here.

Kacey and I raced down the stairs, her laugh a bright noise behind me. Kiran stood in the hallway with his back to the door; his eyes met mine with a warmth that made my pulse skip.

"Hey, Kacey," he said.

"Hey there!" She said enthusiastically.

We said goodbye to Nan and stepped outside. The air had that sharp autumn bite to it now, leaves skittering across the pavement. Steve's eighteenth birthday was just around the corner. I couldn't help wondering whether he was hiding powers the way Taylor had.

Kacey stopped short in front of me. "Holy crap," she said, gaping. "That's your truck?"

Kiran smiled widely, "It is."

I turned to see Steve pull up behind us with Taylor and Scott in tow.

"I'm going with Rhi and Kiran," Kacey said, ducking inside Kiran's truck.

Steve rolled down his window, "Nice ride." He said, eyeing the cherry red truck.

"Thanks," Kiran said, turning the key, the truck rumbling to life beneath us.

Darkness settled around us as we took off, headlights flickering across the houses and pavement. The city lights glimmered sharply against the sky as we turned onto the highway. I smiled to myself, feeling the warmth spread from where Kiran's hand rested on my knee. He drove smoothly for someone who hadn't been doing it long, navigating the roads carefully. We'd spent late afternoons circling through neighborhoods, Kiran learning the feel of driving.

I hoped tonight would turn out to be normal, the kind of night where people were just... people. I sighed, knowing that was highly unlikely.

We came in two vehicles. Parking was impossible near the club, and we finally found a spot two blocks away. "Let's go!" Kacey bounced out as soon as the truck stopped, her excitement pouring out.

We could hear the music growing clearer as we approached the club, its bass thrumming in the air like a heartbeat. A neon sign flickered above, casting a shifting glow over the crowd buzzing outside. The line stretched down the block—girls in tight skirts, guys leaning and laughing under streetlights.

Taylor waved at us, her hair contrasting sharply against a sea of dark shirts and leather jackets. She tucked herself closer under Scott's arm as he shrugged deeper into his hoodie. I pulled at the hem of my skirt, Kiran's arm slipping easily around my waist.

When we reached them, Taylor rolled her eyes at the thick line in front of us. "This is insane," she said.

"No kidding," Scott added. "Place is packed already."

Kacey beelined past us towards a burly man guarding the entrance. "We're on Phen's list," she announced over the noise. She pointed to each of us, giving him our names.

As he glanced over a clipboard and frowned, I saw a side door crack open near the alley. Phen slipped smoothly into view, his lean frame silhouetted in the flickering glow from inside.

"Look," I said, nudging Kacey's shoulder. I nodded towards where Phen lounged against the doorway. Tight black pants hung low on his hips and nothing else. He had no shoes or shirt on. Kacey squealed and dashed to him, leaping into his arms.

He immediately bent down and kissed her; she wrapped her arms around his neck and returned the kiss. When they finally stopped, she waved us over excitedly.

Taylor's face was grim as she said, "That's him? What has my sister gotten herself into?"

Phen smiled at Kiran and me when we got to the doorway. I glared at him. "Do you own a shirt?"

His grin spread wider. "I run hot...if you know what I mean."

Boy, did I.

Kiran's hand never left my lower back as we wove in past bodies already swaying to the music from a band on stage.

Scott motioned toward some open seats along the balcony that overlooked the main floor. "Might as well claim those before they're gone," he shouted over the noise.

Phen leaned closer to Kacey's ear, murmuring something that made her giggle uncontrollably before she nodded and hugged him tightly.

"I'll catch you guys up there," she yelled, clearly not planning to stay with us.

Kace!" Taylor called after her sister, but Kacey was lost to the music and Phen's pull. "He really does have her wrapped around his finger." Her voice darkened as she turned to me. "We've got to do something, Rhi."

Steve came up next to us, his mouth a hard line. "I don't like that guy."

I sighed. "You're in good company," I said, watching Kacey disappear with Phen behind the stage.

Scott put an arm around Taylor's shoulders as she glowered toward the back. "She'll be fine," he said with only slight conviction.

"Let's get those seats," Scott said, leading the way to chairs closest to the railing that ran along the balcony. It was already packed with people perched along the edge, bobbing their heads to a band down below. Several girls pretended not to notice Kiran as we passed, but couldn't keep their eyes off him.

I sank into a seat next to Kiran, who drew me closer as I peered nervously over the crowd, trying to catch sight of Kacey again.

"Do you see Kace down there?" Taylor leaned towards me.

I shook my head, scanning the floor below with growing unease.

I checked the side stage area, hoping to catch sight of her there. Still nothing. Frustrated, I scanned the floor below, and my eyes fell on Sorcha with her arms raised up around Sam's neck.

A rumbling noise rolled over the crowd, then suddenly, blackness engulfed the room. High-pitched screams cut through the air. An electric guitar riff splintered through the room, followed by rapid drumbeats and a wailing bass line. Lights shattered the darkness, exploding around us. Phen strode across the stage still naked to his waist. I spotted Kacey on the side stage, completely enthralled by him.

The band crashed into their first song, and Kiran squeezed my hand tightly as he pulled me against him. Scott was right; it got loud fast. Bodies packed like sardines below surged closer to the stage—an energy flooding from girls near fainting directly into Phen's hands.

Mia shrieked from next to Steve, "This song is insane!" She grabbed onto Taylor, pulling her toward the railing for a better view.

The lyrics wrapped around me, lights slicing across the ceiling and walls until I forgot to breathe. Phen stalked the stage like a predator—taunting, circling, owning every inch of it. His voice was low and throaty, almost a growl. The girls below screamed every word back at him as if he had already reached inside their minds and taken hold.

I could feel his magnetism swelling through the building, pulling at every person there. Then his dark eyes seemed to lock on me. His mouth curled into a smirk, and he lifted one arm out toward us, suddenly growling the lyrics that roared over the music and crowd.

"I fell from the choir, wings turned to coal

Dragged down by a whisper, burned into soul"

His gaze swept across Kiran before sliding back to me. I knew it was some kind of challenge, but refused to let it rattle me.

"One eye to the stars, one knee in the dust

Power's a poison—they told me I must

Hold it like fire, carve it in bone

Now I stand in the ruins, throneless and alone"

I trembled slightly against Kiran. *"His lyrics...they're so...,"* I mind spoke to him.

His lips brushed my ear gently. "It's his story."

There was something deeply unsettling about watching Phen command a room—the way people leaned toward him like plants toward light, as if they'd follow him anywhere. They would. My blood ran cold. They had no idea what he really was.

"Heaven closed its gates, Hell won't take the blame

Now I burn with both—

And I wear their flame

I speak and they tremble, they kneel or they run

But I forgot what it means to be anyone

Grace is gone, and guilt's my flame

Still I rise—

Still I rise—"

Chills moved through me as the last note faded. My mind twisted with it—Phen. Phenix. A phoenix. My eyes dragged over him slowly, and something snagged my attention. The tattoo looked different. It had shifted since the last time I'd seen it—more of it now spread across his chest, wings stretched wider than before. But it was the eyes of the bird that stopped me cold. They were fiery and bright, and disturbingly, terrifyingly real.

Phen prowled back to center stage, shirtless and vibrant under the searing lights. He lifted a fist into the air as drums and guitar thundered together. A frenzy rippled through the mob below, girls screeching madly with their hands reaching out towards him.

"Kiran," I mind spoke to him. *"Phen's tattoo...it's different now. Its head was on his back the last time I saw him, and now it's on his shoulder."*

The crowd below erupted in cheers as a hazy red fog spread across the stage, and Phen's lips curled into a smile. Phen's chest glistened with sweat as he glanced over towards Kacey, never missing a beat. She danced at the side of the stage, spellbound. I watched her with an uneasy ache knotting in my stomach.

I felt Kiran slide his arm behind me, pulling me close. His eyes stayed hard on Phen. "There is a power in that tattoo," he said into my ear. "It must be a being that has sworn fealty to Phen. A vassel."

My breath caught. Of course—the swirling image of fire—it made haunting sense. *"So his vassel is an immortal bird that's reborn from fire?"*

Still I rise...

"That doesn't make sense. Phen himself is a phoenix. Why would he need a vassel of a phoenix?" Kiran replied.

"Maybe it isn't an actual phoenix?"

The drummer pounded out percussion like exploding stars. The notes spun like galaxies as Phen dropped to his knees, singing straight to Kacey, who was hypnotized by every word.

Taylor slumped into a seat beside me, eyes wide with concern. "She's in deep. I'm serious, Rhi."

"She'll be okay," I said into her ear, unsure who I was trying to convince.

Phen's voice dropped into something velvet and low for the last verse. I gripped the railing as he moved toward the edge of the stage, slid a hand along Kacey's side, then pulled her up onto the stage like he owned every inch of it. Like he owned her. They embraced, and he swept back her hair, kissing her deeply in front of everyone.

The sound that tore through the room was primal. Taylor's eyes went narrow with disbelief beside me. I took in the ripple along the floor—the response prompted by Phen and Kacey's sudden display—and felt my nails dig tightly into my palms.

Phen's lips left Kacey's neck as he curled an arm possessively around her waist. He moved his mouth back to the mic, "Do you all know my girlfriend?"

The crowd erupted into a booming noise. Some screaming with enthusiasm and others with dismay. "This is my heart," Phen said thick with emotion so deep, it stopped even me cold for a second. "We'll be back in five," Phen said as they disappeared off stage together to a chorus of disappointment.

Taylor launched out of her seat, mouth set in a determined line. "Let's go," she said. Scott followed her up as she wove quickly through the crowd. Kiran and I scrambled after her.

I darted past Steve, who was engrossed in conversation with Mia. She whispered something into his ear before his lips met hers, and they were lost in each other, oblivious to us taking off.

Kiran pulled me past a cluster of people to catch up with Taylor and Scott. The crowd was packed in tightly—bodies and noise folding around us as we squeezed through waves of fans still screaming for Phen. Taylor bulldozed the crowd, her focus on nothing but getting to her.

Sam hovered by a doorway at the back of the club like he'd been expecting us, Sorcha at his side. Sam smiled at me, letting a small flicker of light slip over his fingertips, barely perceptible through the darkness. The door swung open on its own, unlocking smoothly into blackness beyond.

Taylor's tight steps bounced against the dingy floor as she stormed ahead of us. "Kacey!" Taylor yelled, disappearing around a corner with a sign labeled Bands Only.

Taylor shoved the door open. We crowded into the doorway. Kacey's eyes flew open—startled—from where Phen had her pressed against the wall, his mouth trailing slowly below her jaw.

Phen pressed one more kiss against Kacey's neck, pulling her tightly against him. "Oh, Hello," he purred, dark eyes rolling over each of us.

"Get your hands off my sister!" Taylor's voice cut through the haze that swirled around the two of them.

Kacey squirmed in Phen's embrace, her face flushed crimson with anger. "What are you guys doing?" she said sharply. "This is none of your business!"

Phen lowered her gently to the floor, running a finger down her cheek. "Show them around back. I'll be there soon."

She pouted up at him but nodded. "Fine," she said with an exaggerated sigh as Phen slid his arm away. He began to move away from her, but Kacey tugged on his arm, catching his mouth with hers for another kiss. She glared at Taylor while she did it, making a point.

Taylor moved instantly, grabbing onto Kacey's wrist. "Let's go!" she snapped, pulling Kacey with her as Scott followed.

Phen watched with amusement, leaning against a wall.

The air felt charged as Kiran spoke. "We need to talk, Phenix."

Chapter Twenty-Six

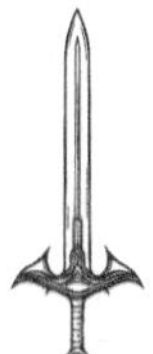

Kiran

Rhi leaned against me as I leaned down to speak into her ear, "You should go with your cousins. Sam and I have this."

She shook her head vehemently. Of course, she wouldn't listen. Rhi tilted her face up to mine, eyes determined. "I'm not going anywhere. I can help."

Stubborn. My heart ached with both exasperation and fierce admiration.

I caught Phen's eye as he pushed off the wall and picked up a beer from the table.

"Did she tell you what we chatted about the other night?" He gestured at Rhi with the bottle.

"She did. What about it?"

He raised an eyebrow. There was a subtle timing to Phen's movements, like he had all the time in the world. "Is it not obvious? Do you know who she is?"

"Like I would tell you if I did." I snorted.

Rhi took a step away from me, "Your tattoo," she said, eyeing him cautiously. "You have a being in it? A vassel?"

A look of shock crossed Phen's features, then smoothed out. "Clever girl."

Sam moved abruptly, stepping in to glare at Phen. "Seriously, Phen? What is wrong with you, man? You've always been so chill. Never cared about power or glory. " He spread his arms wide in disbelief. "Since when are you binding souls as vassels? And what do you want with Rhi?"

Phen didn't appear threatened. "Maybe I simply want to be her friend." His voice was calm, still carrying that bemused half-smile.

"Sure you do." Sam sneered as he studied Phen, "Are you planning to take over Hell?"

Phen set his beer down on the table, then turned back around to face us. "You think I'm after rulership? Please. Who in their right mind would want that much responsibility?"

"Then what?" Sam insisted.

Phen crossed his arms over his muscled chest, and I swore I saw the tattoo move. "All kings find thrones heavy, and draw courtiers like moths to flame. You mistake my ambitions, Sam. Some men want to rule. Some simply want to be free."

My mouth formed a retort, but he kept going. "You think power tempts me?" He shakes his head, mocking. "No. Only autonomy. Only the blessing of choosing one's own damnation."

It's...weirdly beautiful, in a way that makes my skin crawl.

Phen's expression becomes dreamy, but the way he looked at us was anything but gentle. "You want prophecy? Or poetry?" He swirled his beer and tipped it in Rhi's direction. "There's a difference, you know. All prophecy is poetry, but not all poetry is prophecy. Sometimes it's only a way to let the pain out."

"I'm not asking for a riddle, I'm asking for honesty." Rhi snaps.

"Honesty?" The word is a challenge tossed between him and Rhi. "That's a dangerous wish, Rhiannon. The world wobbles on polite lies. You pull the pin on a real truth; you'd better be ready for shrapnel."

"So go ahead then. Why am I so interesting? Or is your real secret that you don't know either?" Rhi says between clenched teeth.

"From the beginning, people like you...you disrupt things. No carefully scripted order, no balance." I'm not sure if he means Rhi's family or just her, or if it makes a difference. "I respect your bloodline, but I'm not your family therapist."

Sam bristled, and I can feel Rhi's anger boiling over.

"Look, if it helps—what you want, what you're poking around for—none of it matters to me. The only game I play is my own. None of this is my problem." Phen says with a bored tone.

"Whose problem is it then?" Rhi asks.

I reached back to find her hand and squeezed it tight.

Something cold and dangerous coasted beneath Phen's smile as he spoke. "Yours."

The silence lingered like smoke; no one moved.

"Mine?" Rhi whispered, placing her hand on her chest.

"It's about setting things right," Phen said, staring intently at Rhi.

"Whose version of right is that exactly?" Sam's hands ball into fists at his side.

Phen shrugged and took a long drink before speaking. "Consider this version of right: The original state of things. The way it was meant to be."

"You're talking in riddles again," I growled.

"Not riddles." Phen's tone softens like he was trying to get through to us. "How do you suppose girls like you are made, Rhi? Do you think it's an accident?

Rhi flinched. Her eyes darted to me, questioning.

He locked eyes with me, a strange glow pulsing in their depths, and for once, his voice dropped the bravado and went flatly honest. "You think it's chaos, but it's always about balance. No matter which side you're on, every Heaven needs its Hell. Every martyr needs a devil for contrast.

I arched an eyebrow at him. "And do you think you are the one to bring balance or chaos?"

Phen laughed, "Me? No. But I know that imbalance is why people like Kiran and Justin never should have existed."

I clenched my fist, blood roaring in my ears. "People like us?"

"Half-breeds," Phen said coolly.

"I am not a half-breed!"

"Yes, you are," Phen cut me off. "You are half angel and half human."

"I am not!" I shot back, my voice thunderous. "Michael—"

"Pfft-Michael. He's been interfering since the dawn of time." He gave Sam a pointed look. "Sam knows what I mean."

Sam seemed to go pale.

Phen took a step closer to me, looking me straight in the eyes, "Michael took your human soul to try and maintain balance. You and Justin are twins, correct?" Phen's expression was infuriatingly calm. "One would be born a Nephilim, and the other soul made into an angel. That does not negate the fact that you, my friend, are a half-breed."

I felt Rhi tense beside me, and Sam shifted uncomfortably.

"And you," Phen turned to Sam, "didn't your kind start all this by falling in love with humans?"

"My *kind?*" Sam looked like he might leap at him.

"The Watchers," Phen said. "Losing focus on your true purpose. To watch. Correct?" He lifted an eyebrow.

We could hear the crowd outside, chanting for Phen. A low rumble was building like an oncoming storm. A grin spread across his face. He lifted the beer and chugged the rest before slamming it on the table.

I don't trust him. Why should I? He's a demon, and a powerful one. He told Justin he would cage me in Hell for him. I wrapped my arm around Rhi's waist again, desperate to feel her warmth.

"Sorry, kids. Got to run. The natives are getting restless." He gave a mocking bow. "Keep in mind what I said. My blood is on the line just like yours." Phen was already moving toward the door.

Rhi slipped away from me and stepped in front of him, a defiant spark in her eyes. "Why are you with Kacey?"

Something crossed over Phen's features. It was softness, a crack in the callous exterior. "I get it," he said quietly. "I understand wanting what humans have. To feel their warmth and be the recipient of love that is given so freely." He grinned wolfishly, "Demons crave it too."

Phen moved his shoulders, and fiery wings erupted from his back. Rhi screamed, putting her hand over her mouth with disbelieving eyes. "I will admit, I just wanted Kacey as a plaything. His fingers grazed over some of the flamed wings until small flames danced on his fingertips. "She is so...good though. So...happy. And her hair.

The color is so much like my fire." His eyes watched as the small flames grew bigger, and he twirled them in his fingers. As fast as the wings appeared, they disappeared.

He put a hand on my shoulder, and I glared menacingly at him, "I'm not really against you half-breeds. But there has to be a balance. And tilting it one way or the other? I'm sure you know how devastating that can be."

He seemed to look through us as he spoke. "Even if you wanted to tilt the balance for good to use on some evil being like Vince," he continued. "It'd still give one side too much power. The Principalities knew this." He glanced directly at me. "Maybe you should find one of them and ask about it."

The Principalities? Did he know about the Ossaris? About Rhi? Coldness seeped into my bones at the thought.

The phoenix tattoo definitely moved as Phen looked at Rhi, then the rest of us. "Now, I have a show to put on." His eyes flashed red as he opened the door. A loud guitar riff blared from the stage, nearly drowning out the sound of the door banging shut. My mind was in a state of confusion, anger, and disbelief at everything I had just heard. I didn't believe he was telling us the whole truth for a minute.

The rain had settled into a drizzle outside as we left the club. Kacey had found Phen again; her arms wrapped around him, refusing to let him go and whispering something that made him laugh. I couldn't tell if she was truly oblivious or just that in love with him already. Either way, she was clinging so tightly I half expected him to get annoyed. He didn't, though; he seemed to languish in her attention. Finally, Phen pried himself away, blowing a kiss as Kacey made her way to us.

Both Kacey and Rhi were silent in the car. I drove through the streaked lights of the city, my thoughts racing.

Kacey said dreamily, "Phen is so...wow." She hadn't wanted to go home with Steve with Taylor in the car after the blow-up between them.

"That's one word for it," Rhi muttered. I reached for her hand at a red light. She squeezed back, but her eyes remained distant, lost somewhere I couldn't follow.

We dropped Kacey off at her house. She slipped out of the car, shooting Rhi a glance, and then turned to me with a slight smile. "Thanks for the ride, Kiran."

I arched a brow at Rhi as we pulled back onto the street. "I still don't get why Phen's with her."

Rhi shrugged, "Maybe he does really care about her as he said."

I watched the streetlights flicker past, the rain blurring them into streaks of color. "Or maybe it's just another part of his game," I said, glancing in the mirror.

She exhaled heavily. "Maybe."

Rhi was silent as I walked her into the house and to her room. I could see the strain of the night wearing on her. Once we reached her room, she sat on the bed, looking at me with tired eyes. "I still don't know what to think of all this," she said, her voice quiet.

I knelt in front of her, brushing hair from her cheek. "We'll figure it out. I promise."

She nodded, but I saw the doubt hovering like a shadow. She changed into a long white t-shirt and scooted under the covers as I stretched out beside her. Her breathing softened into sleep, and I watched the tension release from her shoulders. Her hair fanned over the pillow in waves, her lashes delicate shadows over her pale cheeks. It was so difficult not to touch my lips to her hair, to protect and hold her close.

Her face smoothed into a quiet peace, and I got up to watch the rain. The sound, the smell of rain always brought me peace. Something flickered in the backyard. I squinted into the darkness, and there he was, that Guardian I'd only glanced a few times, lounging in the rain, which didn't seem to touch him. He had a pipe in his mouth, and the smoke spiraled lazily above him.

He glanced up and gave me a nod. Strange. He'd never acknowledged me before, but then again, I never really acknowledged him either. His clothes belong to another century: high-waisted pants, a pinstriped vest, a maroon jacket with long coattails, and a derby hat sitting low on his forehead.

I turned back to Rhi. Still sleeping soundly. Her face was calm, and I wanted to keep it that way. I focused, shifting into the backyard and appearing beside the Guardian.

"Hello," I said to him.

"Hello," he said, tipping his hat towards me. "I'm glad you finally decided to speak to me." He took a long drag from the pipe. A smile flickered at his lips.

"You could have spoken to me."

He laughed through his nose, a single amused snort. "I suppose I could have, but I needed to see how this all played out."

"You're Mrs. Crandall's Guardian." It wasn't a question because what else could he be?

"Something like that." He exhaled a plume of smoke that seemed to take on shapes, twisting and turning into vague figures before dissolving into the damp air.

I watched it dissipate. "Something?" I frowned, not liking that answer. "Why are you here then?"

"I was watching her. But you? You're the interesting one now." He studied me, silver eyes glinting. "Quite the scandal you've made of yourself."

"Scandal?"

"Mmm." Another cloud of smoke, this one forming wings. "You know, boy loves girl, girl loves boy. Girl finds out she has a Guardian Angel, angel loves girl. Girl falls for angel too. Oh and the two she loves are brothers."

An invisible pressure squeezed at my chest. "You make it sound so…"

"Enticing? Devious? Scandalous?"

I shook my head, "Why do you even care?"

He shrugged, "I don't really. It's just entertaining. Everyone likes a good story."

"Why aren't you around more often? I barely see you protecting your ward."

"Stay around humans too much, and they awake…feelings." His words were steady. He packed more tobacco into his pipe and lit it with a silver lighter, the tiny flame reflecting in his eyes like incandescent stars. "Those human feelings."

"She didn't awaken them." I tried to keep my voice calm. "They've been there all along."

He nodded, as if conceding the point. "Such is the problem, you know. Especially for an angel created from a human soul."

He gave me an unsettling grin like he knew something I didn't. I tensed. "How do you even know? How do you know I'm…"

"The Archangels are always trying to keep balance. Always trying to fix things by creating new problems. Michael, Gabriel, Raphael, the rest of them. They are more like Lucifer than they would like to admit, don't you think?" He paused, gauging my reaction.

I stiffened, Phen's words tonight sounding eerily similar. I forced out with a scoff. "You're wrong. Michael is nothing like that."

"Isn't he?" He let out a sharp laugh. "He thinks he knows better than the Creator. They all do."

"Who are you?" I asked, examining him skeptically.

"Oh, forgive me. My name is Ophaniel, Principality of Mirrors."

I blinked at him, my breath catching.

"You have heard of me," Ophaniel said, watching my reaction with an amused tilt to his mouth.

I nodded slowly, trying to make sense of it.

"You're not a Guardian then?"

"I am not." He spread his arms like he was welcoming the rain. "She has no guard, and frankly, it is quite odd that your ward has you."

"Ossaris are given Principalities." My voice was rough in my own ears.

"Indeed, they are."

"But you don't guard them?" I asked.

He chuckled softly, "More like guide them."

"Not always on the right path, though, do you?"

The corner of his lips lifted. "There's no thrill if there's no danger."

I fought the tremor in my voice. "Why are you here? Why now?"

"Balance." He shrugged. "Or imbalance." The smoke from his pipe slipped into the air like an ornate signature before being swallowed by the rain.

I narrowed my eyes at him. "So Ms. Crandall is an Ossaris?"

"Yes, and when one of her heirs comes of age, the powers and the Principality will go to the heir. That leaves her without a Guardian." He shrugged. "It's not like everyone on Earth has one."

"What about her children? She has a daughter —Rhi's mother, and a son — her cousin's father."

"It skips a generation...usually." He paused, fingers tapping lightly on the pipe. "It's not like everyone has a Guardian, and she has more knowledge than most mortals." Ophaniel leaned back and gestured with his pipe. The smoke blurred, almost forming letters like a message he expected me to read. "When her husband, Mr. Crandall, passed, Nireth was his Principality. She should have gone to the eldest heir."

"But she didn't. Taylor didn't even know what she was until we found the books left by Rhi's grandfather." A sudden gust of wind blew my hair across my face, and I let it cover my eyes for a moment as my thoughts collided. Pushing it out of my face, I stared at the Principality, "Where is Nireth?" I finally said.

"Mmmm," Ophaniel hummed. "That is something I don't know." Ophaniel packed his pipe again. "I told you, the Archangels are more like demons than they care to admit." He paused again, waiting for me to speak.

"Michael wouldn't—"

"Michael has always interfered as he sees fit," Ophaniel cut in. "Caging Fallen ones. Mapping out his own tidy little universe." He leaned back, watching me with an unsettling calm. "He has a history of tying up loose ends."

A chill ran through me.

Ophaniel brushed at his clothes. "I suspect even you are one of those loose ends."

I felt like the ground had disappeared beneath me as he began to walk away, smoke trailing from the pipe behind him.

He turned once more. "If I were you, I'd help your ward and her cousins explore their powers."

"Wait!" I yelled after him, but Ophaniel's silhouette faded into the shadows of the night.

First Phen mentioned balance, and now this Principality does. It would seem this is one of the missing pieces to this bizarre puzzle. I hadn't trusted anything Phen had said, and even though Ophaniel was an angel, I didn't trust his words either. It seemed no one did anything for the better good of everyone. They all had an ulterior motive, a selfish motive. If I thought about it, I was the same. I chose to show myself to Rhi in the hopes she would love me.

The drizzle fell into a heavier rain. It was cold and damp. I teleported back inside, to where Rhi was still sleeping soundly. Her face was so soft, so peaceful. I wanted to protect it, to protect her, from this chaos that seemed to follow us everywhere.

I sat on the bed and rested an arm over her, and then a wing to cocoon us together and away from the world outside. I didn't want to be a piece on someone's board. Not Phen's, not Michael's, not any of theirs. I wanted to belong to her completely, without the interference of the immortals. The rain was slowing. I watched it pattern the window in long streams. It mirrored the thoughts streaming through me in a frantic race to sort it all out.

Rhi was an Ossaris, or would be when she turned eighteen. But she had me, a Guardian, when the others did not. A direct suggestion from Michael to make her my ward, but it was our soul song that had sealed our bond, not Michael. Was me being her protector enough to deal with the chaos that surrounded us? Or was I a loose end? The scope of it all was staggering, but this I knew for certain: Rhi was in danger. From whom or what, I didn't know.

Ophaniel said that an Ossaris's power could be used for selfish purposes. No matter what the intent was—angel or demon—the power of an Ossaris tipped the balance, and it tipped it in a way that affected all of us.

The word balance haunted me. Half-breeds...Justin and I were abominations to the celestials. Ossaris should not exist. They were created by the Archangels.

Balance, it seemed, was gone.

Chapter Twenty-Seven

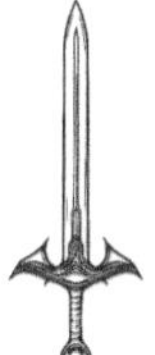

Justin

I slid out from under an old Buick, hands black with grease. This...this was the only thing that kept my mind off of *her*. What it didn't do was keep my mind off of Vince, Phen, and this whole being a supernatural thing. And Rhi had Ossaris blood running through her veins? I wondered if she even knew what she truly was. The irony wasn't lost on me—after all my anger about secrets being kept from me, here I was withholding crucial information about her own identity. I should never have let Sam take that book.

"Justin's Car Palace," Blue called out from somewhere over by the parts shelves.

"Nah, that's lame," Taz said, sifting through some tools. "What about Lube & Lube?"

I shook my head, laughing despite myself. Blue snorted, elbowing him. "Geez, Taz, you really do have the brain of a junior high kid."

"That's what makes me so valuable," Taz shot back, tapping a finger on his head. "Market insight."

The shop smelled like oil and burnt coffee. It was Vince's. His name was still on the sign outside, a reminder of everything I was trying to forget. Vince. Phen. Rhi.

Taz tossed an oily rag at my head. "We could just call it Vengeance?"

I caught the rag mid-air. "Doesn't sound very welcoming."

"What about Fallen Autos?" Blue said, ducking out from between the shelves with a mischievous grin.

Fallen. My mind went there too quickly. *To him. To her.* "No," I said, a little harder than I meant to. Both Taz and Blue paused. "Keep going. We'll think of something."

They shrugged it off. Blue grabbed a wrench and started tinkering with an old carburetor. Taz moved on to another brainstorming session with himself, comically serious. "Horsepower Nation? RPMs R Us?"

I looked around. The place was mine now. If you could call an inheritance from the guy who tried to kill you an inheritance. Everything Vince ever owned he forfeited when he made his choices.

"Could just call it Justin's," Blue said over her shoulder. "Since, you know, you're trying to make it yours."

Simple. Clean. She meant it sarcastically, but it wasn't half bad.

My phone buzzed in my pocket. I took a clean rag to wipe off my hands. Mom. Wanting to know if I'd come for family dinner this week. I hadn't been since everything happened.

I shoved the phone back in my jeans.

Taz lined up spark plugs like chess pieces. "You should just call it Justin's," he said.

"Hey, I'm heading out," I said, grabbing my old leather jacket draped over a chair.

Taz looked up, half-surprised. "You coming back later?"

"Nah. Probably not."

The air felt colder than it probably was, like a premonition. I slid into my car and felt that same pull — dragging me toward the same places. The park. Sal's Bakery. The whole town was soaked in memories of Rhi and me, back before everything exploded.

I kept driving. Avoiding. It was the only thing I was good at these days. Mom's text flashed in my mind. She'd texted me nearly every day. I barely answered, and when I did, it was just to say I was fine. I slammed the gas and nearly took out a garbage can.

I had half a mind to just keep going, past her place, past this screwed-up town, but I turned left on Eighth and circled back to the house I grew up in, shutting off the car in the driveway. I let myself in. The door had been unlocked. I had warned them. Warned them Vince was out for all of us, and she still kept the door unlocked.

"Justin?" Her voice wavered as I walked down the hall.

"Yeah," I said, doing my best to sound solid. Like nothing bothered me. Like, I didn't care. She hurried in from the kitchen, looking like she hadn't slept in weeks. Dark circles under her eyes, hair pulled back with strands spilling free. Her shoulders hunched beneath a loose blouse. "I didn't know if you'd come," she said, voice small and hopeful. She stepped forward and wrapped her arms around me.

She felt so small. So breakable. I held on longer than I meant to. It hit me harder than I expected — the worry and love written all over her face. All these years, I'd blamed her. For Vince. For my whole life, I've felt like a lie. But it was never her. She'd been just one more person he'd manipulated.

She leaned back as her eyes searched mine like she was trying to read how much of me was left. Her hand rested gently on my chest. "Where is the cross I gave you?"

The cross. I had pulled it from my neck when I learned the truth. What that cross did was hide my true identity from me and others. I gave it to Kiran. Something inside me telling me I should. Telling him to give it to her...to Rhi.

I rubbed a palm over my face. "I still have it. Just taking a break from wearing it."

She looked hurt, pulling her hand back. She didn't know what it really was or who the real person was who gave it to her. Sam. She smiled up at me. "Well, I'm glad you're here. I have lasagna in the oven."

I heard voices coming from the hallway. It was Taylor and Scott. Taylor carried the baby carrier, Scott trailing behind. As they made their way towards the kitchen, they stopped and stared. Shocked, I showed up, I suppose.

Mom was already reaching for the baby carrier in Taylor's hand. "Come here, little princess," she cooed, unbuckling the tiny, wriggling baby fastened inside.

Taylor walked right up to me. "Can we talk? Privately?"

"Sure," I said, not needing to hear what Taylor had to say to know it would involve scolding me about something. "Let's go outside."

"Don't take too long," Scott said. "Dinner's almost ready, and I'm starving."

Taylor tugged at my arm, pulling me towards the back door. My dad was in the garage, sifting through some boxes. Rick looked up when he heard us coming. My dad. With the kindest blue eyes. He was probably the most hurt by all this. He had no idea what Vince did; he just thought my mom cheated on him, and the son he thought he knew wasn't really his. But, I was his — much more than Vince's. This man raised me, and guilt washed over me, realizing that he raised me to act better than how I had for years now.

"Justin, my son." He hugged me to him tightly. "I'm glad you're here."

His son. Yes, I was Rick Rizzo's son. I would not claim Vince.

Never.

"Dinner is almost ready," Taylor said. "You should go inside."

That was weird, like really weird. I never heard Taylor's voice sound like that. She always had a near-annoyingly chipper voice.

We walked around to the side of the house. "What's up?"

She turned her blue eyes on me. "That guy, Phen? He's staying with you at Vince's place, isn't he?"

I almost laughed, but the look in her eyes made me stop. "Why?" It was the last thing I thought she'd want to talk about. Taylor and I never really talked.

"He's dating my sister, and I don't want that demon around her."

Taylor had called the night after Rhi and Kiran showed up at her place while I was there. Her voice was tight and measured. "Please call me, Justin. I need to talk to you about Rhi and...what you are."

That phone call was awkward.

I lifted my eyebrows. "Kacey? Is he dating Kacey? But she's so..."

"So?" Taylor prompted. She crossed her arms, the hint of annoyance around her mouth.

"So...sweet. Don't ever tell her I said that."

Taylor looked stunned for a second, and then smiled, a real one. "I'll take it to my grave."

"Does she know? Know what he is?" I asked.

Taylor's smile faded. "No."

She gave me a long look. "If he brings her to that house, I need you to keep her safe."

"I'll do what I can," I said. "Not like she's a fan of mine."

"Yeah," Taylor said, biting her lip. She looked down at the ground. "But at least you're there, right? At least there's someone to keep an eye on her." Taylor looked deflated. Her shoulders sank, and she glanced at me with real vulnerability. "How did you do it? Accept all this crazy stuff? This new world you didn't understand?"

"I didn't. Not really. Not at first." I laughed to myself. "Hell, I don't know if I do now."

She nodded. I saw a different side of her. One that didn't have it all together. One that maybe didn't hate me. "It's exhausting, pretending it doesn't exist. Sometimes I just want things to go back to normal."

"Normal's overrated," I said and leaned back against the side of the house.

Taylor's expression cracked, and I could tell she was close to crying. I'd rarely seen that. She always seemed so solid, so sure of everything. "It's overwhelming," she said. "I just don't want her to get hurt."

I didn't say anything for a minute. I just watched her. It was like reassessing a person you thought you knew. "Listen," I said finally. "I can't promise it'll be fine, but I'll let you know if I see her getting in too deep."

Taylor's shoulders relaxed a little. "Thanks," she said quietly.

"Justin! Taylor!" Mom called from the back door.

"I guess we should go in."

"Yeah," Taylor said. "And try to act like we're normal."

Inside, the house was warm, thick with the smell of lasagna and herbs. I stepped into the kitchen, catching my mother's eye. She smiled, but a shadow of worry crossed her face before she turned to toss a salad.

We sat at the table, silent for a while, only broken by the clinking of forks. I pushed my food around, nodding at all the right moments, my mind miles away.

"So, you're staying at Vince's house?" Mom asked, her voice too casual. She passed a dish to Taylor, not quite meeting my eyes.

"Vince is gone, for good, I think. But you should still be careful. He's dangerous."

After dinner, I slipped away to my room. It felt foreign, like a hotel room. I stared at my bed and the floor where I first kissed Rhi. That was one reason I didn't want to stay here anymore. I grabbed a duffel bag and started throwing in clothes.

I looked around, remembering how things used to be. I zipped the bag, hoisted it over my shoulder, and headed downstairs, leaving those memories behind.

Taylor stood at the bottom of the stairs. "I think you should come over to Kiran's tomorrow."

Kiran's? I didn't know he had a house. "Why?"

"We have books and papers. A lot of information. I think you should be part of it." I started to shake my head when Taylor added, "Also, we're bringing Steve over after school. He needs to know what he is, and you might help him grasp it."

She sounded so sure. I wasn't. "I don't know."

"It'll help," Taylor said. "It'll help all of us."

I nodded, "Text me the address. I'll be there."

Mom caught me on the way out. She had the baby in her arms, bouncing and swaying as moms do. "You don't have to leave so soon, do you?"

"She's right," Dad said, coming up behind her. "We haven't even had dessert."

"Next week," I said, already edging towards the door. "I'll be here. Promise."

I threw the duffel bag in the back of my car. I sat behind the wheel and released a long breath. I twisted the ignition, not sure where I'd end up. The pull was strong, dragging me back towards the place I said I wouldn't go. To her house. I could sneak into her room like I used to. Kiss her, hold her...

I sat there in front of her grandmother's house, half hoping she'd see me, half dreading it. I pressed my forehead to the steering wheel and willed myself to drive away. It should've been easy. So why was I still here? I looked up at the house and felt it — how much I missed her. More than I'd ever missed anyone in my life. I wanted to see her so damn bad. The way her eyes lit up. The way her hands felt on my face. The way she made me feel like I was the only thing in her world — before Kiran came and took all of that away. My hand drifted to my phone. I could text her. Just one message. She'd come out. I knew she would.

Leave Kiran behind.

I could convince her. Make her realize that what we had was more. More than she's ever felt for him. I felt it, saw it.

My fingers hovered over my phone. Itching to just hit send.

Another text came in. I felt the irritation rise, but I checked it anyway. It was from Taylor. The address for Kiran's house. I felt my eyes grow.

The address was on this road.

"Seriously?" I said to myself. I stared at the glowing screen.

For a second, I thought I should just walk up to that door and say what I needed to say. But the other part of me — the part that still couldn't decide, the part that was terrified of what she might say back — went cold.

Cold like a coward.

I drove off, leaving the house behind me, leaving her behind me.

For now.

Chapter Twenty-Eight

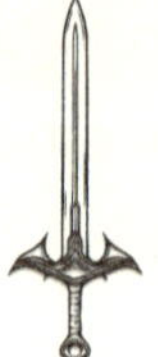

Rhiannon

Taylor and I had discussed telling Steve about all of this. Kacey too. But she felt Kacey was too wrapped up in Phen, and she didn't want her accidentally slipping up around him. It was dangerous. It was better that she and Phen both thought she was just a normal teenage girl.

Then Taylor called last night, telling me she had invited Justin over. "Why?" I had asked.

She seemed to think it would help Steve understand this new reality. Like my word and hers wouldn't be enough?

So now we sat in Kiran's house as he leaned against the wall, his silver eyes watching me as baby Eva lay in my lap, pulling at my hair.

"It's gonna be fine, Rhi. You'll see." Taylor said, taking the baby from me.

Kiran gave me one of his unshakably serene smiles, though a flicker of tension passed through his jaw. Whatever he was feeling—jealousy, anger, defiance—he was keeping it buried deep.

"Let's see," Taylor said, sitting cross-legged on the floor. Her pale blonde hair fell down her back as Eva reached for it now. She flipped through the latest box Kiran had brought over from my grandfather's office. "This looks interesting. It says something about a bound soul or a tethered shade."

Kiran's face seemed to stiffen as Taylor handed the notebook to me, and I thumbed through the brittle pages. The ancient doorbell rang, and I jumped.

Kiran left the room as I searched over the handwritten text. *These spirits or humans are bound to a demon's will.* Fear skittered down my spine.

I raised my head at the footsteps coming down the hall. Kiran came through the doorway, Steve and Justin in tow. Both of their eyes were filled with wariness as they scanned the room. Then Justin's eyes locked onto mine.

"Make yourself at home," Kiran said.

Steve sat down in a chair near Taylor. Justin stayed standing, his gaze never leaving me. "I feel like I walked in on someone's garage sale. What's all this?" Steve asked.

"Old stuff from Pop's office," Taylor said. Then, leaning closer to Steve, she whispered, "Remember, keep an open mind."

"Sure," Steve said, picking up a notebook. "Totally open."

Justin finally moved, settling against a corner of the room, hands shoved deep into his pockets. He looked like he wanted to say something, but he kept silent.

"Maybe it's better if you just tell him, Rhi," Taylor said.

Kiran came and stood behind me, his presence a warm reassurance. "I know this sounds crazy," I started, feeling the heat rise to my face. "But it's all true. Pop's was...involved in some supernatural stuff. And, well, so am I. We all are."

Steve laughed, but his eyes darted around the room nervously, landing on each of us. "Okay, okay," he said, throwing up his hands. "Who put you all up to this?"

"It's not a prank," Taylor insisted.

He tossed the notebook back at Taylor. "You guys know April Fool's is months away."

The doorbell rang again, a shrill echo through the tension. Kiran gave me a quick look before heading down the hall.

Taylor leaned in closer to Steve, her eyes big and serious. "You have to believe us. There are these things called Ossaris—"

"Taylor," Steve interrupted, shaking his head, "when have you ever known me to fall for something like this?"

"It's not a joke," I said, as firmly as I could with my heart pounding loud in my ears. "Pop's had all these notes. He knew about Ossaris, how they..."

Steve cut me off with another laugh, more uncertain this time. "Have you all lost your mind?" He turned towards Justin. "Are you in on this, too?"

Before Justin could answer, footsteps sounded in the hallway, and Kiran reappeared, followed closely by Sam and Mia.

"Got room for the rest of us?" Sam asked, grinning. He flopped down in one of the big chairs, crossing one booted foot over his knee.

Mia crossed the room towards Steve, sitting lithely on the arm of his chair. Her eyes danced as she looked around. "Are you finally telling him?"

Steve turned to her in disbelief, "Wait, so you're in on this, too?"

"You have to believe us, Steve," Taylor said. "It's not a joke."

Just show him," Sam said, waving a hand towards Kiran.

Kiran frowned, his silver eyes darting to mine.

"Maybe you should," I said hesitantly, feeling a knot tighten in my stomach, "Show him what you are."

"What he *is*?" Steve asked, confusion in his voice.

"Ohh, you're gonna love this," Mia said, her lips curving into an amused smile.

Kiran seemed to accept it, the tension easing from his shoulders. He moved to an open part of the room and unfurled his wings.

They were huge, white with a silver iridescence shimmering across each feather like moonlight on water. A bright, soft glow enveloped him, bathing the room in ethereal light.

Steve stared, his mouth hanging open. The color had drained from his face. "This isn't..." he started, his voice a dry whisper. "It can't be real."

"It is," Taylor said, clutching Eva a little closer, her eyes wide with awe even after she had seen Kiran's wings before.

"But he's—" Steve's brain seemed to falter, lost in a universe unknown to him.

"He's an angel," Taylor finished softly, a small smile playing at the corners of her lips.

Kiran folded the light back into himself, the wings vanishing in an instant.

Steve ran a hand through his hair, wild disbelief written all over his face.

"As I said," Taylor said gently. "It's not a joke."

Mia slid down into Steve's lap, swinging her legs as she leaned in close. "See? I told you!" She wrapped her arms around his shoulders, her bracelets clinking. "And Sam's one too....an angel, well actually, a Watcher. And I'm a witch, but you knew that already."

Steve blinked, trying to comprehend. "I didn't think you were serious about that."

"Why would I lie?" she retorted, almost indignant.

Sam cut her off, more amused than impatient. "Anyway, Steve. Your sister and cousin brought you here to let you in on your family legacy. Your birthday's coming up. Big eighteen. You're gonna come into some powers, man."

Steve's eyes widened, his mind slow to catch up. "Powers?"

"Yeah," Sam said, kicking back, "Pretty sweet, right?"

Steve looked from one face to another, like he'd woken up in a world he didn't recognize. His disbelief was palpable, his attempt to process everything almost heartbreaking. "And you've all known about this?"

"No," I said. "We only recently found out. Well, about being Ossaris. I've known about Kiran for a while now." Justin snorted. I glared in his direction. "He's my Guardian Angel."

We all took turns telling him what we knew, filling in the gaps, making the unbelievable feel somehow real. When we finished, Taylor handed Steve one of the notebooks, the one with all our names in it. He opened it with trembling fingers, his eyes moving over the list of names and powers Pop thought we'd have.

Taylor leaned in, fingers dancing over his. "It's all written in here." She pointed to what I assumed was his name. "It's okay," she said. "I'm still getting my head around it too."

He stared back at her, almost bewildered.

"I have coercion. And mediumship, although I have never actually used that one," she added with a grin.

Steve looked at her like she'd lost her mind. "Coercion?"

Taylor got a conspiratorial gleam in her eye. She stared at Mia. "Get off Steve's lap," she said, her voice commanding, "and go into the kitchen to get him a drink of water."

Mia's eyes widened in surprise, but she slid off, a little bewildered, and made a beeline for the kitchen.

Steve stared after her. "What the hell..."

Justin finally peeled off the wall where he had stood this entire time, "Yeah, Taylor, what the hell? Did you do that to my dad the other night?"

Taylor looked embarrassed and nodded her head, "This was the part I thought you should know about."

His mouth twisted, eyes flashing with anger. "So not only are there angels and demons, but you guys have some special powers too? And nobody thought to tell me?" His voice was like a whip, cutting through the room.

He turned to me. "You said you were Ossaris the other night. Not that you had these powers. Only that you had angel blood."

I felt my own anger flare. "Because I didn't know if it was true until I talked to Taylor. She confirmed what the notebook says. She's the only one of us over eighteen, so she's the only one with powers."

"Awesome," Justin said, pushing off the wall. "Just amazing. Can't wait to find out what else you're keeping in your back pocket."

"Justin, come on," Taylor said, a note of pleading in her voice.

Mia came back with the water, blinking like she wasn't sure how she'd gotten there.

"We would have told you," I said, my voice rising, "but you took off to Florida."

Justin glared at me, fury coiled tight in his stance. "And whose fault is that, Rhi?"

Kiran stepped in before I could answer, a calm presence trying to diffuse the storm. "You need to take a breath and calm down."

Justin turned on him, eyes blazing. He laughed, a harsh sound. "You think being brothers means you know me? Means you get to tell me what to do?"

"Wait, what?" Steve interrupted. "What do you mean you're brothers?"

"We haven't gotten to that part yet," Taylor sighed.

Kiran didn't flinch as he stared down Justin, "We all need to work together."

"Oh, right," Justin sneered. "You being all noble again. The great Guardian." Justin mocked.

"That's not what this is," Kiran said, gentle as he tried to reach his brother. "You know that."

"Whatever you say, man. I'm out of here." He was already moving towards the door.

"Justin!" I shouted, pushing past Mia and Steve, who were watching with wide eyes. "Wait." I followed him into the hallway, my heart a hard stone in my chest. He yanked the front door open, the wind from outside rushing in. "Please." The word came out small, almost too soft to hear. "Please don't go."

He was halfway down the porch steps when I caught up to him, grabbing his arm. "Let go, Rhi." His voice was hard, but he didn't pull away. I stepped around to face him, and his eyes met mine. There was something in them, something angry and hurt and almost lost. But he stood waiting.

"Please, Justin." I felt the desperation crack in my voice. "I know I hurt you. God. I'm so sorry. This whole situation is completely my fault. I don't deserve your forgiveness, but I'm begging you for it anyway."

His eyes softened for a second before he hardened them again. "You got what you wanted," he said. "What's it matter now?"

"It does matter," I said, my voice breaking. "It matters so much. I don't deserve it, but I'm begging you to forgive me. I'm begging you."

He looked at me, really looked at me, and I felt that familiar spark. "I don't want your guilt, Rhi," he said, his voice rough. "I just want you back."

He took a step back, running a hand through his hair. "But I know you need time. I know he loves you. Really loves you. He told me in Florida."

I stared at him, stunned. "He did?"

Justin nodded and then closed the distance between us, pulling me into him. I could feel the heat of his skin, the wild pounding of his heart. "I can make it work," he said against my hair. "I know you still love me, and I can deal with him being your Guardian if you just give us a chance."

I breathed in sharply, the nearness of him overwhelming, filling my senses.

"Please, Rhi," he said to my silence. "Just tell me you'll try." He pulled away, looking at me with a fierceness I had missed.

I hated myself. Hated that no matter who I chose, someone would get hurt. And there it was, the pain I caused, continued to cause, clear in Justin's eyes, a raw wound.

"Just go out with me," he said, sounding desperate. "Out without Kiran around. Just you and me. Please."

He pulled me to him again, and that pull was there. Was it our angel blood calling to each other, or was it my love for him?

"I'll text you," he said before letting me go.

I'm just making this worse. Worse for all of us.

He backed away, his face a storm of longing and frustration, then turned and walked down the path to his car. I stood there, the front door open behind me, and watched him drive away. The wind blew my hair across my face, and I brushed it back, trying to steady myself, trying to breathe. I wanted to call out to him, to say something, anything that would make it better, but the words tangled in my throat.

I turned back toward the house and found Kiran standing in the hallway. He looked at me with those eyes that could see straight through to my soul. He knew everything already; I didn't have to say a word.

"Rhi," he said, soft and full of understanding.

I went to him, suddenly exhausted, everything catching up to me at once. He wrapped his arms around me, and I felt the warmth of him, the safety, the love.

"I'm sorry," I whispered.

"It's okay," he whispered into my hair.

We went back into the living room, where they were all poring over the books and papers. I went to pick up the one I had been holding. The one about souls being bound to demons. I scanned it as Kiran sat beside me, peering over my shoulder. It listed types of these bound souls or tethered shades as if they were breeds of dogs.

"Is he gone?" I heard Mia ask.

"Yeah," I said. "He needed some time."

Steve looked over at me, his eyes still wide with disbelief. "Okay," he said. "So, Justin knows about all this?"

"Not about the powers part until now," I said.

"He needs to learn how to control his temper," Taylor added.

Kiran made a small noise in his throat as he picked up another book.

"So, that whole thing about them being brothers?" Steve asked, his eyes moving from me to Kiran. I could see him trying to fit this new piece of information into an already overfilled puzzle. "Is that for real?"

"Yes," I said, feeling worn out by the weight of it all. I proceeded to tell him everything that I knew and what happened to us all at Vince's that night, that Justin almost died, and that Vince was a Fallen Angel.

"I feel like I'm in a bad movie," Steve said, shaking his head.

"Just wait," Mia said. "It gets even better." She filled him in on everything with Vince and Mrs. Rizzo in typical flamboyant Mia fashion.

Kiran crossed to the other side of the room in three strides, and when he reached Steve, he crouched beside him. "You're an Ossaris. You need to see if you can access your powers as soon as possible."

"How?" Steve asked. "I'm not eighteen yet."

"Your grandfather said your powers are heightened senses and accurate intuition. Try to hone in on those powers."

Steve looked at me. "And we're supposed to all work together? Each of us having different powers?"

I nodded, feeling the weight of it all. "We have to. We have to look out for each other."

Taylor passed Eva to Steve, and they exchanged a long look, as if they were having a silent conversation we could never hear.

"Kacey won't come into her powers for a couple of years." Taylor said, "And she's dating a demon." She patted Eva's back as the baby napped on her chest. "Phen cannot know what she is, and we have to get her away from him."

I caught Kiran's eye as he stood. "It will take some time. But we should plan to meet like this as much as we can."

Taylor stood up, Eva starting to fuss in her arms. "Scott's gonna be home soon. We should get back." She picked up another notebook. "Mind if I borrow this?"

"Take whatever you need," I said.

"Do you have all of Pop's journals?" Steve asked, looking at the boxes piled on the floor.

"Not yet," Taylor sighed. "We're working on it."

"What do we do about Phen?" Taylor asked Kiran.

He gave her a reassuring smile. "We keep Kacey safe. We'll have to watch Phen for now."

"Great," Steve said, a little uneasily. "Kacey is stubborn and won't listen to any of us."

Mia leaned in to Steve. "You should come over to my place. I'll help you practice some of those powers." Steve's eyes went wide. "Well, not *those* powers. Not until later," Mia said with a sly smile.

When they left, the early evening lay itself out silent and endless. Almost oppressive.

Kiran closed the door and stood in the stillness of the room, watching me with an unreadable expression. I felt his eyes on me as I moved to straighten the papers on the coffee table.

"You're not okay, are you?" His voice was gentle, more of a statement than a question.

I put the box down and sat on the floor. "No. I'm not. I'm really not."

He sat beside me, close but not touching. "Rhi," he said, searching my face, "what happened with Justin...I know it wasn't easy."

I leaned back, closing my eyes for a moment. "It's ripping me apart. I can't stand how much I'm hurting him, hurting you, everyone." My voice shook, and I hated how it sounded.

"You're not at fault," he said.

"It's ripping me apart," I confessed, eyes stinging.

He touched my hand, a featherlight reassurance. "All I want is for you to be happy, Rhi."

"I don't know if I know what that is. What will make me happy." I leaned in, pressing my head against his shoulder, feeling the warmth of him, the steady presence. "We should go to Nan's," I said, feeling emotionally exhausted. "Dinner's probably almost ready."

Chapter Twenty-Nine

Kiran

I sat in the dark room of the house... my house now, I supposed. We had a good dinner, and Rhi seemed fine on the outside, but I felt her emotions. She was scared, overwhelmed, and anxious. I couldn't blame her. Her life had never been what one would call easy. She was strong, though. But this? This whole thing with angels, demons, and Ossaris. It was even a little much for me. And I was an angel.

She was my ward and I her Guardian. It used to be so clear. I had a purpose, one simple mission—to watch over her, protect her. It was the guiding light I returned to a thousand times. Now, everything seemed dim, clouded by these new feelings, hot and bright as wildfire. What was once easy had become tangled. Instead of entirely worrying about her safety, I worried about her heart, her happiness.

I could already sense the change in me—the way I tried to reason with things I had no right to question. Missing signs, losing focus, acting more human every day. Feeling, longing, wanting.

My old self would have known the answer, echoed Heaven's rules with unwavering certainty. I ran my hand over the polished wood of the table, thinking how it had been touched by her hands only hours ago, and I knew that this—love, longing—was more powerful, more important than any threat of consequence. She was my Ahavah. She had to be, even if it meant losing everything else.

"Kiran..."

My name, sudden and sharp, cut through the silence. I jerked back, the book I held falling to the floor. The voice sounded strangely familiar, like a whisper pulled from a half-remembered dream.

All around, shadows held their breath, stretching long and thin across the floor. The room was empty, yet my name still hovered in the air like smoke that wouldn't clear.

"You don't really seek answers, Kiran. You pretend there are none."

The voice slid inside me, a cold current. I peered deeper into the dark, expecting a figure to emerge, familiar and unwelcome. Instead, the silence thickened, and I began to doubt, wonder if it was all in my head.

"We have much to discuss, you and I."

"Who are you?" I demanded, "Show yourself."

"I am a path. Bring yourself to me. Learn about your history. Learn of her future."

The words pulled at me like a current beneath still water. I felt them on my skin—a creeping frost, a pressure behind my ribs. My mind snapped with a thousand warnings.

Don't listen.

"I know Kiran, I know her fate, your fate..."

"You're lying." My heart rate kicked up with uncertainty. "Leave me."

But the room was already empty, the voice receding like an ocean tide.

I sat there, waiting for the world to still, a quiet drum in my chest. I breathed out, unsteady. Demon, I thought. It had to be a demon.

I got up, reaching for Rhi's mind. It was quiet and content. No bizarre dreams like she was prone to getting, no shadows lingering near her. I teleported to her backyard, hoping the Principality would be there. Maybe he would have some insight into what that weird voice was.

The wind blew through the empty yard, a soft rustle in the trees. There was no sign of the Principality's presence, but I stayed, scanning with my senses.

I called for Ophaniel, but all I heard was the song of crickets in the night air. Silence wrapped around me. Even the stars, sharp and aloof, seemed to flicker indifferently. I felt the edges of despair creeping in. Would they all turn their backs, abandon me with my human feelings and human heart? All those I had called my brothers and sisters since my creation?

"Kiran." A voice gusted like a dry wind from the side of the house. I turned, half-expecting the voice to coil back around me, but it was only Ophaniel, his form glowing gently in the shadows.

"You look restless," he said, stepping closer, his gaze steady and knowing.

"There was a voice," I said, trying not to sound desperate. "It knew me. It knew her."

He frowned, thoughtful. "Did it manifest?"

"No."

"You sound uncertain."

"I am. And that scares me." I paused for a moment, "I don't feel them anymore. Other angels."

The Principality nodded, as if agreeing to the weight of my fears. "You will find that much is uncertain in your new state. But you're stronger than doubt. You made a choice, Kiran. Now you must live it."

Live it. Live for eternity walking this Earth, never to see Heaven again. I would have Rhi even if I were just her Guardian and not her lover—but only for the span of her mortal life. Then what? An eternity of after, without her. The thought cracked something open in me that I wasn't sure could be closed.

I would not regret my choices; I made the choice the moment she said his name as he was dying. Leave him, the angels had said. Give him to us, the dark ones whispered. This is his time. But how could I? Even if he turned against me, even if he despised me for loving her, I would make it again and again. I would have always saved Justin.

And Rhi...I would be here, if only to witness her life, each heartbeat, even if it meant breaking mine a thousand times. Heaven had been my world, but it was nothing without my Ahavah. I wanted to live—truly live—whatever eternity I was given. With her.

"You can learn to block voices of evil. They always speak in half-truths, so you think they know things—personal things. Don't let them deceive you. Don't answer them. It just gives them more power."

His voice penetrated my thoughts, and I welcomed the interruption.

"Now, I answered your call because I need a favor. You are still an angel, even if you're a Fallen. Things are getting much more unbalanced. I need you to work with that witch friend of yours and do a spell to open your ward's Ossaris gifts as well as her cousin's."

I stared at the Principality, unable to sort through all the chaos in my mind. "But I thought—"

"You need to do this, Kiran." The ancient angel's eyes burned silver, unwavering. "Or it will be a bigger mess than even you can imagine. Help me restore some order, and in turn I shall help you."

"Won't that put them in danger? Opening their powers too soon?"

"You will be here to make it safe. You and..." He didn't need to say Justin's name. "Will you do this, Kiran?"

"I will. For her."

"Do not delay. Time has become a luxury." Ophaniel reached into his pocket and pulled out a pipe, tapping it against his palm. "Listen carefully, and we'll get to work." The flick of a match, the mustard tang of sulfur, and a plume of smoke curled into the air.

I stopped him, the question tumbling out before he could continue, "Kacey too, though? She's so young, and she's...she's infatuated with Phenix."

"Young and in love." The Principality looked on with a strange glimmer, his voice slowing. "They never heed the warnings, do they?" he released a plume of smoke. "Not an easy situation. But difficulties are not impossibilities." He was silent for a moment, his eyes narrowing with remembered thought. "Phenix. Phen...he was a powerful and caring Throne. I've known him longer than you could imagine. Before he made his choice. Before he began working for Lucifer."

The name hung between us. I tried to picture Phenix as a Throne, as anything other than the demon he was now. I couldn't.

Ophaniel's eyes grew distant, as if he were watching years unwind. "Phen was always...intense. Powerful. But caring."

"And now? What is he now?" Skepticism clipped my words.

"In his own heart, he thinks he still serves Heaven." A moment passed, heavy with doubt. "He will not give the girl up easily."

"I'll do what I can to protect her."

"I'm sure you will. But prepare for obstacles." He motioned for me to take a seat next to him on the steps. "Now, back to this spell."

He leaned in, fixing me with a serious gaze, explaining in detail what needed to be done. My head spun with instructions, the steps of the spell folding into one another like the pages of an elaborate book. I had to give some of my angel blood for it, which was fine, an easy price for their safety.

"Taylor." He shook his head, his brow furrowed. "Her Principality is still missing. It's troubling." The thought of her unprotected, weighed heavily. She was a mother; she shouldn't have to put herself in such danger.

Ophaniel cut in, quick to reassure. "Have faith, Kiran." He tilted his head, his brow furrowed. "I know you doubt, but your heart will take you where you need to go."

I watched him get up and disappear into the night. The echo of that other voice haunted me.

I know her fate, your fate...

The next day, Mia had her backpack slung over one shoulder. "You need me to bust out a spell? I'm your girl."

By afternoon, Rhi and I were in her room. Sunlight streamed in, catching the highlights in her hair. Rhi elbowed through trigonometry problems, her focus pinched and determined. She chewed on a pencil and threw me a glance.

"What are you reading? Anything that helps?"

I shook my head. "Your grandfather took meticulous notes," I said. "Which is good but, also a bit tedious."

I went back to scanning. Rhi shut her book and came to sit with me on the floor, her sweet smell enveloping me. It made it hard to concentrate. Her phone pinged in her pocket. I could tell it made her anxious.

"It's Justin." Her voice tightened. "He wants me to go to this private release party of Phen's band on Friday...without you."

"No way," I said. "Not at a party with Phen. I don't want you anywhere near him."

"I promised him I would go out without you."

I held my ground. "Then tell him you want something simpler, just the two of you."

Rhi shook her head, burying her face in her hands. I reached over and pulled her against me. My touch seemed to calm her—or maybe I just hoped it did.

"No matter what I choose, I hurt someone," she said, looking straight at me, her eyes glassy with unshed tears. "If I don't go, Justin will think..."

"That you love and want me." I finished her sentence, my voice low. "And if you do go, I'll know you love and want him."

"Kiran," she started, and then snapped her mouth shut, breathing out a long sigh.

I kissed her forehead, allowing my lips to linger against her skin. "I know you love him, sweet girl."

She opened her mouth to protest. "I can feel what you feel, remember?" I tucked a stray curl behind her ear, "Which is why I also know you love me."

I took her hand, feeling how small and fragile it was in mine, feeling the pulse there thrumming like butterfly wings. "You're worth so much to both of us." My own voice came out hoarse.

I smiled, but it wasn't real. I didn't want her to be with Justin. Him touching her or worse, kissing her. I felt possessive over her, and my next words killed me to say. "You should go, not to Phen's party, but meet with him. It is only fair to you and both of us to figure out your true feelings."

As if on cue, her phone pinged again. Rhi's fingers moved over the phone, typing quickly. She let out a breath, drew one in, and then slowly released it.

"I told him I want to meet him today instead." Her eyes shifted from my face to the screen. "He's on his way." Her eyes searched mine. "I'm sorry."

Before I could respond, she kissed me—quick and soft and over too soon. She pulled away so fast that the air seemed to thrum between us, heavy with everything we couldn't say. Then she grabbed her phone and was gone, the door clicking shut behind her like a period at the end of a sentence I hadn't finished writing.

Chapter Thirty

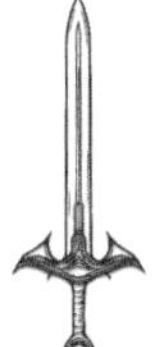

Justin

I was nervous, and since when was I ever nervous? Except she wanted to meet now. Like she just wanted to get this over with.

I slammed the door behind me. Called myself an idiot. This was supposed to be on my terms. My time. My rules. But then there was Rhi and her eyes and her hair and that mouth that looked like trouble, and suddenly here I was, keys in hand, ready to jump when she said jump. I started the engine, and the roar of it loosened the knot in my chest.

I wanted to see her smile, to lose the weight that hung between us. But what if I couldn't find the right words? What if being with me wasn't enough? Her quick text had thrown me. Too determined, like she'd already made her mind up. It clawed at me, the not-knowing.

I took a sharp left, the tires squealing like a taunt. Let her underestimate me, let both Kiran and her do that. I was ready for it. I needed to see her, to chase the doubt from her wide eyes, to make her remember why she wanted this—wanted me.

I pulled up in front of her house. She was already on the steps, hugging her knees, chin tucked down like she was protecting something. My heart rate kicked up into a gallop at the sight of her, as if my own body was reminding me what I stood to lose. She raised her eyes, and I rolled down the window, giving her every ounce of charm I had in me.

She smiled back, but it was crooked and cautious. Almost like she was sorry. Was I imagining it? My gut knotted again as she got up, dusted off her shorts, and made her way slowly to the car. She opened the door and slid in without a word. My hands ached to reach out, to touch her hair, her shoulder, and reassure us both. Instead, I just gripped the wheel and worked up a smile like I was okay with all of this.

"Where to?" I asked, trying to keep my voice light and unfazed. I could see her bite her lip, feel the air fill with the things she wasn't saying. This was not how I wanted it.

"Anywhere," she said with a small shrug.

I revved the engine and pulled us back onto the road, the tension pressing between us like a third person. Maybe Kiran. Maybe her own doubts. Or maybe just the mess of us, tangled and tight. I sped up and turned towards the reservation. It was close, and it had good memories for both of us.

Tall pines blurred past, dark green smearing into each other beneath the wide and cloudless sky. The road wound like a spilled ribbon; I pushed the speed up, hungry to swallow the distance between us and wherever she thought this was going. Rhi tugged at the bottom of her shirt, fidgety, as she'd rather be anywhere else. The trees thickened, and I turned onto a dirt path, the car rattling beneath us until I eased off the gas. I pulled to a stop where the road disappeared behind us, out of sight.

Just us.

I cut the engine, and everything went still, the silence deep enough to hear the slow rhythm of her breath.

"So," I said, trying to find a start. "Why do I feel like this isn't going the way I thought it would?" I said, and it came out rougher than I wanted.

She let out a breath, a tiny sigh that I felt more than heard. "I don't know."

Dammit, I needed to slow down, to work this right. Where do we start? I thought. I can't screw this up. I hooked my arm around the seat, turning half towards her, trying to sound cool and steady.

"Thanks for picking me up."

"Of course." I traced a crack in the dashboard with my eyes, avoiding her face, afraid of what I'd find there.

"Do I need to worry about Kiran lurking around?" I said it and instantly wished I could take it back.

Her eyes flared. "No, but he can feel whatever I'm feeling, so he'll come if he thinks I need help."

My chest tightened, heat flaring up through me. "Help? From me?"

"That's not what I meant. I just—" She turned away, her fingers twisting together.

My laugh came out sharp and biting. "I'm the one who's been waiting around, Rhi. You've been with him for weeks."

Her eyes came back to me, bright and fierce. "You think it's been easy for me?"

"Why don't you tell me? How easy is it to have someone who loves you around you every minute of every day?"

She bristled at my words.

"And what about what it did to me?" My voice cracked, and I hated that she could hear it. I was afraid of myself in this moment, of how much she saw. "I can't keep waiting, Rhi. I need to know."

She flinched, but her voice didn't waver. "I don't know, Justin. I hate seeing you hurt. I don't want either of you to be hurt....especially over me."

"Then why meet me?" It came out hard, accusatory.

"Because I felt I owed it to you." Her voice cracked, a rawness underneath.

"Owed?" I echoed, softer.

Her eyes found mine, wide and dark and pleading. "I don't want to hurt you."

The memory hit hard, flashing behind my eyes. The bridge, the slide, and swings, her laugh cutting through the rain. She was soaked to the bone, and I'd demanded then, too, demanded that she show me if she wanted this, if she wanted me. It was a line drawn clear and sharp. Maybe I should do the same now.

I reached out, ran my fingers down her cheek, watched her become utterly still. "Remember that night on the bridge, Rhi?" I asked, and the words came thick with need. "I need to know like I did that night."

She froze, eyelids fluttering shut for a moment. I held that moment as if letting go meant everything would fall apart.

"Justin," she said, soft and small.

"What do you want?" Desperation cracked through every word. "What do you really want?"

Her eyes opened, softer now. She swallowed, and I could see the answers fighting in her, tearing at each other. I felt her flinch again, weaker this time, like she was too tired to keep it up.

She leaned her head back against the seat, her hair catching the light slanting through the window. "I'm scared," she said, almost a whisper.

"You weren't scared then," I said. "Or you didn't show it." I saw her lips press together, felt the heat of her right next to me, and it was harder than anything I've ever done not to pull her close. "Kiran's not here now," I said. "It's just you and me."

I had never been nervous to kiss a girl, to touch them. Now, though I was unsure, but I drove through my doubt and reached for her. My thumb gently ran the curve of her jaw and down her neck to rest at her pulse, which fluttered beneath.

She sucked in a breath, and the color rose in her cheeks; her pulse quickened under my thumb. Her eyes held mine, and for a moment I was drowning in them.

Then she blinked, shattered the stillness between us. "Justin, please..."

I wasn't sure if that was a plea to take the lead, take her in my arms, and kiss away any feeling she had for Kiran. Or, if it was a plea to stop. To let her go.

My hand fell away, cold without her. I turned from her and shoved my fingers through my hair, tried to steady the rush of blood and anger and loss. There had to be a way. There had to be. I wanted her to feel the way I felt. But didn't she feel that way already? I couldn't have been that wrong.

I slammed my hand on the wheel and turned back to her. "You have to decide." It came out low, barely more than a breath. "You can't keep this up." I was shaking now, more than my chest could hold. The car was a cage, restless with unspoken words, the leather tangling her scent and memories up around us. I replayed a million other ways this could've gone. Where she would have leaned in and kissed me. Where her smile had been full and real, not crooked and sad.

"Justin," she said again.

I opened the door, the sharp air stinging my skin. "I need a minute," I said, and I didn't look back as I walked towards the shadows of the trees. I was pissed at her.

I was pissed at Kiran and, ultimately, level-ten pissed at myself. Because I was sure I could make her feel what she felt when it was just her and me on the bridge.

I didn't know where I was going, just that I needed to not be near that car, in that damn silence, that look in her eyes as she pulled away.

My foot caught on a root, and I stumbled, catching myself against a maple. The bark scraped under my fingertips. I crouched down, my breath coming jagged, and pressed my forehead to my arm. How was I supposed to do this? Get her out of my head? She was the only girl I'd ever—my mind snagged on the word.

Loved. Yeah, loved. Angel blood bond be damned.

When I stood again, the forest spun around me, and that heat, that familiar heat, built up until I couldn't keep it in. My fist flew out, slammed into a tree with a thick, ugly thud that cracked the bark. "Dammit," I muttered, clutching my hand. Blood welled across my knuckles.

"Justin!"

I turned, and there she was. Just like always. Running to me. She stopped short, looking desperate and torn, and I hated that I wanted her close.

"Rhi," I said, low and raw.

She reached for my hand, her touch gentle and cool. "You're bleeding. Let me take care of it. We can go back to my house." Her voice was soft, close.

I pulled my hand back, the cuts stinging.

"No way. Not with Kiran hovering around. I can't stomach the way he looks at you."

Her eyes widened. There she was, the girl I would do anything for.

"Come back to my place," I said, low and quick. "No one will bother us there." Her eyes turned uncertain, and I couldn't stand it.

"Okay," she finally said, voice small.

The sky burned orange as we picked our way back to the car. I got in and started the engine. She was watching me as if she'd never seen me before, like I was not the same person.

She tugged at her seatbelt, fussed with it until it clicked. I pulled us onto the road, the reservation rattling in the rearview. I drove faster than I needed to, faster than was safe. Part of me wanted everything to blur, just get us there before she changed her mind. I took the turns sharp and tight until we skidded up to Vince's—well, Sorcha's.

"Come on," I said as I got out, like if I didn't keep moving, she might slip away. Inside, the air was cool. Quiet. I could feel her behind me as I headed to the closet bathroom, rummaging for bandages.

I returned to where she waited in the hall, trying not to hold my breath as I asked, "You wanna go up to my room?"

She nodded, but I saw the reluctance, the way her arms wound tight across her stomach. I tried to tell myself it didn't mean anything. We reached the landing, and I heard giggling, a high-pitched cascade of it.

Rhi froze in the hall, her face gone soft and stunned. "That's Kacey!" She was off, running towards the noise. I caught up and took her arm, stopping her just as her fist came up to bang on the door. Her eyes were wild, like she didn't understand why I'd stop her. I put my finger to my lips, pulled her along to my room. She tried to say something, but I pushed the door shut and leaned against it.

She turned on me, eyes blazing. "Why did you do that? I need to help my cousin."

I shook my head. "Let me stop you right there. All you're going to do is piss Kacey off. She won't listen to you, and you know it." I lowered my gaze, "I said I would watch over her if she shows up here, and I will."

She seemed to understand, but didn't look happy. "He's a demon, though, Justin."

"I know what he is, Rhi. I can handle him."

Rhi pressed her lips together.

"Okay." I put my palms up. "I'll go check. Stay here." Her mouth twists, but I'm already halfway back down the hall before she works up a protest.

I rap on the door with my uninjured hand. The door creaks open, and Phen appears, his lips curling into something predatory. "Justin. What a pleasure. To what do I owe the intrusion?"

I crane my neck past him. Kacey sits cross-legged on the carpet, furiously mashing buttons on a controller while explosions light up the TV screen.

She glances up, eyes landing on my hand. "Justin! What happened?"

"Nothing important. Everything okay in here?"

She frowns. "Why wouldn't it be?"

"She's perfectly fine," Phen interjects. "I was just teaching her the nuances of vehicular theft." His gaze drops to my hand. "Though you might want to address that bleeding before you ruin the carpeting."

"Right," I mutter. "Kace, I'm just down the hall if you need anything." I hold her eyes a moment longer—she seems content, not frightened.

I pull the door closed and slump against the wall under the hallway light. My head throbs. My knuckles are torn raw, and I press them gingerly, hissing through my teeth at the sting.

I head back to my room, where Rhi is waiting impatiently.

"She's fine. Just playing video games." I said.

"She's still with a demon."

"She is. Sorcha, Sam, and I are all here. Phen won't do anything to her with all of us here." I strode past her to the tiny bathroom attached to my room to wash my hand. The cold water stung, and I hissed.

When I came back, she was standing where I'd left her. She motioned for me to sit on the bed. "Let me see your hand."

I stayed where I was, not ready to give in. To let her think this was all okay with me. Not after today, after what she'd said. Or what she wouldn't say. Her eyes were on my hand, not moving.

"You're bleeding all over," she said.

I held her stare. We were both just too stubborn.

She whirled away from me, and I watched her shoulders sag as she sat down on the edge of the bed, the space between us stretching further than I wanted it to.

I stepped to her, sitting gently beside her. Our legs touched, and without a word, she took the bandages from me and started to wrap my hand.

"So that's it?" I asked. "You're okay with me waiting around until you've sorted out your feelings?"

She didn't look up. "I'm not okay with any of this."

"Then stop it."

Her head lifted, and there was fire in the way she looked at me. "I can't just ignore the way I feel, Justin."

"You love me too, though."

Her hands stilled, and the air went quiet. She didn't reply, but the silence filled in the way her words couldn't.

She finished wrapping my hand, and I thanked her, like it wasn't a big deal, like my heart wasn't tearing itself into pieces. I knew it shouldn't take long to heal. Sam had told me that because I'm a Nephilim, I would heal faster. I thought about it. It made sense. I've rarely been sick.

Rhi was quiet beside me, and I hated the smallness of what I felt. I hated that I felt so inadequate, but I needed to know. "You do still love me, don't you?"

She raised those beautiful dark eyes to mine and nodded. I let out a breath I didn't realize I'd been holding. "Then maybe there's hope for us after all."

She shook her head. "You don't understand."

"Then make me," I said. It was a challenge, but not a mean one. Just wanting. "I'm not going to give up."

One thin line of tears spilled over, and she swiped at it fast, before I could say anything. Before she let herself really cry. "Hey," I said, softer this time. "This isn't how I thought this would go, but I am glad you're here." I put my arm around her then, pulled her against me, and let my chin rest on the top of her head. I could feel the push and pull in her, the confusion.

"Rhi," I said softly. "Just lie with me." Her pulse quickened against me, and I couldn't stop. "I know you can't stay the night, but let me just hold you for a while."

I felt her breath catch, like she was going to say no, or maybe cry, or maybe just break apart right there.

I stretched out on my bed, not letting her go, her warmth folding in against me, where she fit.

Perfectly.

How could she not feel that? How could she not want this as I did? I could hear her heart but not her thoughts.

Never her thoughts. My arm tightened around her, and I listened to her breath, slow and even.

It was enough.

Enough, for now.

Chapter Thirty-One

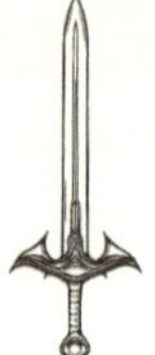

Rhiannon

Time seemed to drag. I loathed math, even with Kiran and Sam to keep me entertained. The teacher seemed to love them both, so they got away with more than we mere mortals.

It was Friday. We had a spell, and Mia, with the help of her friends Jess and Sofie, were going to do it tonight.

I glanced at the clock on the wall. The second hand moved slower than a snail. Three ticks were a lifetime.

I could see him through my hair. Kiran. Next to me, his head bent over his papers. Ignoring the formulas to write a little note he'd pass to me in a moment to help me understand the math problem, just like he did every day.

I needed a distraction. I kicked Sam under the desk. He looked my way. "What?"

"I don't know. I'm sure you did something to deserve it." I smirked as he rolled his eyes.

Kiran's hand appeared on top of my paper and slipped away just as quickly, leaving a slip of paper there. I unfolded it, and he explained the problem so I could understand it and get it right. I knew I was technically cheating, but I didn't care. You didn't need to be a genius at everything, and math was my Achilles heel.

Finally, the bell called out in a shrill burst, and we were free. A tidal wave of kids pushed out the door, backpacks bumping in the rush for freedom. I gathered my things, Kiran falling into step beside me, his silver eyes catching the light and flashing playfully.

"I think you're getting it…the math problems, I mean," he said, brushing a finger against mine.

"Maybe you didn't notice how every second was pure torture," I teased.

We weaved through the students milling around their lockers. I was impatient to get to his place, where we needed to prepare for this spell.

"Are we ready for this?" I asked as we headed out of the building, the sun spilling soft, warm light over us.

"We're as ready as we can be."

Kiran unlocked the door, and I dropped my backpack on a chair. Stanley was lounging in the sun. Kiran eyed me as I walked over to the cat and began to pet him. He really was the sweetest cat.

"I really don't think there's much more to do except wait for the others to get here," Kiran said.

Nerves tightened in my stomach. I had fallen asleep at Justin's. He had taken me home later that night. He seemed lighter and more relaxed. I, on the other hand, was upset at myself. I had to just make a choice and stick with it.

Kiran was there as always when I walked into my room. He didn't say or ask anything, which actually made me feel worse.

"What are you thinking about?" Kiran asked, watching me too carefully.

"Just hoping this spell works." I flashed what I hoped was a convincing smile.

It wasn't.

"I can tell you're lying." He crossed his arms over his chest.

"About the other night…"

A flash of light, and there was Sam, in the middle of the room, grinning like he'd solved world hunger.

"Don't you knock?" I said, startled.

"Sweetcheeks, you should be used to us just popping in and out by now." He nodded at Kiran. "Got something for you." In his hand was a small, ancient-looking clay bowl.

"Is that what I think it is?" Kiran asked, coming to stand beside me.

"Indeed, it is." Sam held it up like a trophy. "One genuine incantation bowl, straight off the black market."

"Give me that," Kiran said, taking it from him. "You can't just steal something this important."

"Borrow, buddy, borrow. I figured certain supernaturals would be happy to donate a little something to the cause."

The bowl was covered in strange swirling symbols, dark lines that seemed to pulse against the clay. I reached out to touch it, and a tingle ran up my fingers.

"I bet it doesn't even work," I said, trying to act unimpressed.

"It'll work," Sam assured me. "Got it from a real nice demon. Trustworthy type."

Kiran shook his head, but a hint of a smile tugged at his lips. "And the other things for the spell?"

"A glittery unicorn will deliver them," Sam said, collapsing onto the couch like he owned the place, propping his feet up on the armrest. "But seriously, Mia's bringing everything else we need over with Jess."

"We need to prep the room." Kiran handed me the bowl. "Sam, you up for some heavy lifting?"

"If I must. I do hate ruining my nails."

I huffed a laugh. "Like using your angelic powers ruins your nails."

Sam snapped his fingers, and I had to jump to get out of the way as the furniture moved to one side of the room. Empty space stretched across the floor, waiting.

Sam waved his hand, and a cheeseburger appeared on a plate, a pile of fries beside it. Kiran and I stared at him. "What?" He took a bite, grinning. "I'm hungry."

"Angels don't get hungry, even Watchers," Kiran drawled.

On cue, my stomach growled. I flushed with embarrassment.

"You want one, sweetcheeks?" Sam asked.

"Would you please stop calling her that?" Kiran sounded exasperated.

"She likes it. Don't you?" Sam waggled his dark brows at me.

"You can call me whatever you like," I said, "as long as you get me one of those cheeseburgers and fries, not regular boring fries though. Disco fries with extra gravy."

Sam looked delighted. "Coming right up." And there it was, steaming and perfect. I sat on the couch next to him, the savory smell making my mouth water. "You gonna eat that? Or just drool on it?"

I waved a fry at Kiran. "You sure you don't want some? You're missing out." I teased, popping it into my mouth. "Extra cheesy, gravy, goodness with a side of awesome." I leaned closer, holding a fry to his lips. "Come on, try it."

Sam groaned. "Get a room, you two."

Kiran smirked and then took a bite. "Not bad."

"Not bad? That's it? It's like Heaven for your mouth." I picked up another fry. "Here, maybe you needed one with more gravy."

Finally, he relented, moving closer to me on the couch. I fed him the fry,

and he bit it gently, making sure not to get my fingers in the process. I watched Kiran wipe a bit of gravy off his lip, his smile lopsided and unguarded. I nudged him with my shoulder and watched as he grabbed a few fries and stuffed them into his mouth.

"Told you."

I shared my burger and fries with Kiran, who seemed to enjoy them more with each bite. I went to wash my hands in the kitchen, and when I returned, Kiran wrapped an arm around my waist, pulling me against him.

"Seriously, Sam, we really should go over the plan for tonight," Kiran said.

"Oh, the plan is simple," Sam said, as he reclined on the couch again. "Rhi and her cousins get their powers, demons get their asses handed to them, and we all live happily ever after."

I laughed. "You make it sound so easy." Stanley wove through my legs and stretched. I reached down to pet him.

Kiran's eyes flicked to Sam. "What exactly did Mia tell her witch friends about all this?"

Sam waved a hand. "Just that she missed practicing magic with them. Made it sound like a small party." He sat up with excitement. "Speaking of the party, we need some music and more food for the mortals." He got up and strode to the dining room, waving his hand around. A moment later, he had created a small stereo and lined the table with goodies.

Kiran was making small circular motions on my hip, sending shivers along my skin. His lips grazed the shell of my ear. "Are you ready for all this?"

"Do I have a choice?"

Sam called out from the other room. "You better be, sweetcheeks, because the witches are here!" Sam sped to the door, opening it with a bow. "Ladies. Welcome to the madness."

Mia dropped a bulging backpack onto the floor. Her eyes glowed with excitement as she looked around the room. "I see someone's been busy."

Jess and Sophie followed close behind, Jess hesitating at the entrance. She clutched her backpack, eyes darting uneasily as she spotted me.

I waved them over, relieved Jess had shown. I worried she wouldn't. She was upset finding out about Steve and Mia, and he would be here tonight.

Jess twisted a strand of dark hair around her finger, her ponytail slipping loose. Sophie's bright red spikes glowed atop her head from the sunlight coming in through the window.

"Hey, Rhi," Sophie said, flashing a wide smile.

Mia sized up the room, a gleam in her eye. "Help me set up, girls?"

Kiran unwound his arm from my waist and stood, crossing toward them, ever gracious. "I'm Kiran. Welcome to my home."

"Holy sh—" Jess began, looking at Kiran, her eyes darting to me as she lowered her voice. "Sorry, I mean...wow. Whoa."

Sophie was more subdued. "Weird eyes."

"I get that a lot," Kiran said, smiling. "There's food and drinks in the dining room."

"Thanks to me." Sam chimed in.

The girls opened their bags, and we all got to work, lining the floor with candles and chalking symbols on the walls and floor. I took several breaks to play with Stanley, who seemed to think the whole thing was just for him.

I chewed my lip, the nerves clawing back up my stomach. Kiran noticed and traced his thumb over my chin.

"Everything will go fine," he assured me, brushing his lips against my forehead.

I lowered myself onto the couch and let my head flop back.

"You okay?" Kiran said softly with concern.

"Yeah, just worried we won't be able to pull this off."

My phone buzzed. I glanced at it.

Justin: *Busy tonight? I'd love to have you in my bed again.*

I flushed red hot.

Actually, I am busy. Ossaris stuff. I replied.

I waited for the gruff response, but only got: *Maybe another time then.*

We were just waiting for Taylor and Steve. We collectively decided it was too dangerous to include Kacey. Not when she was so wrapped up in Phen.

The air felt heavy. I sighed and shut my eyes. It was so much simpler before I met Kiran and Justin.

I'd dated a few boys and crushed on even more. But being with them was nothing like that. It was more. Better. Bigger.

It was an addiction, and I didn't want to give them up. But it was wrong having it both ways. I had to make a choice. It hurt to think about letting one of them down, but it was the right thing to do.

Once all this craziness was over, I'd have to let one of them go. I'd be whole and broken all at the same time.

The bell rang, and Kiran glanced at Sam. "Can you get that? I mean, since you seem to think you own the place."

"You rang, my liege," he said as he swung the door open with a flourish.

As Steve and Taylor entered, I scanned Jess's face as she saw him. She stiffened, a hard line pressing her mouth together. "What's he doing here?"

Mia tucked herself under his arm. "This spell is for him, too."

"Everything's set?" Steve said, avoiding Jess's glare.

"Ready to begin as soon as the candles are lit." Sam chimed in. "Then Rhi and Steve get all powerful, and we mere mortals will worship their awesomeness."

Sophie scowled at him. "Yeah, sure. Whatever, dude."

Jess wouldn't look at anyone. "Let's just get this over with." She dropped to the floor, crossing her arms.

"Girl," Mia said, putting her hands on her hips. "I told you I wasn't going to be tied down my senior year. I'm sorry you're hurt, but you need to get over it or leave."

Jess stared at her, open-mouthed. I glanced at Steve, who looked a little hurt by her words.

"Everyone, chill," Sam said. "Here's some advice about relationships. Don't have them. They suck."

Jess fumed silently, and I started to worry she'd leave before we could start the spell. But she uncrossed her arms and glowered at Steve.

Sam turned to the rest of us with a wide grin. "Time to kick it into gear, folks. Everyone, get in a circle. You two," he pointed to Steve and to me, "in the center."

He motioned us in, the rest forming a loose ring around us.

"So," Mia said, breaking the moment. "Ready, Rhi?"

I nodded, nerves and excitement twisting in me.

"Let's light 'em up," Sam said.

Mia clapped her hands, and all the candles blazed.

"When did you learn to do that?" Sophie said, her eyes wide.

Mia grinned at her, "I practice and have a Mёteìnu for a grandmother."

Everyone joined hands, and Jess, still glaring, took Sophie's. "Can we just do this already?"

"We got plenty of time before Rhi and Steve turn into magical dragons." Sam's voice rang out, and he seemed to be enjoying every moment of the tension.

"Just start," Jess snapped, shifting uncomfortably.

Mia gave her a look and then led us through the incantation. Her voice, low and musical, wound around us, and I felt my skin begin to prickle. The symbols on the walls seemed to shift and glow.

The glow slipped into my pores, a surge of energy that sent my senses spiraling. The walls pulsed and blurred, and I had the dizzy feeling that the room was spinning around us, faster and faster until I couldn't tell where I ended and it began. The words of the spell flooded my mind, strange and familiar at once. They beat through me in waves, rushing through my blood, filling me up, spilling over.

Steve's shape wavered beside me, and his face had a look of awe and fear. He tried to say something, but his words were lost in the roar that filled my ears. I opened my mouth to speak, to shout, to tell them all to stop, but the world tilted sideways, and light exploded in a blinding flash.

Then silence.

I was floating, suspended in blackness so deep that I couldn't tell if my eyes were open or closed. Was I dead? I felt like I was drifting through a dream. There was no sound, no sensation except the vast dark pressing in on all sides. I felt for the ground beneath me, pushing myself to sit, and then I saw it. A glow, soft at first, growing brighter.

A warm, resonant voice emerged from the glow. "Hello, Rhiannon."

I shrank back, a tremor of fear racing through me. The being was shrouded in brilliance, human-shaped but without features. "Am I dead?" My voice was a thread of sound in the emptiness.

Laughter, light, and strange, filled the void. "No. You are far from dead."

"Then what is this?" My mind reeled, trying to make sense of the figure before me.

"I am Caleth," the voice said. "Principality of Fire Without Smoke."

I could feel myself trembling, helpless and small in the presence of this burning form.

"Do not be afraid." Caleth's tone was like embers in a hearth. "You have not yet reached the age of power, but I will grant it nonetheless."

A pulse of heat washed over me, and I was struck by the certainty of his words. "Why?" I forced out, my voice wavering.

"I know what lies ahead," he said. "And I believe in exceptions to the rule."

The air shimmered around me, and still I shook. "Does it hurt?" I managed.

"No." His words wrapped around me like smoke. "It will not take long."

Sudden light flared again, white and searing. I felt myself falling through that brightness, collapsing inward. Images surged through my mind—a whirlwind of faces and sounds, moments and memories. Kiran's silver eyes, his soft wings wrapped around me. Justin and his teasing arrogance, his burning lips upon mine.

Then I was soaring again, a breathless rush of blazing light. I reached for something, anything to hold on to, and it was all too bright and too much and then…

I gasped, choking on air, Kiran's face inches from mine.

"Rhi!" he cried, relief and fear tangling in his eyes.

"Get back in the circle," Sam called, his voice shaking.

I glanced to my side. Steve lay sprawled next to me, pale and still. "Go!" I cried to Kiran. "I won't lose my cousin."

He hesitated for one heart-wrenching moment, and then went back to the circle. I saw the raw, desperate fear in his eyes, and I wanted to go to him. But I stayed, gripping Steve's hand with everything I had. "Wake up!" I said, my voice a choked whisper. "Please, Steve."

The others chanted, their voices urgent and insistent this time. I could feel the energy gathering, pulling tight like a string about to snap. Heat rolled off my skin, and Steve's body seemed to drink it in, drawing it from the air around us.

It felt like an eternity, every second a piercing ache. Then, with a shudder, Steve gasped beside me. "Thank God." Taylor cried, her lips trembling. "Did it work?"

Steve rubbed his head slowly, disoriented. "I'm not sure. I met some guy named Auraziel. He was dressed in some sort of armor."

The candles flickered and died, smoke curling towards the ceiling. I threw my arms around Steve, holding him as tight as I could. "You scared me," I said, my voice cracking.

"Whatever it was," Mia said, "it worked. I felt it."

Steve pushed himself up. "What about you, Tay? Did you, uh, see anything? Meet anyone?"

"No. It was nothing. Just black. Like sleeping," she said, voice thin. Taylor's eyes landed softly on me. "What about you?"

"I saw someone too." My words were small. "Caleth. I saw Caleth." I didn't mention the suffocating darkness, the thorns in my lungs, how I felt peeled back to nothing.

Mia leaned in. "Was he creepy as hell? I bet he was creepy as hell."

I tried to smile, but it slid off my face. "Yeah, Mia. You could say that."

Chapter Thirty-Two

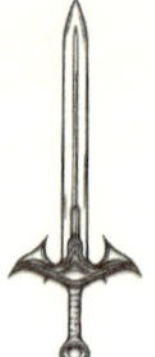

Kiran

R hi waved from the door as everyone left. I waited and then took her hand. "Let's go outside." She looked up, obliging, though her eyes were still stormy from the spell.

I led her to the pool. The moon bleached the water silver. Rhi sat on the edge of a lounge chair, pulling her knees up. "This is all," her head shook back and forth, "this is all so much."

I sank down next to her, my heart heavy. "I know."

"It's like these beings, these Principalities know something. Something big. And they're not telling us everything."

"Probably not," I admitted. "They didn't exactly get top marks for transparency."

Rhi was quiet, searching my face. The silence pressed down on me. I steeled myself to tell her about Ophaniel — something I knew I should have done a long time ago. "Rhi," I said, my voice more serious than I wanted it to be.

She looked at me quizzically. "What is it?"

I let out a slow breath. "I met a Principality before. Ophaniel." Her eyes widened, and I rushed on. "I thought he was your grandmother's Guardian. He was the one who told me about the spell."

"When were you going to tell me?" There was no fight in her words, only weary confusion.

"Why should he have?" a voice floated up from behind us.

I spun around. Ophaniel stood at the pool's edge, smoke curling from his pipe as though he'd been there all along. Rhi went rigid beside me.

"What are you doing here?" I said, my own anxiety spiking as Rhi's eyes stayed on him, wary.

"You're ready to know more," he said, carefully. "The rest will come when you need it."

Rhi leaned forward, the lines of worry easing just slightly. "Can you tell us what all this means and how to access our powers? What do all of you want with us?"

"It's all Ossaris that powerful beings will seek, but you," he said, gesturing to her, "are the Veilbreaker. The Seventh Flame. You will learn to bind or banish celestial beings as well as dark ones. Be they the highest Archangel or the lowest demon."

Rhi reached for my hand, squeezing hard. "And Caleth, what will he do?"

"He will watch. He will let you fail or succeed on your own."

"Why?" Rhi asked. Her voice was small but determined.

"Because you might be more powerful than any of us," Ophaniel said.

She shook her head, a slight, disbelieving gesture. "I don't want that."

"The truth does not change," Ophaniel said, "because you do not want it."

Rhi's eyes widened, but there was a fire building behind them.

"The Veil that separates immortal worlds from mortal worlds is thinnest for you." Ophaniel's gaze was steady, unblinking. "The Seventh Flame carries great risk. Rhiannon, you are a Veilbreaker — the last in a long cycle. Archangels, demons, Watchers. They will all want you for your power."

"Even..." I didn't want to say the words. "Even Lucifer?"

Rhi turned to me as Ophaniel said, "Especially him and all who covet his throne."

"So basically," Rhi said, her voice clipped, "everyone is out to get me? I'm not safe from demons or angels or even my own Principality?"

Ophaniel exhaled a long stream of smoke as his eyes stayed steady on Rhi. "I am the oldest of the Principalities. But I cannot leave my station with your grandmother until she leaves this world."

"Don't ever, ever say that!" Rhi said, her eyes suddenly bright with fear. "I cannot think of losing Nan."

"I guard her," Ophaniel said, nodding slowly. "Now that she is older, her powers as an Ossaris have become less and less over the years."

"Does she know?" Rhi asked, her voice quieter. "That we are Ossaris too?"

Ophaniel shook his head. "Not yet. She suspects that any of her family can become one, but she cannot tell who."

"My grandfather knew, though," Rhi said, her voice growing steady. "He left all those journals."

"Yes," Ophaniel said, a touch of respect in his voice. "He was a determined man. He left those believing you and your cousins were, but he was not a hundred percent certain."

Rhi was silent for a long moment, her face half-hidden in shadow. I wanted to reach for her, to tell her it would all be okay — but I didn't know if that was true. She turned to Ophaniel, chin lifted. "And how do we know you're loyal? That you won't harm my cousins or me?"

Ophaniel's expression did not change. "You don't." He studied Rhi with those strange, unreadable eyes. "Trust is never given freely. But you will find there are some who prove true." He puffed his pipe, watching the smoke curl like a serpent into the sky. "Now, I must get back to my poker game. Things will be clearer in time."

"But—" Rhi started, but he was already gone, a lingering haze of smoke the only trace left behind.

Rhi's face broke, and she threw herself, sobbing, into my arms. "I don't want this, Kiran," she cried, her voice raw and shaky.

My heart cracked open at the sound of it. I pulled her closer, wishing I could take every bit of this from her — the weight, the fear, all of it.

She pulled back, looking at me with a desperation that almost split me open. "Why me?" she cried. "My life hasn't been easy and now...now I'm in danger, and I have the weight of the universe on my shoulders?"

"Rhi, I—" I stopped, my words failing me, knowing the comfort I offered wasn't enough.

Her eyes flickered, softening for a second before the turmoil took hold again. "I can't, Kiran. This is too much."

"Come on," I said, as the night air wrapped around us. "Let me take you home." She nodded, but there was distance in her eyes. "Sleep on this. We'll tackle it tomorrow." She gave another brief nod, and I knew she was only agreeing because she didn't know what else to do.

I took her to her room. Her curtains swayed gently, casting shadows like restless ghosts on the walls. She lay in bed, her body tight and defensive, curling beneath the blanket. I lay beside her, my hand brushing through her hair.

It was a long time before she found rest. I had to hold her close, letting my light comfort her, letting the song of our souls wind gently together. When her breath finally evened out, I stayed still, letting the night close in around us. I lingered in the quiet, watching the moon trace a pale path over her sleeping form. She looked delicate, almost fragile, and I wished I could take her place in all this.

Chapter Thirty-Three

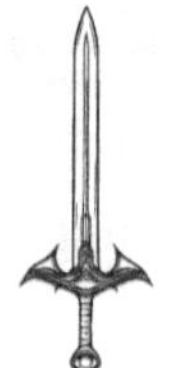

Rhiannon

The house loomed ahead, darkly familiar. I pushed through the door. The rooms stretched and deformed as I moved from one to the next. Empty. Then not.

They drifted in and out of focus: Taylor, Steve, Kacey, Jess, Sophie. Collapsed on the floor, lifeless heaps of limbs, eyes wide and blank.

I couldn't breathe.

I raced through hollowed shadows, my heart a war drum in my chest. Mia and Sam lay tangled beside each other, smoke curling where their bodies touched the wood.

"NO!" I shouted, feeling my voice swallowed by the house.

I turned, frantic and searching, my hands reaching blindly through the dark.

I screamed, my voice cutting somewhere deep and tight. "Kiran!"

The shadows held their breath.

Beyond a flicker of movement, I heard something crash. The noise drew me and I ran, shoving open a door and stumbling into a room.

My steps faltered.

Standing over Kiran, her dark eyes bright and fierce, was the Ossaris, the Veilbreaker, I had seen in my last dream.

Dread gripped my spine. Kiran was on his knees, a flaming sword extended from the Veilbreaker's hand, its blade burning white-hot at his throat. His face was drawn with fear and disbelief.

The Veilbreaker looked so much like me that it hurt to stare. Her expression was steady, unreadable. She turned her gaze on me, a mix of indifference and certainty. "You cannot save him," she said. Her voice was calm, sure. "No one can."

Everything in me screamed in protest. "What are you doing to him?" My words broke, raw and panicked.

A hint of a smile crossed her lips, wry and knowing. "Only what he cannot do himself."

With a silent cry, I was at Kiran's side. Flames from the sword cast wild shadows over his face. "Rhi," he choked out. His voice was hoarse, edged with pain.

"Don't," I said, my voice trembling, "don't do this."

The Veilbreaker moved closer to Kiran, the sword still hovering. She looked like me — older, harder, more muscular — a reflection I couldn't deny. Her laugh was cold and sharp as shattered glass.

I flung myself between them, the heat of the sword scorching my skin. "You will not hurt him!" I screamed, heart pounding.

"You can't stop this," she said. "You can't do anything. You don't even accept who you are."

I shifted my body to block Kiran.

"You're pathetic. You don't even know who you are, do you?" She sneered.

"Leave her alone," Kiran gasped, trying to stand. I held him down, a fierce desperation clenching my heart.

She smiled, but it never reached her eyes. "The Veilbreaker. The Seventh Flame." Her words were taunting. "You're nothing."

Blood roared in my ears, defiant and alive. "I may be," I said, breathing fast, "but I'm glad I'm not like you."

Her mouth curled coldly. "You will be."

Kiran grabbed my arm, pulling me against him. Even now, even here, his touch was electric, primal. "I won't let her!"

The door behind us rattled and cracked as if punched by an unseen fist. The noise of it startled the Veilbreaker, and she looked to the doorway, doubt shadowing her face. The edges of the room seemed to tremble.

The Veilbreaker's eyes flashed with something sharp, angry. "You're blind," she said. "And so is he." She turned, she and her sword passing like a ghost through the walls.

The room shuddered and went black.

"Rhi?" I heard my name being called from far away, and then a form appeared. It was Kiran. "Rhi?" He looked down at me and then at himself. The Kiran I was protecting.

"Awaken." He commanded.

My eyes fluttered open, and I gasped for air like I hadn't been breathing. I felt sweaty and cold. Kiran pushed my hair back from my brow. "What were you dreaming about? Why were you in my house in that warded room with me on the floor?"

The Veilbreaker's words clung to me like shadows. The Veilbreaker. The Seventh Flame. I turned my face into Kiran's palm. "You were there," I breathed. "The sword. It almost..." My voice faltered.

"It was only a dream," he murmured, but I saw the worry in his eyes, silver now dimmed to muted grey. "You're okay. I'm okay."

"But it felt real," I said, clutching the front of his shirt. "And her...that Veilbreaker from my last dream." I rested my cheek against his chest. "And that flaming sword...she had it pointed at your throat."

He wrapped his arms around me tighter, as if anchoring us both to this moment. "She said I couldn't save you. That I..."

"That's not true, Rhi."

"But the dreams..."

"Stop," he said, tipping my chin so I had to meet his eyes. "Dreams are just manifestations of our unconscious desires, fears, and thoughts." His thumb grazed my cheek. "They are not real."

He began to rock me like a small child. Our soul song hummed around us—through us until I was able to breathe easier again.

I didn't remember falling asleep, but I awoke with Kiran wrapped around me, the blankets twisted tight around us both. His eyes were shut, lips parted in a soft curve — but I knew he wasn't sleeping. I watched him, the strange, aching beauty of him.

I traced his eyebrow with my finger, and he smiled with his eyes still closed. "Feel free to touch me," he said, the words slow and husky. "Wherever you want."

And I did, pulling up his shirt and over his head so I could feel his skin, warm and real, as I rested my head against his chest. "Kiran?" I said quietly. "That Veilbreaker. She looked like me." My voice wavered. "I know she isn't, but still."

He stroked my hair, his touch gentle and sure. "This is you. Here, with me."

"She looks like a more badass, evil me."

He breathed a soft laugh, his fingers threading absently through my hair. "And dreams can't hurt me. Even if other Ossaris and Veilbreakers existed at one time, they are gone now and can't touch me." The conviction in his voice settled over me like a warm blanket.

I let my eyes flutter shut. "Promise?" I murmured, the word barely more than a whisper.

"Always," he said, and I felt the vibrations of it in his chest, the steady beating of his heart

I shifted my head to look up at him, the angles of his face soft in the dark. "But what if…"

"Don't. Just stop with the what-ifs. I know there is a lot to take in, understand, and do. But for now, let's just enjoy this quiet time together."

Later that day, we sat cross-legged on the floor of Kiran's living room, our breaths in sync as we exhaled slowly. Incense smoke curled above us, heavy and sweet.

"Are we supposed to think about nothing?" Taylor broke the quiet.

Kiran's voice drifted from the shadows. "Just be open. Let images come if they want to."

Steve shifted beside me, breaking my concentration. "I feel like an idiot just sitting here."

"You are an idiot." Taylor snorted.

I tried to ignore them, settling into my breath. A soft sound filled the air—strings, slow and lush. I opened one eye. Kiran stood by the stereo, and when he saw me looking, he frowned, motioning me to close my eyes.

"Dude," Steve said, "what is this? Enya?"

I could hear the smile in Kiran's voice. "Close." I heard Kiran's footsteps, and his voice was closer. "Center yourself, Steve. You're not even trying."

We fell silent, the music pushing at the edges of thought. My mind floated, untethered. Images began to bloom behind my eyes. At first, they were pale and swift, but as I relaxed, they sharpened, took form.

Light splintered around me, bright and absolute. An old man stood in the center of the sunburst, his face wrinkled and wise. He reached out, hand gnarled but strong. I felt myself pulled toward him like I was made of nothing more than starlight and endless space. My body felt unreal, translucent, and light.

The old man pointed, one gnarled finger directing my gaze. Suddenly, I was flipping through history at warp speed, images rattling past like a freight train. The old man. Guardians. Ossaris. Watchers and demons. Somehow, I knew what they were.

Battles.

The Ossaris standing sword-drawn over fallen supernaturals, flames rising as angels and demons were cast down like stars falling from the sky. The images slowed, and I saw the old man standing over an Ossaris, sad, shaking his head, before the scene flickered again.

I saw several figures, their robes woven from strands of silver starlight. Principalities. Again, I just knew who they were. Their eyes were fixed and bright as they looked at a row of people, of Ossaris.

Flashes of lightning struck, and all the Ossaris crumpled, their bodies going limp. One remained. The Ossaris from my dream—the Veilbreaker. Her face set in fury. She stood against the Principalities as at least seven of them encircled her. A rift opened, gaping behind them, seething and dark. The Veilbreaker moved, feral and fierce. She screamed words I couldn't understand before her final words came through to me clearly.

"Bye bye," I heard, malice dripping from the words. As she aimed the sword at them, a flame erupted from its tip.

But one of the Principalitie's eyes flashed, quick and resolute. At the last moment, he caught the flame from her blade, wrapping it around his arm. The Veilbreaker's eyes widened in shock as he pulled her toward the rift, throwing her inside as the other Principalities sealed it shut.

The visions collapsed inward, and Caleth appeared before me. He was human-looking this time. Ruggedly handsome with a twist of smugness in his lopsided grin. Like someone I might have seen skateboarding down Main Street.

"Why?" I asked, my voice cracking like my heart. "Why did you kill so many Ossaris?"

Caleth regarded me in silence, as though weighing a response. "Knowledge is the most important thing to keep safe. Some Ossaris wanted to use it for themselves—including your ancestor."

His words crashed into me, and I shook my head. "What do you mean, my ancestor?"

"She realized her full potential and became power hungry. We had no choice."

I tried to blink back the tears.

"And she's not the last one of you who will think they know better than the rest of us." He looked at me with what seemed like pity. "You're here for one purpose, Rhiannon. To keep the Watchers—both the good and bad ones—in line. To keep the balance between good and evil."

His words tightened in my chest. "I won't be like her," I said, but it sounded small, a weak protest.

"Maybe not." His eyes drilled into mine, truth and doubt mingled in them. "You are the daughter of the Warrior and the Veilbreaker as well as the Seventh Flame."

"I don't even know what that means!" I screamed.

Caleth knelt before me. "Your father is not just your father, but a powerful angel. It is his angel kiss sealed in your skin." He glanced around, as if someone might be listening. "The Veilbreaker is as it states. You can break through the Veils between worlds — that is what you witnessed your ancestor do. I was forced to throw her into the void she was trying to cast us into."

"And the Seventh Flame?" My voice sounded weak to my own ears.

"Only six before you could wield that sword you saw in your visions. You are the seventh."

He grabbed my shoulder. "Now tap into your powers. Learn to grab the energy from those around you. You must do this, must be able to keep the balance."

The light around me exploded, and I felt myself spinning away, Caleth becoming a blur. His voice carried on the wind, "Keep your heart pure, Rhiannon. Do not misuse the powers that are granted to you lest your fate becomes the same as the one we had to banish."

Kiran's voice, low and anxious, pulled at me. The light dissolved, and I opened my eyes, seeing him hovering over me. The world slowly came back into focus.

"Rhi," he said, his voice edged with panic. "Wake up."

The room was filled with smoke from the incense, and the others were still sitting cross-legged, eyes closed. I opened my mouth to speak, but a sob came out instead.

Kiran's face twisted in concern, and his eyes didn't leave my face. "Rhi…"

I wanted to look away, afraid he could read the terror still ricocheting inside me, but I couldn't. Behind him, Steve made a strangled noise and gasped.

"Whoa," he said, his voice a disbelieving whisper.

Taylor remained cross-legged, her face peaceful and distant, while Kiran and Steve exchanged swift glances.

"What did you see?" I whispered to Steve, my voice unsteady. A sick, heavy feeling pooled in my stomach.

"Auraziel," he said. "But not like I saw him before. He looked like—" He paused, a bewildered laugh escaping. "A freaking biker. Covered in tattoos, ravens flying everywhere. He said a promise is just a spell with blood on it." Steve shook his head. "What does that even mean?" He laughed with disbelief. "Then he told me to follow my gut instincts. Like that's ever been a problem."

Kiran frowned, his face thoughtful. "That was all?"

Steve nodded, still bewildered. "That's it. Don't you think that was enough?"

"You didn't see anything else?" I asked, my voice tentative. "Like battles?"

Steve shook his head, eyes bright and certain. "Just Auraziel and all those ravens." His eyes flicked to Kiran and back to me. "Why'd you ask about battles?"

Kiran searched my face, still holding me close. "Because," I said, my voice small, "that's all I saw."

"What kind of battles?" Kiran's voice was calm, but I could hear the edge beneath it.

I pulled away so I could see his eyes. "Ossaris fighting. Some of them were..." I sucked in a breath, "unconscious or dead, and flames were..."

His eyes went wide.

"There was one Ossaris—the Veilbreaker," I said. "The one from my dreams. She was fighting back, all alone. She threatened Caleth. He..." I hesitated, feeling the words catch. "He overpowered her and threw her into a rift."

Kiran exhaled slowly. "And then he told you it was just a vision?"

"No." My voice was unsteady. "He said...he said she's my ancestor."

Steve drew in a sharp breath. "And she was fighting a bunch of Principalities?"

Before I could answer, Taylor let out a startled cry. Her eyes snapped open, bright and wild, her breath fast and uneven. We all turned toward her, "I know!" she said, like she couldn't quite believe it. "I know what happened to my Principality."

"What?" Steve asked, eyes wide.

"She's tethered to another," Taylor said, like she was struggling to grasp what she'd seen. "To a demon." She looked between us. "She called out to me. Begged me not to let anyone know I was an Ossaris."

"What else did you see?" I asked.

She shuddered. "Nothing. Just darkness and a wall of flames."

Kiran and I exchanged glances, and he squeezed my knee.

A shadow of unease crossed Steve's face. "So what does this mean for us?"

Taylor looked at him, her eyes wide. "I don't know."

Steve stood and stretched, disbelief still etched across his face. "That was intense."

Kiran got up and turned off the music. "From what we've learned, all of your innate powers were already in you," Kiran said. "You just need to learn how to use them."

"And how are we supposed to do that?" Steve asked, a note of frustration in his voice.

"By practicing," Kiran said. "Experimenting. You'll figure out what you're capable of." He glanced at me. "You'll know who the Watchers are."

"But, Taylor can't let anyone know who she is, and Kacey doesn't even know about being an Ossaris."

"That leaves you and me, cuz." Steve smacked me on the back.

I guess it did.

Chapter Thirty-Four

Justin

Rhi and I had been texting on and off. Sometimes I felt she was coming back to me, and other times it felt like I had lost her forever. I got it. She was now some powerful supernatural Ossaris. I felt like my sweet girl was gone. She was always busy learning about what that meant for her. Maybe it wouldn't upset me as much if it weren't for the fact that *he* was with her and I wasn't.

"Still brooding over her little bro?" Sorcha asked, leaning over the kitchen island where I sat eating some sugary cereal.

"I'm not brooding."

"You're brooding like nobody's business," Sam said as he walked into the kitchen.

I rolled my eyes, took my bowl to the sink, and rinsed it out.

"Wanna keep practicing teleporting today?" Sam asked me.

"Maybe later."

"You won't learn if you don't keep trying."

"I'm aware," I said over my shoulder, leaving them in the kitchen and heading up to my room.

I sprawled across the bed, staring at the ceiling, wondering how this whole Ossaris thing would change her. Maybe she'd become unrecognizable, powerful, and indifferent, and I'd get over it. Maybe that would be the best option for me. My phone buzzed on the nightstand.

Hey man. Party this Saturday for my b-day.

It was Steve. His birthday. I had almost forgotten.

You sure you want me there? I texted back.

Steve replied almost instantly. *Of course, dude. been friends too long for you not to make it.*

Where at?

American Legion Hall.

I held the phone against my chest. Thinking about Steve's party made me think about my birthday party when Rhi was just a girl who blushed when I looked at her. Before any of us knew she was an Ossaris, before Kiran showed up. Just a normal life full of normal drama. I found myself staring at the ceiling, feeling like nobody understood how hard it was, watching her drift away.

"Don't hide in your room all day," Sam's voice called from the hallway. "If you change your mind and wanna practice, let me know."

I heard Sorcha laughing, saying something I couldn't quite make out, but I was sure it was at my expense. I shook my head and grabbed my phone again, tapping out a message to Rhi.

Want to meet up later?

I knew she was busy with him. I tossed the phone aside, not expecting an answer. I wasn't even sure what I'd say to her if she did meet me.

Every time I thought of them together, it felt like acid in my chest. Rhi was something more now, something I could barely understand — and I didn't know anymore if I wanted to understand it, or if I just wanted her back the way she used to be.

It's complicated, she had said, the last time we'd talked. It was always that now.

A knock came at my door. I didn't move, hoping whoever it was would leave. "Maybe later, Sam," I yelled.

"It's not Sam," a smooth voice called.

Ugh. Phen. Even worse. I got up and opened the door. There he was in his usual outfit — too-tight black jeans with holes in the knees, a white shirt in the same condition. His copper hair fell into his eyes like he'd just rolled out of bed. Girls loved it, apparently.

"Still can't get over her, huh?" he said.

"Don't you have Kacey to badly influence?" I mocked.

"Oh, you know the good girls love a bad boy. Doesn't hurt that I'm also so very pretty." He leaned against the doorframe, a smirk playing on his lips.

"What do you want?"

"Just came to see if you wanted to mope together," he said, his eyes scanning my room with mild interest. "I'm on my own while Kacey is out shopping."

"Right," I drawled, unconvinced.

"You going to Steve's party?" He picked up a stray book from the floor.

"Maybe."

"Rhi gonna be there?"

I shrugged. "Probably. She is his cousin."

He laughed, placing the book on the shelf. "Man, you are hopeless." He turned to face me. "She'll come around, you know."

"Yeah? I'm not so sure of that anymore."

He studied me with a lazy grin. "Maybe you've gone soft. All this alone time stewing in your own angst..."

"I'm just giving her space. So she can figure things out."

"Space," Phen said, "That's what you're calling it?"

"What else would I call it?" I said, annoyed.

"It's a coward's word for giving up."

I gave him my best death stare.

"If he breaks her heart, it'll be your fault, you know. You could save yourself a lot of brooding if you let me help."

"I'm not locking Kiran in Hell."

Phen sighed dramatically. "Suit yourself." His head tipped sideways. "I'll be playing at Steve's party. Just me...going acoustic."

"Steve agreed to that?"

"Well, he loves his baby sister, and she insisted. I was going to go with her anyway."

"Why are you dating her? She doesn't seem to be your type."

Phen smiled, holding up his fingers. "She's hot, she adores me, she tells me all the time how awesome I am...oh, and she's hot."

I almost laughed...almost.

I really couldn't stand this guy, but I would play along with him. I needed to know what he was up to.

"Seriously, though. I do like her. Maybe I'm even *in* like with her."

I raised an eyebrow.

"What? You don't think I can like a girl?" His mouth twisted into a mocking pout. "It's because I'm a demon prince, isn't it? You think a demon prince can't have feelings? Why does everyone think I am so untrustworthy?"

"Gee, I wonder."

"Hey, I have a heart. It's deep, deep down, but it's there."

I shook my head, smiling despite myself. "If you say so. Just don't hurt her."

"Man, you are so suspicious." He flashed a grin. "I'm offended you'd even think such a thing."

"I'm sure you'll recover."

The smug look fell back into place. "You let me worry about Kacey," he said. "You should be more worried about Rhi. Maybe you should be practicing teleporting. You can teleport right into her room. Prove you're not as soft as you seem."

I shook my head. "I don't think so. I don't want to see her with Kiran."

"It's not like you don't know what will happen if you keep being the nice guy." His eyes flicked over me, and he shook his head. "You're coming to New York with me."

I frowned. "New York?"

"Yeah. The big apple. I have to check out a club for our release party." He paused dramatically. "You can teleport us back. It'll be great practice."

"I can't—"

"You can. Trust me. It's easier to teleport to a place you know." He leaned closer, as if letting me in on a secret. "It'll be fun. You do remember what fun is, right?"

I hesitated. Every part of me wanted to stay here, or at least stay away from Phen's idea of fun. But maybe if I went with him, I could find out what he was really up to. "Fine. I'll go."

"Now you're talking," he said. "Get ready. We can leave in five."

He turned and sauntered back down the hallway, his voice echoing through the house. "Hey, Sam...Sorcha...I got him out of his room!"

I sat back on my bed, rubbing my temples. I wasn't sure what was worse, the fact that I was going to New York with Phen or that he was probably right. Maybe I had gone soft. Maybe I should go see Rhi and make her talk to me.

Phen showed up barely five minutes later, a pair of ratty combat boots on his feet. "See? Told you I'd get you out of here," he said, bouncing on his heels. "They're already planning a we-freed-Justin party downstairs in your honor."

"Ha." I stood reluctantly and walked over to him. He grabbed my hand, and his customary mocking grin spread ear to ear.

The room blurred and spun — wind, light, nothing. The floor dropped out from under me, and for one breathless second I existed nowhere at all.

We landed in a flash of light and electricity on a shadowed street. Lights blinked from every window, and a low rumble of music filled the air. People clustered in front of shops and bars lining the block, their laughter cutting through the chilled evening. "Welcome to New York," Phen said, releasing my arm. "You didn't even throw up. Nice work."

The sidewalk was crowded with what seemed like every kind of person. Punks with bright mohawks, artists with paint-splattered jeans, girls with perfect hair and tight dresses. A couple of street performers played a saxophone and a drum on the corner, and the scent of hot pretzels tangled with the bite of passing cigarette smoke.

"You with me?" Phen asked, already moving down the sidewalk with his confident, effortless stride. "I didn't bring you here to cry about her."

"No crying," I called out, but he was already turning down some narrow side street, dodging between a couple making out against a brick wall.

Grungy guitars blasted from the door of a club, strung with fairy lights and a crooked neon sign. People huddled outside, smoking, laughing, their voices rising above the clamor.

I stared at the sign above the door. "The Underworld?"

"Cozy, right?" Phen slipped into the crowd, grinning.

The bar wasn't too crowded yet, still too early. A band was setting up, tinkering with amps and mics. A guy with dark, messy hair adjusted his guitar, a gorgeous vintage Gibson that caught my eye even from across the room.

Phen was already talking to a pretty woman sitting on the bar, her legs crossed and swinging. Her hair was streaked with electric blue. I could hear him working his charm. "Isn't it past your bedtime?" he asked, smirking at her.

"Funny," she said, her voice smooth. Her eyes landed on me with curiosity and a hint of appraisal. I nodded in her direction. "Justin," I said, offering a wave. "Tess," she replied, leaning toward Phen with an easy familiarity.

I walked over to the band. The guy tuning his guitar was tall and lanky, with a studded leather belt slung low around his hips. "Nice Les Paul," I said, nodding towards the guitar's vibrant red body.

His fingers paused over the strings. "Thanks, man," he said, his eyes meeting mine. They glowed as if lit from behind, red-rimmed with a silver light, a lot like Sorcha's. He must be a half-demon, half-angel...a cambion.

"You play?" he asked, his voice shaded with interest.

"A little," I admitted.

"Really?" Phen cut in, suddenly behind me. "You should get on stage."

The guy shrugged and went back to his tuning. Phen nodded toward the girl sitting on the bar. "She's a fan."

"Of the band?" I asked, glancing at her.

"Of me," Phen said, smirking. "I do have other fans besides Kacey, you know."

I turned back to the cambion. "You play here a lot?" I asked.

"Often as we can," he said, plugging the guitar into an amp.

"So what do you think?" Phen asked, glancing around.

I shrugged, taking in the exposed brick walls and the dim red lights casting everyone in an eerie glow. "It suits you."

He laughed, brushing a hand through his hair. "Perfect for the release."

"It's cool, I guess," I said, shifting on my feet. "But are you sure this is where you want to do it?" I glanced at the tiny stage.

"Exactly where," Phen said. "Tell me it doesn't have a certain ambiance about it."

"You mean dark and loud?" I said.

His grin widened. "Exactly." He clapped me on the shoulder. "See, I knew you'd love it."

Tess watched us from the bar, amusement dancing in her electric blue eyes. I could see what Phen meant about ambiance—if your taste ran toward seedy and sketchy. "So, what now?" I asked.

"We hang out, see how the night goes. Maybe meet more of my adoring fans," Phen said, throwing a casual glance at Tess.

"I've got nothing better to do, I guess," I muttered.

Tess called over, curiosity in her voice. "When's the release, rockstar?"

"A month," Phen answered, leaning against the stage.

I watched him, suspecting there was more to this than the album. "You sure it's not too small for your ego?"

Phen gave me a look. "It'll be intimate," he said, winking at Tess.

"Right. Intimate."

"It's a go!" Phen called over to Tess and gave her a thumbs-up. Phen's red eyes flicked to mine. "You ready to head back?"

"We just got here. I thought you wanted to hang out for a bit?"

"Nah." He grabbed my arm, dragging me toward the back of the stage. "We can leave," he said. "And Justin, the maybe rockstar, teleports us back." He pulled me into a utility hallway, dark and narrow.

"Sure, we should just disappear in plain sight?" I asked. He didn't answer. Instead, he gave me his smug grin and squeezed my wrist. The world folded in on itself, the air crackling around us. I felt my stomach plunge, the bar winking out, and a rush of cold, salty wind hit me. The world snapped back into place. I staggered forward, catching myself against a railing. My breath froze in my chest. The towering silhouette of the Statue of Liberty loomed beyond the railing, and the black waters of the Hudson stretched all around. "What the hell?"

"Surprise." Phen shoved his hands in his pockets, looking entirely pleased with himself. "An empty Liberty Island. Ideal for practicing teleporting. No one here to see you fall on your face," he said, smirking. "And in case you were wondering, it's closed. No people."

"An empty island to practice?" I asked. "That's your brilliant plan?"

"It's genius, right?" He looked so full of himself that I wanted to throw him in the water. "No distractions, no interruptions, just you focusing on one thing."

I stared at the massive statue, so close I felt like I could reach out and touch it. My pulse pounded in my ears. "You're insane."

"Only a little." His eyebrows arched, daring me. "You need to get us back to Jersey on your own, and the only way to do that is to just do it."

"I get it," I snapped. "I'll teleport us back."

He clapped his hands together. "Excellent. Go ahead, then."

I looked around. "This is a really bad idea."

"Keep your eyes open," he said, ignoring me. "And forget what Sam told you."

"Forget what Sam told me?"

"Sam likes to make things complicated." Phen's voice took on a mocking tone. "Focus on your soul finding its way. Just pick a spot and go there. Sam has you thinking. Thinking is bad. You don't think. You do."

I glared at him, but he only leaned back against the railing, watching me with amused patience. "Easy," I muttered to myself. I focused on the opposite side of the chain-link fence, willing everything to line up, to fold and collapse.

Nothing.

Phen laughed, the sound echoing across the empty island. "I'd say it was the effort that counts, but..."

I tried again, clenching my jaw as I pushed every thought to the other side of the fence.

Phen was calling to me in a sing-song voice. "Hurry up, or I'll start singing breakup songs about letting her go."

I ignored him, stubbornly focusing. Everything felt heavy, like I was trying to push a boulder uphill with my mind. I clenched my jaw. I refused to let him win. This time, I forgot everything but the fence.

The world spun, and the wind whipped past me. I landed hard on my knees, breathless, the gritty pavement scraping through my jeans. "I did it," I said to myself.

Phen appeared next to me. "Damn, that's what I'm talking about!" he said. "You're almost competent."

The ground hummed beneath me, a strange sensation like a steady, vibrating pulse. I pressed my hands flat against the ground, trying to figure out what it was.

"You feel that?" I asked, my voice edged with confusion.

"You mean the pavement you just kissed?"

I shook my head. "No, smartass. The buzzing or whatever."

His dark eyes widened, just a little. "Yeah. It's from the statue. Kind of intense, huh?"

"Intense?" I sat back on my heels. "It's...weird."

Phen pulled me up, still laughing. "Ready to try again?"

"Give me a minute." I rubbed my temple, feeling the same vibrating pulse beneath my feet. "You know something about this, don't you?"

"Me?" He blinked innocently. "Never."

Phen played it cool, examining his black, polished fingernails. "If you don't try again, I'm leaving you here. You'll have to figure out how to get back on your own. Hope you don't end up in the middle of the ocean."

I blew out a frustrated breath. "Fine."

"Teleport to the base of the statue." Phen tapped his boot on the pavement. "Any day now."

"Don't rush me." I closed my eyes, focusing past him, to the Statue of Liberty. I took a deep breath and tried to clear my mind, to let the space between here and the statue shrink. The world jittered around the edges, closing in, and then it snapped away sharply.

The world flickered, and I hit the ground hard again. I looked up. "I'm inside?" Pale light crept down from high windows, and the floor beneath me throbbed with that strange vibration — worse than outside, like the entire lobby was alive with something buried just beneath the surface.

A sharp thrum pulled at me, drawing me to a narrow door tucked into a shadowed corner. Neon light seeped out from beneath, casting an eerie glow across the floor.

Phen appeared at my side, looking entirely too pleased with himself.

"Nice work," he said. "You might even get us back to Jersey without drowning."

I pointed toward the door. "You see that?"

He barely glanced at it. "Probably just a creepy old janitor's closet."

"You're not curious?" I asked.

"What I'm curious about is why you're still here," he said, flipping his hair out of his eyes. "Meanwhile, your brother is probably stealing your girl. He is the handsome, charming type, you know, and you need to man up to get her back."

I ignored him, watching the glow pulse from under the door, pulling at me. It was like some strange magnet, growing stronger, louder, tunneling through me.

I took a step toward it, the pull beneath my feet growing stronger.

"Need you to zap me back to Jersey," Phen said, looking bored. "Gotta get back to the girl."

I rolled my eyes. "Kacey?"

He smiled, shrugging.

Part of me didn't want to leave, like I was caught in some invisible grip. I wasn't sure if I could look away long enough to teleport us. "This feels..."

Phen grabbed my wrist, and the world tilted until we landed in the alley outside the club. The music was loud now.

"What the hell, dude?" I growled.

"You were getting distracted by that weird door. Now, get us back to the Jersey."

I scrutinized him. He was hiding something — he knew what that sensation was, and he hadn't expected me to feel it. That much was obvious from the flash of surprise he'd failed to hide. And the door? He knew exactly where it led. He just didn't want me finding out.

But I would find out.

I grabbed his arm, and this time I didn't feel any hesitation as I teleported us back to the mansion.

Chapter Thirty-Five

Kiran

I wasn't looking forward to Steve's birthday party. I liked him — a lot, actually — but this wasn't the time for celebrating. Still, they all deserved a chance to breathe. Rhiannon and Steve had been working tirelessly, almost feverishly, diving into harnessing their powers with more focus than I'd thought possible. I felt a swell of pride thinking about how they juggled the weight of their responsibilities alongside school.

Still, there was the constant, looming threat of the power shift. I couldn't shake the feeling that we might be celebrating at the brink of a storm.

Justin would be there tonight, haunting the corners with that easy, magnetic charm that pulled Rhi toward him and twisted my heart. I couldn't deny the draw between them, though. Still, Rhi and I had become even closer. She had feelings for Justin, but I felt deep in my soul that she loved me more.

It wasn't just my love for Rhi that tangled inside me. It was this new, raw feeling of kinship with him. My twin, my brother—unfamiliar words that lodged in my throat. Some days, I thought I understood him; most days, the gulf between us seemed immeasurable.

"Hey, you okay?" Rhi's voice cut through my thoughts.

I nodded because I was more than okay with her near me.

"Are you sure?" She moved closer, her eyes searching mine. "You've been... distant."

"I just wish we weren't stretching ourselves so thin," I admitted. "Everything feels...precarious." I hated feeling this way, but everything was changing so fast.

Her face softened, a mix of love and resolve. She slipped her arms around my neck, stood on her toes, and kissed me on the cheek. "Everything will be okay," she whispered.

The warmth of her skin lingered, a tender balm to my restless mind. Did I deserve the trust she placed in me? Fallen and flawed, I grappled with this new fragility of my heart. And yet, wrapped in her embrace, there was a comfort that everything would be okay.

"I'm gonna meet Kacey at my uncle's to get ready," she said, sliding her fingers through my hair and making me bite back a moan of pleasure. She turned, the ends of her brown hair flicking against her back as she headed towards the door.

"Go ahead," I said, smiling to reassure her, or maybe myself. "I'll be right behind you."

"Promise?" Her smile was gentle.

"Promise."

I watched her walk away, filled with longing. She disappeared around the corner, and I heard the front door click shut. I turned my attention back to the newest journal we had found in her grandfather's office, its cover worn and the pages full of secrets.

A storm was coming, and though I wanted to believe Rhi, uncertainty gnawed at the edges of my hope. How did you protect someone when you didn't even know where the real danger was?

Where was the imbalance happening? Were more demons rising, fueled by some new, vicious power? I grimaced at the thought of more Watchers siding with evil. Or was it something entirely different, a swell of angels and righteous souls upsetting the order? What if, in our dedication, we were simply shifting the scales too far the other way?

Each possibility roiled inside me, and I flipped through the brittle pages, desperate to find something we'd missed. Some answer.

"Looking for me?"

The voice was like ice poured through my veins.

Vince.

I turned, body tense, as the air in front of me shimmered and he emerged, his smile sharp as a blade.

"Still reading your bedtime stories?" Vince gestured to the journal with a casual flick of his hand. "I hear they're quite thrilling."

"What do you want and how did you get into my house?" My voice was steadier than I felt. His presence churned the air around him, oozing menace, and I struggled to mask the quickening beat of my heart.

"You know what I love about you, Kiran?" he said, ignoring my question. "Even as a Fallen, you're just so...earnest." He took a step forward, and I could sense the dark energy coiling beneath his skin. "The way you care. It's adorable."

I took a breath, eyes locking on his. "Get out and stay away from my twin and me. Away from all of us."

He laughed, a harsh and sour sound. "Is that what you tell yourself? You've found your long-lost twin and are a happy family now?" He sneered. "Keep that faith, little angel. See how far it gets you."

My house was warded. Sam and Mia helped put them in place. There was no way Vince could slip through them. I stood, barely trusting my legs.

"You aren't real." I took a step toward him and raised my hand to obliterate him.

His shape wavered, but the mocking smile remained. "Oh, I'm real enough."

"You're the one who was calling to me?" I asked, confused. Reluctant to believe, but knowing it was true. I blinked, the room tilting as his laugh rattled the walls.

The air crackled. Then I felt him — inside my head, an oily presence slithering around my defenses like smoke through a cracked door.

"Stop this!" I shouted.

I fell to my knees, fists clenched. How was this possible? The wards were working. This was something else, something worse. He could reach me through my own mind.

Vince's voice seemed to expand, vibrating through me and filling every crevice of the house. "Let me help you. I don't want to hurt you anymore."

The words wound through my mind like a snake. Help me?

"You've stumbled upon a dangerous imbalance," his voice continued, both inside me and around me. "I can fix it. I can help you both."

His voice thrummed inside my head. "I know exactly where the imbalance is and how to fix it."

Through the haze of my panic, I caught sight of him again — that smile, a dark promise carved into his face. There was no way he could know that Rhi and her cousins were Ossaris. My breath came in ragged bursts. He was lying. He had to be.

His eyes flickered, like coals sparked to life, blazing suddenly bright red as the truth hit me.

"You've turned demon?" I whispered, horror coating my words.

"Fallen, angel, demon—what's the difference, really?" His voice was smooth, smug. "Maybe you should reconsider your loyalties."

I staggered to my feet, willing strength back into my limbs. "Go to Hell."

"I'm already there," he taunted. "And soon, you'll be too." Then he was gone, his presence a cold stain on the room.

What was that supposed to mean? I will be there soon. No, that was impossible. I would never turn demon. Never.

I needed to get to Rhi. My soul called to hers, and it was strong and pure, and I held onto it with everything I had. She was safe.

I needed to know how Vince was doing this and how to block him. I popped right outside of Mia's room. I banged on the door.

"Come in!" She was perched on the edge of her bed, mirror in hand, halfway through her makeup, wearing nothing but a towel. "Blondie?"

As she looked at me, she must have seen the fear in my eyes. "I need Sam," I said, my voice barely holding.

"What's wrong?" Her dark hair was still wet from the shower, and her brow creased with sudden concern.

"It's Vince," I said. "He's turned demon."

I heard her sharp intake of breath, and then her expression hardened. "That bastard."

I nodded, too numb to find words.

"And you think he wants Rhi? He's not getting his filthy hands on her." Her voice was fierce, protective.

"Where's Sam?" I asked again.

"Where do you think? With Sorcha. He's always at that mansion." She tugged a jacket on and walked to me, "Come on. Let's get him."

"We're teleporting," I warned. I grabbed her arm and jumped us to Sorcha's. I stood on the doorstep, hand raised to knock, when Mia hammered ahead of me and shoved the door open.

"Sam! Sam!" Her voice bounced off the walls as she barreled down the hallway.

Justin was the first to emerge, a slight scowl on his face. "What's going on?" he called, his eyes narrowing when he saw me.

"Vince!" Mia snapped. "He's turned demon."

Justin's expression shifted to stone as he squeezed the beer bottle he was holding. It exploded into a million tiny glass fragments. That was...weird.

"Whoa," Mia said, stunned.

Sam and Sorcha came in from the back porch, looking alarmed. "We have to strengthen the wards," I said, finding my voice. "Or something." I scraped my hand down my face.

Sorcha's expression was grim. "He got into your house?"

"He got into my head. If he can do that..." I couldn't finish.

"We need to find Rhi," Justin said, already pulling keys from his pocket.

"She's safe," I said.

"Oh yeah, you're all knowing when it comes to her." Justin clenched his teeth. "I don't care what you say, I'm going to find her."

"Take it down a notch, Romeo," Mia said. "Rhi is fine for now."

"Kiran?" Sam asked, voice tinged with urgency. "What happened?"

"I thought we were warded," I said, finally finding my voice. "I don't understand—he was in my head, mocking me. Said he knew how to fix this, that I'd be joining him soon."

Sorcha's eyes were wide. "How is he getting in?"

"I'm not sure," I said, "That's why I'm here."

All their eyes were on me. "He called to me a couple of weeks ago. It was just his voice. I didn't know it was him then. Tonight, it happened again, but this time he manifested."

"Manifested?" Justin asked.

"Yes, like he was in my house in front of me. But, he kept getting fuzzy like he wasn't really there."

"He's manifesting an image of himself, but he's not actually there," Sam explained. "Only very powerful angels or demons can pull that off."

"He's blocking my defenses. It's like he's...in me. Even with the wards up."

Sorcha put her hands on her hips. "But angels can't get through wards. Demons definitely can't."

I turned to her, desperation making my voice rough. "He's inside my head!"

Sam turned to me. "We need to block him. It's like closing a portal link. We'll build shields over your mind."

Sam turned to Sorcha, grabbing her hand. Then he instructed Mia and Justin to gather around me, holding hands as well. "He has a link to you. For Hell's sake, he's your father." He gave me a pitying look.

"Shouldn't we all be shielding our minds?" Justin said, his face set with determination. "Especially me? Since he's my DNA donor, too."

Sam nodded. "Yeah. He'll likely use your connection to his advantage, too."

"Great," Justin muttered. "This is what I've always wanted—a family reunion in my brain."

"Ready?" Sam asked, eyes darting between us.

I nodded. Sam gave a quick jerk of his chin, and the room seethed with sudden energy as he drew power from the others. I felt the brush and hum of their presence sweep around me — warmth flooding in over the cold Vince had left behind.

"Focus on blocking him out," Sam instructed, his voice firm. "Think of the boundaries you need, and then solidify them in your mind."

I tried, breathing through Vince's words that still clung like a bruise to my insides. But this time, instead of panic, a growing strength rose with each breath I took. They were sealing me off from Vince. I could feel it working.

Sam's voice was a low hum, soothing and instructive. "Don't fight it. Let it cover everything."

A molten glow filled my mind's eye, a shield against Vince, against anything. I let out a shaky breath as the last gap closed and the oily presence inside me finally recoiled.

They all stared at me, waiting. "I'm good."

"Justin, you're up, and then Sorcha. Then she and I will add more protections here. We'll head over to your place and add more there as well."

"And we'll be ready for him." Sorcha's voice was full of steel.

God, I hoped so.

Chapter Thirty-Six

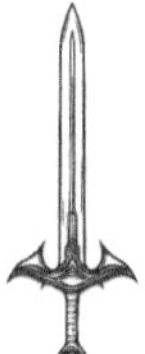

Rhiannon

The party was in full swing. Steve was obviously popular, judging by the crowd that had spilled into every corner of the room. He moved through it all with an easy confidence, face lit up, riding the energy like a current—and he deserved every second of it. He'd been pushing himself hard lately, honing his Ossaris powers until they were almost frightening. His intuition was razor-sharp, and his senses? The way he could see, hear, and smell things that no one else could made him seem less like a person and more like something wild, something ancient.

My eyes wandered through the room until they landed on Taylor and Scott. They looked happy and carefree on this night out without the baby, who was with Scott's parents. Kacey was practically attached to Phen's hip, sitting on his lap and whispering into his ear. Mia was dancing, eyes closed, as if she were lost in her own world.

And then there was a sight that made me blink twice. Kiran and Justin. In a corner.

Talking.

It was surreal. Kiran honestly looked like he was listening, his silver eyes intent, nodding along to whatever Justin was saying. I wouldn't have believed it if I hadn't seen it with my own eyes, the two of them standing there with no bloodshed, no visible tension. Justin's tall frame leaned casually against the wall, his dark hair falling across his eyes. Kiran's posture was more rigid, his silver eyes looking concerned.

I hadn't had a chance to talk to either of them. I took another sip of my drink, wondering what they were saying.

It had to be about me. Everything was, lately.

Kiran caught me staring. For one breathless second, something pulled taut between us—invisible, electric—and then he turned back to Justin like it had never happened.

"Rhi!" Mia called to me, and I knew I should join her, but I couldn't stop staring at the two figures in the corner.

I had to know what was happening, what Justin could possibly be saying that required that level of attention, what was making Kiran look so concerned. I set my drink down, determination knotting my stomach as I made my way toward them, weaving through the clumps of people.

"Hey, sweet cheeks," Sam grabbed me by the elbow, pulling me off course. "I was just about to come find you."

"I—" I glanced over his shoulder. Kiran was talking now, and Justin was nodding, arms crossed, like he was weighing Kiran's words. "I was just on my way to—"

"Dance with me first," Sam said, taking my hand and pulling me toward the center of the room. "Remember how much fun we had last time?"

My words caught in my throat as he took my hand, pulling me toward the center of the room. The music was loud, the beat quickening around us, and I was spinning, caught in the blur of lights and laughter. Sam twirled me, pulling me close, then pushing me back with a playful wink. "Come on," he said. "Don't be so serious!"

I tried to protest, my eyes darting back to the corner, but the view was blocked now. "Sam, I—" He was spinning me again, and I couldn't help but laugh, despite myself.

Mia appeared next to us, her face flushed with excitement. "There you are! I thought you disappeared!" Her hands joined mine and Sam's, the three of us forming a circle, laughing.

"You're relentless!" I shouted over the music, letting myself spin into the chaos, trying not to care for a moment about the two figures still in the corner.

I was whirling, dizzy, breathless. Sam spun me around again, and the music and laughter swallowed me whole. Then, suddenly, the air was knocked out of me. I hit something solid. I hit someone solid. I looked up, startled, and there he was. Justin.

His hands gripped my waist, steadying me, but they lingered—too long, too firm, like he was testing the waters. His fingers pressed into the curve of my hips, sending a shiver up my spine. A sliver of his black silk hair fell across his cheek, and I took a breath, trying to ground myself.

"What are you doing?" I asked, my voice trembling more than I wanted it to. Out of the corner of my eye, I saw Kiran still standing in the corner. Watching, his face a shadow, unreadable from this distance.

"Rescuing you from Sam," Justin said, a teasing challenge in his voice. He let one hand drop to his side, but the other stayed glued to my waist, his thumb brushing against the fabric of my dress in a way that made my skin prickle. "Unless you're having fun?"

"Of course she is," Sam chimed in, shooting us a grin.

"Thanks," I managed, the word coming out smaller than I intended.

He looked down at me, green eyes darkening in a way that made it hard to think straight. The corner of his mouth curved. "Miss me?"

I pulled away, my mind catching up to my body, and then the music slowed.

Justin laughed, a rumble low in his chest. "You think I'd let this idiot keep you all to himself all night?" He motioned to where Sam and Mia were now dancing next to us.

Sam shrugged, a mock expression of defeat crossing his face. "Can't blame a guy for trying."

Justin's smile faded a little, replaced by something more intense, more dangerous. His eyes burned into mine, and I felt like I couldn't breathe. "We need to talk," he said, his voice barely audible over the music.

I nodded as a knot formed in my stomach. "Now?"

He looked around, his lips twisting. "Not here." He pulled me close again, his hand warm against the small of my back. The music slowed further, and people around us paired off, swaying to the romantic notes. But Justin didn't move. Instead, he pulled me closer until his chin rested on my head. "I've missed this," he murmured.

He took my hands, placing one on his waist and the other on his chest. I could feel the hard planes of his body beneath my fingers, the steady thud of his heartbeat under my palm. I scanned the room for Kiran, but he was gone, vanished into the shadows.

Justin's hand slid lower, and I felt my breath catch. "You're not getting away from me this time," he whispered, his lips brushing against my temple. His grip tightened, pulling me even closer until there was no space between us. I could feel every inch of him pressed against me, and it was all I could do not to melt into him.

The music swelled around us, but all I could focus on was the heat of his body, the way his fingers traced patterns on my back, the way his breath hitched when I shifted against him. "Justin," I whispered, my voice trembling.

"Shh," he murmured, his lips grazing my ear. "Just dance with me."

And I did. Because how could I not?

The song ended, and a hyped up dance mix came on. His fingers wrapped possessively around my wrist. He was pulling me through the crush of bodies, toward the door.

I half stumbled, my voice caught in a mix of surprise and excitement. "What are you doing?"

"Let's go somewhere quieter. Where can we actually hear each other."

He led us outside, the cool air biting at my skin. Distant shouts and laughter trailed from the party, the door swinging shut behind us. Justin's grip had loosened, but he was still holding my hand tightly.

"What's going on?" I demanded, trying to catch my breath as we stepped into the dimly lit street.

He stopped and turned to face me. "Run away with me." The words landed like a stone dropped in still water. His eyes were dark, searching my face for something—hope, maybe. No. Desperation.

"What?" I took a step back.

He released my hand, running his own through his hair. "This is suffocating you, Rhi. I can see it. You need to get away. Just for a little while. With me."

"I can't just leave," I said, my pulse drumming in my ears. "I have school and my family. I can't—I can't just disappear."

His hands moved to my shoulders, gripping them fiercely. "You can. We can. You know you want to."

"It's not that simple, Justin."

"Yes, it is." He reached for me again, but I stepped back, wrapping my own arms around myself.

A voice came from the shadows, and I turned to see Kiran stepping toward us, his expression stormy. "After all we talked about tonight, Justin. This is what you do?"

"Kiran," I heard myself say around the knot in my throat.

"Rhi, there's something you need to know," Kiran said, coming closer to us.

"Kiran, don't," Justin warned, stepping in front of me.

"You really think I can keep this from her?" Kiran shot back, "I saw him, Rhi. I saw Vince."

A cold shock rippled through me. It was the last name I expected to hear, a ghost from the past rising with new life. "Vince?" My voice wavered, "How?"

Kiran moved closer, his eyes seeking mine. "That's what we were discussing."

Justin glared, his jaw tight. "It doesn't matter how. What matters is I get you far away from here."

Kiran took another step forward. "He's back, Rhi. He's dangerous...he's turned demon."

I stood frozen between them. "When did you find this out?" I looked from Kiran to Justin, searching for answers, for something that made sense.

"He appeared in my house soon after you left." Kiran looked around like he thought Vince would pop out of the shadows.

"But your house is warded!"

"It is. And now it is even more so, as well as yours, the mansion, and all of your cousins' homes."

"I don't understand."

"He wasn't actually there. He was in my head and manifesting an image of himself and his voice."

"I didn't want to drag you into this," Justin said, his voice low, conflicted. "Not again."

"You mean you didn't want her to know," Kiran countered, his expression fierce. "You think running is the answer."

My heart thundered frantically in my chest. "What does he want?"

Kiran shook his head, his voice taut with urgency. "Balance. He kept talking about balance, saying that he knows what the shift is. He claims he doesn't want to hurt us."

Justin snorted, stepping closer to me. "He's lying. He's only ever cared about himself."

"I agree." Kiran said, "I don't know what he is after, but he said things similar to Phen. About the balance of power being disrupted. He also said he knows our fates." He motioned between himself and me.

"He's toying with us," Justin cut in. He turned to me, his eyes fierce. "He's trying to mess with our heads. I'm telling you, Rhi, getting out of here is the best thing you can do."

Kiran ignored Justin's interruption. "He said we'll need him soon. That things are changing."

"Did you forget what a lying bastard he is?" Justin's eyes flashed, one hand clenching into a fist. "I haven't."

"Of course I haven't!" Kiran groaned, scrubbing his hands through his hair. "Look, I know what you're trying to do, Justin."

"Oh, do you?"

"Yes, I do, and I know it's because of your feelings for Rhi. But trust me, please. Vince scared me, and he can't kill me. You, though, are not immortal, and he can kill you and Rhi if it is just the two of you."

Justin looked away, a muscle ticking in his jaw.

"We all have a better chance if we stick together."

The door swung open behind us, and all three of us turned as Steve bounded down the stairs, his breath misting in the cool air. "Did something happen?" he asked, concern lacing his words as he came closer.

"Steve," I said, breathless. "What are you doing out here? You're missing your party."

"Intuition," he said, tapping his head. "Got this crazy feeling I needed to see you. Like something big was about to go down and I had to be there."

"Vince is back," I said, the words feeling heavy and strange on my tongue. "We don't know exactly what it means, but it's bad."

Steve's eyes widened, and his whole body tensed like he'd been shocked. "Are you serious? How?"

I glanced at the brothers. Justin was silent, his eyes filled with turmoil. Kiran spoke first. "He appeared at my house. Said he knows what's coming, and that we'll need him." His voice was grim. "He's a demon now."

"Demon?" Steve ran a hand through his hair, looking between our faces. "That's—that's bad, right? Really bad?"

Kiran nodded. "He was powerful before, but now? I'm sure his power has grown."

"So what's the plan?" Steve asked, his eyes flicking between us.

I looked at them, my heart heavy. "I...I don't know."

"The plan is staying together," Kiran said, his eyes cutting to Justin with a warning that left no room for argument. "It's the only way any of us stand a chance."

Chapter Thirty-Seven

Justin

Kiran to the rescue again. I ground my teeth as I pressed myself into the farthest, darkest corner of the room. He'd filled me in on every detail of his run-in with Vince. Kiran said it had shaken him. I wasn't scared of my DNA donor. I had enough rage coiled inside me that fear didn't stand a chance.

Kiran had insisted we keep Rhi close, maintain a united front. "We can't leave everyone else exposed," he said, his eyes all serious and silver, like that would make me listen. Everyone else be damned. I could not let what happened to Rhi with Vince ever happen again. Hiding her away was the only thing that made sense. I'd watch over her and keep her safe.

Kiran thought hiding her away wouldn't work; we had to fight and work together. With what army? A Fallen Angel, a half-demon, a Watcher, and a witch? It sounded like the beginning of a bad joke. I glanced over to where he stood with Rhi and Steve, and I thought that maybe, just maybe, he didn't understand how far I'd go for her. Or maybe he did, and that's what really scared him. I looked over again and caught his eyes on me, as if he could hear my thoughts aloud from across the room. Maybe he could.

Phen walked to the center of the room, acoustic guitar in hand. A mic and wooden stool were set up for his performance. "This one's for the birthday boy," he said, grinning over at Steve.

I knew that Phen had his own set of secrets, and something about him gave me the creeps. Maybe it was his sudden appearance or the way he weaseled his way into our circle so easily. I didn't trust him as far as I could throw him. And Kacey looked at him as if he were a god, her eyes glued on his every move. I watched from my vantage point, drowning out the music, my thoughts circling back to the Statue of Liberty. I still needed to get back there, to see what was behind that glowing door.

No time like the present. I pushed off the wall. I figured I could slip away, check things out, and then get back here before anyone knew I was gone. Demon-boy would keep them entertained long enough.

I slipped out the side entrance of the building, toward the alley, where Phen's van loomed in the shadows. The chill wrapped around me, and my footsteps sounded loud against the pavement. I turned the corner and paused when I heard it. A muffled cry. At first, I thought I'd imagined it, but then there it was again.

I followed the sound, my eyes adjusting to the darkness when I saw her, Trina, crumpled against the wall, her hair veiling her face. "Tri?" I called out, quickening my pace.

She straightened at my voice, a hurried hand brushing at her cheeks. "Justin?"

I crouched beside her. "You okay?"

Her lip wobbled, and then she collapsed into me, her shoulders shaking. "It's Steve," she said, her words tumbling out between sobs. "He didn't even try, you know? Like he didn't want to talk to me at all."

I wrapped my arms around her, feeling the ache of her confusion. I knew that ache because I had the same feeling every time I saw or even thought about Rhi.

Trina was a lot for anyone to handle. A whirlwind of drama, insecurity, and desperation. But she was also one of my oldest friends. We had history. I stayed holding her while she cried about Steve. I didn't blame him for breaking up with her. She would have had them married with matching tattoos by Christmas break if she had her way.

"Hey, you'd have him chained and shackled if you could," I said, my voice teasing but gentle. "Why don't you try giving the guy a little space?"

She sniffed. "Did Rhi put you up to this?"

"Nah. I just know a thing or two about how guys think, that's all." I squeezed her shoulder. "And I know a thing or two about you, too."

She sighed, easing back against the wall, some of the tension leaving her shoulders. "I don't know what I'd do without you," she said, her voice softening.

I smoothed her hair, and she shifted closer, her sigh rippling through me — sad and hollow. I thought of my own loss, self-inflicted but still raw. Maybe I needed to take my own advice and give Rhi some space. But hadn't I been doing exactly that? And still she hadn't made a choice between Kiran and me. Or maybe she had, and I just refused to see it.

Being that close to her was its own kind of torture — everything I wanted, always just out of reach. But tonight, when we danced, something shifted. She didn't pull away. That pull between us was real, undeniable. I refused to chalk it up to angel blood. It had to be more than that.

Trina shifted beside me, pulling me from my thoughts. "So, what are you doing out here anyway?"

Good question, I thought, but I couldn't tell her about the glowing door. "Needed some air," I said, my eyes flicking over to the shadows. "Too much drama in that room."

A sudden noise pulled my attention. A thump. A strange, metallic clatter. "Did you hear that?"

"Hear what?" She tilted her head.

I listened, picking up a faint whisper I couldn't quite make out. "Nothing," I said, shaking my head. It must be my Nephilium hearing getting stronger. All my senses had gotten better since ditching that shielding necklace.

"What's up with you?" Trina asked, watching me like I was losing it.

I heard it again, louder this time. It was definitely coming from farther down the alley. It made the fine hairs on the back of my neck stand on end.

"It's her, isn't it?" Trina asked.

"Her who?"

"Rhi."

I felt my irritation flare, "You should get back inside."

She blinked at me, her expression a mix of hurt and stubbornness. "Justin…"

"Seriously." I stood and offered her my hand, pulling her to her feet. "I'm right behind you. Just need a minute." I walked her to the back door, making sure she got inside before I turned back to the alley.

I hesitated for a moment, scanning for shadows, for wings, or for anything that didn't belong. The sound of a metallic crash rang through the air, louder now, and then more shuffling.

I moved slowly, scanning the alley. I could just make out movement by Phen's van. A figure. I crept closer, listening hard.

Another crash, and the sound of wood clattering to the ground. It didn't sound like a fight. I stepped closer, my eyes adjusting to the dim light through the van windows. It was too damn dark to see much, but whoever was at work in there was getting busy. I slipped back, skirting the van silently, but not before I heard another smash followed by two voices.

I listened for Phen still singing inside to make sure I wasn't walking in on him and Kacey doing things I didn't want to see. I caught a high note that was unmistakably Phen's voice singing.

"So not demon-boy," I said to myself.

I waited for a moment, listening for anything else, when I saw a flicker of movement by the van. I took a step forward and then froze.

It was the girl from the club in New York. What was her name again? Tess…that was it.

I ducked back, flattening myself against the wall. Who the Hell was she talking to? I leaned out, trying to catch a glimpse, but then a clang broke through the air again.

"It has to be here," she said, her voice edged with frustration.

"It's not. I've gone through the whole van already." The male voice sounded agitated. "We need to hurry before he finds us."

"Relax!" Tess replied. "He'll just think someone was trying to rob his band equipment and got spooked."

A chuckle reverberated from behind the van. "You should have just come to me if you wanted an autograph," said a voice with oily charm.

I stilled. Phen. How did he get out here so fast?

A nervous yelp cut through the air. "I told her it was a bad idea!" The male voice shook with panic. "She made me do it. Please—"

He sauntered toward the van, a smirk playing on his lips. Tess looked stunned, her mouth gaping like a fish out of water. Her accomplice cowered beside her, wide-eyed and pale.

"It's just a misunderstanding," Tess stammered, trying on a bold smile. "We're just..."

"Stealing from me?" Phen finished, cocking an eyebrow.

"You wouldn't believe us if we told you," Tess said, less bravado now.

"Try me," Phen said, like he had all the time in the world — like he wasn't half a second from snapping in two.

I peeked out again and watched Phen lean in close, stopping right in front of the guy and Tess. "Tell me quick, before you lie, what waits for you under the sky?

A pocket knife? A girl's embrace? A hunger hollow as your face?" he said, his voice strange and syrupy.

The guy's eyes glazed over, his panic turning to a dull monotone. "Some guy came to the club...a demon," he started. "He knew you were playing there in a few weeks. He threatened Tess—said he'd burn her place to the ground and drag her to Hell."

"What is he looking for?" Phen asked.

"A knife. He said it was his and described it. He said you were the most likely to have it."

"Did he now?" Phen's voice turned sharp. "And what was his name?"

"Moretti." Tess said flatly.

What!? It can't be. They can't mean Vince.

"And you're more scared of him and what he said he would do then me?"

"Yes." Tess said flatly. "Moretti is now the right hand of Lucifer."

"What!" Phen growled. The look on his face made me grateful I wasn't in their shoes.

Tess tugged at the guy's arm, her face crumpling with fear. "Please," she begged. "He'll come after us. We just thought—"

"We didn't have a choice!" The man wailed.

"We all have a choice." Phen circled them like a lion about to pounce. "Isn't that the wonderful thing about free will?"

"Everything we are telling you is the truth. I swear."

"Of course it is." Phen's smile, even in the dark, was predatory. "I coerced you so you cannot lie."

The guy blinked, awareness snapping back. "What will you do to us, Lord Phenix?"

Phen laughed. Then his eyes darkened. "Maybe I should burn you from the inside out." Then fire erupted from his hands. I slid back into the shadows, fear crawling over my skin. I took a deep breath and peered back again.

Phen's eyes were glowing red. "You will return to New York and tell Vincent you didn't find anything." He paused, "You will not remember our encounter, only that you did your best to find the knife. Now go."

They didn't wait, scrambling off into the dark. I stayed hidden, my mind racing. What knife did Vince want that was so important?

Phen lingered, gaze sweeping the alley. I held my breath. He swept his hands, and the mess around his van was cleaned up. Then he turned and went back toward the building, his silhouette elongating in the dim glow from street lamps.

I waited a few minutes before I moved, making sure I wouldn't bump into Phen. I pulled the door open and slipped back inside. Nothing had changed. Kiran and Rhi were huddled together in a corner. Kacey was draped over Phen, and Sam and Mia were dancing.

I pushed through the crowd to get to them.

"Where's the fire?" Sam asked, grinning. He had a cup in one hand and the other wrapped around Mia's waist.

"I need to talk to you."

His eyebrows shot up, and he set down his drink. "What's up?"

"Not here," I said, nodding toward the side, away from Kiran and Rhi and the cluster of people around them. I wanted to keep this as under the radar as possible.

I jerked my chin toward the back door. I turned and walked out, Sam behind me. Once we were away from prying eyes and ears, I took a deep breath and let it all out at once. "You won't believe what I just saw."

He raised an eyebrow. "Try me."

"There were these two people. They were going through Phen's van. They said something about a knife. They mentioned Vince."

"Holy shit." Sam's face turned serious. "Was Vince there?"

"No. But they were scared out of their minds about him."

"Did you recognize them?" Sam asked, leaning in close.

"Some chick from the club in New York Phen has booked. Tess. She said Vince was the right hand of Lucifer now."

Sam reeled a little as if the words punched him. "What?"

"He told them to find a knife." I looked around again, making sure no one was eavesdropping. "The guy with Tess said Vince thought Phen was the most likely to have it."

"And Phen caught them?" Sam blew out a long breath. I could see him try to wrap his mind around this. "What did he do?"

"Scared them with his demon tricks and then coerced them or something. Then he set them loose and told them to go back to New York."

Sam pushed his hands through his hair. "Damn," Sam's eyes darted, calculating. I could see his mind working a mile a minute. "We gotta keep this on the down low. If Vince is after this knife, we need to find it first or get it from whoever has it."

"Phen's involved in all this way more than he's letting on," Sam mused. "Do you think he knows what's up?"

"He looked pissed when he found out Vince was behind this." I said, "And just as stunned to find out Vince was Lucifer's right-hand man."

He studied me for a second. "And you're sure they didn't know you were there?"

I shrugged, trying to seem cool, but my heart was thrumming like mad.

"I'll take care of Phen," Sam said, eyes bright. "You don't mention this to any-one...for now."

I nodded. I wasn't planning to let anyone else know anyway. I still needed to get to New York and that weird door at the Statue of Liberty.

I turned to leave when the door swung open. It was Trina crying again. "Justin?" She sniffed.

"What's going on now?" I didn't have time for this.

"I..."she staggered down the steps.

"I'm out of here," Sam said, eyeing Trina. "Good luck with that."

"Thanks a lot." I huffed at him.

"Justin, I found Steve in the kitchen...he was..."

I rolled my eyes. "What was he doing, Tri?"

"I walked in on him and Mia!" Her bottom lip was quivering. "I can't stay here, Justin. Would you take me home?"

"Sure." I wrapped an arm over her shoulder. I'd get her home and visit that door another day.

Chapter Thirty-Eight

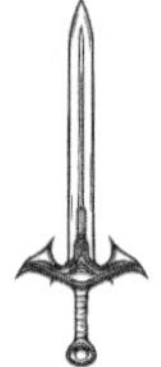

Rhiannon

Tonight was just weird. The ups and downs made me dizzy. I was excited for Steve's birthday party. We have all been working so much; it was good to celebrate him and enjoy ourselves. I expected Kiran and Justin to lunge for each other's throats, but then, I saw them talking. It was strange enough to watch, like seeing a panther and a lion sharing tea. I didn't dare get my hopes up that they might get along.

Then Justin asked me to dance. He had spun me, and I couldn't help it—I laughed. "You're not bad, you know."

"You're surprised?" He dipped me low, his hair swinging like a curtain, and I found myself grinning up at him.

"Just a little." He brought me back up, pulling me close. He was warm and real, his smile a mix of arrogance and something deeper. It made me breathless. For a while, I forgot all the reasons our lives were so impossibly complicated.

But then nothing could have prepared me for the last surprise of the night. Vince. Vince, who was supposed to be long gone, had appeared to Kiran.

The drive home was unnaturally quiet. Kiran's hands gripped the steering wheel until his knuckles were pale, his jaw tight with thoughts unspoken. I touched his arm, felt the tension rippling under his skin, "Are you okay?" I asked for the thousandth time, and he looked at me with those liquid silver eyes.

"I am now."

When we got inside, he let out a long breath and went over everything that had happened. How Vince got into his head, the things he said, and how he went to Sam for help once Vince was gone. "We will do the same for you, Steve, and Taylor tomorrow. Plus, we increased the wards around all of our homes, including the Rizzos' and Taylor's homes."

"But what does he want?" My voice was a small, worried thing in the room's half-light.

"Revenge, power, maybe me. It doesn't matter. We're going to stop him." His voice was fierce with conviction, but I sensed the turmoil underneath. He pulled me close, his breath warm in my hair, and I closed my eyes against the steady beat of his heart.

I think I fell asleep somewhere in the comfort of his arms. But then I reached for him, and he was gone.

My eyes flew open to the dark and the cold absence where he should have been. I lay there, my mind spinning with fear and endless questions. There was no chance of sleeping without him beside me.

I knew if I called to him he would come, but I wanted to find him instead, to see what he was doing and if I could help. My footsteps were quiet through the hushed night. I threw on some clothes, slipped out the front door, and let it click softly behind me.

The air was cool on my skin as I hurried down the front steps. Kiran's place wasn't far, and soon, I was edging around to the back of his house. "Kiran," I called, stepping into the moonlit space.

He looked up, his eyes glowing silver in the night. "Rhi," he said, a crack of surprise in his voice.

I hesitated, taking in the sag of his shoulders. "I woke up, and you weren't there. Is it—did something happen?"

He shook his head. "Just thinking."

I moved closer. "Is it Vince?"

"Everything," he sighed, a resigned smile pulling at his lips. "You. Justin. What happened tonight. It's like everything's changing, and I'm..." He stopped, drawing a shaky breath. "I don't want to lose you, Rhi.

I settled beside him, our toes just skimming the water's edge. "Why do you think everything's changing?"

He watched the pool ripple, his jaw tense. "Ever since I fell," he began, like it hurt to say the words aloud, "I've been different. I feel...different. More human. It's confusing."

"But that's not a bad thing, is it?" I pressed, trying to catch his eyes.

"Sometimes, I don't know." His voice was so quiet, "I'm afraid these changes, my...my emotions, make me weak."

"It's so much stronger, these human feelings," he went on, his fingers tightening around mine. "Sometimes it overtakes me, like tonight. Seeing you with... with Justin..."

He trailed off, a tightness in his expression that made my chest ache. I could see him pulling back, holding something in. "I've felt jealousy before, but this..." His eyes closed for a moment, and when he opened them, they were so intense that I almost flinched. "This is different. It's stronger. It eats at me."

I touched his arm, the muscles taut under my fingers. "I'm sorry," I whispered, wanting to take away his worry. "I'm so sorry, Kiran."

He shook his head, but I caught the flicker of pain that crossed his face. "I don't want you to be sorry. I just—Rhi, I need you to know how hard this is for me."

"I know. I know it is," I said, "And I know it's hard for Justin too. I'm making this harder on both of you. You're being so patient, so...perfect, and I...I love you for it."

He stared at me, his silver eyes a storm of longing, as if he was trying to memorize every part of me. "Say it again. Tell me you love me."

"I love you," I whispered again.

Then he was kissing me, an urgent, breathless kiss that spoke the words he couldn't say. I felt it—the truth of what he felt for me—and I kissed him back with everything I had, willing him to know that he didn't have to hold back, that I was his even though I was torn.

I touched his face, felt the warmth of his skin, the soft, uneven beat of the pulse in his neck. "Kiran....I want you. All of you," I breathed, and the fire in his eyes made my whole body hum with longing.

He kissed me again, slower this time, as if we had a lifetime to spend on this moment. "I don't deserve you," he murmured, his lips brushing mine. "Not after everything. After what I am now."

"Don't," I said, sliding my fingers in his hair, that impossible shade of honey blonde even in the dark. "You're still the same to me. Still Kiran. Still everything."

The weight of his gaze was almost too much, a mixture of disbelief and devotion. "Rhi..." It was a whisper wrapped in all the human emotions that tangled around us. I felt the truth of them, and instead of fear, I was full of something wild and reckless, a love that no longer had room for hesitation.

I pulled at his shirt, slipping my hands beneath it, touching his warm skin. His breath tangled with mine, his fingers brushing my skin with a softness that made me shiver. He pulled back, his eyes searching my face, full of wonder and something that left me undone.

"Are you...?" This time, his voice was a raw mix of need and disbelief.

"Yes," I said, a simple word, but it carried all of me, showing him everything—how ready, how sure, how much I wanted him. "Yes." My heart was a wild thing in my chest. "I want this, Kiran. I want to be with you."

He looked at me, searching for doubt, but I had none. I wrapped myself around him, pulled him down to me. The grass was cool beneath us, and the world faded until there was nothing else but the press of his body and the night around us.

He pulled me closer, and I melted into him, losing myself in the warmth of his touch, the way his breath quickened against my skin. It was everything I needed, everything I wanted, and I felt the last of my resolve slip away as I gave myself over completely, feeling a new kind of freedom.

"Are you sure?" His voice was rough, unsteady, and he held me like I might disappear.

"Don't doubt it. Not tonight. Not ever."

He kissed me again, harder this time. Then he moved against me, and I was on fire, burning with him, for him.

I gasped as the sky above us cracked open, rain falling in scattered drops. Kiran paused, looking up at the sky. Then the rain came in earnest, soaking through my clothes, the wind wrapping my skin in goosebumps.

Kiran stood in one smooth motion and pulled me up with him. I laughed at the suddenness of it all, the feeling of abandon in the storm. "You're not getting away that easily," I teased, reaching for him. But I was shivering now, and with a soft sound, he swept me into his arms, holding me close.

We made it inside, the dark, quiet house wrapping around us like a secret, and I barely noticed as he carried me upstairs to one of the bedrooms. All I knew was him, the warmth of his body radiating through my wet clothes. "I want you so badly," he whispered, setting me on my feet, but I was already pulling at his shirt, my fingers clumsy and impatient.

"Don't stop," I murmured, tugging him down to me, the need in my own voice startling me.

He kissed me deeply, and I felt his disbelief turn into something fierce and un-stoppable. The storm outside was nothing compared to this. There was an intensity in his touch, and it filled me with a wild, dizzying need. I was trembling against him, my whole body alive with the feeling of him everywhere at once. I was sure of this, of him, of us, in a way that left no room for doubt or fear.

I pulled away only briefly. "Do you have…um…do you have protection?"

His eyebrows rose. "Yes, well no, but…" He snapped his fingers, and the small foil packet appeared. "I do now."

I giggled, and his smile was magnetic.

His hand curved around my hip, then onto my stomach, pushing my shirt over my head. Skin to skin, I felt him tremble against me, his breath a shuddered warmth that melted through the cold. All my senses were alive, each touch sparking something fierce, something new. He kissed me again, his lips trailing fire along my skin, and all my thoughts dissolved into the perfect, dizzying whirlwind of us.

Thunder cracked outside, and we both startled, a rush of airless laughter escaping me. Kiran looked at me, eyes luminous with so much love it was almost unbearable. "I've waited to have you like this," he said, his voice rough with wonder. "I never thought—never believed this was ever possible." He traced my face, every touch deliberate, as if carving the memory of me into him. "I love you. All of you. I've loved you for so long, and I'll love you long after I'm dust."

I gave myself over—completely, utterly—to his arms and the raw, perfect desire in his words. All I could do was hold on to him, my breath tangled with his in the dark. I was full of him, full of love and longing and a fierce certainty that this was right, that even though the world might tear us apart, this moment would stay with us, holding us together.

He rose above me searching...searching as our soul song filled my heart. "I tried to stop, tried to let you go." Each word was ragged, like pieces torn from him. "But I couldn't. I can't."

He kissed my hair, dizzy, tender kisses like he couldn't believe I was here with him like this. Wrapping me in his arms, he let out an unsteady breath, and it sent a shiver cascading over my skin. His touch was like an unravelling, the barriers between us dissolving until nothing was left but a sweet oblivion.

I was breathing him, holding him, everything else fading to nothing. Stars exploded behind my eyes, a universe of light and heat and Kiran. I felt a shudder run through him, and then we crashed into each other, our bodies finding a rhythm that was breathless and everything we wanted, everything we needed.

This was different; everything was. Need and love and raw, new feeling entwining us so tightly that I couldn't tell where he ended and I began. He fell into me, a glint and flare of light, of sensation, and the last of our barriers slipped away. I gasped at the intimacy where our bodies met. He stopped, fear in his eyes. "Am I hurting you?"

"No, this is all new to me, and I wasn't sure how it would feel. Just go slow for a bit."

His hands glided along my face, holding me steady to look him in the eyes as he pushed a little farther and then stopped.

"What is it?" I whispered.

"I feel so much. It's overwhelming. I feel all my most potent emotions, but I feel yours as well and well…" he paused, pushing inside me slightly more. "I'm consumed by you."

I bit down on my lip feeling my tears hover along my lashes and slid my hands down his muscled back. His tattoos flared as I pulled on his hips and raised mine to meet him.

Kiran let out a ragged sound of disbelief as he filled me completely. A full, impossible feeling as our soul song roared. Heat coursed through my veins, and every inch of me responded, dizzy and alive and wrapped up in a love so deep it burned. I'd never felt so near to anyone, so known.

We were urgent, breathless—the world outside forgotten as we moved together. He gripped me tighter like he was afraid I might vanish. There was only us, crashing and colliding, a fierce and perfect unity.

My voice was thin, an airy cry of his name as each sensation crested higher, as everything else splintered away, and I was consumed, consumed, consumed. I was lost in him, in the exquisite, dizzying freedom of giving ourselves over to each other. I arched beneath him, abandoning everything but the blinding joy of becoming one.

The newness of it all was electric, wild, and I clung to him, everything inside me burning. "Kiran," I gasped, each breathless syllable a testament to how right this was. Each movement brought a new, consuming wave that built and built until I thought I might break apart with the intensity of it. "Please," I gasped, a needy, desperate sound that I couldn't hold back.

He answered my plea with a newfound intensity, letting the last of his restraint unravel. His breath was hot and quick against my skin, the sweet intensity swelling between us, and I was lost to it, breathless.

"I'm here," he said, his voice rough with love and need. "Always."

I clung to him, my body trembling, as the pressure inside me built and built, unstoppable, until I was a live wire of sensation. I thought I might drown, might be swallowed by the ecstasy of it, and then—I was breaking open, and everything was white light and fire. I cried out, the force of it ripping through me, and Kiran followed, a shuddering release that left us undone and breathless, holding on to the only thing that mattered—each other.

Chapter Thirty-Nine

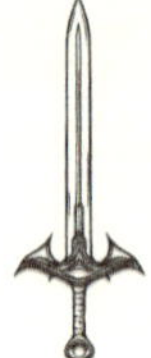

Rhiannon

I lay there, watching the way the early sun played across his skin. Before dawn, he had teleported us back to my room, where we made love again. Slower this time with his wings enveloping us. He wanted this...this unbelievable bond in his angel light, and it was so much more intense than the first time.

He seemed so peaceful as he lay beside me, a calm I hadn't seen in him since he fell. I touched his face, the line of his jaw, and he stirred, silver eyes blinking open.

"Hi," he said, a hint of disbelief in his voice.

"Hi," I whispered back, feeling a smile spread across my face.

He pulled me closer. "I can't believe you're here with me...like this," he said, motioning our still naked bodies entwine together. He kissed me then, soft and lingering. I curled into him, the warmth of his body chasing away the morning chill. "Last night," he began, kissing my temple. "Thank you."

My chest tightened around the quiet sincerity in his voice. "For what?"

"For choosing me," he said, a fierce light in his eyes. "I know how difficult it has been for you."

"Difficult for everyone," I said. Even now, I could see Justin's eyes, stormy green, and it sent a pang through me.

Kiran tucked a strand of hair behind my ear, his gaze searching mine. "What is it? You're holding back."

"I just…" I took a breath, feeling the weight of it all. "I don't know how to hurt him."

"There was never a way you could avoid that. You must know that." His voice was gentle, but there was an edge to it, a flicker of worry in his eyes. He pulled me closer, and I felt the strong, steady beat of his heart against my cheek. "I want you to be happy," he said. "Really happy."

"I will be," I promised. "With you." And I meant it, more than I'd ever meant anything. But the thought of Justin's face, the way he'd looked at me with such consuming need, twisted inside me. I didn't know how to hurt him like that.

How to shatter him.

"He's your brother. This will break any relationship you both have with each other."

"Possibly," Kiran said, a shadow passing over his features. "And I broke angelic law for him."

"You mean for me."

He smoothed my wild waves away from my face, placing a finger under my chin to look him in the eyes. "Do not carry that guilt. We have been through this before. Yes, you begged me to save him, but even if you hadn't, I would have." His silver eyes burned unrelentingly into my own. "My fall is not your burden to carry. He is my brother, and saving him was more important than my grace."

I swallowed, feeling the tears press at the back of my eyes. "I want him to be happy. I want him to be—"

"Whole?" Kiran finished for me. "Rhi, he needs to find that on his own. You can't do it for him. You can only be honest."

I kissed him softly, the tears unshed and glistening in my eyes. "I know."

He met my kiss fiercely, and the shadows of doubt receded, replaced by a sweet, consuming fire. Kiran pulled me beneath him, and I felt the whisper-soft brush of his wings. There were no words, just the slow, beckoning language of his body entangling with mine. His lips traced the line of my shoulder, my neck as I became lost in him again.

Everything spun.

Dizzying. Twisting.

The memory of Kiran's skin against mine faded to a blur as darkness swept over me like a wave, pulling me into a tangled dream. A mist surrounded me, thickening until I could see nothing but the ghosts of old streetlights flickering in the haze. I staggered through the streets of my town in Colorado. It was years ago, and my hair was shorter, my body thinner. I felt everything, all the pain and hope and confusion, all at once.

Moments collided and shattered and reformed. Justin's lips on mine, the fierce blaze of his gaze, the sense that we already knew each other, as if it was written in stars and blood. Kiran's touch, turning my soul inside out, his voice whispering love and devotion.

The mist cleared, leaving me breathless. I was in an unfamiliar hallway, heavy with shadows. A door loomed in front of me, green light seeping from its edges, pulsing, alive. My heart pounded as I stepped towards it.

"Rhi, don't!" Voices behind me. Urgent. Desperate. Kiran's and Justin's.

I turned, the pull of them like gravity. Kiran's silver eyes were bright with fear. Justin's hands reaching towards me. "Leave it alone!" Justin shouted over a rising roar between my ears.

I turned and reached for the door. I couldn't stop myself. The door latch was cold under my fingertips, and the light grew blinding.

"Rhi, no!" Kiran's voice broke through my haze, but it was too late.

I fall. Plunge into a searing heat, into flames licking and devouring my skin. The burning is so fierce, so absolute, that I am certain I will die from it.

I scream.

"Rhi!" Kiran was there, shaking me awake. My breath came in ragged gasps, my chest tightening with the remnants of panic. I blinked, the room coming into focus, shadowed with early morning light. "Rhi," he said again, leaning over me, fear etched into the lines of his face.

I wrapped my arms around him, holding tight, feeling his solid, reassuring presence. Just a nightmare. Just a nightmare.

He stroked my hair, his voice softening. "I felt how scared you were."

I trembled against him, the fire of the dream still vivid in my mind. He pulled me closer, shielding me with his wings, and I breathed in his familiar scent, letting it ground me.

"Are you alright?" he asked, his words edged with worry.

"It was so real," I said, my voice still trembling. The tears I'd been holding back spilled hot and sudden onto his shirt.

He was dressed now, wearing the faded grey Black Sabbath shirt I loved on him. There was a softness in his eyes, but also a tangle of fear. "Do you want to talk about it?" he asked, brushing my hair away from my face.

I nodded, wiping the remaining tears with the back of my hand. "I was back in Colorado and parts of my life rolled by me like a movie... and you and Justin..." My voice broke, but I pushed on. "There was a door. There was a glowing light leaking from behind it. I reached for it, and then..."

"Then what, my love?"

"You and Justin both yelled for me to stop, but I couldn't help myself. I opened it and fell...fell into flames, and the heat was unbearable."

"Fire can represent intense emotions like anger or desire, or it can be a sign of transformation and new beginnings. All of which you have had the past few weeks."

I shook my head. "I felt the fire, Kiran. It was real. It was more than a nightmare."

His silver eyes held mine. "You've had dreams before," he said. "None of them have come true."

"That's not exactly true." I pulled back a little, needing him to understand. "Remember the one I had about you? I saw you die. And then you did. In a way."

He held my gaze, a flicker of something crossing his face. He didn't speak, but I felt him listening, really listening.

"They're more than dreams, Kiran." I let the words tumble out, desperate for him to believe me. "They're warnings."

He shifted, pulling me back into his arms, his warmth soothing but not enough to calm the frantic rush inside me. "I won't let anything happen to you, Rhi."

I buried my face in his shoulder, the dark panic receding but not gone. "I don't want anything to happen to you either," I whispered. I thought of the fire, of how real it felt on my skin.

"It won't," he said resolutely as if his will alone could bend the universe.

I wanted to believe him. I needed to. "Promise me," I said.

I felt him hesitate. "I promise it was just a dream," he said at last.

I exhaled and lay back against him, letting my eyes close for just a moment. Outside, the town was awakening. Cars moved down our street, and birds were calling to each other.

"I'm going to my house for a while and study your grandfather's journals some more," Kiran said as he brushed his lips across mine.

"It's okay, I have homework, and I should spend some time with Nan."

He smiled, and I wrapped myself around him before letting him go. I blinked, and he was gone.

I made myself get up, pad barefoot into the bathroom, and splashed cold water on my face.

When I came out, Nan was at the sink, peeling potatoes. She looked up, sharp eyes catching me before I could slink by.

"You look like you've seen a ghost," she declared, raising an expressive white brow, "or wrestled one, by the state of your hair."

She looked at me in a way that made me feel like she could see straight through me. "Just a nightmare." I tried for a casual laugh, but it came out shaky.

She set the paring knife down and ambled over to give me a gentle hug. "They run in the family, you know. The dreams." Her voice was soft, almost apologetic.

Nan gave my back a quick rub, then nodded to the kitchen table. "Sit. You look like you could use some breakfast." She rooted in the fridge while I blinked at the sunlight streaming in through the lace curtains. A few minutes later, she brought me a slice of homemade coffee cake and a mug of steamed chamomile tea.

"Aren't you going to be late for church?" I asked.

"I can miss a Sunday or two, the Lord knows where to find me." She set her own mug down and fussed with the edge of her apron as she sat across from me. "There are things we need to talk about, anyhow. About our family."

I nearly choked on my first bite, which seemed to amuse her. "Don't look so terrified, Rhiannon. There's nothing you don't already suspect."

I placed the fork down and wiped my hands on the napkin. "Okay. What things?"

She sipped her tea, considering. "You've always had them, haven't you? The dreams that stick around in the morning? Sometimes even the air is different after." It wasn't really a question.

I nodded, not trusting my voice to speak.

"You see, Rhi, dreams are a means of communication between God and humanity."

I swallowed hard. I wasn't sure if it was just God who used dreams to communicate.

Nan's thumb traced the rim of her cup, slow and deliberate, like she was choosing her words the same careful way. "There's more to it, though," she said, and her eyes flicked up to me, banded with a kind of worry I'd never seen there before. "I know you want answers. But certain things can't be spoken until the right time. Sometimes words act as keys, and if you unlock a door too soon—"

I felt a strange chill slide through me.

She took off her glasses and set them on the table with a soft click. "It's not in all of us. But you, your mother, and my mother—it's a line, handed down. Sometimes a blessing, sometimes a curse."

I let that settle. "So... you're saying they aren't just dreams?"

Her mouth quirked. "I've certainly lived long enough to know the difference between a bad dream and a message. So have you, I suspect."

My head jerked up. "Mom never told me she had dreams like this."

"She saw things. Didn't always talk about them, but I knew. Your great-grandmother, too, though she claimed it was the 'Irish' in her, a trick of the mist." Nan poured herself more tea casually, but I could feel her watching me, weighing what I could handle. "But that's not for me to say. Not all at once."

"But you are saying it, Nan," I whispered. It came out louder than I expected. "You think I'm dreaming future things—like predictions?"

Her eyes softened. "Let's just say there's a knowing that comes with dreaming. Sometimes, it's only a warning. Sometimes, if you listen, you can change the ending." She reached out, her soft hand closing over mine. Her eyes bored into me, fierce and sad all at once. "But if you ignore it, you end up wherever the dream wants to take you."

My stomach flipped. "I don't want it."

"Nobody does, at first," Nan said, her hand squeezing mine.

She let her hand linger over mine another moment, then picked up her teacup again. "I'd wager your cousins Taylor and Kacey have it too, though they've never said anything to me about it." She took a bite of her coffee cake. "Taylor gets those headaches, right? The kind that come out of nowhere and leave as quickly?" She tossed a glance my way, the corner of her mouth quirking. "That's often the sign, and I know you deal with the headaches as well. They just last much longer."

Nan's mouth turned down at the corners. "But you, Rhiannon, you're the one I hear upstairs sometimes, screaming like you're being chased by Hell itself."

A flush crawled up my neck. I hadn't realized she could hear me.

She glanced sidelong at me. "But you're stronger than the rest of us, Rhi. There's something about you, like you were meant for more."

I stared down at my hands, at my bitten-down nails and the scars that didn't show, and all the anger I had buried finally surfaced. "I just want to be normal, Nan. I don't want to be haunted or warned or...meant for more." The last words came out strangled, edged with more bitterness than I'd meant to show. "Why can't I just be normal for once? Why can't I just be a teenager?"

Nan's eyes narrowed, not unkind, but wary. "Rhiannon—"

"No!" I shoved back from the table. "It's not fair. I didn't ask for any of this. All I wanted was to just be with...someone. To have a normal, happy life."

Nan's face softened, and she held out a hand, so small and unthreatening it almost broke me. "Come here," she said. "Sit, baby. Sit."

I stayed standing, my fingers gripping the edge of the table.

"You have a right to be angry," she said, as if she'd practiced the line. "But running from it won't stop the dreams. Best to learn from them, that's all I was saying."

I pressed the heels of my hands into my eyes. "I just want to buy bad coffee and ditch class and pretend none of this exists—" I broke off, voice cracking. "I don't want the burden of all this."

Nan got up, slowly moving to put her hands on my shoulders from behind. She didn't say sorry or try to fix it. She just stood there with me as the morning sun sketched little golden prisms along the kitchen table.

I want to ask her, so badly, about the Ossaris, about what we are. But I hate confrontation almost as much as I hate being left in the dark. Still, the question claws up my throat. "Nan?" My voice comes out wobbling. "Why haven't you told any of us what we are, about being an Ossaris?"

Her hands stall, one palm heavy on my shoulder.

Nan's never at a loss for words, but she is now. When she finally breathes, it's a whisper, filled with dread. "How do you know that word?"

"I found some of Pop's old journals." I turn to look at her.

Nan's eyes close tight for a second, and when she opens them, she looks haunted. "How?" She lets out a breath. "They're locked up...and..."

She doesn't finish. I look at her, and the questions pile behind my lips. Maybe I should have waited, figured out more before confronting her about it.

"Does it really matter?" I say, trying to sound braver—and failing. "The point is, I know. So does Taylor. And Steve."

"What do you want to know, Rhiannon?" she finally asks.

I try to answer honestly, picking through the mess of longing and dread inside my chest. "I want to know if we're in danger. If something's coming for us. I want to know if I'm...if I'm cursed. Or if I can fix it."

She waits for my breathing to slow, then steers me gently back into my chair. She sits across from me, face creasing in a way that makes her look even older than she did a minute ago.

"Rhiannon. You are not cursed. Do you hear me?" Her thumb sweeps over my knuckles. There's a tremor in her hand that I've never noticed before. "You think this is some ancient affliction set loose on you? No, love. It's a gift, no matter how wretched it feels."

Then, with a long, steadying breath — like she's been holding it for years — Nan begins to unfold the truth about who and what we are.

Chapter Forty

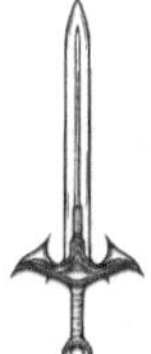

Kiran

I had already been through all the journals and papers several times. Taylor was keeping meticulous notes so we could return the journals to the office before Mrs. Crandall noticed. I had found two more in the closet and was going through them now. I hadn't shared them with the others yet.

It was hard to keep my focus. The lines of text swam before my eyes. All I saw was the memory of her. Her perfect skin and loving eyes. The radiant spill of Rhiannon's hair over my bare chest while I held her in the dark. I remembered every detail, as if it were stitched into my soul—her body moving against mine, each time more certain. The lines of her, the warmth of her, the way she'd touched my face with such devotion. Every time she said my name, it was with such wonder and awe.

I remembered the curve of her waist and the sound she made when I traced fingers down her thigh. She kissed my face like she was afraid I'd vanish, her hands mapping the lines of my jaw to convince herself I wasn't some vision she'd lose when she woke. If I concentrated long enough, I could conjure the taste of her.

I closed my eyes and let my mind run over our bodies fitting together. I had been told desire was dangerous because it made angels covet. They weren't wrong. I had wanted her in a thousand small ways before this, but our night together was the first time I'd been truly hungry. It was surprising how human I felt—the selfishness, the sheer need to keep her for myself, to leave the shape of my hands on every part of her. I now understand why the angels who fell for mortals would leave our world behind.

Because now I had something precious to lose.

My hands shook as I turned another page, my body and soul aching to touch her again. The journal tumbled from my lap and hit the floor with a hollow clank. I stared at the book for a long second, irritation and curiosity prickling together. It had landed splayed open, and something metal was glinting from within.

I crouched and pried the book from the floor. There was a small, old-fashioned key wedged in the gutter of the binding. Brass, maybe, and worn smooth at the edges like it'd been passed from hand to hand for years. I held it between my fingers, the light glinting off its edges. I flipped the journal's cover and ran my finger along the inside. There—a tiny slit cut into the leather.

"Clever," I muttered, with admiration.

I replayed the last trip to the office in my mind, forcing myself to reroute the current of longing for her. There'd been nothing locked. No cabinets, no drawers, not even a safe.

I scanned the journal's spine for other notches or broken leather. Nothing. I flipped through the pages. The last third of the book was filled with numbers and formulas—diagrams in margins, lines connecting initials and cryptic dates. I flipped to the front again. There was an entry that ended mid-sentence. The ink was smeared, the lines curling awkwardly over the edge of the page.

Underneath, in different handwriting — cramped and urgent, as if written in haste — someone had scrawled: KEY IS IN THE SHADOW.

It gave me a chill the way only mortal warnings can.

"Key is in the shadow," I murmured. Shadows need light to exist. If the key was in the shadow, maybe the shadow itself was the answer.

I angled the key toward a stream of light from the window and watched as the edge of the brass key cast an elongated shadow onto the surface. It looked nothing like the key I held. Instead, the silhouette was unmistakably a cross with four notches.

I closed the journal, taking out a piece of paper Taylor had been writing notes on. I drew a picture of the cross as best I could. I swore I had seen this design before.

The air behind me shifted, and I knew there was a presence in the room even before I looked up. Ophaniel stood in the space by the window. He offered a thin smile, his pipe hanging from his lips. His gaze drifted down to the key in my palm. "I see you've found it."

My grip tightened around the key. "What am I supposed to do with this?"

Ophaniel's head dipped, and for a moment, he simply watched dust spinning in a beam of light. "Did you ever wonder," Ophaniel mused, "why men go to such lengths to lock away the things they cherish most—and the things they fear?"

I rolled the weight of the key in my palm as my irritation flared. "You're speaking in riddles." I held up the jagged silhouette, the uneven arms. "This key. What is it?"

Ophaniel's shoulders rose in something like a shrug — or maybe he simply enjoyed watching me writhe a little longer. "Not everything is a matter of locks and doors, Kiran. Some things are a matter of memory." He looked down at the crude sketch I'd made. "What do you see there?"

"A cross with four notches around it." I twirled the key in my hand. "I've seen it before," I admitted, "but I don't know where."

He smiled like we were coconspirators, and maybe we were. "It's at the edge of every story that ends, and every story that refuses to. Humans call it a grave marker, but the symbolism means more than that."

I tried to think—there had been a cross like this, or at least a shadow shaped like it. I'd stood in a snowy field, watching mourning doves flit around a headstone while Rhiannon knelt in tears, her family surrounding her. The memory fluttered up, sudden and fierce. I looked at Ophaniel. "It's at her grandfather's grave."

I waited for some explanation, but Ophaniel only tamped his pipe, eyes half-lidded like he was somewhere else. "So I take it you want me to go to the grave," I prompted.

He tapped ash into his palm and blew it into the stream of sunlight, a miniature constellation between us. "That would be a start."

I stared down at the journal and the relic key, willing myself not to ask the question I knew I needed answered. Instead, it slipped out, the way all hard things do. "Why are you helping me?"

Ophaniel's gaze sharpened, and for the first time, I saw fatigue behind his smile, as if centuries of playing a sentinel had worn his moral compass thin. "Do you believe the world is served by knowledge left to rot in the dark?" He set the pipe aside and leaned closer, the silver flecks in his irises glinting. "Most of my brothers keep their oaths. They know power and memory are too dangerous for mortals. For what you are rapidly becoming, doubly so."

"What am I becoming?"

"You're a bridge, Kiran. And the point of any bridge is to be crossed. Not simply admired from either shore."

"Again with the riddles." I pinched the bridge of my nose, trying for patience.

His gaze fixed on the cross drawing. "I am loyal to what survives. You've done impossible things out of love, and you did not even have to be taught." Ophaniel smiled sadly, fingers drumming on the windowsill. "When you see Rhiannon, what is it you want?"

The question caught me off guard. "To keep her safe," I replied automatically. Then, softer, I said, "And to love each other forever."

His grin was more a wound than a smile. "There is always a cost, and always a choice. You ask why I help you? Because you and I are the same species of fool." He reached past me and tapped a single pale finger on the cross sketch. "Nireth." The name burned the air between us. "She is Taylor's Principality and was the brightest of us, and she is gone." His gaze went distant. "Principalities love nothing—not mortals, not the world, and certainly not each other. It's why we survive millennia. We're bred to shed attachments and serve the idea of order, not its casualties." He weighed the key in my palm with a hollow gaze. "I broke that rule by loving Nireth."

The silence between us hummed. "So, you, who is tasked with keeping the knowledge for the Ossaris, who in turn are supposed to keep the Watchers in line, have become just like them, except they fell in love with humans."

Ophaniel nodded. "This conversation goes nowhere. Not to Rhiannon, not to her cousins, not to your brother or Sam. Especially not to the other Principalities. Are we clear?" His eyes bored intensely into mine.

"Crystal."

He relaxed by a fraction and resumed his study of the journal, a finger tracing the cracked leather with reverence. "Go to the graveyard. Bring Rhiannon and the key." He paused momentarily, "You'll need her, and you'll need the key."

He reached into the folds of his coat and withdrew a yellowed envelope. "Do not open this right away. You'll understand as time goes by."

I took it, tucking it into my back pocket, careful not to crumple the edge. "What aren't you telling me?"

His mouth flickered, perhaps with pity. "What I can't." His expression soured. "Sides change, Kiran. And you'll find there are more than two." He was already fading, little more than a ripple of shifting air.

After the Principality vanished, I spent the rest of the afternoon cross-referencing the drawing I had made with every coded entry in the journal. I pieced together a plan, stone by coded stone. The grave marker wasn't just a memorial. The cross was a sigil—a composite of angelic and alchemical magic meant to safeguard whatever it held.

I was half-mad with exhaustion by the time Rhiannon walked through the door. She wore an oversized sweatshirt, her hair scraped into a soft, unruly knot — and somehow she still looked like the answer to every question I'd ever asked.

"Nan made enough chicken and potatoes to feed an army," she announced, studied me a beat longer, then softened. "You've been in here all day."

I looked at her, and the ache of wanting made my voice catch. "I found something."

Her palm trailed down my jaw, and her thumb caught at the corner of my mouth. "What is it?"

I wanted to tell her everything, but I remembered Ophaniel's warning. Instead, I smiled, stealing the warmth of her hand and bringing it to my lips. "I love you."

Her smile warmed every dark corner inside of me. "I love you too."

I pulled the key from my pocket. I told her how I found it and the symbol it cast in the shadows. Then I showed her the sketch I made.

"Do you recognize it?"

Her slim brows came together. "It looks like my grandfather's headstone."

"I think we need to take a ride to the graveyard after dinner."

We sat in silence as my truck ate up the miles of tree-lined road, headlights sweeping the trees as the road led upwards toward the old cemetery. I stole a glance at her as we crested the hill. She was biting the inside of her cheek, the way she did when she was looping old sorrow in her head. "You okay?" I asked, my hand brushing her knee.

"I haven't been back since..." Her voice dissolved, but I didn't need her to finish.

"Since they buried him," I said, as gently as I could.

She nodded. "Yes, since then."

We turned off into the gravel lot. I cut the truck's engine, and a secretive quiet fell—just the wind through autumn leaves. Rhiannon hesitated when I opened her door. I let her come to me, her breath fogging in the chilly fall evening as she laced her fingers in mine.

She didn't need my hand to guide her. She led me unerringly through the wind-carved rows. Each stone was different, but in growing darkness they all looked the same—tablets of gray memory, some grown over with moss, others nearly erased by rain and time.

The path curved past a bare-limbed bush, its last few leaves clinging stubbornly to the branches. She stopped short, her breath clouding in the crisp air. I squeezed her hand. The cold was sharper here, the silence heavier, and I could almost feel the layers of grief radiating from her as we reached her grandfather's grave.

Someone had left a bouquet.

Yellow roses. Wrapped in butcher paper, tied with green twine around the stems. The cold had bitten the edges, but the petals were still bright. She stopped short, blinking hard.

I stepped back, giving her space, and watched as she knelt, fingers trembling over the petals. "Someone's been here," she whispered.

I crouched beside her. "Your grandmother?"

"She never said anything about visiting, but of course, she would. She loved him." She sat with her knees drawn up, her fingers tracing the engraved letters as if she could will her grandfather back. I waited with her silently. The wind lifted tiny tendrils of her hair that had come loose from the knot on top of her head. Everything was quiet except for the low cry of a blue jay and the distant hum of a passing truck.

I busied myself studying the stone. It was tall and upright, the cross carved deep near the top, and everything about it—the slant of the lines, the way shadows caught in the carving—matched the sketch I'd made. The cross was not just a cross. At its center was a circle, and each quarter of it was notched, exactly like the negative space the key had cast in its shadow.

I circled the stone. On the back, pressed faintly by weather and time, was a small, nearly invisible seam.

"Rhi?" I called softly. "Can I show you something?"

She didn't answer for a moment, but I could hear her shifting, brushing loose the memory that clung to the grass and the cold.

"I see it," she said as she tilted her head, then reached to brush her fingers over the seam I'd found.

"Look," I said, holding the key up to catch the last streaks of dusk. Its shadow fell across the stone, a near-exact replica of the notched cross. She pressed her lips together, then shuffled on her heels and lined the key directly against the carved sigil, slotting the notches over the grooves. It was almost a perfect fit; only the narrowest gap between the brass and limestone remained open.

Nothing happened.

"That's it?" Rhiannon frowned, her mouth tilting sideways. "Shouldn't it, I don't know, glow? Or open a magic portal or something?"

"You want special effects now?" I joked, but my voice sounded thin. "Maybe it needs more light."

"Let's try this." I lifted my hand, palm open. A small, steady beam of light appeared. We both blinked at the sudden intensity. "Angel perk," I said, trying to seem casual.

I maneuvered my hand until the light fell in a flat line across the stone. The shadow from the key stretched long and sharp across the marker. Slowly, I rotated it, letting the cross's outline rotate over the engraving like a sundial.

For a second, nothing happened, and I felt an absurd pang of disappointment. But then Rhi gasped.

At the intersection where the shadow's notched edge overlaid the stone, a faint line shimmered. Not quite a glow, more like a line of mist or heat distortion. Rhiannon exhaled, her breath visible in the cold, and pressed both hands on either side of the seam.

The line began to move. Just a twitch. I braced my other hand against the grave as Rhiannon pushed outward, and the stone gave way with a long, low moan like an old ship's hull in ice. I felt the vibration in my knuckles as the crosspiece on top of the grave loosened, then lifted free, as if on a hidden hinge.

We both stared inside the cavity. In a hollow, not much larger than a shoebox, was an ornate knife.

My reflexes anticipated hers; I caught her wrist as she leaned in, the tips of her fingers inches from the blade's hilt. "Careful," I said, low. "It could be protected. Or worse."

She looked up, a challenge blooming in her eyes. "I can handle..."

The words cut off as I reached in myself. The air inside felt charged—too cold, but burning at the same time. My fingers wrapped around the hilt, smooth and warm, and then a jolt shot up my arm straight into my bones. I jerked back, hissing, and the knife clattered against the limestone lip, sparks arcing along the blade before fizzing out. I shook out my hand, cradling it. The skin across my palm bore a faint, cross-shaped welt that flared red, then faded. "Warded," I said, voice rough. "You see?"

Rhi's eyes went big, but she chewed at her lip and said, "Or maybe it's just meant for someone else." Before I could protest, she plunged both hands in. Her fingers curled around the hilt, and when she drew it out, the gold lit up in her hand, brightening the fading light. Then the knife grew into something larger and more deadly-looking.

A sword.

She dropped it, and the light blinked out as soon as it hit the ground. The sword shrank in an instant, flickering smaller and smaller until it was the size of a regular knife again.

"Are you okay?" My voice cracked. I searched her for blood or scorch marks, but there wasn't any that I could see.

She curled her fingers inward, knuckles white. "I'm fine. It didn't—" Her pupils were blown wide, brown eyes churning. "It didn't cut me. It's just—"

I saw then how pale she was, how sweat beaded at her temples even in the chilly autumn evening. "Hey," I said softly, "Talk to me."

"It's...that thing." She pointed, almost recoiling from her own outstretched finger. "I saw it, Kiran. In my dream. The Veilbreaker—she used it on those men to murder them." Rhi's hand trembled harder. "It's the same one."

"Maybe it's just a coincidence. Or some symbolic thing."

Rhi shook her head, the knot in her hair almost coming loose. "No, it's not a coincidence. I didn't tell you this, but my grandmother said we—my mom's side, the women—we sometimes have dreams that show the future. Not always, and sometimes it's completely wrong, but when I touched that, and it became a sword-the Veilbreaker's sword." She wiped her palms on her jeans. "I saw what it did to people."

The confession tangled in the air between us. I eased to my knees, careful not to crowd her. The golden knife—sword—whatever it was lay between us in the grass.

There were a thousand shields I wanted to throw up between her and this thing. "We can't leave it here," I said. "It's bound to you. Whatever it is, whoever hid it, whether your grandfather or someone else, they meant it for you. Not for me. Not for anyone else."

She looked at the blade. It was dull now, as if sulking at being denied. When she spoke, her voice had a faraway flatness. "My grandfather used to say that the objects left behind are never really just objects. They're memories. They want to be carried." She reached out, plucked the knife from the grass, and held it in both hands. Her arms steadied. It flickered and elongated, flames licking across the metal. "I can't just walk around with a flaming sword."

"Here." I manifested a towel. "Wrap it in this until we can figure out how to handle it properly."

She did, and when her fingers lost contact with it, it shrank again to an elaborate, but normal-looking knife.

"Come." I reached a hand out to help her up.

She wrapped her hands around my waist, snuggling into my chest. "I just want to go home and sleep and pretend I'm a normal girl."

Chapter Forty-One

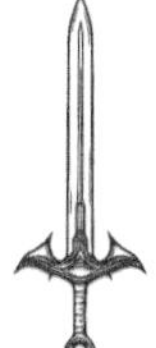

Rhiannon

It was impossible to concentrate in class when I had a magic sword, a family of Ossaris, and a demon-Fallen Angel out there waiting to do who knows what to Justin or Kiran or...me.

I watched the minute hand slouch around the clock's white face. Second by second, minute by minute, stubborn in its progress. I'd spent hours on my laptop researching flaming swords. The closest parallel to what I'd pulled from my grandfather's headstone was Michael's sword. What was I supposed to do with an angel's sword?

Kiran had forged a sheath out of shadow and scripture for the thing, a weird act of angelic magic that seemed to exhaust him. Now the sword lived in that warded master bedroom in his house, so even he couldn't touch it. He said the sword needed to be kept far from any supernatural radar.

What I hadn't told Kiran was how many times I'd dreamt about that sword since we discovered it. It never looked the same. Sometimes it was just a rod, weightless and cold. Sometimes it was a haloed sabre with an intricate hilt, or a straight-bladed Viking-looking thing that seemed to resonate with the memory of hands and blood. Once it was just a column of white fire, dissecting the world with its murderous light.

Kiran had come up with rules. No touching the sword unless he was with me, and don't discuss it with anyone. He'd trust Taylor and Steve because of my insistence. They could hardly believe what I had told them about finding it at the graveyard.

The bell's electric screech yanked me out of my reverie. Sam's chair screeched as he bolted out the door, notebook lassoed under his arm, orbiting immediately back to Kiran and me in the crowded hallway.

"Bro, seriously," Sam said as we merged into the tide of bodies. "You guys are like, straight up in a witness protection program now. You're never around anymore." He rounded on Kiran with mock suspicion. "You're holding her hostage, aren't you?"

"Trig is just killing me, not to mention…"

He made a disbelieving pfffft and leaned in, as if he expected us to whisper some monstrous confession. "You're probably just hiding because you finally did it," Sam said, eyes bright with the sparkle of gossip. "I'm right, aren't I?"

I rolled my eyes and blushed, which only fanned the flames.

"Holy crap. You did!" His laugh bounded off the lockers.

"Sam," I said, but he wasn't letting up.

"No, no, it's adorable," he pressed. "But I'm not letting you off the hook for Phen's album release party this weekend.

Sam's mention of the party was the only thing that got me to glance at Kiran, who was suddenly fascinated with a fire alarm above the office door. We hadn't exactly broken the news to anyone that we had lost our virginity. After our first time together, there'd been a second and then a third and, well, enough that my entire sense of self felt rearranged around his existence. Maybe it was the cosmic trauma-bonding, but most times it was all I could do not to launch myself at him.

I knew Kiran wasn't comfortable with how desperately he wanted me. That was the part that undid me. He was this celestial being, and yet when our lips slid together, he was wrecked by it. When we parted, he needed to remember how to breathe again. It made every time feel cataclysmic and sacred.

Sam kept up a running commentary as we walked. I caught Steve making out with Mia by her locker. "Hey," I said as our trio came to a stop in front of them.

"Hey, yourself, Lady Bug." Mia said, dislodging herself from Steve. So much for her remaining single senior year.

Kiran pressed his hand to the small of my back—a casual, unconscious touch, but my knees still went weak, damn him.

"Did you two know—" Sam began.

I turned on Sam with my most demanding expression. "Don't."

He just smiled wickedly at me.

"Know what?" Mia asked.

"I'll tell you later." She looked at me skeptically. "I promise."

Mia slid her arm through mine and started walking toward the parking lot. "While we're here, can we please address the more urgent question? Which is what the heck are you wearing to Phen's party?"

I blinked at her.

Mia's eyes went flat. "Rhi. It's on Halloween. You can't just wear regular clothes to a costume party."

"I haven't even thought about it. I've been a little preoccupied with, you know." I never knew who was listening. It hadn't totally hit me until now, but yeah—of course we would go. Wild horses couldn't drag Kacey away from anywhere Phen might be, especially not a Halloween bash where he was playing host. Still, my mind was a knot of competing terrors and desires.

"Rhi?" Mia questioned.

I tried to reorient. "Sorry. I'll figure it out."

Kiran was smiling as sunlight filtered through his hair. "You'd be beautiful in anything." The sincerity of it made me want to melt. I was definitely taking off his clothes when we got back to his place.

"There are so many options," said Mia, "You should go as like, Persephone, or Joan of Arc."

"Nah," said Steve. "Something tougher."

"Like those women weren't bad asses," said Mia, and punched his arm harder than necessary. "Ignore him. Think about it. We can go shopping when I get out this afternoon."

Sam piped up, "I think I'm going as Batman. Because I've always wanted to walk up to people and say- I'm Batman." Sam slung his arm around my neck, zip-tying me into a one-armed hug, and whispered, "You could be my Catwoman."

Kiran's hand closed around my wrist as he peeled Sam's arm off me and inserted himself. Sam let go at once, palms up in peace. "Bro, chill. I'm joking." But his smile flickered. "Sheesh."

"He's jealous. It's cute." Mia winked in my direction. "You guys are going to need matching costumes. Just saying."

"Excuse me while I go ice my broken heart," Sam said, making fake sob sounds as he veered off.

We split off from the group at the parking lot, Kiran steering me toward our street with a single-mindedness that let me know the rest of the afternoon would be spent away from all outside interference, mortal or otherwise. I motioned to Mia that I'd text her, and she called after me, "Six o'clock, Rhi! We're going!" as if I had a choice.

I barely made it three steps into the house before Kiran grabbed my elbow and pulled me against him, his mouth finding my hairline, then my jaw, and then my mouth. He pushed the door shut with his heel, not breaking the kiss. And then I was kissing him. Not the gentle, feathered kind, but a bruising, full-body collision. I heard him gasp—that tiny break in his composure.

He dropped my backpack and swept me up so fast I barely got my arms around his neck. I clenched my legs around his waist, laughing into the corner of his mouth, startled by the suddenness and the way we collided—bodies, breath, everything we'd been holding back in front of our friends. He pressed my spine into the wall, hands everywhere, until he looked me full in the face. His eyes—those molten silver eyes—burned with a hunger that made me feel like I was the only one in the universe.

"I love all the ways you make me weak," he growled, and kissed me again, harder.

His palms slid beneath my sweater, blazing brands into my skin. I braced myself, expecting him to slow, to gentle the moment, but instead he hoisted me higher, and the hungry shudder in his breath made me dizzy. He nearly tripped on the threshold to his room, which sent us both toppling onto his rumpled bed, and for a moment we could only laugh, mouths pressed together, tangled in the heat and need. He hovered above me, knee braced on the mattress, fingers tracing my cheek.

"If I'm your weakness," I whispered, my voice threatening to break, "then you are mine."

He shivered at that, and I reached up, curling my hands into his hair as he lowered himself to me, lips mapping the line of my throat while his fingers toyed with the waistband of my jeans.

"You make every sin I've committed feel like it was worth it. Every mistake. Every choice. All of it. You make me wish I'd fallen sooner."

I pulled him against me. The ache in my heart at his words burned through me.

He was careful, always, as my skin lit up under his mouth, and he guided me out of my clothes with a slow reverence that almost—almost—made me believe I was sacred. His hands cupped my face. "I'd fall from Heaven a thousand times if it always led me here," he murmured against my skin.

Words failed us for a while. There was no before, no after, only the now of us. Kiran's breath soft on my ear, our bodies threaded together. When it was over, neither of us moved, not at first. Our arms and legs remained tangled, my head pillowed on his chest. I felt him trace idle circles along my shoulder.

I pressed my nose to his chest. "So what do you want to be for Halloween? Should we go in couple costumes?"

He made a quiet noise in his throat. "Halloween?"

I poked him in the side until he stirred, rolling toward me so our faces were inches apart. "Yes. Remember, Mia will be here soon to take me costume shopping."

His expression sobered as he tucked a strand of hair behind my ear, thumb lingering just under my cheekbone. "I don't want you to go."

"You can't keep me away from the world. That's not how this works. If I don't go, it'll just look suspicious—to everyone."

He went quiet, his jaw flexing. I sighed. "Besides, Kacey is going. She doesn't know what Phen is. We need to protect her."

He slipped his hand over my stomach possessively. "You never listen to your Guardian."

I turned to face him, pinning him with my most disarming look. "You do realize that you literally fell from grace for not following the rules, right?"

He made a sound, almost a chuckle. "Touché."

"We'll be fine. It's a club full of people. What, am I supposed to never leave your room again?" His look said he wouldn't mind that one bit, and then he crawled over me once again.

Mia honked three times, each sharper and louder than the last, and buzzed my phone for good measure. I threw on Kiran's hoodie, the one that swallowed my hands and smelled deliciously of him. I jogged out to her car. She was in the driver's seat with both feet on the dashboard, painting her nails neon green while an alternative rock station thumped through the speakers.

She assessed me with one glance. "Get in, loser, we're going shopping."

I snorted, but obeyed.

She flicked her sunglasses down her nose. She drove into traffic, reckless as a race car driver, but careful with her wet nails. The sky was October gray and overcast, but Halloween colors bled out of every lawn and shop window we passed, pumpkin orange and black, purple ghosts and skeletons blowing in the wind.

Mia adjusted the radio till it was all high-energy pop. She handed me an iced vanilla latte, studied my face for a second, and then made an exaggerated o face. "Oh, my God. You totally did it."

My cheeks hurt from smiling, but my stomach did a small, traitorous flip. I crammed a mouthful of whipped cream in my mouth and tried to act normal.

"Girl. So. Are you in love?!"

I nearly choked on the latte. "What kind of question is that?"

"The only question! Are you, like, obsessed with him, or just addicted to the...you know."

My smile spread so much that my cheeks ached.

Mia gave a conspiratorial squeal. "Is it true what they say about, like, angel stamina?"

I spluttered. "That's not—do people say that?"

"No girl. But what's he like? I mean, he's an angel? Did he levitate? Did you?"

I tried not to laugh. "He did not levitate, but it was magical and still is every time."

Mia squealed. "Every time?! Best friend privilege, you realize I get every detail."

I gave her the edited highlights. Not the things that I thought too precious that were just between him and me. Just the softness and the way he listened, all the simple things that had made the rest of it feel right.

"Are you happy?"

"Yeah," I said eventually. "It's overwhelming, sometimes. But he's...he's everything. He makes me feel safe."

Mia nodded, thoughtful, letting the car crawl into a parking spot. "Well, you can't just torch your V card with one twin and never talk about the other again," Mia said, lip gloss glistening as she studied me. "We both know what's coming, Rhi. Halloween, Phen's party—Justin's going to be there."

"I don't know," I said, and twisted the straw in my cup until it squeaked. "He hasn't messaged me. Sam said he's—" I couldn't finish. "He's not himself."

"Steve's been texting with him, and it's just...different. He's different, Rhi. I'm kind of scared for him, honestly."

I have been scared, too.

"I'm sorry, Rhi. I didn't mean—" She chewed her lip, searching my face, really looking. "Sorry. I'm not trying to make it weird for you. I want you to have your storybook ending, okay? I just—" She took a weirdly big breath. "Rizzo was a different person with you. Like he was healing. I just hope he can get back to that."

She let her words hang for a moment and then nudged my shin with her sneaker. "Okay. I refuse to get mopey. Let's get you a hot costume just so I can see Kiran's face when you wear it."

Inside the mall, Halloween was in full swing. Fake cobwebs, grinning skulls on every kiosk, and throngs of kids trailed by frazzled parents. Mia steered us straight into the costume store, sampling each pair of fangs and devil horns. I drifted behind, picking at a rack stuffed with velvet mini dresses and fishnet tights.

"OMG, Rhi," Mia said, holding up a silk slip dress so small it could fit in a tissue box. "This, with your hair? You'd shatter the glass ceiling of hotness." She pressed it into my arms, eyebrows raised. "Try it. And bring the wings."

I ducked into a dressing room and texted Kiran. I knew he'd answer immediately. I was sure he had felt my anxiety and sadness talking to Mia about Justin. He agreed to stay behind and give me some girl time, knowing he was only a thought away.

Hey you. He replied to me instantly.

I slid the slinky fairy dress over my head. *I'm in a dressing room. Mia is threatening my life if I don't model something ridiculous.*

I have immediate concerns. Came his reply.

This thing is basically see-through. I bit my bottom lip.

Hmm. Interesting.

This was fun. *I bet you'd like it.*

I'd like it better if you were back here, not trying it on for everyone in the mall.

Option A is I text a fitting room selfie. Option B is you wait until Halloween. Suspense builds character, Kiran. There was a long pause, enough to imagine the way his silver eyes would darken, the way his voice would drop half a register, seeing me in this.

I choose option C. Come home now.

My laugh startled a woman two stalls down. *Something tells me you'd like to rip this off me.*

His response was immediate. *I'd prefer to do it gently.* Then, *Show me?*

I grinned and texted back, *You'll have to wait for Halloween, my love.*

You're cruel. Came his reply as my whole body warmed from this flirting.

Mia burst in, arms full of more costumes. She stopped short, open-mouthed. "Holy...Lady Bug, you look like a fairy and a supermodel had a baby and then raised her in Vegas." She thrust a fake flower crown on my head and turned me to the mirror. I stared at myself. The dress was silver and green, skimming my collarbones and barely brushing my thighs. The wings caught the overhead lights and cast fractured rainbows along my arms. It was not at all what I would've picked—but now?

"Does Kiran know what you're about to unleash on him?" Mia asked, tightening the crown.

I bit my lip. I didn't think I could wait until Halloween to wear this in front of him. In fact, I couldn't wait to get back and show him so he could gently take it off.

Chapter Forty-Two

Kiran

We stood in Mia's room. The girls decided to get ready here, Rhi saying her grandmother wouldn't let her out of the house in the Halloween outfit she chose. I was thinking the same thing. I didn't want her out in public in that fairy costume.

She had been giddy when she returned from shopping with Mia, running into the bathroom to change and making me close my eyes until she came out. She had been right. I wanted to tear it off her.

Mia looked me over. "What are you thinking about, blondie?"

I couldn't tell her I was remembering that evening, slowly taking off that fairy costume from Rhi's perfect body.

"Never mind, I think I know," she said, winking at me. She swept her hands in a flourish. "Well, bitches, bow before your Vampire Queen." She bared her plastic fangs. The blood at the corner of her mouth was disturbingly realistic.

Sam pulled up his Batman mask. "Can I get a bite?" he asked, deadpan, eyes flicking to Rhi, then to me, then back to Mia.

Steve lingered in the doorway holding a phone in one hand and his car keys in the other. His shirt, stark white, had *This Is My Halloween Costume* in blocky letters across the chest.

Rhi spun in a circle, and her wings sparkled in the light. She looked over her shoulder, eyes conspiratorial. "I need fairy dust."

"I have glitter," Mia said, digging in her makeup bag.

"What are you supposed to be?" Sam motioned to Steve.

"He said he's 'apathy,'" Rhi said, tugging carefully at the hem of her dress. "You mock, but it's a lifestyle," Steve said, not looking up from his phone.

Rhi perched on the edge of the surprisingly neat unmade bed, legs crossed, wings sitting prettily on her back. Mia flourished a bottle of sparkly shadow and, almost tenderly, dusted it over Rhi's eyelids. I could see Rhi's throat working as she tried not to smile, the pink at her cheeks betraying her happiness. It made my heart happy. But, beneath it all, I felt her anxiety. She wanted so badly to be normal, but nothing about any of us was normal.

"Not too much, I don't want to look like a hooker," Rhi said.

"Shut up, you," Mia said, bopping Rhi's nose.

"Anytime now, girls." Steve drawled.

"Are Taylor and Scott really skipping this?" Mia asked.

"She vetoed it. I offered, but apparently dirty diapers and a baby with glitter in her hair is spooky enough. But, seriously. Taylor loves Halloween and wouldn't miss Eva's first one."

What Steve wasn't saying is that we had talked to Taylor about coming. Even though she was an Ossaris, she was also a mom. The baby came first. Besides, Kacey would have the rest of us to look after her.

"She just wants free peanut butter cups." Rhi joked.

Mia looked me over expectantly, eyebrow quirked. "Don't tell me you aren't going in costume, blondie," she demanded.

I rolled my eyes. "I don't do costumes."

Mia planted her hands on her hips. "You're not leaving this room until you're in costume. I demand it as your Vampire Queen."

Rhi came to my side. "I TOLD him he should go as a tooth. Get it? Tooth—fairy?"

I gave her my best are you kidding me look. "I think I'll pass on the dental cosplay, thanks."

Rhi's eyes glimmered, a dare in them. "You lack vision." Then she cocked her head, half-hidden beneath a wild tangle of glittery hair. "Unless you got something better?"

I let out a dramatic sigh and swished my hands around for effect. My normal clothes disappeared, and I stood in full-on Viking garb. Helmet, tunic, furs, and an unnecessary amount of dramatic leather strapping. I even grew my hair out longer.

"Yesss, blondie! Let's go!" Mia shrieked, "We are not missing one more minute of this party."

"We'll meet you there," I said, taking Rhi's hand in mine. I pulled Rhi into my arms and kissed her.

"Wow, I've never been kissed by a Viking before." She placed her lips on mine again as I snapped us to the club in New York City.

Rain had left the streets glossy and black. Sam stood with his hands jammed in his Batman belt, Mia tucked close to his side. Her plastic fangs glistened white in the streetlights; she waved wildly when she saw us.

"Where's Steve?" Rhi asked, looking around the alley.

"He went to find Kacey; she's here with Phen somewhere."

"Let's go then," Sam said, heading towards the front of the building. "There's a line starting already."

Rhi locked her fingers through mine and pulled me toward the line by the door, where humans and not-so-humans clustered together, indistinguishable to the un-trained eye. A demon in a suit of actual gold paint stood three people ahead of us — a literal horseman of the apocalypse, complete with glowing red eyes.

Inside, the air was warm and thick with humidity and the scent of beer. Fog machines created a thick haze, and jack-o-lanterns with twisted faces hung from the ceiling. The venue throbbed with hundreds of heartbeats as people danced and mingled. The stage took up the back wall, crowned with tattered muslin cobwebs. A band was already howling through a set. The lead singer was in a phantom costume, and the guitarist in a massive devil mask. Their music was a scream of distorted chords and rough melody.

Mia bolted for the front of the stage, Sam's cape billowing as she dragged him through the crush of bodies.

Rhi's hand squeezed mine as we pressed forward. The dance floor was already packed with drunken pirates, ghost brides, and angels in every flavor from slutty to gothic.

I caught a flash of strawberry blonde hair at the edge of the stage, and then saw Steve and Kacey mid-argument. I nudged Rhi, and she followed my gaze; her face lit up, and she grabbed my hand, towing me through a gauntlet of costumed bodies.

Kacey's costume was a short white tulle wedding dress trimmed in black lace, her veil speckled with blood spatters and glittering crystals. Blue and gray makeup carved her cheekbones sharp, her lips painted to look stitched shut, bruises blooming artfully around her eyes.

Kacey shrieked when she saw Rhi, immediately breaking into a run—she collided with Rhi so hard they almost both hit the floor. Kacey pulled away, adjusting her veil, and fixed Rhi with a conspiratorial look. "Rhi, you look like an actual woodland nymph."

Rhi grinned, glitter sparkling at the creases of her eyes. Kacey laced her arm through Rhi's, and with a fishtail flick of her skirt, began towing us toward the hallway to the side of the stage. She called over her shoulder, "Steve, go find Mia. Maybe you'll loosen up."

At the end of the hall, Kacey stopped at a door labeled 'BAND ONLY' and rapped out a rhythm with her knuckles. It swung open, and the sound of laughter spilled out. The green room was lined with black-lit posters, a folding table covered in cheap vodka and grocery-store cupcakes, and a mountain of empty chip bags.

Kacey strutted inside like she owned the place and plopped herself onto Phen's lap. She nuzzled into him as he licked his way up her neck to whisper something in her ear. Phen's band was done up as skeletons, black bodysuits airbrushed with ultraviolet bones, and massive strokes of white and blue makeup across their faces.

Phen wore nothing but a robe of tattered cheesecloth and a face painted like a demon of death. His eyes, rimmed in black, caught sight of us as he grinned. "Didn't think you had it in you to drag Rhi out on All Hallows' Eve, let alone in a get-up like that." He set his painted chin on Kacey's shoulder and gave my Viking ensemble a once-over. "Are you supposed to be Thor? The god of thunder and lightning?" He lifted Kacey right off his lap like a featherweight and settled her on her feet. He swaggered towards me, "How very pagan of you."

"And what exactly are you supposed to be?" Rhi asked, staring him down.

He bared his teeth at her. "Original Death, baby. The only horseman that matters." He swept in with a gothic bow, stretching out his arm for effect, the cheesecloth fluttering.

"I like the hair, Kiran; you should keep it that length." He reached out to touch my helmet and leaned in close enough that I could smell the vodka sting on his breath. "You haven't figured out what she is, have you?" he whispered, eyes darting to Rhi and back.

"Not yet," I whispered back. A lie, and it felt strange on my tongue — one of my most sacred rules, broken clean. But there was no way I was letting Phen know that I not only knew what Rhi was, but that her cousins carried supernatural powers too.

Phen squeezed my shoulder and straightened, an odd look crossing his features. Someone started pounding on the door. "Five minutes!" a voice bellowed.

Kacey bounced on her toes. "Let's do this!" Her Veil fluttered as she jumped up and down, ignoring the way the band scrambled for their gear. She squealed and then rounded on Rhi, snatching up both her hands. "Promise me you're going to dance with me in the front row."

Rhi bit her lip as she nodded. "You know I will."

Phen raised his arms in a grand benediction. "Tonight, my pretties, we ride!" His gaze flicked to me, lazy and wolfish. As the band scrambled out the door, he paused so close we nearly touched. "You'll want to stay sharp in the crowd tonight, angel," he said, low enough that only I could hear. "The air is crawling with fierce things." His face, for once, lost the knowing smirk. He hovered a beat, then clapped my back. "Don't trust everything you see." Then, with a wink at Rhi, he disappeared with Kacey, her arm slung through his. The rest of the skeletons followed, lugging amps and instruments. The door slammed, leaving us alone.

"What was that about?" Rhi asked.d.

I shrugged, but even Rhi could tell I had been rattled. The words Phen had used—*tonight, my pretties, we ride* echoed with a chill, a kind of prophecy. I tried on a smile, but it felt brittle. "He warned me not to trust anything I see tonight." I tugged at some stray glitter in her hair, letting my hand cup the back of her neck. I glanced down at her, at the fine shimmer of sweat already dewing her collarbone. "I don't like it."

She looped her arms around my waist. "What, you afraid Phen is going to drag me to Hell?" She tried to say it like a joke, but there was a little shake at the end of her voice.

"Not him," I said, tucking her under my chin. "But something. I told you, the Veil—" I gasped as I felt her lips against my neck. "Is thin, right now."

I dipped my head and kissed her—hard. Her lips caught mine, and for a second, I didn't care about Phen. All I cared about was the taste of her, the little gasp against my mouth, her hands tangling in my hair. I felt her push back into me, fierce, her mouth hungry as mine. I let my hand tangle in her hair, and she made a faint whimpering sound at the back of her throat. My guard shattered; I angled her jaw up, kissing her like I wanted to own the oxygen in her lungs.

I heard the doorknob rattle and turned, dragging Rhi behind me, my hand never letting go of her wrist.

Justin pushed the door open. He wore all black and had smeared fake blood around his neck. He didn't speak, just watched us.

Rhi's voice went tight and a little breathless. "Justin," she managed.

"Is this a bad time?" he asked, voice low and hard.

Chapter Forty-Three

Rhiannon

Justin looked so angry, but there was more burning behind his green eyes.

Despair.

I watched him, the metallic tang of our shared silence spreading out between us, and I realized I'd never hated myself more. The way he flexed his hands open and closed, trying not to punch something. The way his eyes watered, just a little.

All me.

This was a pain I had conjured just by existing — by wanting them both and having to destroy one to keep the other. I still hadn't found it in myself to tell him what was going on between Kiran and me. I'd been avoiding this. Him. And that exact look in his eyes.

Justin motioned behind us with his hand. "Look, I wouldn't even be back here if Phen hadn't asked me. Said he forgot some of his scarves and needed them for the performance or whatever."

Justin stalked past us, scooping up a duffel bag from the table and unzipping it with a furious motion. Black t-shirts, half-drunk Gatorade bottles, a battered deck of cards tumbled out, but he dug until he found the bundle of scarves.

When he turned, he ran straight into me. Literally, almost bowling me off my feet, and for a split second, our chests touched, and the world kind of stuttered.

He said nothing. Just let his arm fall against mine, dragging down until our hands brushed. I must've looked so dumb, mouth half open, because he grinned. "Nice costume."

He left then, the door smacking shut behind him.

Kiran cleared his throat. "He'll be okay."

"He hates me."

"He wishes he hated you."

A ripple of noise from the main part of the club. Not the usual holler of the crowd when a band swapped in. The voices escalated in my ears, hearing "PHEN! PHEN! PHEN!" like they were conjuring a demon. Which maybe they were.

"We should go," I managed, adjusting my fairy wings.

The floor of the club had the sticky sheen of spilled drinks. People pressed up against the stage, elbows knifing for a better vantage. Mia and Sam stood together, Sam's arm flung around Mia's shoulders. I couldn't see Steve and wondered where he had gone off to. Kacey leaned near the front, waving frantically at us. I pushed through the crowd until I reached the front. Kacey turned and opened her arms wide, enveloping me in a hug.

"You missed soundcheck!" she said, but then her voice dropped. "You okay, Rhi?"

I nodded. Liar.

I felt Kiran at my back. His hands were laid lightly on my waist as I covered them with my own and let my head fall back against his chest. The house lights dimmed, and an underwater blue washed over the stage.

A figure stepped into the spill of light—Phen. He took his time crossing the stage, letting the crowd's chant crash around him. There was a brief second where Phen just stared out into the crowd, and then he grabbed his mic and screamed into it as the band exploded into song.

Next to me, Kacey and Mia screamed and let their voices snake into the hurricane of sound. The band, ghouled up in skeleton paint, carved out a sound so loud I felt it in my teeth. The lyrics didn't make sense at first—just fragments, the sharp, intricate syllables tumbling out of him.

"Blood honey on your windows, Smoke in your eye,

And the shadow-wings, folding,

And the body that forgets how to die—

Oh my beautiful, broken,

Let us burn for a minute in time."

The crowd ate it up, surging toward the stage. Kacey pressed forward, eyes enormous, her whole face tilted upward like she was drinking in every note. It wasn't just a crush. She moved with Phen's voice — every curl of his lip, every flinch of his fingers on the mic stand.

Phen slithered toward the edge of the stage, voice boiling above the band. He crouched and winked at us.

Suddenly, Mia was in front of me, grabbing my shoulders and shrieking over the music, "You look so good, it's criminal!" Then she dragged me into a three-part hug, sandwiching me between herself and Kiran. Her fake vampire teeth glowed blue in the club lights. Kiran's hands slid lower as Mia mashed us all together, and I could feel the vibration of his low chuckle against my back. "Loosen up, you fey goddess!" Mia crowed. "It's Halloween!"

For half a song, we became exactly what I imagined normal teenagers felt like. The way I used to feel.

The song crashed to an end, and the lights went dead, blacking out the room except for strobes that froze every expression in the club. Somewhere behind the stage, a metal door shrieked. I saw, for a heartbeat, a shadow-shaped form on the back wall. I watched Justin ghosting around the band's equipment and wondered what he was up to.

Like he knew I was watching him, his eyes bore into mine. He raised a dark brow in question, but I lost sight of him when the lights illuminated the crowd.

Phen prowled the edge of the stage, fingers twisting in the air, teasing the crowd with a come-hither motion. When the music dropped away for a second, the club was so quiet you could taste the expectancy. He grinned and rolled his tongue over a pointed canine. Then he leaned down and crooned into the mic, "You beautiful sinners know what tonight is?"

The crowd howled back. "That's right, freaks," he purred, "it's Halloween and you look delicious tonight. I wanna bite each and every one of you."

A shrieking cheer answered him, and he gave a little bow and tore straight back into another song with the band. Girls at the edge of the stage clawed at the air to touch him, Kacey included.

The guitar ratcheted up, and the crowd went from screaming to howling. "We got new music tonight, just for you. Been working on it for months. We call it The Human Fault, on account of how every one of us is tragically..." his gaze reached me, "so so beautifully broken."

The band started up on the next song, and I felt myself being spun, Mia's hands gripping my elbows and forcing me to dance. Kiran twirled me back, and I was shocked by how good a dancer he was.

The last chords reverberated like aftershocks, and Phen dropped the mic with a dramatic flourish. The house lights snapped on, and for a second, everybody blinked, dazed by the sudden banishment of the blue and red. Then the noise picked up again, all whoops and the clatter of excitement.

I saw Kacey climb up the stage, slipping around the amps until she was at Phen's side. He grabbed her hand and spun her in a wide circle, like they were the only two people in the world. Her laughter broke through the noise of the crowd. It was brighter than the lights, sharper than the feedback whine still drifting through the monitors. Together they waded through the clutch of people calling Phen's name, making their way to the merch table.

I caught sight of Justin, not behind the table but next to it. His hair pulled back in a low, quick knot now. He scanned the crowd and found me, holding my gaze. The corner of his mouth twitched, then he looked away, letting two girls argue over who got the last signed poster.

I turned away as the house music started. Kiran pulled me against him and began to sway us to the music. "I didn't realize you were such a good dancer."

"It was always one of the things I loved about humanity, and now I have someone to dance with."

I smiled up at him and then felt someone hug me from behind. "Rhiiii!" Kacey squealed in my ear. It nearly jostled me out of my shoes. "We're going," Kacey demanded, "to the after party and you cannot, cannot, cannot bail on me, or I will be so mad."

I caught Phen threading his way through the knot of bodies already back in his street clothes. "Hey, Fey Queen," he said as his smile landed on me for a second, then flickered to Kiran. "Party's on a boat, by the way."

"A boat?" Kiran echoed.

Kacey and Mia both shrieked. "Shut up, that is the best idea ever." Kacey grabbed Phen's hands, "You didn't even tell me it was on a freaking boat!"

Kiran leaned close and whispered, "Are you sure you want to do this?"

"We don't really have a choice if Kacey is going," I replied.

Steve made his way through the crowd until he was standing with us.

"Where have you been?" His hair was disheveled, like he'd been running.

"Long story."

Kiran's hand grazed mine. "Who's actually invited, exactly?"

Phen's smile sharpened. "Just us. Inner circle. VIP only." His eyes flicked over to Steve and Mia. "You guys in?"

Steve grinned, but not in a friendly way. "Always. Love an adventure."

Mia faked a bow. "Lead us to the carnage, master of ceremonies."

Phen flashed a toothy grin at our motley circle, and then jutted his chin toward the hallway. "C'mon, children of the night. This way."

We snaked down the back hallway, Phen in the lead with Kacey at his heel. The air outside was wet and smelled of October. I could see Phen's silhouette in the spill of street lights as he motioned for us to follow. Behind him, parked askew on the dingy alley curb, was his van.

Justin was there, sitting on the battered hood, staring into the orange haze of a distant pizza place. He looked up at the sound of our footsteps, regarded us with that careful blankness he did so well, and then slid off the hood, hands shoved deep in his jacket pockets. For a second, I almost turned back. I didn't think I could face him again, not with what I'd seen in his expression and not with Kiran's hand still woven through mine.

My phone buzzed in the little bag I carried. I pulled it out and checked the screen. It was Taylor. *Everything going okay?*

I hesitated, thumbs hovering. Was everything okay? We were about to head onto the water with Phen.

Band was amazing. Kacey is still obsessed with Phen. We're heading to an after-party on a boat. Steve and I are both with Kacey.

Her reply came instantly. *A boat?*

"Let's go, fairy queen!" Phen called from inside the van.

Yep. I typed back, *I'll keep you updated.*

Kiran helped me into the van. Justin was in the front seat, bracing his foot against the dashboard. He didn't look back once. I crammed in next to Kacey and Mia.

"Slide the door shut," Phen said to Sam.

"Isn't your band going with us?" Sam asked as he reached for the handle.

Phen just shrugged. "They've got other plans." He winked and turned the key. The engine rasped to life, twin headlights stuttering through the mist.

As the city blurred past, I caught Kiran staring straight ahead, his jaw set into a hard, worried line.

He turned towards me like he felt my stare. Then his voice spun through my head. "Do not leave my side tonight, Rhi. I have a weird feeling about this."

We rolled into a converted warehouse district, half the buildings faceless and dead, the other half housing luxury condos and coffee shops with glass windows that reflected the sodium streetlights in jittery orange strips. Phen hooked a hard left, and the van scraped into a parking lot beside a patch of broken curb and steel gates. "Everyone out," he called.

Kacey and Mia exploded from the van like confetti. Kiran helped me out, and his hand stayed locked around mine. Moored to a derelict wooden dock, a boat glinted against the night. Not a fishing trawler, not a party pontoon, but a full-on yacht.

Justin glanced at Phen, one eyebrow up. "Yours?"

Phen shrugged. "The world belongs to us, my friend." He made a courtly gesture toward the gangplank.

A guy in a pea coat and captain's hat waited by the gangplank. A cigarette was glowing on his lips. His face didn't look like it belonged on a boat. More like it belonged in a dive bar. "That's our captain," Phen said, skipping ahead. Phen introduced us all with a flourish. "Captain Krell, my loyal psychos."

The Captain flicked his butt into the sludgy water, looking us over and, without a word, motioned us up the ramp. At the threshold, Steve hesitated.

"What?" I whispered to him.

"My intuition. It's telling me something is going to go down tonight."

"I don't have Steve's particular intuition," Kiran said softly, "but I feel it too." He swept his gaze over the water, "Something's not right."

I kept my voice low so only Kiran and Steve could hear, "Can you teleport us out if things get bad?"

Kiran looked at me for a long second. "I'll keep you safe," he said quietly. "I swear it, but Kacey is the issue. She doesn't know about our world."

"Let's go!" Kacey squealed, oblivious to the tension coiling around us.

"We're coming." I forced a grin on my face.

Phen herded us onto the deck, where the air instantly changed. It was cooler, cleaner, with the promise of open water. Within minutes, we were drifting, the shoreline's lights becoming smaller.

We followed Phen below deck, where the room was strung with flickering multicolored lights and paper bats. A makeshift bar was already set up with cans and a champagne bottle; someone had scribbled "BLOOD OF THE DAMNED" in marker on it. Phen was in his element, holding court with a red plastic cup while Kacey hung on his arm.

"We should change into regular clothes," Kiran said at my side. He guided me down a hall away from Kacey's eyes. A whip of his hand, and he had jeans and a thick flannel on. My clothes changed as well into jeans, a warm, heavy hoodie, and my favorite sneakers. "Don't worry, I saved the costume." He winked at me, leading back to the rest of the group.

"Bottoms up, baby!" Kacey crowed, shoving a cup in my hand. She looped her other arm through mine, tugging me toward Phen.

I started to take a sip from the cup just to make her happy when Kiran's voice entered my head. "Don't. We don't know what Phen might have put in it."

Phen clapped Kiran on the back with force that would've staggered a normal person, but Kiran didn't even blink. "You know," Phen said, gaze sliding to me, "When I was a kid, I always thought Halloween was for monsters. Ghosts, vampires, devils." He arched a brow at me. Who was he kidding? He was never a kid, but an angel turned demon. "But, now I know there is a monster in us all."

Chapter Forty-Four

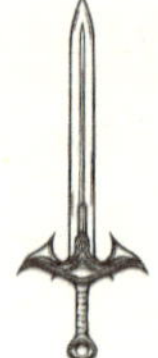

Kiran

Something wasn't right, and I didn't need Steve's intuition to know it. I didn't let go of Rhi's hand as I made my way over to Sam, who was still in his Batman costume. "Sam."

"I'm Batman."

Rhi huffed. "Are you drunk, Sam?"

"Pfft. It takes a whole lot more than this to get an immortal drunk."

"Sam, seriously. There is something not right about all this."

Sam seemed to consider looking around at the rest of our crew. "Do you think we can't handle it? I mean, we have you, me, Justin, and…" He waved a hand at Rhi, "Our very own Veilbreaker."

"Don't say that out loud." I hissed.

The captain, who was definitely a demon, called down to Phen that we had arrived. Where could we have arrived so quickly?

"Oh, yeah. We're here, minions! And it's almost the witching hour."

Phen made his way to the stairs. Pulling Kacey behind him. "Well, come on." He yelled back to the rest of us.

"Sam, listen. We need to get out of here. Now." I said urgently.

"Wait," Rhi squeezed my hand, "What about Kacey?"

"I'll wipe her memory," I promised. "Sam, you take Steve, Mia, and Justin. I'll get Rhi and Kacey."

Phen's head popped back into view. "Hey! You're still coming, right?" he shouted. "We're at the Statue of Liberty."

Sam's face went slack behind his mask, and Justin's eyes grew large.

Phen whistled from above. "Tick-tock! You don't wanna miss the main event!"

"Let's go," Justin said sharply, "Don't think, just get Kacey and get out of here."

The night air on the deck was thick and misty. Manhattan glittered softly to the left, but Lady Liberty towered ahead, bathed in floodlights. For a second, she looked alive, the flames in her torch flickering like a real fire.

Kacey didn't even hesitate—she bounced off the ramp and onto the dock, heels clacking, tripping but not falling because Phen kept his grip. She spun, dragging Rhi with her, "What are you waiting for? This is literally a once-in-a-lifetime thing!"

"Ladies first!" Phen bellowed, grinning ominously.

I scanned the surroundings, looking for threats, but every instinct told me the threat was already here. I made it to Rhi's side, taking her other hand.

Phen led us right to the base of the statue and then through a door so old it had to be original.

Inside, the air changed. The black marble floor of the statue's atrium gleamed with sparse, almost supernatural moonlight. The echo of our footsteps sounded off, warped by the amount of empty space. I stopped, suddenly. My hand found Rhi's again. "Wait. Where's Sam and Mia?"

She craned back, peering through the wavering yellow light from the old bulbs. "He was right behind us."

Steve appeared, eyes blazing. "Sam got Mia out."

"Why are you here?" I pressed, keeping my voice low. Steve was supposed to go with them.

He set his jaw hard. "I'm not leaving my sister."

Phen, halfway across the floor, stopped and peered over his shoulder at us, lips tightening in mock disappointment. "Hmmm. My surprise seems to be running late." He eyed Steve and then Rhi, not seeming to care that Sam and Mia were no longer with us. "Ah, but what's a party without late guests?"

The echo of Phen's words had barely faded when a voice like murderous silk —
the kind that made you want to run but held your feet to the floor — rose from
behind us. "Well, well…" he purred.

I turned, pulse ragged in my throat, just as Vince came through a metal door with
glowing green light illuminating behind it. "And here I thought you boys didn't
get along." His gaze flicked from me to Justin and back. Vince's steps drumrolled
across the marble, "The twins together again, with their little harrower in tow." He
grinned wider, showing canines a little too sharp. "Honestly, I expected Rhiannon
to come with better chaperones, but the company of failures suits her."

Kacey let out a sound too raw to be called a scream. Phen's hand flew to her
mouth, crushing her jaw closed, but her terror throbbed through the air.

"Quiet love," Phen murmured. "Nothing is going to happen to you."

Rhi's grip on me trembled. Her voice barely pierced my mind, but she got
through. *"Kiran, do you see that door? It's…it's the same one from my dream. The one
with the fire."* She stared at the corroded seams of the entryway behind Vince, face
white beneath her makeup.

I stepped in front of her, blocking Vince's line of sight with every ounce of my
body. "It's not going to happen," I said, more to her than anyone else. I stepped
forward. "Rhi's not going anywhere with you."

Justin shifted closer to her protectively.

"Cute," Vince deadpanned, making a dismissive gesture. "You remember, don't
you, Rhiannon?" He jerked his chin at Justin and me. "And who's going to save you
this time? The brothers…or yourself?"

Justin stepped in front of Rhi, shoulder brushing mine. For the first time, we
stood in solidarity. "You're not calling the shots," Justin said. "Not tonight."

Vince looked delighted, raising his hands. "Oh, I'm terrified."

Kacey let out a string of curses, stomping her feet. "What is going on, Phen?"

"Such a mouth on you, my little vixen." Phen cooed.

"Get your hands off my sister!" Steve's voice ricocheted through the marble
chamber.

Phen laughed low. "Relax, she's not who Vince wants, kid." He tightened his arm around Kacey's ribs, "Nothing is going to happen to her. In fact, I'll even get you out of here with her."

"What do you want, Vince?" Justin bristled. "You've got us. We're here. Stop screwing around with the girls."

Vince circled us with predatory patience, every movement measured. He smiled, and my blood went cold. "I want to see what she becomes."

Kacey thrashed so wildly her heel snapped off and clattered across the floor, but Phen only lifted her into his arms like she was nothing but air. "Let go of me," she shrieked, beating her fists and clawing at his arms. "What have you led us to, Phen?"

Phen didn't budge, didn't even wince. "No!" His voice resonated off the statue's bones, rattling the glass around us. "I won't let you go, Kacey. Not now, not after all this. I love you! Do you hear me? I love you, and that's why I couldn't let him take you!"

Kacey froze, her fury turned inside out, eyes disbelieving. "What are you talking about?"

Phen's eyes widened. "It's not a game! I'm trying to save you." The vulnerability in his stare was all the more terrifying for how human it was underneath the brutality.

"Oh, how endearing," Vince said, voice syrupy. "Little vixen, is it? That's the pet name you use for her, Phen?" He made a show of sighing. "So sentimental."

He strolled up to Kacey and Phen, less than a foot away, his eyes never leaving Kacey's. "Do you know why you matter to him, Kacey? Do you even know what you are?"

Kacey stopped moving.

"It's not just you, you know. It's the boy," Vince said, a soft gesture at Steve. "And that adorable blond sister of yours." He turned his head, his eyes narrowing on Rhi. "Your cousin, too. She's the most powerful."

My skin burned cold. Vince couldn't know. But the gleam in Vince's inhuman eyes said he knew it all. The true nature of Rhi, Taylor, Kacey, and Steve.

Phen's eyes shot to Vince full of venom. His face twisted, the human mask sliding for a second as something ancient and furious boiled up through it.

Vince showed his teeth in a savage smile. "Phen was the youngest Prince of Hell in a thousand years. Gifted, but soft."

"I'm not like you." His gaze locked on Kacey, "I needed out. I made a trade." He looked away, jaw tight. "Vince for my freedom."

Vince let out a triumphant sigh and made a broad, theatrical gesture. "Phen really is an artist when it comes to betrayals. He promised me up, but Lucifer required something extra."

Phen didn't look up, but his voice carried. "My boss—he wanted more than just a traitor Fallen." His jaw jutted at Vince, who gave an ironic salute. "So I found Vince, sold him on being a Prince of Hell. But the real prize Lucifer required? An Ossaris and a Principality."

Vince, smug, folded his arms. He jerked his head at Justin. "You and your brother? You're the final pieces." Vince allowed himself a long, appreciative look at Justin and me, like a shopper deciding between two cuts of meat. "The symmetry's delicious," he purred. "You'd almost think it was fate."

Phen dropped the showmanship. "The plan was you at first, Kacey," he said, looking at her with a rawness in his eyes. "I thought you would be the easiest of the Ossaris to snag. You were so into me." He smiled slightly, "But the more time I spent with you, the less I could go through with it. I meant what I said. I fell in love with you."

"So instead you're offering my cousin and my brother?" She spat in his face. "How could I ever love someone who hurts my family?"

"Because you won't remember." He touched her temple, and she went slack in his arms.

Rhi screamed and tore her hand from mine. She got right in Phen's face, clawing at his arms. "You twisted, evil—" Her voice shook. "Love is not manipulating someone into believing you're something you're not. It's not standing by while their family gets torn apart—"

"Enough!" Phen yelled. He gathered Kacey against his chest. With one long finger, he touched his arm, and a red-and-orange mist was drawn from his body where part of his tattoo sat. It grew into something solid, and he let it fall to the floor.

I couldn't breathe. It was an angel.

"Here's your Principality." He pulled Kacey tighter against him as flaming wings erupted from his back. "My deal is done." He drifted closer to us, and I could feel the heat from his flaming feathers. "I told you, Kiran. I told you to find out what Rhi truly was." He whispered. "I didn't want this to happen, and if you had done as I asked, you would all be safe."

I went to grab him, but he was too fast. He grabbed Steve, and dissipated with Kacey and Steve in his arms.

Vince's hand flicked, and the limp Principality rose like a macabre puppet, blood streaming down her brow. She hung there, ankles brushing the black stone floor, lips parted, eyes glassy and fixed on nothing.

Vince was distracted, so I pulled Rhi against me and reached for Justin's hands, pulling them toward each other, toward me. We only needed a second—just one, and I could snap us out, and then I would come back to take Vince down.

For an instant, all I saw was Justin's clenched jaw and Rhi's panic.

"Such devotion, dear boy. Thinking you can save them." Vince crooned — and before I could blink, I was on the ground, his power slamming into me like a freight train. The air contracted. Rhi was dragged across the marble before I could reach her, skidding hard, landing at Vince's feet.

Justin roared. An actual, inhuman rage. His hands twisted, knuckles cracking. His voice was a growl in his chest, and then his skin rippled. It started in the lines behind his shoulders—the flesh shuddered, fissured outward, and split. Black wings clawed themselves from Justin's back, at first shriveled and tarred, then snapping wide, leaking shadow like smoke. The marble under him spiderwebbed, shrapnel crackling out from where his fist hit the floor. Justin roared again, and the windows high above shattered, sleeting glass across the atrium.

"There it is," Vince said softly. "Now you show your true face."

Justin was locked on Vince, wings arching high and monstrous, "You're not touching her again."

Vince's smile thinned. "Oh, Justin. You always did have a flair for dramatics."

Chapter Forty-Five

Rhiannon

I couldn't believe what I was seeing. Justin, with giant feathered wings sprouting from his back. His eyes scorched Vince with their fury, jade flames burning hotter than the circles of Hell. Almost the same color as what seeped from that door. The wings were the same as those I saw him have in my dreams, and I choked at the realisation. Black, but up close, all the iridescence of a raven-purple and blue and even a shimmer of emerald green flared as the feathers snapped, unfurling to their full span.

But for a moment, he was just standing there, letting all of us stare. His chest ballooned and hollowed with each breath. Blood dripped down his arm where the new wings had ripped through skin. He didn't seem to feel it.

I touched the floor to steady myself, and my fingers brushed the cracked tile. Justin's eyes snapped to mine, dangerous, almost feral.

And beautiful.

"Ahh," Vince crowed, his face a parade of sharp teeth and wild disbelief, "the Underlord will thank me for bringing him you at full strength." His gaze devoured Justin's wings. "What a lovely mess you make, boy."

Vince was so enraptured that he barely saw Kiran move. He was a bolt of white and silver, slamming full-force into Vince's chest. The room sang with the collision as Kiran's fist split the air, seizing Vince by the throat and driving him backwards until they crashed through a wall. The sound was like a shotgun going off. Vince squirmed, but Kiran's grip was iron, every muscle trembling as if he could throw him back into Hell himself.

Justin sprang, wings slicing the air, ignoring the blood that slicked his bare shoulders. He landed next to me, his hand landing lightly on my wrist. "Get back, Rhi."

Sorcha and Sam materialized out of nowhere, the air shuddering the way it does before a lightning strike. Sorcha's face was pure focus, a white-hot ferocity that looked too big for her small frame. Blue sparks jumped from her fingers as she rushed to flank Vince, plucking an obsidian dagger from her belt.

"Now would be a good time to move!" Sam yelled.

I half-crawled, half-scrambled across the wrecked floor to where the angel Phen pulled from his tattoo lay like a rag doll. She was staring straight up at the ceiling, eyes wild and glazed. I pressed my fingers to her jaw, felt a fluttering beat. "Hey," I whispered, "wake up. Please."

She looked impossibly small. Then her eyes snapped open. Pure white radiance, so bright it hurt to meet her gaze. She groaned. "You..." She blinked. "You're an Ossaris," she said. Her voice was bone-dry, ancient, and raw.

I nodded as the battle roared around us. There was a crash behind us, the sound of Kiran's fist thundering Vince into another wall. The whole room shuddered. Justin's wings unfurled again, haloing me in shadow. He stepped closer to us, putting his body between me and anything that might come.

The Principality rolled to her side, clutching at my arm with a grip made of desperation. "Child," she rasped. "Your gift...what is it?"

My voice wouldn't work at first. I tried to swallow the air, turn it into words, but my mouth was too dry. "Energy," I croaked. "I can—" Another crash from across the room, Vince shrieking as Kiran wrenched him by the throat, slamming his head against the metal railing. "I can channel energy from anything living," I said finally.

"Then do it," she said, yanking me forward so we were nose to nose. "Pull the energy from that demon so we have a chance."

"I don't—" My body felt drained, useless, every muscle trembling. "I've only done it with plants. I don't think I can." Barely even that — Steve and I had only just started practicing a few weeks ago, and half the time the rose bushes barely wilted.

She twisted my chin toward her, eyes burning. "Show me," she growled. "It is the same with any living thing. Pull his energy from him just like you've done with plants."

My hands shook, blood and ceramic dust smeared along my palms, my heart thrumming so hard my ribs ached. The Principality's stare was so unrelenting it felt like it might char me from the inside out. I steadied myself. This was it. My only shot. I closed my eyes and tried to reach for the current that I felt in the backyard garden every morning, the pulse of dewy leaves, only now the room was filled with the smells of blood, burned ozone, and sulfur. I could taste it. I could taste Vince's rage.

Then Sorcha screamed as sharply as broken crystal. My eyes flashed open, and I saw her launch across the room, glass exploding as her body shattered a window. "Wretched children," Vince sneered, his voice inhumanly deep, "I'll drag you all to Hell."

The whole place shivered like a living thing. I pushed past Justin and tried to focus on Vince. The air vibrated with energy, strobing violet, red, and a sickly neon green. Kiran was still locked with Vince, both of them bleeding, snarling, but Vince was gaining. Even from here, I could see the way Kiran's muscles strained, his mouth tight with effort. Sam was beside him, slamming beam after beam of white light into Vince's chest.

For one second, Justin flicked his gaze at me, eyes wide. I tried to step in front of him but he grabbed my waist, shoving me behind his wings. I wormed past him again, locking eyes with Vince.

"Go help them!" I yelled at him. "They need you!"

His eyes revealed the inner turmoil he felt. He didn't want to leave me wide open for attack.

"Go!" I screamed again.

"I don't have their powers. I can't help them!" He yelled back. "But I can get you out of here."

"No," I shook my head, "I refuse to leave without them." I shoved him and raised my hands. I could almost taste Vince's life-force, burning and ancient, the energy pouring off him like gasoline on a match.

I saw Justin head into the thrall. He landed beside Kiran, who looked at him in shock, then anger. He pushed something into Justin's hands and then threw his hand out, sending Justin sliding back towards me.

I shut my eyes and pictured a tree's root system. I remembered the surge of green when I'd brushed my thumbs over the rose bushes in Kiran's garden. The rush, the ache, and then the nothing as the plant wilted in my hands. This was the same. Underneath the sulfur, the hate, Vince was alive, and what was alive I could take the energy from.

I reached for him. I didn't even have to move because my will found the ragged edge of his essence and clamped down. It was like plunging my hands onto a burning wire, the current so fierce it jerked my teeth together and made my spine judder. The taste was worse than anything I'd ever known, sickly and rotten. I could feel him coil away, burrowing deeper into rage and fear to fend me off.

"You dare," Vince hissed, his pupils going wide and black as he felt the drain.

I sucked at his power like it was air, threading it through me, past all the terror and doubt, straight into the depths of my chest. I was a black hole, and he was the doomed star. I opened my mouth and gasped because I couldn't contain it. My body began to vibrate, every nerve and cell burning. I could see it. The flicker of green and grey and blood orange in the air between us. His energy.

His essence was pure rot, every draw of it sickening. It curdled in me, hit my stomach like arsenic. Still, I couldn't let go. My hands were shaking so badly that I thought they might break. I barely noticed Justin's hands clenching my shoulders, trying to yank me away from the line between me and the demon that was Vince. I was on fire, burning from the inside, hungry and sick and wild.

I opened my eyes to see Vince grinning at me, teeth slick and black. "You want to play thief, child? Try this on."

He hurled what was left of himself. The room shuddered as a lastconvulsive burst of his energy flooded the air in a shockwave. I watched Sam get lifted clear off his feet, limbs flailing as he flew backwards, crashing spine-first into a wall. Sorcha was crawling back in through the window, blood bubbling at her lips, and then Justin dove forward, wings first, to shield me.

My bones crackled with the aftershock. I felt the punch of it, like standing too close to an explosion. My ears rang. I heard a sound in the wake, a grotesque, wet pop, and saw Kiran lifted clean off the ground, limbs pinned by nothing, head thrown back. Vince had him in an invisible vise, not even a muscle moving, but Kiran's body was jerking, arching in agony. Vince squeezed, and the room filled with the scent of burning vanilla sugar. Kiran, my Kiran's sweet vanilla scent burning.

I tried to reach for him, but Justin's wings blocked out everything. "Stay down!" he said, voice hoarse. There were cuts all over his skin, the blood wet and bright across his side.

Kiran's breath hissed between his teeth. I could see his eyes, silver, flicking to me, desperate. Vince leaned in, savoring the moment.

But Vince wasn't looking at Sam, Sorcha, or even Justin.

He was looking at Kiran.

I screamed, "Kiran!" but Justin already had me, arms a shackle, crushing me to his blood-warm chest even as I clawed at him, even as I twisted and bit and went for his bruised side. He grunted—shocked, pained, refusing to let go. He was so strong. The wings, the muscles, the desperate need to protect, it was more than I could ever fight off. Still, I kept fighting.

"No!" I shrieked again, a wild animal, sweat and tears stinging my face. "Let me go!"

Kiran's head wrenched toward me. His face wasn't just agony, but a desperate, shattered love. "Rhi—" He choked the word out. "Ahvana, I—" But his teeth ground together. Vince squeezed invisible claws, bending Kiran's spine, and every muscle in his body was fighting to keep from shattering.

Through the white-hot auger of hate, Vince's face was nothing but glee—he was enjoying it, feeding on all of our pain. Even now, his energy snaked through the room, through the wounds in all of us. It touched me, too, oily fingers that slid along my skin. I could almost hear him, in my mind, laughing.

"You think the girl will save you?" Vince jeered, voice pitched high with something close to hysteria.

Kiran's body convulsed, and a crack ran up his cheekbone like ice fracturing. Then his eyes locked with mine. All the world collapsed into those eyes. "I love you. My Ahvana, I love you." His gaze jerked to Justin. "Get her out of here. Now."

With the last charge of his body, he tore himself forward, catching Vince off-balance. They tumbled together, a blur of pale and darkness, Kiran's hands finding Vince's skull. There was a sound like thunder and glass breaking at the same time. The world filled up, for one second, with wild light.

I fought Justin, slamming my fists into his arms, his chest. "Let me go! I will not let him sacrifice himself for me."

The room fractured into slow motion. Kiran and Vince thrashed through the tangles of energy and ruin. Every lamp and bulb exploded, strobe shadows stuttering across the burnt walls. In that flicker, I caught Sam's face — swollen with bruises, his shirt dark with blood. He pressed a trembling hand to his stomach and wiped his mouth. His eyes flicked up, past the chaos, and found Justin's.

Sam gave a single grave nod. Without a glance, he seized Sorcha around the waist. She was half-conscious, clutching the obsidian blade in bloody fingers. Then the two of them fizzled out of existence.

Gone.

"No!" I screamed. The word came raw, tearing my throat. I lashed at Justin's grip, my nails splitting his skin, smearing us both with red. "You don't get to leave him! You don't get to—"

A voice sliced through my mind. *"Rhi. Ahvana, listen to me. I can't hold him for long. I love you. But I will not let you fall with me. I will not see you in Hell."*

His agony echoed inside my own head, the clash of rage and tenderness and terror so pure I might have dropped to the floor if Justin wasn't crushing me to him. "Go. Sam and Justin will take care of you."

I could feel Kiran losing. That invisible thread between us pulled tighter and tighter — and if it snapped, it would take my heart with it.

I screamed, "We don't leave people! Justin, please—"

Kiran's jaw was set, but his eyes glistened wet with unshed tears.

His voice was so tender in my head. *"Goodbye, my love."* "Now, Justin."

Justin reached for the Principality, and then the world blurred.

Chapter Forty-Six

Rhiannon

I scream, and the sound cracks the world. It is animal, elemental, a scream so huge it breaks open my throat and fissures the air like lightning. It is not a girl's scream, not even a human scream. It's the howl of every cell as it tears itself in two, a sound so loud the room itself holds its breath in horror. It doesn't matter that Justin's wings are around me, that his arms are a cage; my scream drills through him, through the ceiling, through all the dimensions.

All around, time shudders to a halt. I am suddenly outside myself, floating behind a scrim of smoke and blood and flickering lights. The world drains of sound except for the hollow roar in my head. Everything slows, blurs, and then stutters frame by frame, as if I am watching the end of us flicker across a broken screen.

But there is another version of me. Or maybe it's just my mind, snapping. I'm there, pressed against Justin's sweat-slick chest, but I'm also above it, seeing Justin's wings wrap the pair of us in brilliant, oily shadow.

I turn my head, and there are Kiran and Vince tangled across the room. They look wrong, like a film sped up, slowed down, and paused. Every feather and blade and drop of sweat is suspended. I blink, and the world splits open. A line down the center of reality, a seam ripping wider and wider as I stare.

The seam is brightening, drawing me to it, devouring every other color in the room. I don't know what I'll see if it opens wide enough—another world, a pit of fire, maybe nothing at all—but I can't look away. There's a hand on my shoulder.

It isn't Justin's; it isn't familiar at all, but the fingers are cold and a little too long. I jerk, spin, and every atom in my body knows him.

Azrael.

"You," I gasp.

Azrael does not move. His eyes are on me, but also the seam. His mouth curls at the edge, like he's never meant to smile and has only ever read about the concept. "Welcome to our side, little Veilbreaker."

He's close enough that I see the grain of his irises—there's no white, only striations of grey and moonstone. "You know what I am." It isn't a question, but an accusation.

"I do," he says simply. "You, Rhiannon, can pierce, weaken, or momentarily dissolve the Veil that separates Heaven, Hell, Earth, and everything in between."

He sweeps his hand across the frozen chaos surrounding us. "You do not fit neatly into our cosmic order. Angels will fear you, demons will want to use you, and humans will not understand you. You are living proof that the boundaries everyone relies on are not absolute." His moonstone eyes fix on mine. "Once you see past the Veil, you can't unsee it. Your existence is dangerous, even though your heart is kind." His eyes glitter with something between reverence and hunger. "A Veilbreaker doesn't have to want chaos. Your mere presence destabilizes reality."

"I don't want to destabilize anything," I rasp. "I just want to keep everyone I love alive."

Azrael nods, neither approval nor mockery in the tilt of his head. "That is always how it begins. A single will, refusing to be bound by rules that have held since the beginning."

"What do you want from me?" My voice is raw, and it hurts to focus on anything but Kiran's dying light.

He sighs. "What I want is irrelevant. What is inevitable is that you will be forced to choose. Save those you love and risk the order of all worlds, or bow and let the universe define its own justice. Even now, your presence here is fraying all the lines."

A flick of his gaze behind me, to the spot where energy still bleeds from Vince and Kiran, locked in their hate-dance. "You want it to stop?" he says. "You wish to save your Kiran?"

"Yes," I plead. I don't care how desperate or pathetic I sound. "Please. Let me."

Azrael looks at me with something terrifying—a silent apology. "You are the child of my most revered brother," he says, "but I warn you, Rhiannon: every Veilbreaker in history has believed themselves noble at the start. And every Veilbreaker has turned the world into a battlefield of their own longing, whether they meant to or not."

I swallow and drop my eyes to my own hands, and for a split second, I think about what it would mean to say yes—to burn the rest of the world to save one. I see Kiran's face, the way he looks at me as if I am the only thing worth saving. Then my eyes flick to Justin, battered and desperate, wrapping those impossible wings around me like a promise. I know what Azrael is saying without him even needing to say it.

I am selfish.

I know I am not supposed to matter this much. That the world is bigger than my grief. My whole life, I have been told to shrink, to hush, to make myself small. My stepdad, my mom, every teacher who hated the way I raised my hand when I already knew the answer—but most of all, every celestial or demonic asshole who thinks the world is a story they get to write, and I am just some expendable line in the margins.

I look at Azrael, and I want to spit in his face, or maybe just weep at his feet. I want to clutch his sleeves and tell him that nobody's life is a footnote for someone else's cosmic order. But the words won't come, and all I can do is grind my teeth against the scream growing in my heart.

Azrael takes a step forward and raises his arm. I stare at where his hand should be, because his hand isn't a hand at all — it shivers, collapsing into a sleeve of black fog until his sword slides from nothingness into his grip. He holds it upright, and for a moment, I think he's going to finish Kiran.

Azrael examines me for a long, cold moment, and my veins freeze. I realize that he is not here for Kiran.

No. No, no, no.

My legs remember how to move, and I stagger back. He raises the sword—not a flourish, just a deliberate, final motion. Heat crashes against my face and, for a split second, I'm sure I'm about to combust. I curl my arms over my head, expecting death, but the only thing that touches me is impossible warmth.

When I look up, wings of pure fire are all I see. There's a form in the heart of the fire, haloed so bright I can hardly force my eyes to look upon it. But the light dims, contracts, and an outline steps forward. He is angelic and so enormous that the walls seem to bend to fit him. His armor glows, not gold but molten, as if it's smelted sunlight. His eyes aren't eyes at all but literal orbs of fire.

Azrael bows his head, the motion almost human. His sword vanishes into vapor, and I can see a tremor at the base of his jaw.

"She is not yours to touch, Azrael," the angel's voice booms.

"But you see what she has done, what she is. Look." He gestures—not at me but at the seam, at where the world is still torn open, trembling at the brink. "She is a Veilbreaker," Azrael continues. "Even now, she unravels the fabric separating death and life, Heaven and Hell, and that is without intent. See what will become of her if she learns to crave it?"

"Again, I say she is not yours, Azrael," the inferno-angel says.

Azrael's jaw clenches, eyes narrowing. He looks at me, then back up at the angel of fire. "You cannot protect her. Not forever."

The angel's wings flared wider, and the heat doubled. "That is not for you to decide. Now leave my sight."

Azrael opens his mouth, but the retort dies on his tongue. He bows his head in submission. The world folds around him, and just like that, he is gone.

The fire gutters and drains down, collapsing in on itself until it's just a single, human-shaped figure. His hair falls in a wild, wavy mane, the color of deep walnut. His arms are sleeved with old scars, and as he steps closer, heat still warps the air around him. I see his eyes; they are dark brown, flecked with gold like the fire that was there before is just waiting to come forth again. His face is familiar. Muscular jaw, nose a little too long, the same arch to the eyebrows, and the same swerve to the cheekbones as...no.

The resemblance hits like a punch. My brain rejects it, but the features are more than familiar—they're mine. I stagger, dizzy, and whisper, "No," even as my eyes refuse to look away.

He takes another step closer, reaching out, and the heat is still dangerous, but it's not for me. It's for the whole world around us, as if he'd incinerate anything that tried to reach me.

"Who are you?" I hear myself say.

He speaks, and there's a shock of recognition, a cadence in the way he forms my name. "Rhiannon. My daughter. I am Michael."

I make a strangled noise. "No," but it's a whimper.

The angel—my father —looks at my confusion with unbearable tenderness. "I hoped you might never see beyond the Veil." His eyes—my eyes, I realize, flick to where Kiran and Vince are still frozen in battle.

He smiles, and I see the frightful sadness in him. "I know you have so many questions. But the wall you have broken—" He gestures at the gaping seam in the air, "means we have almost no time. Listen to me, Rhiannon." He kneels so our eyes are level, somehow making even that look powerful, as if the whole world bows with him. "You have stepped entirely out of time. Your scream, your pain—it moved you here, to this threshold. You have become what our kind always feared." The words tumble out of him, fast, and I wonder if he's been rehearsing this speech for centuries. "You can stitch the Veil back together or tear it beyond mending. You are both the lock and the key." There's a trace of pride in his voice, but the weight of terror, too. He cups my face in both hands, and the heat is close to scalding, but I do not flinch. I need this. A touch, an anchoring point. "The act of loving makes you fragile," he says, thumb smoothing the blood at my cheekbone.

"But I have to save him if I can...all of them." I point, and the air around Vince and Kiran warbles.

He follows my gaze and smiles, sad and proud at once. "Time stops, briefly, for children like you. You see past everything. You can even stall the machinery of fate, if only to say goodbye."

"I don't want to say goodbye," I choke. "I want him to live. Isn't that what you do? Isn't that what angels do—save people?"

His whole face seems to crack open with feeling. "I wanted more for you—I want more for you. But I am not the only power here, and the others will demand a price."

"I don't care what it costs!" I howl, the tears sliding down my face. "None of this is fair. You—you're just going to let him die or be taken to Hell? Kiran, Justin, all the others—why do we have to be pawns in your game?"

Michael—my father—crumples at the edges, something in his face shattering. He bows his head, trembling. "I can turn back time, but only for a breath, a single instant. Just enough to—"

"Then do it!" I lunge at him, fists curled up, not knowing if I wanted to hit him or hold him. "What are you waiting for?"

"You are your father's daughter," he says, and it is not pride, not exactly, but awe. "You're right. This is not fair. We pretend it is, but we have never been fair. We are only constant." He reaches for my hand, bigger than mine and calloused with old battles, and pulls it close. The old scar puckers across my palm. Michael brushes it with his thumb, and something sparks, hot and silvery, from his skin to mine. "I release Samyaza from his oath. He can freely tell you what you ask of him. My protection stays."

Michael's eyes go glassy, gold fire dimming along the edges. All that light, all that heat, spooling down into something unbearably small—a single tear catching in the fan of his lashes before it falls. He should not be able to shed tears. "I wish there were more I could do. But the universe is not all mine to bend. I love you, Rhiannon. Remember that—always."

It floors me, the sight of him so torn up—my father, an Archangel, so humble. I open my mouth, but nothing comes out except a sob.

"My daughter," he whispers, and the sorrow in that word threatens to drown everything else. "I have watched a million worlds spin from darkness to dawn, but I have never known a light like yours." His broad palm lifts to cradle the back of my neck, pulling me in so our foreheads touch.

"Will I?" I ask, and my voice is so thin I barely recognize it. "Will I see you? Ever?"

His arms pull me in, heat wrapping me in a tight hug. "I am never gone, Rhiannon. Just on the other side of the Veil." He cups my face between his large hands. "If you ever wish to see me, speak it with your heart. I will come if I can. Even if the whole host pursues me, I will find a way."

He lets go, and the world around us warps, the smoky filaments rearranging themselves. Everyone is still paused, like plastic figurines, until Michael gestures. I feel every molecule in me skid sideways. I am torn apart and then sewn together. Suddenly, I am back in that room—Justin's arms caging me. The air snaps, and everything flickers into motion.

"Make it count," Michael says, but I don't see him; I only hear his voice, smoking through the fracture in time.

I shove hard at Justin, so hard it surprises both of us, and I slip through his grasp.

"Goodbye, my love." Kiran's voice whispers softly into my head. No, no, no. This is not enough time! I need more time! "Now, Justin."

The scream caught in my throat as Justin reached for the Principality, and then the world blurred.

We landed hard on the wood floor of Vince's mansion. I wrenched myself free of Justin's arms. I stumbled and crawled, the carpet burning into my skin. All the air seemed to be gone from the room except the noise that tore out of my lungs raw and wild. Justin reached for me, but his hand just hovered and then fell, uselessly, against his thigh. His green eyes, wet at the rims, never leave my face.

"Take me back," I rasped, then screamed it, "Take me back! Take me back to him! You can't just..." A wave of white-hot ugliness boiled out of me. I choked, gagging on words and snot and the taste of blood in my mouth.

Justin slumped to the floor in front of me. His hair hung wet across his cheekbones and his breath came out in torn, shuddering gasps. "It's not safe. You know...damn, Rhiannon, I wanted...."

I slammed my fist against his chest. "You take me back there! Now! He needs me!"

Sam and Sorcha had appeared in my periphery. Sam lurched forward, arms extended as if to hold me, but thought better.

"Sam," I gasped, arms out. "Please. Please. Take me back. I can't—I can't live without him."

He winced, as though I'd stabbed him. His face was more haunted than any living thing should look, but his voice was even. "It's not that easy, Rhi," he said. The words scraped like broken glass. "He's gone, Rhi—Vince took him. No one gets back from there."

My scream blistered the air between us. I didn't recognize the sound as mine. My nails dug into the carpet. "You can't know that! He's not...he can't..." The next sob was too big for my throat, and I choked on it. I felt like I was bleeding on the inside of my own skin.

"We'll find him," Justin said. The certainty in his voice was so absolute it would've been laughable under any other circumstance. "We'll get him back. I promise you, Rhi."

"I don't want promises. I want him," I sobbed, and hated my own voice, how it reverted to a child's wail. "I want him, I want..." and there was no language for what I felt, so I screamed again.

After that, I couldn't hear anything. Not from them or the world. There was just this massive, sucking roar inside me like an ocean crashing into black space. The room spun with the slow, tilting spirals of grief. I couldn't stop my hands from shaking. It was as if some vital cord inside me had been snipped, a tether to whatever made me breathe, sleep, accept the next moment as bearable.

Kiran had been my anchor, my gravity. Every day since the day he appeared to me, I'd felt his presence vibrating at the root of everything, a kind of secret frequency humming behind my ribs. When I was awake, it colored my vision; when I slept, it threaded itself through my dreams. Now, the absence was a hungry, biting thing.

Sam tried to guide me to a chair, but I crumpled to the floor, back against the sofa, palms pressed to my temples. If I squeezed hard enough, maybe I could press the pain to a small, manageable kernel. I didn't think I could survive this.

But deep inside, beneath the panic, something stubborn sparked in me. The bond where our souls wound together still pulsed faintly. So fragile and far away, I almost missed it.

The notes of our soul song.

The Principality ran her fingers through my hair. "There, there, child."

I was a ghost, not responding to her words or touch. "My name is Nireth, Principality of Silence Between Heartbeats."

I glanced at her then. "You're my cousin Taylor's missing Principality."

"I suppose I am. I was to be used as a bargaining chip for that demon prince's freedom. Now I doubt he will have the leverage to be free of Lucifer's grasp." She swiped a hand down my back, and I felt angelic healing magic wash through me.

"You're more than just an Ossaris. Am I correct?"

Sam answered for me. "She is the Seventh Flame and the Veilbreaker."

Nireth nodded. She was an ethereal beauty. Now that she had started to heal, I could see the pink in her cheeks, her hair flowed down her back in white waves, and her eyes were the darkest blue I had ever seen. "I felt your power, and you are indeed powerful. You just need to hone those skills."

"I don't care. I don't care about any of it."

"I know your heart is breaking, but your powers may be the only thing that can save your angel."

"Tell me." And she did.

Sam had teleported us back to my room, where it still smelled like Kiran. Vanilla swam around my senses, and I tumbled into my bed, pulling the pillow he used tight against my chest. Sam settled on the edge of my bed. He was hunched with his elbows on his knees, staring at the pale stripe of moonlight that sawed across my floor. His dark skin was creased with worry, his black hair wet with perspiration; his knuckles gripped the edge of the mattress. He didn't speak, but I felt his weight, the tired anxiousness radiating from him like a fever.

My body caved into itself, this empty, useless vessel. Every few minutes, a fresh, stupid hope bloomed that he would just pop in, his arms would be around me, but each hope collapsed. I must have said his name, because Sam finally looked at me. "I know," he said softly.

"No, no, you freaking don't," I rasped, and he didn't contradict me. My eyes burned. I couldn't do anything about all the water leaking from my eyes.

He let me lie there, wrung out, for a small measure of time. Then he handed me a glass of water. I didn't want it, but I drank.

The silence was a heavy, choking blanket. "Nireth said there were entrances to Hell."

Sam nodded. "The one in the Statue of Liberty is one. Though I am sure it has been demolished now."

"Where are the others?" Nireth had told me that with my powers, I could pass through the Veil that separated Earth from Hell.

Sam chuckled without humor. "The Morning Star only uses grand places for his doors into Hell. He's so full of himself."

"Where Sam?"

He turned to me, his eyes tired. "One at the Eiffel Tower in France. One in The Great Pyramid of Giza. One at the Taj Mahal, one at Buckingham Palace, and the last at the Lincoln Memorial."

"Then the Lincoln Memorial it is."

Sam started to speak, but then seemed to think better of it. He lifted his head like he heard something. He cleared his throat. "Justin is outside."

Justin's shadow blotted out the moonlight for an instant as he teleported in. He was an angel now, or so I assumed with his wings showing. And he could teleport.

He made a little sound, seeing me broken down, biting his fist like he could punch his feelings into silence. He looked at Sam, then me. "I texted Kacey," he said finally. "She was home," Justin said. "She's fine." He uncurled his fingers and wiped his eyes with the heel of his hand, "She, uh...She doesn't remember anything except that it was the best night she's had in ages."

"Thank you," I whispered, hollow and hoarse, voice barely scaling the distance between us. "Thank you for checking."

All the hate I had for myself was turning sideways, stretching to fill the room like a gas, and suddenly it was aimed at Justin. At Sam. How dare they talk about anything else? How dare they sit, breathe, soothe, when every atom of me was on fire for the one who was gone? I clutched the pillow tighter. "You should have let me stay," I said, glaring not at them but at my hands, knuckles white as teeth. "You could have helped him. Instead, you…" I bit my tongue, aware of the cruelty blooming between my lips, but I wanted to hurt, I wanted to dig nails into someone else.

Justin's fingers raked through his hair. His face lost all its color. At first, he just stared, slow and slack-jawed, like he'd been punched in the temple by the blunt force of truth. Then he looked at Sam, wild and pleading, but Sam just looked away, studiously picking at a loose thread on my duvet.

"Rhi, I—" Justin started. "I was trying to—"

"You shouldn't have pulled me out," I said flatly. "I could have saved him."

"I wasn't going to let you die," Justin's voice was a low grumble.

"You can't just decide for me. Not with him. You knew what he meant—what he means."

He clenched his jaw, veins visible in his neck. "You don't understand, do you?" He made a low, wrecked noise. "If Kiran had to pick, he'd pick your life over his every damn time."

Part of me wanted to crack his teeth for saying it, but what was left of my heart stuttered and bled at the truth. There was no scenario where Kiran didn't choose me. That was the problem. He'd always chosen me. Even when I should have given him up, to let him go, and save us both. And now I was just supposed to what? Move on? Just breathe and wait for a plan? When he could be…when anything could be happening to him. Nothing made sense outside of him, and all of me felt useless and too heavy.

"You think I don't know that?" My voice wasn't mine. "That's the point, Justin. I don't want there to be a world where he's not—" I closed my eyes, pinched the bridge of my nose to stop the stupid, constant leaking from my eyes. "He's the other half of my soul. He's not just a…" A cold, ugly laugh clawed up my throat. "He gave up everything for me. That was his choice. Do you get that? I'm the reason he's in Hell, Justin. Don't talk to me like I don't understand what sacrifice means." The words were knives, and I kept cutting myself on them. "I'm nothing without him. I'm something else. Something broken."

Justin's expression crumpled. "You're not broken. You're—" He searched the air like there might be a script for this, and finding none, let his hands fall. "Damn it, Rhi, you're still here. And I promised him—"

I flung the pillow at him, hard, missing. "Well, I didn't promise anything!" He stared, mouth working at words, but none came. Sam didn't move, but his own eyes were full of regret. "Don't you ever say I don't understand," I spat. The words burned my mouth, "I know exactly what I did. But you—you dragged me away like I was something you owned. Like you were the only one who got to make the call."

He opened his mouth, but I kept going, the tide of anger rolling through my body. "You don't get to save me from him. You don't get to save me for you. If you ever cared about me at all, you would've let me go back." My voice cracked, a splinter running down every word. "You would've let me burn with him, if that's what it took."

I struggled upright, gathered my knees in tight, and turned away from them both. The ache of Kiran's absence was growing claws, tearing up my insides. This was what I'd always been afraid of—letting myself feel, and then losing everything. I was supposed to be the Veilbreaker and the Seventh Flame. All I knew was that I was a hole shaped like Kiran, burning at the edges.

Sam's hand landed on my shoulder. His voice was so soft it made my chest ache. "I'll take you," he said. "You want to walk through Hell for him? I'll help you. If only so I don't have to sit here and watch you tear yourself apart." It shocked me, the quiet sincerity. For a second, it was too much. I turned and pressed my forehead into Sam's shoulder, clutching at the muscle of his forearm.

Justin let out a breath, long and uneven, and then scrubbed his face with both hands. When he took them away, his eyes were puffy and livid, his green irises gone glassy. He flicked his gaze from me to Sam. "Screw it," he said, and his voice was low but determined. "If you're going, I'm going too."

I started to protest, but was too tired, too raw.

Sam looked at us both, his face unreadable, and then he let out a slow breath. "It's suicide," he said.

"I know," Justin and I said at the same time.

Sam pressed his lips together until the shadow of a smile haunted his face. "Not an adventure," he said, "but a pilgrimage. No one walks into Hell and comes back unchanged. If they come back at all." His brown eyes flickered in the soft light from my lamp. "Most of my best days have started like a bad idea, and this is the worst I can imagine."

The memory of what my father — Michael — said to me whiplashes back. "Sam," I say. "My father. Michael. I saw him."

Sam goes so still he all but stops breathing. "So you know?"

I nod, brushing my thumb against the scar on my palm. "He said he released you from your vow."

His hand wraps around mine, thumb tracing the scar with reverence. "I thought I'd feel it when it happened." He rubbed his palm over his chest. "Yes — the burden has lifted. Now I can tell you everything: both my knowledge and the contents of Michael's book." His eyes darkened. "Justin discovered it at Vince's mansion. I don't know how it came into Vince's possession, but the book rightfully belongs to you alone. You are Michael's heir, after all."

Chapter Forty-Seven

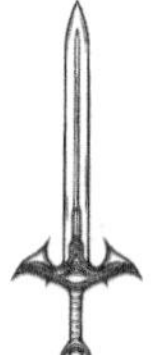

Kiran

Hell was not how I had once been taught to imagine it. There was no biblical fire, no lake of sulfur churning with damned souls. Instead, I woke into silence so dense it pressed around my head like a thickening fog. There was a scent of rot woven through the coldness and a faintly metallic taste in my mouth. My whole body shivered, but not from cold. I remembered the demon prince's claws—Vince's claws, tearing through the air just before blackness enveloped me.

I tried to move. Pain crackled from my ribs up into my neck, but I forced my eyes open. I was inside a cage of black iron bars. The ground was slick and red-black with oil, or maybe old blood. Somewhere in the distant darkness, something gigantic breathed. The slow rise and fall of it stretched the very air. I remembered my wings were gone because the pain where they were ripped from my body was not. I rolled my shoulders, and the ache of their absence was so precise, so total, it nearly choked me. A sob, or its leftover, sat at the root of my tongue.

I forced myself upright, bracing my weight on my elbows, and breathed through the pain as I sized up my surroundings. There was no sky above. Just a sweeping shroud, like a cathedral ceiling built of charred velvet. Shadows moved somewhere beyond the bars.

I saw the world through rivers of blood. My first thought, clear as a lightning strike, was that she hadn't made it out. Maybe she was dead, carried here to Hell with me. Maybe she was already in the next cage over, or shredded in the teeth of a demon. I fell forward, hands gripping the bars, and retched. A shadow moved on the far side of the bars. I blinked hard, but it wasn't my brother or Rhi.

I reached for the piece of myself that was Rhiannon. My love, my heart. There, through the thickening dread, her soul's bright light faintly hummed our soul song. She was alive. She was...safe. It was too much to hope for, but she was not dead. I let myself clutch that one absolute until my breath stopped trembling.

Something scraped behind me along the bars, and I heard my name in a language I should not have known. A chorus of syllables shuddered through the black iron and straight into my gut.

"Kiran." The voice was hollow, thick with decay. "Guardian. Fallen. And now — Brother."

I blinked hard, wrenching my focus off the blood-damp ground. A thing that was shaped like a man, but built entirely of ash and spidery bone, crouched just outside the cage. Its head was an eyeless oval, and veins or cracks ran through its body. What looked like insects writhed through the shadows within the ash. Its mouth, lipless, craned into a smile, and then parted to reveal a forked tongue. "It's time," it said. "You know this."

I forced myself up, hands braced on the bars. "Time for what?"

The thing only grinned — if grinding bone could make a smile. It reached through the iron, and the cold slap of its palm flattened against my chest. Every atom of my being ignited.

I arched against the touch, agony flaring so suddenly my hands spasmed around the bars, and I thought, this is how you unmake a soul. I tried to shout, to call to Rhi, to anyone, but the pain was bigger than my body, bigger than breath. It tunneled fire through my nerves, crawling up my throat. Its forked tongue flicked out, and the thing's voice bent the air. "You don't get free, angel. You don't get love again. You belong to us."

I wanted to say no, to shriek out my refusal — I belong to her, only her — but my body was a paper scrap being devoured by a blaze. Every bone and muscle convulsed. Then I did scream. The sound was a high static whine echoing off the stone.

Our song, the one thread of brightness in the dark that surrounded me, shivered. A single, high note, stretching farther and farther out, like Rhiannon was reaching for me across a worsening chasm. I lunged toward it, desperate to hold onto the bond one more second, but the demon's vice grip deepened.

"It's time to kneel," said the demon, "and to rise. To become." It dragged the syllables out, relishing every twisted word. "You are no longer angel. No longer her Guardian. With your wings torn and your body lost, all that's left is..." It inhaled deeply, and I felt my own lungs fill and contract in tandem, "us."